PETER LAMBERT

INVOLVED BY ACCIDENT II

THERE BUT FOR GRACE

Printed in the United States of America
Library of Congress Control Number: 2025917091
ISBN: Softcover   978-1-969213-04-5
          e-Book   978-1-969213-05-2
Republished by: TwinVerse Prime
Publication Date: 09/08/2025

To order copies of this book, contact:
TwinVerse Prime
Phone: (725) 257-6538
clients@twinverseprime.com
www.twinverseprime.com/

DEDICATION

Thanks has to go to my 'Soul Mate' Elaine for her patience, continued support, and encouragement while I've worked even struggled at times to complete this second book. Also Joanne Richards, Jennifer Cotton, and Mary Hunter for their time, hints and suggestions; collectively you have been the gel that has stuck this story together.

Bless you, thank you.

FOREWORD

It is late September, six months since Stephen Leigh-Grace first met Nita Patel and left Portbridge. He is bringing his boat, *Finbar II* back up the river to her winter mooring having spent the summer cruising around the Channel Islands and South coast of England with his daughter Emma and family, Mary and Richard. He has kept in touch with the detective whom he'd met while hospitalized following an attack he'd suffered at Eastertime. He has arranged to meet her at the NCB wharf in Portbridge to catch up on what has happened in their lives since April.

CONTENTS

INVOLVED BY ACCIDENT II

There but for Grace

FRIDAY

The CB radio on the shelf above Mick Holmes's office desk crackled into life, and a moment later the familiar voice of one of the barge crews spoke.

'You there Mick, its Joe come back.'

Mick finished putting some invoices into a box file, flicked the spring clip down and placed the file on the shelf next to the CB set. The voice came on the CB again.

'Mick pick up if you're there mate, come back.'

Reaching for the mic from its magnetic clip on the side of the set, he keyed the button and replied.

What's up, Joe? You've only been gone two hours...what've you forgotten this time? Come back.'

'No, nothing mate, nothing, just thought I'd give you a heads-up. You remember the bloke that got involved in that assault six months ago, then got attacked himself. We've just passed him working through County lock on his way upriver. Reckon he should be up to you 'bout fourish, back to you.'

'Thanks for that, I'll keep an eye out for him. Safe trip Joe out to you.'

Joe replied quickly.

'Okay, see you next trip Mick... I'm out.'

The CB fell silent, replacing the mic on the clip of the set he got up from the desk and went through to the back room of his office. A couple of minutes later he re-emerged carrying something that resembled a small bucket rather than a mug, and half a packet of biscuits. Sitting back at his desk he picked out a couple of biscuit and dunked them in his drink. For the rest of the afternoon he continued dealing with a mass of reports and paperwork. Much later, with the September sun low in the sky opposite his window bathing the office in a glorious amber glow, he knew he needn't look at the clock, it would be home time soon. A loud knock on the office door frame startled him, spinning around in his chair he saw a dark silhouette standing in the doorway.

'Judas bloody priest!' he spluttered, 'you scared the shit out of me!'

Pushing himself out of his chair he went towards the person in the doorway trying to make out their features against the strong evening sunlight.

'Who is it anyway? What can I do for you?'

'Hello Mick,' the figure said. 'It's me you daft sod, Stephen.'

He smiled remembering Micks strong dialect from six months ago. Watching the man move across the office he thought he'd definitely put a on few pounds since Easter. His NCB boiler suit seemed to be struggling to contain the body of the man wearing it, some buttons down the side were unfastened, his face looked a little fuller too, more jowly than the last time they'd stood face to face.

'Don't do that again you bugger...you've just shortened my life by ten years.' Mick held out his hand and shook Stephen's. 'I knew you were coming upriver but I never heard your engines where've you moored then?'

As he spoke he looked over Stephens shoulder towards the wharf scanning the edge until he saw the familiar outline of *Finbar II's* cabin and flying bridge.

'That's okay, you remembered that's the better end of the wharf.'

Stephen, inside the office now, closed the door. Both men stood looking at one another, Mick broke the silence first.

'Well you look a damn sight better than you did six months ago, must have been a reasonable summer 'cos you've got a tan and you've lost a pound or two, I reckon.'

Stephen grinned, 'Wind and sea air Michael... better than anything for making a person look well, what about you?'

'Oh you know, still here Monday to Friday,' he replied, 'scratching out a living to hold my bones together.'

Chuckling he hugged his well-rounded belly through his boiler suit. Stephen nodded.

'Looks like too much beer or too many curries to me, Mick.'

Giving another little chuckle Mick replied.

'Both, more'n' likely.' then in a reflective way added, 'You know Steve, you took a real beating that night you should've stayed in hospital at least another couple of days. By heck mate you didn't half upset a lot of folk. That detective...'

He searched his memory trying to remember her name.

'Nita...' Stephen said.

'Yeah, Nita... she was bloody mad at you. Think she fancied you and that staff nurse wasn't too happy either, if looks could kill she'd 'av had you back in bed for days. Anyhow you're better then?'

Nodding Stephen answered, 'Yes thanks, it took three months nearly before I was pain free but an easy summer, some sun, wine and good food made all the difference.'

Mick turned going straight into the back room saying over his shoulder.

'Want a brew?'

'That would be good thanks.' Stephen replied moving across the room to one of the easy chairs by the gas fire.

Three miles away in the first-floor office of a building in the centre of Portbridge, DC Nita Patel looked at the wall clock in the office as the Parish Church clock across the road chimed the three-quarter hour. A colleague passing behind her chair sang quietly.

'All the nice girls love a sailor... la lala la la...la.'

She smiled a little embarrassed, opposite her Alan Syms her partner grinned.

'Erm... I'll bet you,' he began to say then hesitated for a moment thinking, 'a drinks night that the boss gives you a job before four.' Mimicking their boss's voice, he continued, 'but there's no-one else who can do it detective... I'm really sorry.'

She looked at Alan throwing him a sour grin, yet deep down she knew he could be right. Glancing across at the clock again, an hour and a quarter to go before she could get away. From across the office someone called.

'See you all Monday, have a good weekend folks, hey... Nita If you're missing on Monday, we'll get Interpol to look for you.'

A ripple of laughter ran around the room. The detective leaving added before walking out of the door.

'Dave, Katie, pub in twenty minutes, yes?'

From different parts of the room two detectives answered together. 'Yep, okay.'

Another detective in the office, Linda walked past Nita's desk and gently touched her shoulder.

'Have a great weekend lovie. Don't let him get you on a slow boat to China that's all!'

Looking up at her she smiled and nodded. Linda, Dave and Katie all left the office together, as the church clock chimed the full hour. A little later the door of Detective Inspector Allen's office opened and he stood there scanning the office, searching for someone. Alan Syms glanced at her quickly.

'What did I tell you?'

She felt the pit of her stomach tighten into a knot. 'Not this weekend, please.' she prayed to herself.

DI Allen finally found who he was looking for.

'Ah, there you are, Syms my office lad I've got a little job for you.'

Alan's face was a picture, Nita couldn't help a little giggle as all the tension inside her was gone

'Drinks on you then...?' she said softly.

'Bastard!' Alan muttered pushing back his chair and reaching for a note pad and pen. DI Allen called again.

'Before bedtime lad it's the weekend and some of us have to be somewhere before then,' he raised his voice adding, 'Don't we DC Patel?'

Nita felt herself flush slightly but replied as Alan wove his way through the maze of desks to the Di's office.

'Sir.'

~~~~~~~~~~~~~~~~~~~~~~~~~~~~~~~~~~~~~~

Three hundred miles away across the North Sea, in a small sleepy harbour in Belgium. A converted fishing boat gently bumped against the quay wall, its fenders protecting the hull from damaging its new paintwork; its name *Caspian Blue* emblazoned across the boat's stern. Two deckhands busied themselves sorting out lines and stowing other equipment in preparation for leaving the harbour. A large expensive, Mercedes four-by-four turned onto the harbour side and drove quietly towards the fishing boat. It was followed by a people carrier, the windows of both vehicles sporting privacy glass to hide their occupants. They stopped by the boat's gangway, moments later the front passenger door of the leading car opened and a woman's shapely leg emerged. She turned on her seat and elegantly stepped onto the wharf. Dressed exquisitely in a tailored suit, her make up perfectly applied, dark hair cut and styled framing her face and complimenting her features. Draped around her shoulders a three-quarter length trench coat, the belt fastened at the back. Before she could move across the uneven surface of the wharf, the rear door of the Mercedes opened and a smartly suited young man emerged to stand by her side. She glanced at him briefly, then taking his arm moved towards the boat. Two other men emerged from the car now, again both dressed immaculately, the older of the two
~~~~~~~~~~~~~~~~~~~~~~~~~~~~~~~~~~~~~~

who had been driving looked at the younger man, said something to him then turned to follow the other couple onto the boat. The young man glanced towards the people carrier, pointed to it and then at the boat. Both front doors of the vehicle opened and two men stepped out. The one at the passenger side pulled open the door and indicated for its occupants to get out. Three very attractive young ladies climbed out, beautifully made up and smartly dressed. The little group stood for a moment before the young men ushered them towards the boat. The two men left on the harbour side locked their respective vehicles and then boarded the boat.

~~~~~~~~~~~~~~~~~~~~~~~~~~~~~~~~~~~~~~~

Back in Portbridge the church clock struck the three-quarter hour as DC Syms walked out of the Inspector's office back to his desk. Watching his face for any signs, Nita said.

'Are you still going to be able to give me a lift Alan?'

'Yeah sure not a problem, do you want to get off now?' he replied.

She nodded and began to tidy her desk while Alan gathered some papers to add to the pile the Inspector had just given him.

'Ready?' he said looking at her.

Reaching down beside her desk she picked up a holdall and followed him taking an anorak from the coat stand by the door. Together they called to the few people still at their desks.

'See you Monday,' and 'Bye.'

Someone somewhere chirped up singing, '*A life on the ocean waves...*'

Nita smiled closing the door and following Alan down the stairs to the car park at the rear of the building. As they descended the stairs Alan said over his shoulder.

'You know you'll never live this down don't you?'

She smiled, yes she knew!

Later as he turned off the main road onto the NCB wharf he
~~~~~~~~~~~~~~~~~~~~~~~~~~~~~~~~~~~~~~~

glanced at her.

'Listen, have a good weekend okay. I know you've kept in touch for most of the summer but you don't know the guy, so stay alert and take care, okay?'

She looked at him and nodded, she'd heard the concern in his voice.

'Mm... Thanks for that, but I plan to have a great weekend trust me... and I think I know enough about him now so don't worry too much, I'll see you Monday.'

In the wharf office Mick opened his mouth to say something but the sound of a vehicle coming onto the wharf, its tyres scrabbling to grip distracted him. Looking not too dissimilar to a meerkat, he craned his neck upwards to see who it was. Not recognising the car he stood up moving towards the office door. He saw someone taking a hold-all from the backseat of the car, they stepped back and closed the door. As the car drove off they turned to face him. He couldn't help smiling.

'Now why aren't I surprised to see you here just now?' he said.

My, he thought she really was good looking; tall, slim, with her long jet-black hair roughly plaited and pulled around her neck to rest on her shoulder. She was wearing grey jogging pants and trainers topped off with a blue hoodie with the letters 'NEPD' written across her chest, and over that a grey and blue anorak. She smiled, a bright smile that he recalled from some six months ago that would light up any room.

'Hello Mick, long time no-see.'

Mick nodded, 'Detective.' was all he said in reply.

Turning to look across the wharf she saw *Finbar.*

'He's here then?'

'He is.'

'How does he look?'

Behind Mick, Stephen spoke, 'Why don't you ask me yourself?'

'Hello you,' she said, 'it's good to see you in the flesh again and you look very well, all tanned you know.

Stephen shrugged, 'Yeah I am generally, some of this is wind burn though; sea air and salt do wonders for a tan.'

She smiled, 'I'll remember that.'

Stephen continued to look into her beautiful brown eyes.

'It's good to see you too,' he said softly. 'Seeing you here now, I realise just how I've missed you. It's one thing talking online, getting to know a person but it's a completely different kettle of fish being able to see the real you.'

She gave a little shrug and her face shrivelled in a childlike way, 'Mmm...'

The three of them moved into the office and Mick went through to the back, Stephen and Nita sat by the fire.

'Are you sure about this?' he said. 'I know we've been talking on the phone and in e-mails, but you coming with me up to the moorings for the weekend is a totally different ball game, you really don't know me, the real me I mean.'

She reached out and touched his knee briefly, her eyes studied his face. He started a little at her touch.

'I'm sure... I'm a big girl now and can make my own decisions. I mean it's not that you're going to abduct me to sell into the slave trade is it...?' She hesitated briefly... 'Or is it?'

They both giggled as Mick returned with tea and some biscuits, on a tray this time. Placing it on the old coffee table that stood in front of the gas fire, its surface stained with ring marks from years of spillages and the odd cigarette burn, he distributed their drinks.

Stephen commented. 'What's all this Mick, a tray and biscuits, that's a bit posh for you?'

Mick grinned, 'Listen mate, I know how to treat guests. It's not often we get someone in here worth treating as a guest.' Looking at Nita, he winked, 'Let's be honest your last visit left a lot to be desired, it was something of an invasion rather than a social event if I'm not mistaken and one not to be repeated.'

Stephen shrugged. 'Yeah okay... I see your point.'

'I rest my case,' Mick said and turning back to Nita offered her the plate of biscuits.

'Thank you.' She said taking one smiling at him.

'My pleasure detective.' He responded politely.

'Right I've got work to do,' he said returning to his desk.

For the next hour the two of them talked quietly. Their conversation sporadically interspersed with a laugh or giggle. Mick, meanwhile continued working through the invoices and order forms needing his attention. Finally he pushed his chair back from the desk, stood up and stretched grunting as he straightened his back. Walking across to where they were sitting he picked up the array of mugs from the table and the hearth, put them on the tray and walked through to the back room collecting a couple more mugs and his special bucket from his desk as he passed it. Re-emerging a few moments later, he came face to face with Nita. A little surprised he took step back.

'Whoa! Don't do that... What's up?'

'Nothing,' she replied, 'I've come to help you wash them up.'

'Nay, I'll do that on Monday morning when I come in, it's all part of my morning routine.'

'You sure Mick?' she asked.

'Absolutely.'

Stephen had come across the office now. 'Am I okay moored here for tonight or do you want me off the wharf?'

'No you can stay here tonight its Saturday tomorrow and I'm not working so you won't be disturbed.'

Nita went to push past him into the back room.

'So I'll wash them up then.'

'No! leave them.' Mick said firmly.

'Listen Mick,' Stephen started to say, 'we could be down at the Duchess later for a night cap if you fancy joining us.'

He thought for a few moments then replied.

'Okay, thanks... can't promise but I'll see.'

Turning to Nita, Stephen smiled and went to pick up her holdall from beside the chair she'd been sitting in. Surprised that it weighed very little he shook it and looked at her.

'Why bring such a big bag? There's nothing in it.'

Reaching to take it from him, she said.

'There's everything in there that a girl needs for a weekend jaunt!' then throwing it over her shoulder flounced off to the office door with an exaggerated walk.

Stephen and Mick looked at her before turning and following her to the office door.

'Later maybe then Mick?'

'Aye… later.'

They nodded to each other and shook hands. Stephen followed Nita out of the door onto the wharf stopping briefly at the door. 'Thanks Mick.'

Walking with Nita to where *Finbar* was moored they heard the office door bang shut and a moment later turned as he shouted across the wharf to them.

'See you.'

They watched him cycle out of the wharf entrance before continuing to the boat. Boarding *Finbar* first Stephen took Nita's bag then held a hand out to help her step onto the boat's gunnel and down into the sundeck, she followed him through the patio doors into the saloon. He closed the sliding doors behind them and moved through the saloon, the lounge, to the galley area. Filling the kettle he switched it on; Nita meanwhile took a moment to reflect on the last time she'd been here remembering they'd sat in the galley with Shamir, the young girl who with her boyfriend David, Stephen had rescued as they were being savagely attacked by three men. They'd talked and shared tea and biscuits before he'd left Portbridge to continue his journey down river to the estuary Marina. There was a difference now though, the boat felt warm and welcoming, there was a homely atmosphere and smells of her being lived in. To think it was only six months ago since she'd first met Stephen in his hospital bed, hooked up to all sorts of monitors and drips as he himself recovered from the beating he'd received for becoming accidently involved. Turning to Nita he smiled.

'Welcome onto *Finbar* it really is good to see you again. Now are you...

She took a step towards him, putting a finger on his lips.

'Will you stop with the PC thing and relax, like I've already said I'm a big girl now, over twenty-one,' She smiled adding, 'In fact I'm nearly over thirty one so I can decide for myself what I want to do... okay!'

The kettle clicked off, he turned and poured the water into the teapot.

'Okay it's just...'

'Stephen!'

'Sorry.' He held his hands up in surrender.

'Look,' she began. 'we've had this conversation so many times since April about you feeling guilty for cheating on the memory of Suzanne. We had this same conversation just three nights ago as you went down to the marina to pick *Finbar* up. Stephen its fine you're not cheating on Suzanne, I'm not expecting anything. We are friends meeting to have a weekend together getting to know each other, that's it!'

Then with a sparkle in her eye she threw her plaited hair back off her shoulders in an exaggerated way adding.

'Anyway, I'm definitely going to have a good weekend because on Monday I'm going back to work and telling everyone I've spent the weekend on a floating gin palace, so yah-boo-sucks!'

That broke the tension and they both laughed. Holding the teapot up a little, like a toast to someone, Stephen said. 'No milk as I remember... yes?'

'Mmm yes, correct.'

He poured the tea and for a little while they sat in silence sipping their drinks.

'Are you hungry?' he said suddenly, 'do you want to eat here, or go posh and have fish and chips out of newspaper?'

She looked at him quizzically, 'What...?'

'Do you want...?' he began to repeat himself.

'I heard you the first time.' She interrupted still looking a little bewildered at the question, she continued, 'But I...'

'Only joking, how does spaghetti bolognaise sound?'

A little surprised, she smiled. 'And are you going to cook?'

Tutting he replied 'No silly... Keith Floyd is, I keep him in that cupboard for special occasions...' he said pointing to a tall cupboard at the side of the doorway to the front of the boat... 'Of course I'm going to cook it! Is that a problem?'

'No, that would be fine.'

He moved out of his seat and over to the cooker.

'So fill me in on just what the out-come of my case was in the end.'

He moved around the galley area preparing their meal as Nita began to tell him how the case involving him, the young woman and her boyfriend ended up.

'Once the Dutch police had returned Shamir's brother here, he appeared at the county court with the other two men; you remember, his cousin and a friend who'd helped them. He had to plead guilty to the assault on Shamir and David, because Shamir's evidence was unquestionable but he tried to plead not guilty to the attack on you and trashing Finbar; he claimed he was somewhere else when that all kicked off. Anyway his cousin and the friend clearly saw the brother was trying to wriggle out of the second charge and just spilled the beans. They weren't going down for something all three of them had been involved in. Together with the witness statements, the CCTV evidence which clearly showed the van leaving the wharf, remember? It was an open and closed case.'

Watching him for a few moments she said. 'I'm very impressed, where did you learn to cook?'

'After Suz died I realised that if I lost the tin opener or the microwave packed up, I'd starve plus, I had to think about Emma she needed proper food, a proper diet, so I set about teaching myself to cook and although I say so myself, I reckon I'm not bad.'

'I think I'll be the judge of that.' she said quickly. 'Yes, how is Emma by the way, does she know about me yet, that I'm your crew for the weekend or am I still an awkward secret?'

'No, no I took your advice and told Emma, Mary and Richard all about you. Well it could have been difficult us talking on Facebook or getting e-mails all the time while we were away. I was really surprised how well they took it, they seemed quite happy for me.'

When he turned to look at her, she was smiling broadly at him.

'Good, I thought it would be okay if you were honest, particularly with Emma.'

'Yes, it was.'

He said grinning back at her.

'Go on then, what happened in the end?'

'Oh, yes, well he realised that he was on a loser and had to plead guilty to all the charges. The CPS had a field day in court all three were found guilty. The brother got five years, the cousin and their friend three a-piece with an order to be deported after time served. The cousin's family appealed to the Home Secretary and he was eventually allowed to stay. The DS made Inspector on the back of the case you know? Mind you it was already on the cards that he was up for promotion even before this one but seeing it was cleared up in double time he was guaranteed it.'

Taking two plates which had been warming from the small oven he served up the food. Reaching across to a shelf he gathered some cutlery from an in-set box and paper napkins placing them on the table.

'What about Shamir and David,' he asked, 'you said they moved away once David had recovered.'

Disappearing up into the saloon briefly while Nita told him about them, he returned with a bottle of red wine and two glasses. Switching on some recessed lights that bathed the table and the food in a warm and subtle glow he sat down.

'Yes, they moved to the Midlands to start their life together. There were too many bad memories here and far too much interest from nosey people, some of it definitely not nice and not welcome, you know!'

Putting her hands together in a little round of applause she said.

'This is so romantic Stephen. How could any girl not be impressed?'

'Thank you, but hadn't you better try it first before you shower me with praises.'

Picking up her fork and spoon she began to eat as he poured them some wine.

'Mmm,' Nita said, pausing for a moment to fully savour all the flavours of the meal, 'this is really good, I am very impressed.'

Having cleared her plate she sat back and took a drink then dabbed her lips dry, she sighed.

'Mm... that was excellent, really very good thank you. I hadn't realised how hungry I was. I only had a packet of crisps for lunch and an apple this afternoon.'

Stephen set his spoon and fork on his plate as he finished, picked up his glass and drained the last mouthful of wine.

'Good.' he said, 'would you like some cheese and biscuits for dessert?'

'What... no thanks, couldn't eat another thing... I'm stuffed!'

To emphasize that statement she puffed out her cheeks. He smiled watching her across the table as she finished her glass of wine. Re-filling it to empty the bottle, he watched her, this was the first time he'd really looked at her since she'd arrived at the wharf office and sitting here under the gentle glow the recessed lights, he was again taken by how beautiful she was. Returning his look over the rim of her glass, she took a sip.

'What?' she asked.

'Nothing, I was just thinking how lovely you look sitting there. I've never invited anyone on board before for a meal, you know I mean a lady... like on a date; it's usually only been with the whole family around when we're moored somewhere and met another couple or family, and we're just being sociable... Do you understand?' she nodded. He continued. 'I've only really been on two dates since Suz died and, huh... both have been with you.'

His voice trailed off and just for a moment it seemed to Nita his thoughts had focused on past memories. To break the silence and distract him she touched his arm. He jumped, looking directly at her.

'She must have been a very special person Stephen.' she said gently.

He looked down at her hand on his arm and nodded. Sitting bolt upright now she said enthusiastically.

'So do I get a conducted tour, or is it some sort of a treasure hunt to find my bearings?'

Shaking himself out of this momentary mood, he smiled and slid from his seat.

'If you'd care to join me miss, I'd be happy to show you around your accommodation for the next thirty-six hours.'

She moved out of her seat to stand by his side. With a sweep of his right arm he began.

'This, if you haven't already gathered, is the galley... and in sailors twang, the mess.' Turning he added grinning. 'And trust me it can be a mess sometimes, particularly if we're trying to cook or eat and the seas a bit choppy.'

Going up the three steps from the galley to the saloon he continued.

'Moving through here we arrive in the lounge or saloon.'

He exaggerated the word 'lounge' in a feigned county accent.

Nita giggled. 'I always knew you were posh.'

Turning to face her he drew himself up and assumed the pose of a country gent, resting one hand on the control console and waving the other hand around in an over-exaggerated gesture, like a rising spiral, saying.

'Well of course 'mi dear you do know where the origin of the word 'posh' comes from, hmm?'

She gave him a gentle shove, 'Stop it fool. No I don't but you're going to tell me, yes?'

'I most certainly am mi' dear. It comes from the late nineteenth and early twentieth century when people, ladies that is, took passage to India in the old sailing ships and early steamers. It means port out, starboard home. Ladies travelling out to join their serving men in India, or coming home, booked cabins on the shaded side of the boat to avoid the strength of the sun and the high temperatures at the height of the day.' Throwing her a wide-eyed pompous stare he ended with, 'There, what do you think of that...?'

'You're an idiot...' she said, 'can I leave now before we un-hook please.'

'Un-hook!' Stephen spluttered, 'un-hook... Oh no... no, no!'

Turning to a cupboard behind him he searched among some of the books eventually pulling one out. Taking a note pad and pen from a box at the bottom of the cupboard, he said.

'Un-hook... oh we can't have that!'

Handing her the book notepad and pen, he added with some authority in his voice.

'You, young lady are on Captains report. This is a glossary of nautical terms, you will be tested at 0900 tomorrow. Depending how well you do... or not, you will either be scrubbing the decks or steering!'

Standing to attention briefly she saluted with her left arm. He put his arm up to his forehead and swooned in an act of surrender.

'No, no no! Wrong arm... you use your right one to salute!'

Dropping her left arm she raised her right one. He couldn't help chuckling now.

'Better, but definitely needs some work on it.'

Looking sideways at her raised arm then at Stephen she began to laugh unable to keep up the facade.

'What's wrong with it?'

He reached out taking hold of her wrist and lowering her arm to her side chuckling at their silliness. She stood looking deeply into his eyes, there were no words spoken but in a moment the atmosphere changed. It became charged almost electric! They stood apart briefly then came together and kissed gently, their lips hardly touching at first. After a few moments Stephen drew away looking awkward and embarrassed. He opened his mouth to say something, but she came in close to him and touched his lips with a finger.

'Shush...'

'But.'

'Shut up! ...That was fine... in fact it was better than fine.'

'But...'

'Stephen!'

He could see that to continue was pointless.

'Can we continue the tour now, Captain.' she said softly.

To hide his embarrassment he turned his back on her beginning to explain about the VDU screens, dials and levers that adorned the area around the control console at the helm position. The tone of his voice had changed and she sensed his awkwardness. Wanting to show they were okay and he needed to relax, she took a step towards him encircling her arms round his waist. He stopped what he was saying but didn't look at her. Sliding her an arm round his waist she stepped round him to stand at his side to get a clearer view of the consoles, leaving one hand lightly resting around his waist and looked into his face. He looked like someone who had just been caught doing some sort of mischief. Smiling, and giving his waist a squeeze she said.

'Go on, if you're going to let me drive I need to know what does what.'

He remained silent so to reassure him, she said gently.

'Hey... it's alright, okay.'

He nodded, she squeezed him once again trying to change the subject.

'If we're going to make the Duchess for a drink, then we need to get on here.'

That seemed to ease the tension between them and he responded.

'Yes, you're right. Well this is the lower helm position for wet or rough weather. There is another one up on the flying bridge up those stairs there.' He pointed to a spiral staircase ascending from the left-hand side, the port side, of the saloon by the patio doors. 'We steer her from there on fine days or when we're just cruising. I suppose you could say this is the best room really.' His eyes glinted, he smiled adding, 'The posh room, the lounge.'

She chuckled, 'There you go again...posh!'

'Yes, but it is, all the drinks, the fridge, the TV are up here and when the weather is hot the patio doors stay open and everyone just wanders in and out as they please.'

Turning to retrace their steps down to the galley he said.

'This is the toilet here,' gesturing to his left, 'or the heads in sailor talk. There's a shower in there too.'

She turned to look into the room.

'I was going to ask what you do about washing and so-on, so you've got running water then, hot and cold?'

He nodded. 'Yes, there's a 300 gallon freshwater tank plus we have a spoil tank for waste water from the basins, showers and toilets which gets pumped out at some of the wharves we re-fuel at and where we take on drinking water. It's all much more civilised these days you know. However, with regard to the use of water we still have to be frugal how we use it. I mean a bucket on a piece of rope provides the water for washing down the decks or the tender; that's the little inflatable we use to get ashore sometimes. The same goes for washing the outside of the cabin the flying bridge and windows too.' He paused for a moment before adding. 'That's your job tomorrow if you don't get your answers right...!'

He gave a wicked chuckle as he said this, sounding like some old sea dog.

'Now here where we've just had dinner is a double berth, the table folds down to form part of the base. The two long settee's in the saloon make up two single berths and here...' He said stopping at the door at the front of the galley, 'Is the forward cabin.'
Standing by the door, he pushed it open and moved to one side slightly. Nita peered over his shoulder.

'Ohh wow,' she said, 'this looks very grand, I thought you'd sleep in a hammock or something.'

'No no, the crew have hammocks, this madam will be your berth.'

Facing her was something that looked like a state room. The sides of the cabin were panelled from floor to the underside of the deck which, like the rest of the cabin was panelled with a dark rich teak wood. The double bed was shaped to follow the contours of the hull, it had a thick duvet covering it and a number of scatter cushion up against the curved headboard. There were wall lights on either side of the bed and to one side was a dressing table and mirror fixed to the cabin wall. On her left stood a full-length wardrobe and just inside the room was a small en-suite shower room. There were portholes on the side of the cabin with venetian blinds to provide privacy and a hatch above the bed again covered by venetian blinds. Pushing past him, she spun round and bounced down onto the bed.

'Ohh yes... I could really get to like this. What about you, where are you sleeping?'

'Ah,' he replied, 'as I said the table in the galley forms the base of another double berth or the long settee turns into two single berths.'

She pushed herself up the bed and assumed something of a sexy pose, then in a very sultry and seductive tone said.

'Do I get to fraternise with the crew?'

Stephen responded immediately with his country gent's voice once again.

'No madam sorry, the crew live in the bilges with the rats, they're awfully dirty and smelly... you wouldn't like them at all, sorry. The rats aren't much better either.'

He turned and walked back through to the saloon, picked up her bag, and returned to the forward cabin. Nita was sitting on the edge of the bed checking her hair and make-up in the mirror.

'Your luggage madam.'

'Oh thank you steward, come to my cabin later and I'll reward you then.'

Again she threw him a very sultry look, fluttering her long dark eye lashes. He had to admit she was so sexy when she did that. Returning to the galley he cleared the plates and glasses from the table. As he was putting the last of the bits and pieces away in the cupboards, his senses told him that Nita was close by, he could smell the sweet essence of her perfume. Turning he saw she was leaning against the bulkhead frame between the galley and the forward cabin. She'd put her hair up to reveal her beautifully slender neck, changed her top and was wearing a long-sleeved t-shirt in a pale honey colour that set off her naturally dark complexion, beige trousers and to finish off the ensemble a broad belt encircled her waist. A pashmina was draped around her shoulders fastened with a clasp on her left shoulder and turned slightly so that part of it fell over the other shoulder. He stopped and stared at her.

'Problem?' she inquired.

He shook his head. 'No. No problem… you look stunning, just like you did the evening you had dinner with me at the Duchess. Look at me I really do look like a deckhand.'

Closing the cupboard by his leg, he turned and went up into the saloon saying to Nita over his shoulder.

'Just come up here for the moment while I go and change my jeans then we'll walk down to the pub?'

He'd picked up a remote control pad and turned the television on handing her the control.

'Have a seat, I'll only be a couple of hours…'

'What!' she said, her voice surprised at what she'd just heard.

'Only joking… a couple of minutes; mind you I can't compete with you… no way.'

He grinned as he went back through the galley to the forward cabin. Nita sat on the long settee down the port side of the boat and looked around her surroundings. She noticed that all the furniture fittings were made of, or faced with, a richly coloured wood, teak she thought or rosewood. It was the same all through *Finbar*, the galley, the forward cabin all the cupboards and lockers. For the first time too she noticed some pictures here and there, taking a closer look she saw pictures of Suzanne with Stephen and some together with a little girl she took to be their daughter Emma and another couple. Suzanne looked a little taller than Stephen, slim, brown hair, very attractive. Studying them for a while she saw the smiles of the family. Sighing she turned and sat on the settee, 'so sad and so hard for Stephen and Emma' she thought. Picking up the book of nautical terms, she started to flick through it taking in the different words used by boat people.

Beam; The width of the boat at its widest point.

Draft; the depth of the hull below the water; how much water a boat draws.

Stanchion; The posts or guard rails running down the sides of a boat.

Transom; Stern; The back of a boat.

Warp; A strong length of rope used for mooring a boat to bollards, or for towing another vessel.

Stephen appeared in the saloon doorway, he'd put on a pair of chino trousers and a sports shirt and was carrying a jacket.

She looked up at him. 'I'll never learn all this by tomorrow.'

He shrugged, 'Well we'll have to find a suitable task for you until you do, say galley hand, or deckie.'

Throwing the book down on the coffee table she folded her arms saying. 'I won't do it... I won't. I'll rebel or whatever you do on a boat.'

'No you won't...' he chuckled, 'you'll mutiny.'

Holding out his hand, she took it and he pulled her up-right. Standing an arm's length apart, it just seemed the natural thing to do, he leaned forward casually and planted a gentle kiss on her lips. Turning the TV off, he turned and led her out through the patio doors onto the sun deck and held her arm firmly as she stepped up onto a locker and across the gap onto the wharf. He went back closed and secured the patio doors then nimbly stepped up to the wharf to stand by her side. This time it was Nita who kissed him and hand in hand they walked across the wharf to the entrance as if they had been together for ages.

At his home on the other side of Portbridge, Alan Syms picked up the dinner plate he'd just eaten his micro-wave dinner from putting it on the sideboard behind him. Turning back to the table he opened the file Detective Inspector Allan had given him and read the review. It was a case the uniform branch had been originally looking into which had now become something bigger.

Seven weeks ago, a vet reported to the RSPCA and the local police that he'd recently had to destroy a dog that had been found wandering, suffering quite extensive burns to its front paws, chest and snout. It had a microchip implanted and from that information officers had gone to the address given to interview the owner. A woman living at the address claimed that until three months ago she had been the partner of the dog's owner and that they had now separated. She gave the owner's name as Patrick Doyle, she also said that to the best of her knowledge no-one had seen him recently in the locality and she thought he'd probably left the area to visit relatives in Northumberland.

Four weeks ago the charred remains of a man were discovered by a member of the public walking their dog in a disused quarry on the outskirts of Portbridge often frequented by courting couples and walkers. The body was partially hidden by hay and covered with branches and leaves. The victim's hands and feet were bound with a rope dog lead and the dog's collar was fastened around the victim's neck.

Pathology and forensic reports indicate the victim showed signs of having suffered a severe beating prior to death. The report concluded that he probably would have been dead before someone had tried to burn his body. As the case was now a probable murder enquiry it was to be passed onto CID/Regional Crime Unit for further investigation.

Alan started to make notes following up what was known of the victim so far and if there were any known contacts locally. He needed to try and discover the victim's movements over the past three months. He heard a key turn in the front door and moments later a woman's voice called out as the door was closed, 'Hiya.'

Alan replied, 'Hi.'

A blond woman, average height if a little over-weight peered round the door into the dining area.

'Alright?'

'Yeah... okay.'

'What you doing?'

Alan glanced up from the file he'd been reading.

'Writing a letter to the Pope... what does it look like, sis?'

'Sorry... Want a brew?'

'Please.'

Alan's sister went through the door from the hall into the diner kitchen instead of passing by where he was working.

'Alan!' she called from the kitchen sounding irritated, 'When did you last wash up?'

'What?' he replied preoccupied by what he was reading?

'I said when did you last wash up? And how long have these clothes been in the washer?'

'Oh a couple of days I think.''

'What, the dishes or the clothes?'

'Both.'

'Bloody hell Alan, you're useless!'

Opening the washing machine she stepped back a pace.

'Did you put conditioner in with these? They smell a bit, I'll rinse them again.'

Alan answered, 'No, forgot, sorry.'

He was still distracted by what he was reading.

'Where is it?'

'What?'

'The conditioner?'

'In the bathroom.'

'No stupid the clothes conditioner not hair conditioner!' sounding annoyed now. 'Alan...!'

She raised her voice to get his attention it worked. Throwing his pen down onto the notepad he stood up going through to the kitchen.

'Louise, I'm trying to work, okay? Just stop wittering...'

'Alan, since Mum's been gone I've been worried about you.'

Stepping closer to him she stroked his arm affectionately.

'Every time I come around the place is a mess. I'm not here to be your skivvy, to clear up all the time do you understand?'

He looked round the kitchen and dining area and through to the lounge. Shrugging he replied.

'Well apart from this washing up it doesn't look too bad.'

Exasperated at his apparent lack of concern she snapped at him.

'Alan, it's a tip! I'll bet upstairs is even worse, yes?'

His reply was just as sharp.

'Lou, I get up, I go to work for god knows how long each day, I come home and still I work. When do I get the chance to play house... aye, answer that!'

She thought for a moment then said calmly.

'Okay, I accept you work silly hours but that's the nature of the job. You knew that when you applied to transfer to CID. But when you're home instead of buggering off to the club with the lads or going into town and getting wrecked, why not spend one evening a week tidying up. Better still get a cleaner once a week, you can afford it.'

Alan couldn't argue with her reasoning.

'Oh, sod off, sis,' he said and went back to the table.

Louise made some tea for them both placing one by his side then spent an hour tidying the kitchen and dealing with the washing, which she re-rinsed. Taking the armful of clothes upstairs she hung them on the high-dry frame in the bedroom that had been their mothers. She was right, upstairs was nearly as bad as the kitchen. The bathroom smelled of damp towels and sweaty socks. She cleaned the bathroom and liberally bleached the toilet then sorted another load of washing from the overflowing linen basket. Back in the kitchen she set the washing machine on. Jobs done she made them both another drink and setting it down beside her brother said.

'The house is tidy now, think seriously about a cleaner love, if you feel you can't keep on top of it or take one night a week and make the effort. Alan, I can't come home there are too many memories, just putting your stuff in Mum's room upset me. Anyway, I enjoy sharing with Nita and Moira it works and we get on so well.'

She turned to go into the lounge and watch some television, but Alan reached out and held her arm for a moment.

'Sorry Lou... I've been thinking, you're right, as usual. I'll have a word with one of the women who clean for us at work and see if they want an extra hour or two.'

Louise bent and kissed the top of her brother's head affectionately then went through to the lounge and sat down.

The walk down to the Duchess took about fifteen minutes. It felt strange to Stephen as he retraced his footsteps from six months ago only now he wasn't in pain from broken ribs and multiple bruising. They made their way through the entrance to the main bar.

'You find some seats and I'll get the drinks. What would you like?' he asked.

'White wine spritzer please, lem...' They finished the sentence in unison, 'With lemonade not soda.'

'I remember now.' he added.

Going to the bar he recognised the landlady and one of the other girls from his short stay here back in April. The landlady came across the bar to him.

'What can I get you, duck?' she said.

Stephen ordered Nita's drink and a pint of lager for himself. Twenty minutes or so must have passed during which time they talked about his summer with Emma and the family and what Nita had been up to workwise. She asked where his work had taken him since the end of May and through June. He explained that the company had kept him running around the UK until he felt he was able to resume his European runs, the downside was that he had to switch from the jobs he'd been doing in southern Europe to take over the Scandinavian contract.

'Do you want another?' someone said by their side. Startled they both looked up to see Mick standing by them.

'Mick, great you made it. No... this one is on me.' Stephen said standing and shaking Mick's hand. 'You sit.' continuing he asked him, 'Beer, lager... what?'

'Beer, Marston's please.'

Then to Nita he said, 'Another?'

'Why not.' she replied.

As he went to the bar Mick pulled up a chair and sat down. At the bar Stephen waited to be served for some time as the pub was quite full now with lots of noisy animated conversations. Eventually one of the barmaids came to him.

'Yes love, what can I get you?'

'Pint of Marston's, Pint of Lager... that one please,' he said pointing to the pump his first one had been drawn from, 'and a white wine spritzer with lemonade, not soda.'

As the young girl was drawing the lager the landlady walked behind her.

'Jen...' she said, 'these are on the house, okay!'

The girl glanced quickly at the landlady who nodded to confirm what she'd just said and then to Stephen adding.

'I wasn't sure when you came in but now Mick's turned up I recognise you. How've you been duck? Are you better now?'

A little taken aback that she should recognise him as it was six months since he'd stayed here, he smiled replying.

'I'm fine thanks, it took a while but I'm good now.'

'Pleased to hear it duck.'

Stephen called after her, 'Thanks for the drinks.'

Returning to the table, he set the drinks down as Nita finished off what she'd been saying to Mick. Picking up his pint he raised it to Nita and Stephen. 'Cheers...' and took a long draw from the glass almost half emptying it. Slapping his lips together he declared. 'Lovely, just what the doctor ordered I needed that!'

Putting the glass back on the table he looked at Stephen.

'She's just been filling me in on the result of the court case, reckon they got what was coming to them.'

The three of them talked incessantly for the next hour, occasionally breaking off to replenish their drinks. Their conversation covered Stephen's summer cruise, his work abroad where he'd been, his best and worst experiences. Mick told them of his time with the NCB and some of his more entertaining reflections of people's mishaps on the wharf. Both listened to Nita as she related tales from her time in the States with the New England Police. Stephen knew some of it from the evening they'd spent here in the Duchess back in April. Some stories had the three of them in stitches at the excuses some people would give. Suddenly the bar bell rang followed by the landlady's strident call.

'Last orders please good people, we've had enough tonight it's time you got yourselves off home. Last orders please.'

'One for the road anyone?' Mick said. Stephen and Nita shook their heads.

'Not for me thanks Mick, I'm okay with this one.'

Nita said. 'I'm okay too thanks Mick.'

'Well I'm on for one more.' Mick said standing and making his way to the bar.

Nita looked at Stephen.

'I don't know about you but I'm a little bit tipsy.'

'I'm okay, but I've had enough particularly as we have to move in the morning.'

'Is there any rule about drinking and steering a boat?' she asked.

'Not a hard and fast one, but if you have a collision with a boat or some other structure, then the rule is basically the same as drink driving, plus your insurance would be void as you would be deemed unfit through alcohol or drugs.'

She nodded as Mick returned to their table and sat down again. Standing Nita said.

'Just going to the little girl's room.'

A few minutes later the bell rang again, 'Time good people thank you. Time please.'

People drained their glasses, some took them back to the bar others left them on the tables and just left leaving two of the barmaids to collect them. Stephen, Nita and Mick finished their drinks taking their empty glasses to the bar. As they walked towards the doorway Mick called to the landlady.

'Night Jean thanks.'

'Night Mick, night you two.' The landlady replied.

Outside they stood for a moment their eyes adjusting to the dark. Nita shivered as the cooler night air hit them, Stephen put his jacket round her shoulders.

She looked at it draped around her; glancing at him she smiled.

'Chivalry lives on.'

'Right you two,' Mick began, 'I've got a date with a curry, fancy joining me?'

Stephen glanced quickly at Nita then back to Mick.

'No, I don't think so thanks Mick, we'll get back to *Finbar*. I need to be off before eight to get up to the yard tomorrow night.' Holding his hand out Mick shook it.

'Oh well, I'll maybe see you next spring then?' he said.

'Take care Mick, I'll definitely drop by in spring on my way down river.' Stephen replied.

He turned to Nita. 'Detective...'

Putting a hand on his shoulder she kissed his cheek. 'Bye Mick.'

He grinned touching his cheek briefly then turning went down the steps of the pub and walked off towards town. Nita moved closer to Stephen mainly to get warm and they stood for a while watching him walk away. At the same time, across town, Alan hugged his sister.

'Bye, love you, and thanks.'

He watched his sister walk down the street then, closed the door and locked up for the night.

Three hundred miles away in a small Belgium port the navigation lights of the converted fishing boat faded into the darkness as it made its way out to the open sea. The two cars that had been parked alongside the boat all evening had driven quietly away from the harbour and the sleeping village. Had anyone been passing the boat earlier in the evening they would have heard music animated conversation and laughter. They wouldn't have heard the occasional shout or scream from someone somewhere in one of the boats cabins as they'd been subjected to rape and sexually abuse. If they had heard anything then they may have mistaken the sounds for some high-spirited young people having a good time. Eventually, things quietened down until just before midnight the elegant woman, the older man and the four smartly dressed young men all made their way off the boat back to their vehicles to drive quietly out of town. Of the three young women who had joined the party, there was no sign.

~ ~

Standing together on the steps of the Duchess watching Mick Holmes wandering towards the town, Stephen looked at Nita.

'Come on you, let's get you back to *Finbar* you're cold.'

Together they went down the steps and walked briskly back towards the wharf. Turning into the entrance they'd gone three or four yards when the security lights switched on bathing the whole area in eerie amber light, Stephen stopped, frozen to the spot.

Nita took his arm. 'Stephen... what's the matter?'

He didn't reply.

'Stephen...,' she said again, concerned, 'What's the matter?'

Taking his hand she held it firmly, he was looking anxiously around the wharf, she sensed his anxiety, fear almost.

'Sorry...' he began 'I've just had a flash back to the night I was attacked.'

They walked slowly towards the boat as he continued talking quietly, re-living that night.

'The taxi dropped me here and I walked over to where *Finbar* is now. The security lights were tripped on when the taxi drove onto the wharf.'

He glanced around the wharf and the darkened buildings surrounding them trying to reassure himself that everything was okay.

'I noticed she was rolling in an odd way, not what you'd expect on a river mooring and then I saw a light flash on the water.' He hesitated again, just momentarily his voice sounding distressed. 'She was such a mess, they'd wrecked her.'

He looked straight at Nita now the expression on his face spoke volumes to her.

'The rest of it you know.' he said.

Linking her arm through his and squeezing his hand, she said quietly.

'It'll be okay tonight, you'll see.'

Reaching the side of the wharf Stephen stepped onto the boat's gunnel then down into the sun deck. He glanced quickly around the boat, she was right everything was as it should be. Turning back he half lifted her down to the sun deck. Putting her down on the deck she slid her arms round his waist pulling him into an embrace. It was intended to reassure him but she couldn't resist the urge and kissed him this time more lingeringly than earlier in the evening.

All his inhibition, his reticence of becoming involved with a woman again, even though it had been a few years since his wife had died, were dulled by the alcohol they'd consumed. This time he responded, returning her kiss properly, passionately, but gently. Their tongues touched briefly as their lips parted in this first real kiss. In a while they separated, remaining in the embrace looking into each other's eyes.

'Stephen Leigh-Grace, you are a very deep man. A lovely man but oh so very deep.'

Lifting his head up he looked at the sky watching the stars playing hide and seek in the clouds, trying to control his head and the desperate urge to break free from Nita and hide.

'Hmm,' he began to say, 'do you know how much you mix my head up lady?'

He looked into her eyes, beautiful he thought.

'Only you could do this to me. Part of me wants to run and hide the rest of me…' he made a little sound in his throat, 'ohh… the rest of me just wants, yet in a really strange way it feels okay, you know.'

Reaching up she took his face in her hands. 'Good.' she said and kissed him again lightly. They remained in the embrace holding each other tightly their eyes searching, exploring the others seeking a sign or some signal. The gap between them slowly closed and their lips met once more in another kiss, this time a full-on passionate kiss that mixed with their rising passion. Eventually they separated, Stephen turned opening one of the sliding doors to the saloon letting Nita pass him. Following her inside he clicked on the lights and closed the doors setting the locks top and bottom. Slipping his jacket from her shoulders she dropped it onto the end of the long settee that ran down one side of the saloon, turned to face him.

'Night cap?' he said.

She shook her head.

'Tea, coffee then?'

Again she shook her head.

'What then…?' he was lost for ideas now.

She took two steps towards him. Her eyes wide and focused on his face. With each step the tension between them became more palpable.

'You…' she said softly.

'Nita…?'

'I want you, Stephen!'

'Oh god… Nita.'

He was struggling again! Struggling against that urge once more to hide, but at the same time his heart and body's needs were taking control, he could feel that urge growing in the pit of his stomach, that desire to just take her.

'It's been…'

'I know… you've told me how long.'

'So how can …'

'Because you know that it's going to be alright.'

'Ohh Nita.'

He stood before her, arms by his side like someone who was resigned to the fact that all their arguments and reasons for not doing something, something they actually wanted to do, were finally exhausted. Reaching out she took his hand and led the way forward through the galley to the main cabin. He allowed himself to be led, his mind raced between what was happening here now with Nita and his guilt! On one hand he was experiencing those very natural, base instincts any man feels, urges of pure lust. Against them were the overwhelming memories of his late wife, Suzanne and the recurring feeling of not wanting to cheat on her memory. This was something he and Nita had talked about over the past six months. He had finally begun to understand and see her point that if he ever found himself losing control of a situation, he'd use Suzanne's memory as an excuse to hide behind.

'Stephen!' Her voice brought him out of his head. She was holding his face between her hands again and looking intently into his eyes. He could feel the warmth of her breath on his face and smell of her perfume hanging in the air.

'Stephen,' she said again, 'Trust me, it's going to be fine… honestly.'

He realised that he was holding her around the waist. She was still watching him and he saw the concern in her eyes, it was a caring look but there was desire there too; her pupils were dilated and he clearly recognised her 'want', her passion now. Drawing his face to hers again she kissed him gently trying to reassure him that what she'd just said, 'It's going to be fine,' was right. Responding gradually then with a growing sense of urgency, he became more aroused until they both submitted to their desires and the kiss became hot and fiery. Their lips melded together, tongues exploring each other's mouths passionately. They wanted one other now!

Without breaking this deep passionate kiss they began to pull at each other's clothes. Nita reached skin first, her hands exploring Stephen's back under his shirt in a sweeping caress, she circled her hands around and up to his shoulders pulling him into an even tighter hold. Into his mouth she sighed at her victory. Pulling her top from the waistband of her trousers he felt Nita's skin for the first time, soft warm, like satin to the touch of his fingers, he heard her sigh. Sliding his hands around her waist he gripped her in a bear hug.

Pulling away from each other, breathing heavily, their eyes fixed on one another, he pulled at his shirt rushing to undo the buttons and take it off; she pulled her top over her head. Reaching out for her he rested his hands on her shoulders drawing her back into the embrace encircling her waist again. Teasing each other now with tender butterfly kisses that drove their combined passion to even greater heights, he allowed his hands to trace her spine upwards until his path was blocked by her bra strap. He smiled sub-consciously remembering how in times past, when as a teenager beginning to experiment in the art of seduction: if you over-lap your fore-finger and thumb on either side of the fastening then gently squeeze them together it is possible to undo the bra clips one handed, like so…. Bingo! the strap parted. Nita dropped her arms and the bra fall to the floor to reveal her breasts. The nipples were stiff, erect, Stephen cupped one in his hand bent slightly and kissed the nipple. Shuddering at his touch she uttered a sigh from her throat, her legs gave way momentarily and she clung to him for support. Urgently she pulled on his trouser belt releasing the buckle, undid the button and pulled the zip down. Sliding her hands around his waist to meet behind his back she gently pushed them down over his buttocks. Stepping back she allowed them to fall to the floor then moved back into their embrace. Although restrained by his boxer pants she felt his hardness pressing against her abdomen. No reservations now, no pretence, things were beyond any sort of restraint. Drawing apart they pulled at their remaining clothes.

Outside it was pitch black around the wharf, the night air chilly from the September wind. Inside the main cabin the temperature was hot, full of passion, the aroma of Nita's perfume mingled with the scent of their two bodies on fire with lust and pure passion. Together they fell onto the bed exploring each other's body giving vent to their passion, sighing at their small victories as they made love.

Later, lying together in each other's arms, legs entwined stroking one another gently, her head resting on his chest his left arm around her shoulder absently caressing the small of her back.

'Why have you one arm browner than the rest of you?'

'Ah yes that's known as truckers' arm, you can always tell a driver because only one arm gets really tanned, which one depends on which side of the road you normally drive on.'

'Right…' She lifted her head from his chest offering him her lips for a kiss, he responded.

'Are you alright?' she asked.

'I'm fine.'

'Sure?' she quizzed him.

'I'm sure.'

Returning her head to his chest, she allowed her left hand to trail down his body and caress him.

'That was really very good you know. I'm glad it was me for your first time.' She hesitated giving him a squeeze, then corrected herself. 'This time I meant.'

She couldn't help herself giggling a little, embarrassed at her boldness, not just in what she was saying but in what her left hand was doing and the reaction she was getting from Stephen. She felt him tense a little and heard him give a quiet low grunt as he was beginning to feel the effects of her caresses stirring his newly awakened passion once more. Moving into a more comfortable position he found himself face to face, she was watching him, her eyes wide dewy and sultry, all the while her hand was gently stroking and caressing him.

Taken by just how beautiful she really was he closed the gap between their faces and kissed her. He caressed her breast, feeling her hand move in response to his kiss and caress. From that moment, things moved quickly becoming more urgent as they succumbed to their desire to make love again. This time they took an age loving one another until they finally lay together spent and totally satisfied. Stephen slept, his head on Nita's breast. She listened to his slow breaths punctuated occasionally with a soft snore. It reminded her of a cat purring, she smiled at the thought and whispered in her own tongue then in English, 'Sleep well Stephen Leigh-Grace before drifting into a deep peaceful sleep herself.

~~~~~~~~~~~~~~~~~~~~~~~~~~~~~~~~~~~~~~~
~~~~~~~~~~~~~~~~~~~~~~~~~~~~~~~~~~~~~~~

SATURDAY

An unfamiliar smell and strange sounds invaded Nita's senses bringing her out of a deep sleep. Opening her eyes she lay for some minutes gathering her thoughts, recalling the last few hours since arriving back on board *Finbar*. Fully awake she began to assimilate the sounds and smells. Firstly, there was just the slightest aroma of diesel also a strange sensation of movement and a feint vibration. She felt the boat rock very slightly, the motion made her feel a little strange even though she was still lying in the bed. It reminded her of the room spinning after a great night out and a little too much to drink. Also there was the sound of water rippling down the side of the boat just by the side of the bed. Sitting up suddenly she quickly calculated, 2 + 2 equals 4, then the realisation hit her... they really were moving!

Slipping from under the quilt, she sought out some fresh underwear from her overnight bag then slipped into her jogging pants and pulled a t-shirt on over her head. Turning back to the bed, she pulled the duvet back to the end of the bed to air the cover and sheet smiling as she did so remembering last night's passion. Finally she gathered up their discarded cloths that lay around on the floor, folded them and put them on the stool under the dressing table. Sitting on the edge of the bed she slipped her bare feet into her trainers then taking a sponge bag from her holdall stepped into the bathroom placing it on a small shelf. Switching the light on above the vanity mirror she studied herself for a few moments. Looking good she thought, like the cat that's just had the cream. She brushed her teeth and hair, pulled it away from her face and wound a scrunchy band around it into a ponytail. Turning she grabbed her hoodie from the top of her bag and made her way through the galley to the saloon expecting to see Stephen driving the boat. Standing stock still for a moment she was thrown into an immediate panic when she saw he wasn't there and *Finbar* appeared to be moving on her own! What was really spooky was the wheel turned a little one way and then the other all on its own.

'Hello...' she called anxiously, as no reply came she called again, louder this time. 'Hello! Is anyone there?' Still no response! She raised her voice now. 'Stephen!'

From somewhere she heard his voice. 'Nita, up here, come up the stairs.'

Moving to the rear of the saloon she looked up the stairs and saw daylight through the open hatch. Climbing the spiral steps she emerged onto the flying bridge to see Stephen steering the boat, relieved she smiled at him.

'God, I thought I was on a ghost ship, you scared me!'

'Sorry, but this the best place to be when we're on the river, if the weather's good, you get a clearer view of what's going on around the boat.' He smiled back at her.

With the gentle motion of the boat and the mild September breeze blowing in her face, she glanced around at their surroundings quite surprised at the scenery passing slowly passing. She sat watching it for a while thinking that most of the time she travelled around in a car, just like everybody else so never really got the chance to look properly at the countryside. She was surprised by the variations of greens in the fields and the leaves on the trees that bordered the river, some beginning to take on brown and gold autumn tints. She watched as they sailed past a ploughed field intrigued by the optical effect the straight furrows created.

'Right you.' Stephens's voice interrupted her thoughts. 'Your first task this morning is to go and find your way around the galley and make some tea... please.'

Standing to attention she answered, 'Yes sir, captain'

Shaking his head in mock dismay he couldn't help chuckling.

'Oh no... the answer is, aye captain.'

She grinned back at him and this time saluted.

'Yes sir, I mean aye captain.' but moved towards him saying. 'Actually this is my first task of the day.'

She bent and kissed him on the lips, gently but passionately. Suddenly *Finbar* Speeded up, A little shocked she broke the kiss and stood looking at Stephen then around the boat somewhat alarmed.

'Oh dear, you've upset her now, she's jealous.' he said gently reaching out and stroking the surround of the control panel, as you would a child to reassure it.

'There,' he said softly, 'it's alright. This is Nita and she's very nice really.'

He turned slightly, still stroking the panel and said to her over his shoulder.

'Come and say hello.'

She saw the cheeky look in his eye and smiled back. Sitting back on his seat he repeated himself.

'You've got to say hello or she'll think you don't like her.'

Just then the engine stopped altogether and in a few moments they'd lost all way and began to drift, the rivers current bringing her bow round to float back down river. Still a little alarmed at what was happening, she knew Stephen was teasing her but couldn't quite work out just how. Reaching forward she tentatively stroked the panel top where he had moments earlier.

'Hi *Finbar*, I'm Nita.' she said.

Immediately the engine started again and Stephen brought her quickly back on course heading upriver once more. Nita, still leaning over him she saw his elbow resting on two levers, she quickly realised they controlled the engine. Taking a step back from him she gave his shoulder a gentle swipe.

You rat!'

'Oww...' he exclaimed, 'what was that for?'

Holding himself where she'd hit him he feigned surprise and pain looking up at her.

'You know very well what that was for.' and went to give him a second swipe; this time he shied away and she missed her mark. He made a grab for her thigh hooking his arm around her and dragging her towards him. They were both giggling like a couple of teenagers as she put up weak resistance. He kissed her stomach through her clothes, she flopped down next to him on the edge of his seat and they continued their kiss.

'Morning.' someone called.

They sprang apart like guilty children who'd just been caught doing something mischievous.

Looking towards where the voice had come from Nita put her hand to her mouth in a natural gesture to hide her embarrassment. Stephen raised his hand nonchalantly acknowledging the other boat passing them, going down river. He saw a tall well-built man and a slightly shorter woman standing together on the little stern deck of a barge.

'Morning,' he called back, 'lovely morning.'

'Yes it is, have a good trip.' the man replied and waved again.

'You too.' Stephen responded as the gap between the two boats grew.

Nita giggled like a little girl.

'Do you think they saw us?'

'Oh for sure, it'll be all over the river by tonight.'

She saw the look in his eye again and raised her hand.

'Ah... no! Go and make tea cabin boy... girl, now!'

Obediently she stood up and went down the stairs to the galley eventually returning with two teas. Sitting on one of the comfy upholstered seats beside Stephen, drinking tea and sharing slices of toast she'd rustled up, she said.

'So come on then my captain fill me in on the rules of the river and so on.'

Over the gentle rumble of the one engine running he began to explain the ins and outs of inland waterway cruising. She listened trying to grasp all the technical and colloquial terms and phrases, at the same time revelling in this newfound beauty that was the English countryside its sounds and smells. They were so unlike the sights she was accustomed to as a car driver, the miles of tarmac and the dirty grimy verges flashing past at sixty miles an hour. She was amazed that there was so much to see on the other side of a hedge or wall that would normally be gone in a blur in the car. It was only now that she began to really appreciate something of what life at 4 miles an hour offered. Apart from the instant feeling of calm and peace in a person's inner self, there was this kaleidoscope of different colours everywhere you looked.

'Hey sleeping beauty… , wake up. I've got a little job for you.'

She woke with a start and sat up. The scenery had changed there were buildings on both sides of the river now and she could hear the distant sounds of traffic. Still a little disorientated she looked at Stephen.

'Where are we? How long have I been asleep?'

'Oh, about an hour.' he replied, 'I've got a little job I need you to do, okay? First I need you to put some fenders over this side.'

He pointed to the right side of *Finbar*, 'The starboard side,' he said. 'an orange one at the bow and three white ones spaced down the side. You'll see them already fastened to the stanchion posts.'

As she stood up he added a cautionary note. 'Nita! be careful watch your feet.'

He watched her as she put the fenders over the side and made her way back up to the bridge.

'The canal starts here so we've got to go through this lock. We'll be up to it in the next 5 minutes or so and I need you on the bank to take one of the mooring lines and walk up to the top of the lock.'

She looked at him a little surprised at what he was asking her to do. However he just carried on explaining to her what she had to do.

'When I get *Finbar* into the lock you'll need to take two turns round a bollard to hold her steady and then wait for me to come up to you, okay?'

Nodding she replied, 'I think so.'

'Don't worry the lock keeper will talk you through it if you're having a problem?'

A few minutes later as they rounded a bend in the river she saw a huge pair of gates blocking their way, a traffic light was showing red on the wall beside on one of the gates from where water was spewing out in several places. Concentrating Stephen brought *Finbar* slowly alongside the riverbank, the sides were walled here and bollards spaced out at twenty foot intervals. Without looking at her he said.

'Will you go down to the sun deck, you'll see two ropes there. Take the one that runs forward to the front, the bow and go up the bank to that bollard,'

He pointed to one of them some ten feet in front of the boat, 'and tie us up to it please.'

'Okay.'

She nodded and descended the steps once more to the sun deck. He felt the boat rock gently as she stepped ashore and over the edge of the bridge watched her pull the line along the bank as she moved to the bollard. Turning to look at him as she got to it and pointed to the bollard, he gave her the thumbs up. She took a number of turns around it then stood looking at the boat. Putting the engine into neutral, Stephen made his way down the steps to the sun deck and taking the stern line stepped ashore and took three turns round the nearest bollard. Nita was back now watching him as he went back aboard into the saloon, moments later the engine stopped. Coming back to the sun deck he stepped up to the tow path to join her.

'There's another boat working the other way through the lock, so we'll be a quarter of an hour or so. I think we'll walk up and you can watch what happens, alright?'

Walking hand in hand along the pathway they ascended the steep steps that climbed up the side of the lock. As they got to the top of the steps the sound of rushing water made Nita turn and look down over the edge at the river. It appeared like a boiling cauldron as the lock emptied. She watched the barge in the lock sink down as the water drained away.

Grinning she said, 'It's like watching a giant's bath empty.'

Smiling he explained how the lock worked and how the water was released to raise and lower the boats. Holding tightly to him she peered over the side of the lock and saw the barge at the bottom turning, her eyes wide with amazement she said.

'Doesn't it frighten you going all that way down in such a small space?

Giving her a little squeeze to reassure her he replied.

'The first couple of times it's a bit daunting but not all locks are this deep, it's just that this is the first one from the river to the canal proper. That's another reason why this one has a fulltime keeper here.'

The outer gates began to open to let the barge out.

'Come on it's our turn now.' he said.

Taking her hand they turned to retrace their steps back to *Finbar*.

Arriving back at the boat they were in time to wave to the people who'd just worked through the lock as they passed them going down river. Releasing the bow line Stephen passed it to Nita.

'Take this back up to the top of the lock as I bring *Finbar* into the lock then take a couple of turns around one of the bollards at the far end and wait for me to come up to you okay. It's just like walking a dog.'

She giggled as she set off calling back over her shoulder.

'A dog! ... if it's a dog, then it's a sodding great St Bernard, why couldn't you have a little boat instead of a cruise ship...?'

Appearing on the flying bridge he called after her.

'Stop whingeing woman and get a move on!'

Turning back and looking towards him she stuck her tongue out. By the time she'd reached the top of the steps Stephen had motored *Finbar* into the lock. She took a couple of turns around a bollard at the end as he had instructed then waited glancing around at her surroundings. A voice called out, she turned to see some guy leaning out of a window on the opposite side of the lock in a small tower that resembled a railway signal box.

'You all set luv'?'

Shrugging her shoulders she replied. 'I guess so, yeah.'

The man waved and moments later she saw the lower gates close behind *Finbar* boxing her in. Nervously she edged to the lip of the lock wall and looked down at Stephen, he waved to her. Retreating back a few steps she held onto the rope loosely. Suddenly it went taut and she had to grab hold of it tightly with both hand to stop it being whipped out of her grasp. 'Oh shit..!' she exclaimed as the rope continued to try and whip itself from her grasp. She let out a shriek and quickly stepped back to the edge. There were two powerful jets of water spewing out of the upper lock gates which made *Finbar* skew violently from side to side like a mad dog tugging on the rope she was holding.

'Stephen,' she shrieked 'what the hell do I do!'

He didn't seem to hear her. She screamed at him now.

'What do I do for god's sake?'

He looked up at her cupping a hand around his ear suggesting he couldn't hear her. From the control tower the man called out of the window.

'Pull the rope in duck, keep it tight as the boat rises or it'll do some damage.'

She pulled hard on the rope, it sighed around the bollard as she took up the slack. Once she'd caught up she kept the tension on it as *Finbar* continued to rise in the chamber. The radar cone and aerials were visible now then the flying bridge drew level with the lip of the lock, Stephen at the helm grinning at her at face level.

'Alright, I knew you'd get the hang of it.' he called.

She retorted instantly and angrily.

'Bollocks! That's twice no three times today you've frightened me.'

The rest of *Finbar* had risen above the edge now and the keeper was opening the top gates to release her. Looking over the side of the bridge Stephen called again.

'Come on, back on board we'll get some breakfast in another

ten minutes.'

Seething at what had just happened she unwound the rope from the bollard then grabbing the coils, threw them into the sun deck before climbing back on board. She didn't go back up to Stephen but sat on one of the locker cushions surrounding the sun deck. She heard Stephen call to the lock keeper as they cleared the gates and looking up to the tower, half-heartedly returned the guys wave. Some fifteen minutes passed as they slowly motored up the canal, she noticed yet another subtle change in its scenery. It was much narrower and seemed very quiet and calm, her mood changed too as Mother Nature worked her charm on her anger revealing quiet, shady tree lined places on the banks and between them an ever-increasing variety of buildings. Even here there was a feeling of tranquillity, with bird song adding to the overall sense of peace. There were ploughed fields again and some just fallow or with cattle grazing them, apart from the occasional sound of the boats engine echoing back to break the peace and quiet, she began to picture in her mind the canal a hundred years ago, alive and thriving; so different from now, from today. Okay the picture was marred at times by the odd traffic cone or a car tyre floating by, there was even a supermarket trolley caught in some reeds by the tow path. There were the old buildings too standing by the canal side, many of them totally derelict. Nearer the town there were more warehouses and old mills that had been converted into apartments. The developers seemed to have made every effort to retain as much of the history of the buildings, their facades and characteristics as possible. A crane at the top of one particular conversion had even been kept, its wire and hook secured at the top of the sixth floor. Even the doors that had originally given access to each floor were surrounded by balconies allowing their respective residents to sit outside and enjoy the views. She could almost hear in her head the sounds and picture in her mind's eye the sights from long ago, the people working at that warehouse unloading or loading the barges moored below.

Finbar gave a shudder, her engine note changed and she seemed to veer a little. This motion brought Nita back to reality. Looking around she saw that they were drifting in towards one of the banks then the engine stopped. Stephen appeared through the saloon door onto the sun deck, picked up one of the ropes and stepped ashore. He took two or three turns round a nearby bollard then stepped back onto the boat securing the rest of the rope around a deck cleat in a figure of eight knot. Taking the tangled mass of rope that Nita had dropped when she had come back on board, he looked at her, tutted then left the boat unravelling it as he went forward to secure the bow line to another bollard, returning he said.

'Come on, I'm going to buy you the best breakfast you've ever eaten.'

She stood up, 'Do I need my jacket?' she asked quietly still annoyed by her earlier experience at the lock.

He stopped what he was doing and glanced at her, he could see from her body language that she was not happy.

'No you'll be fine as you are, the café's only a couple of minutes away.'

She nodded 'I'll get my bag.'

He closed the patio doors locked them and offered her his hand to help her onto the tow path. In silence they walked side by side to the end of the nearest warehouse around the corner and down an alley between some other buildings. *Finbar* settled gently against the canal wall with a few bumps as the wake of a passing barge disturbed her.

Over breakfast he talked to her about what had happened at the lock. He listened whilst she explained how angry she had been, and why. He apologised and said in future he'd try to explain things more clearly. Later, returning to *Finbar* they slipped their mooring and left the town behind although the atmosphere between them was still tense. By mid-afternoon they were back into the countryside following the gentle meandering bends of the canal as they continued towards the inland marina where he wintered the boat and where he could carry out maintenance jobs. Nita re-discovered the same sense of peace she'd felt earlier and her mood mellowed. A short while later they had to work another lock, only this one was much smaller and there was no lock keeper. Stephen steered *Finbar* to the edge and tied her up. He made his way to the sun deck, opened one of the lockers and took out two handles, each with a short length of rope attached. Calling to Nita, who'd remained legged out on one of the seats on the bridge enjoying the afternoon sun.

'Sorry to disturb you, have you got a minute please?'

Moments later she appeared through the patio doors. He held out one of the levers to her, she took it and looked at him quizzically.

'Put your wrist through the loop and come with me.'

'What for, are we going to have a duel?' she said, brandishing the handle at him like a weapon.

'No… silly, I'm going to show you how we work a lock, okay?'

'Ohh, right.'

Obediently she followed him towards the steps up to the lock as he began to explain.

'The problem this morning,' he said, 'was because that lock was the Lower Leavens lock. It's owned by the Severn Trent authority and is manned because it's a commercial lock. Most of these locks we come across now belong to British Waterways and are much smaller. We have to work these ourselves.' Taking her hand, he continued. 'I'm sorry again that I just dropped you literally in at the deep end.'

Turning, he took her face between his hands and kissed her gently saying against her lips, 'Sorry.'

With their foreheads touching they looked into each other's eyes, she smiled realising she couldn't stay annoyed anymore. They stayed head to head for a moment longer before Nita put her arms round his shoulders and returned his kiss. Arm in arm they continued towards the lock as he continued explaining how these smaller locks worked.

'The ones on the river this morning are nearly all manned because the gates are electric, those locks are so much bigger because they take commercial barges like NCB 9 the one you saw at Portbridge in April, remember?' By now they had reached the lock. 'These,' he said, 'we work ourselves. Look this one is full, that tells me that the last boat through was going the same way we are. Had it been empty...?'

Nita interrupted, 'Then it would have been going the other way and we would have seen it.'

'Exactly, plus the gates at this end would have been open.'

For the next twenty minutes he talked her through the process of working a lock. He answered her questions repeating some of the processes a second time so that she fully understood, finishing off by saying. 'The only way to really understand is to work one.'

Holding up her handle she asked. 'What happens if you drop the handle?'

'Ah yes, that's where the loop comes in, if you drained one of these locks you'd probably find half a dozen or more of these buried in the mud and silt, but be warned! take your wrist out of the loop when you're closing the paddles in the gates or you could break your wrist! Come on let's put this theory into practice.'
Working on opposite sides of one pair of gates, Nita mirrored what Stephen did on his gate until the water level was the same as where *Finbar* was moored.

'Do you know,' he said as they walked back to the boat. 'Some people have been stranded in a lock for hours just waiting for another boat to come along because they've dropped these handles.'

Nita chuckled. 'Really... honestly?'

'Absolutely, yes for hours!'

A short time later they emerged out of the upper lock gates and continued up the canal. Nita disappeared once they were on their way again returning a little later with a tray of tea and a plate of biscuits. Putting the tray down on the moulded table between the seats, she handed one to Stephen. Taking a sip, he slid off the helm seat patting it.

'Next lesson,' he said 'I've put the 'L' plates on. You can drive now.'

She looked at him stunned.

'What! No, no way! No, sorry I can't…no! I might crash or something or run into another boat, No Stephen you carry on driving.'

'Look, you need to learn to steer so that if I need to go…'

She looked at him horror struck. 'Go!' she exclaimed, 'Go where? You're not going to leave me on my own are you?'

He grinned broadly at her expression, she looked genuinely terrified.

'No, I'm not going to leave you but if I need to go, you know to the heads, sorry toilet, then we needn't stop if you can drive, well steer actually that's all, okay?'

Reaching towards her he took the mug of tea out of her hand and put it on the tray, then taking her by the shoulders guided her to the helms seat. Reluctantly she shuffled herself onto it and sat waiting to be told what to do next. He started to explain what each of the different levers dials and switches did.

'This is the wheel,' he said, 'and these are the throttles, one for each engine. On the canal I only run on one engine for economy plus, the speed limit is only 4 mph so I don't need both engines. Here are the rev counters again one for each engine, just like you have on a car. This is the speedo but it's in knots not miles per hour.'

She looked at him, it was an expressionless stare.

'What the hell is a knot…?'

'Ah well, a knot is a way the speed of a boat is measured. It's historic and too complicated to explain now, but a knot is equal to about one and a third miles an hour.'

Nita still looked expressionless. 'One and a third miles an hour… really?'

'Yes.'

'So how fast does *Finbar* go?'

'Flat out around 15 Knots, say twenty, twenty one miles an hour or so.'

'Is that fast then?'

'For a cruiser that's pretty fast.'

Continuing to explaining the controls, he said.

'This upside down fishbowl with that clock looking dial inside is the compass. This is the horn and oh, these you don't touch!' he said pointing to two red buttons on the control panel.

She looked at him. 'Why?'

He threw her a wicked grin. 'They're the ejector seat buttons for rebellious crews!'

Her arm swept round in an arch as she tried to side swipe him. 'Rat…'

Intercepting her arm he said quietly, 'Go on take the wheel and just get the feel of her. Even at these low speeds on one engine she's quite responsive.'

He made a sudden grab for two chrome grab handles near to the helm position as *Finbar* veered one way towards the bank then sharply the other, back to the centre of the canal. Nita glanced up at him quickly, apprehensively.

'Steady,' he said but the tone of his voice was firm. 'You only need the slightest movement on the wheel then wait for her to answer the helm. It's not like steering a car.' Looking up the canal he pointed to a tree standing alone on the bank where the canal began to curve. 'Line the bow up with that tree but keep on the right side of the canal and you need to be able to see the tow path down this side from where you are sitting otherwise we could run aground.'

He watched her for some time as she concentrated on keeping *Finbar* on a straight course. After a while he said to her quietly.

'Take hold of the throttle levers. Now push that lever forward and see if she responds.' Nervously she pushed the lever forward, nothing happened. She pulled it back and looked at him.

'Try the other one then.'

She pushed the second lever forward, the engine note changed instantly and *Finbar* surged forward quickly gathering speed. She screamed at the sudden acceleration, panicked taking her hand off the throttle leaving it in the new position. Stephen reached across and pulled the lever back to its first position *Finbar* slowed immediately.

Touching her shoulder he said,

'Look,' pointing behind them, 'that's why there's a speed limit on all inland waterways.'

Following them like some preying serpent was a wave of water, the wake from *Finbar*'s acceleration. On either side of the canal the wave was breaking against and over the banks as it chased them.

'If there wasn't a speed limit then a lot of the open banks would be washed away, and the canal system would just silt up with the mud and debris that's been washed down. Plus could you imagine if you were moored up somewhere and a boat passed you at speed. You'd end up with your dinner and a glass of red in your lap. Anyway, back to your driving lesson, look here,'

He pointed out some markings on the chrome surrounds set into the control panel that the throttle levers rose out of. They were engraved with the words Forward, Stop, Slow, Half and Full, and the other way. Astern, Stop, Slow, Half and Full. Between stop and slow ahead a mark was etched into the chrome.

'That mark is about 4 miles an hour, okay? And then when you want to stop, you go astern.'

As he said this he pulled the throttle lever back to Stop, waited a moment for the engine note to change, then continued to pull the lever back to astern passing the slow mark and down towards half. As he did so *Finbar*s engine note increased sending a vibration through her hull as she came to a stop. He pushed the throttle back to stop as they came to a standstill in the water. Looking at Nita he nodded.

'Go on you try now.'

Very tentatively taking hold of the throttle lever once again she pushed it forward, looking for the mark. The pitch of the engine increased and *Finbar* began to move forwards again. Stephen stood by her shoulder prepared to intervene should she panic again. After a minute or two, she pulled the lever back to the stop mark and then passed it towards slow astern. A buzzer sounded! Panicking again she turned to look at Stephen.

'That's okay.' he said, 'You've got to wait a moment for the gearbox to change from forwards to astern. The buzzer reminds you.'

He put his hand over hers, pushed the lever back to stop. The buzzer stopped and then he pulled her hand and the lever back towards astern. *Finbar* shuddered and rumbled as her propeller brought her to a standstill. Still covering her hand with his he pushed the throttle back to stop.

'So do you want to drive for a bit?'

She grinned broadly at him, her brown eyes bright with excitement.

'Yeah, for a little while... but don't leave me!' she said anxiously.

'Okay.'

Adjusting her position so she was more comfortable, she put her hand on the lever and pushed it forward to the notch; *Finbar* responded and moved forward. Stephen sat on one of the moulded settee cushions and surveyed the passing countryside. This whole passage, whether up the canal this weekend to his winter mooring, or down to the estuary Marina in springtime never failed to impress on him the wonders of nature. At some point he must have drifted off to sleep because Nita's urgent call suddenly brought him upright on the settee.

'Stephen!' It was more urgent the second time. 'Stephen! Wake up, there's a boat coming, what do I do?'

Craning his neck slightly to see over the wind shield at the front of the bridge, he saw a narrow boat coming towards them. He sat up, 'You're okay,' he said reassuringly, 'Just keep on your side of the canal.' He watched her, ready to help if needed, 'Not too close to the edge. Remember you need to keep the tow path just in view.'

She made a small correction with the wheel.

'That's okay, keep her steady at that.'

The two boats passed each other without any problem. As they did so they each acknowledged the other with a wave. Stephen stood up, 'Right... time for tea I think!'

She glanced at him quickly. 'You're not going to leave me on my own are you?'

'Yeah,' he replied, 'You're doing all right you can always stop if you're not sure.'

As he went down the stairs from the bridge to the saloon and galley, he added.

'I'm only going to be a couple of minutes. Don't panic!'

True to his word he returned to the bridge minutes later handing Nita one of the mugs he was carrying then sat down by her side. Half to himself he said thoughtfully.

'We could make the mooring today if we push on into the evening, or there's a rather nice little pub not much further up here where we can stop for the night. They do some very nice meals.'

Nita on hearing his thoughts, mulled over the options for all of thirty seconds then replied.

'Mm... Pub... food and finish off the trip tomorrow sound's the best option.'

He looked at her then nodded. 'Okay, we're half an hour or so away in that case.

~~~~~~~~~~~~~~~~~~~~~~~~~~~~~~

Just after five 'o clock with the September sun settling low over the distant hilly horizon throwing shafts of golden light through the trees to reflect on the rippling water, the pub Stephen had talked about appeared around a bend in the canal. It seemed to Nita that the water had become a bed of pale diamond and amber stones. They'd moored up a hundred yards from the pub and whilst waiting for Stephen she sat on the sun deck trying to learn more of the nautical terms from handbook, she glanced from the sparkling water towards the pub. The building appeared like a picture on the lid of a chocolate box, its walls all adorned with floral hanging baskets and even though the displays were beyond their best they still made a vivid array of colour. Dotted along the tow path were another half dozen narrow boats all apparently with the same thought as theirs. Wandering
~~~~~~~~~~~~~~~~~~~~~~~~~~~~~~

back through the saloon and down to the galley area she stood close behind him and stroked his shoulders affectionately.

'I need a shower before we go out, I've been in these clothes all day and I'd like to change.'

He turned from the sink to face her.

'Help yourself, there's the en-suite one in the cabin, or this one here,' he pointed to a door set off to one side by the steps up to the saloon.

She moved towards the cabin. 'I'll take this one, all my stuff's in there, it'll be easier.'

He followed her through to the cabin opening the sliding door to the shower cubicle, then went to the nearest, narrow wardrobe and took out two cream towels handing them to her, she kissed him gently.

'Thank you, Mm… I've missed that.' she said quietly.

He put his arms around her waist and kissed her again. The embrace and kiss lasted some time before they parted for breath. 'Go on you,' he said, 'this isn't going to get us to the pub for dinner is it?'

She giggled and scrunched up her nose. 'Consider it as the starter.' she said cheekily and moved back towards him sliding her arms around his waist pulling him firmly into another embrace. The shower was never going to happen now! They kissed one another urgently wantonly before collapsing onto the bed.

Stephen was more relaxed this time as they fumbled to help each other remove their clothes, until finally they were naked. They kissed and caressed, he discovered one of her erogenous zones teasing it with his fingers and tongue. She squirmed under his touch squealing as he paid special attention to this most sensitive part of her body. The effect though, brought her to new heights of arousal so that when he moved to cover her she arched her back to meet him and just as the previous night experienced an instant mini orgasm. Throwing her arms around him she held him in a vice-like embrace, wrapping her legs round his thighs so that he was unable to move, from deep in her throat she emitted low growl.

'Oh… god… Stephen! What do you do to me?'

Her orgasm slowly subsided and they began to move together, gently at first savouring the myriad of sensations that coursed through them. Then as the inevitable moment rushed to meet them, so their rhythm quickened. They were together, in perfect harmony locked in the most passionate of embraces seeking the ultimate sensation of a shared orgasm. Holding one another tightly, their bodies quivering, their muscles twitching it was as though both had just been shocked by some unseen power. Gradually the muscular spasms subsided until at last they lay, arms and legs entwined experiencing the wonderful after-glow lovers speak of. Nita lay nestled in the crook of his arm her head resting on his chest, a leg lying across his. He stroked the small of her back tenderly, taking time to compare the tone of her honey coloured skin to his. Even after two months of summer weather, sea and wind burn, he still looked pale against her skin. She spoke quietly, interspersing her words whilst kissing his chest.

'My god Stephen… you are an amazing lover… do you know that?'

Considering what she had just said for a moment or two, he replied. 'No-one has ever said that before,' then adding, 'mind you, there hasn't been anyone since Suzanne… until now.'

He kissed the top of her head giving her bare bottom a firm, but gentle smack. She let out a little shriek. 'Come on you. Go for that shower or we'll be going hungry tonight.'

He rolled away from her and slipped into the jogging pants and a T-shirt he'd worn through the day. Glancing at her still lying on the bed he said, 'I'm going for a shower.'

As he got to the cabin door her voice stopped him in his tracks. 'Captain.'

Her tone was quiet, sensual and seductive he turned to look at her. She'd rotated herself until she was lying on her tummy at the foot of the bed, resting on one elbow watching him, the pupils of her deep brown eyes still dilated from their shared passion. His eyes followed the contours of her naked body down past her shoulders taking in the soft curve of a half-exposed breast then the curves of her hips and buttocks, her thighs.

'Oh my word,' he thought, 'you are truly beautiful.'

'Thank you Captain.' She said coyly, grinning broadly at him.

'What!' he said surprised and shocked.

'Thank you, for that compliment.' She repeated herself.

'But I... I was just thinking it!'

'Yes, but you said it out loud.'

Confused and embarrassed, he tried to cover his awkwardness.

'I'm going for a shower.' He said again.

'Stephen.' she said, this time firmly.

He stopped to listen to her but didn't turn to face her.

'It's okay. I'm touched by your comment, your compliment it makes me feel good inside, thank you.'

He nodded and left the cabin saying, 'Okay.'

Three quarters of an hour later showered and squeaky clean, dressed for a night out the two of them stepped onto the tow path and walked hand in hand the hundred yards to the pub. Passing some of the other barges and narrow boats moored on the canal, Nita commented.

'I never really appreciated how beautifully decorated some of them are.'

'Yeah,' he replied. 'You can buy the plant pots and watering cans already painted but some of the owners like to do them themselves. You know some of the woodwork and the artwork on the interiors of their boats is quite fabulous.'

She turned around to look back at *Finbar* while keeping up with Stephen but walking backwards.

'Do people ever comment on why you bring *Finbar* this far?'

She turned back once again to walk by his side waiting to hear his answer.

'Some do. You get the traditionalists who reckon she's just a floating gin palace or a piece of Tupperware, an excuse for lazy sailing you know all plastic, little effort required, low maintenance!'

She giggled, picturing the image he'd just conjured up in her mind. She put her arm round his waist and gave him a squeeze.

'Well I think she's beautiful.' she said.

Arm in arm they arrived at the pub entering through the doorway off the tow path and found themselves in a room full of chatter laughter and music, the whole atmosphere felt warm and friendly. Looking around for somewhere to sit Stephen saw only a bar stool guiding Nita towards it, he said, as she slipped up onto the stool, 'Spritzer?'

'Please.'

As she settled herself on the stool a barman came to them.

'Yes folks. What'll it be?'

Stephen ordered the drinks then stood by Nita's side. They watched the people in the bar, occasionally passing a comment on an individual or a group of people. The rest of the time they talked about the day. Later they moved to a table that became vacant and after viewing the menu ordered the chefs 'House special grill' to share. The next two hours was spent talking about their own aspirations and dreams, what they'd do if they ever won the lottery and so on.

Basically this was an evening of getting to know the real person now their fledgling relationship, first begun through long phone conversations texts and e-mails, had become more intense more personal and intimate. Something prompted Stephen to stop talking at one point, looking at Nita he saw she was watching him, he saw a longing in her eyes, he was feeling the same want as well; a yearning to be close to her again, to caress her, inhale her scent; it felt very exciting very intimate. Quickly looking around the bar at the other people, he wondered if they knew what he was thinking, were they able to tell that all he wanted was to be really close to her again separated only by the thickness of their skin! She too saw the look in his eyes and reaching across the table held his hand stroking the back of it with her thumb.

'Do you know what I'd like to do now?' she said.

'No. What?' he answered watching her face, her mouth, as she formed her words?

'I'd like to kiss you until my lips go numb.' She giggled at her own silliness.

He couldn't help smiling at the thought. 'Right home then?'

'Mmm.' she nodded.

Finishing their drinks, he paid the bill and they walked out of the pub onto the tow path. Standing for a moment breathing in the cool night air, savouring it while around them the clear sky revealed a carpet of stars that spread out on every side. Hand in hand at first, then with arms around each other they sauntered back along the tow path. A quarter moon reflected on the rippling water like an arrow pointing the way to *Finbar*. Reaching her side Stephen stepped across the gap between the boat and the path onto one of the moulded locker seats then down into the sun deck. Nita waited, he turned and held his arms up to her, she half stepped half fell into them and into a passionate kiss. Their lips locked together he gathered her up in his arms and moved towards the patio doors, reaching them he said against her lips.

'Doors.'

Taking her hand from his shoulder she reached behind fumbling to find the catches that secured the doors. Finally she give in, broke the kiss to look over her shoulder to see where the catches were. Finding them she released them sliding the door open just enough for Stephen to complete the job with his foot. She turned back to him slipped her hand round his neck once more and drew his lips back to hers to continue the kiss. Carrying her into the saloon he laid her on the long settee and then went to close the doors. Hearing a rustle he turned to see she was gone, he smiled.

For the first time since Suzanne had died he felt truly relaxed, settled and really happy. Until now happiness had been something he'd felt for the other members of the family; Emma and her school friends when he saw how much they enjoyed a holiday on the boat. It was the same feeling for Richard and Mary, his in-laws who'd taken on the role of looking after Emma on a permanent basis. Then there was his Dad who wanted so much for things to be as normal as possible for her, albeit his health issues meant that he was an on-looker most of the time, but that didn't matter he knew she saw him as often as she could home as on as she visited Stephen at home. Nita had been right all the time, he had felt guilty at the thought of being happy again and enjoying himself. In just a few short hours this weekend she had turned his comfort zone upside down, and he hadn't felt a thing. These feelings he was experiencing of contentment and happiness once more, of being able to relax; he'd forgotten just how good they felt. Taking a deep breath, he exhaled in a long sigh turned and followed Nita to the main cabin. The door was closed, he knocked.

'Wait!'

Obediently he waited, from inside the cabin he heard a thud then some rustling.

'Okay. You can come in.'

He opened the door, the cabin was lit by one of the bedside lamps and the bar light over the mirror. Nita was reclined on the bed wearing a deep red silk or satin full length nightdress. The deep 'V' of the design dropped away from the thin shoulder straps to reveal the cleavage of her breasts, her jet-black hair released and free cascaded down over one shoulder. The sight of her lying there reminded him of a painting he'd seen years ago. He stood, his hand still holding the doorknob drinking in the sight of this 'siren' lying before him.

'Captain.' she said seductively.

Almost speechless by the vision on the bed he tried hard to assume the role of Captain and answer her.

'Yes Ma`am…' His voice croaked initially, he tried again more successfully this time and more controlled, 'Ma'am

'I want you… now!'

As she spoke she extended a slender arm towards him. That, oh so simple action sealed the moment for the rest of the night. It was as if he was being drawn towards her by an invisible thread, he moved to sit beside her. Hitching up the nightdress slightly she knelt by his side beginning to undress him, his fingers helping her. They got mixed up in the rush to undo his shirt buttons, the belt of his trousers. The smouldering embers of their earlier passion began to flare again.

Moving across the bed she waited for him to slide up next to her, she was breathing heavily, her brown eyes were moist and dilated. They fell into an embrace seeking each other's lips, it was frenzied and urgent, their hands slid over the others body, caressing, stroking arousing one another. Stephen ran his hands over the smooth satin of her nightdress down her back and along one of her thighs. The touch of the fabric under his fingers excited him he slid his hand back up over her stomach and cupped one of her breasts fondling it firmly. The nipple, stiff and engorged, protruding through the soft fabric; he teased it with his finger and thumb squeezing it gently. She sighed and squirmed under his touch as tiny shock waves coursed through her body. He went to slip the shoulder strap from her shoulder so he could hold the bare breast and kiss its softness. She twisted and turned ending up half lying on Stephen's chest and began kissing him, quick little kisses. Slowly she kissed her way down his body until he felt the moist warmth of her mouth cover him. He reached out to her but she quickly slid her free hand up to his chest and held him firmly flat on the bed.

Later, much later she said against his lips.

'Nice?'

He held her tightly. 'Mmm.' was all he managed to say.

'Good. I want to please you and pleasure you as much as you do me. That was good. Yes?'

For the moment, because his body was still calming down after the myriad of sensations he'd just experienced, he was lost in thought as he tried to find the words to describe the last twenty minutes. She lay by his side aware he would speak when he was ready, she smiled to herself just as she had in the morning when she'd felt like the cat that had just got the cream. For the first time in years she felt happy and content in the company of a man who'd made love to her not once, but four times and one she'd given pleasure to. With these thoughts in mind she gave Stephen an affectionate squeeze and nestled closer into his body, this seemed to bring him out of his own thoughts. Returning her gentle squeeze, he began to say.

'You are just so sexy, so… passionate. Do you know that?'

She giggled snuggling closer to him, draping a leg across his.

'Has no-one ever done that to you before?'

'Yes but not for a while and never like that.'

Hugging him she kissed his chest; responding he kissed the top of her head.

'Are you okay, you didn't get any pleasure or satisfaction?'

'Oh, I got a lot of pleasure, believe me.' She replied.

Nestled together under the duvet they talked of their lives and loves until they fell asleep in the early hours.

~~~~~~~~~~~~~~~~~~~~~~~~~~~~~~~~~~
~~~~~~~~~~~~~~~~~~~~~~~~~~~~~~~~~~

SUNDAY

Wide awake, Stephen listened to the sounds around him that were *Finbar*, sounds he'd grown familiar with over the past seven and a half years. He knew the boat intimately, her little foibles that made her work or stop! It was at times like this he wished Suzanne were here to share all this; there again it was because of her that he was here at all. Then there was Nita, from their first conversation six months ago when she'd interviewed him at the hospital they'd established an immediate rapport. As the police family liaison officer her remit was to build up a profile of the people involved in the case. Later as she'd learned more about him, his life and work their friendship began to form and they talked of more personal things. He realised that over this weekend in her company, she'd very subtly taken him out of the past and brought him back to living in the here and now and having spent this weekend with her he was beginning to see her point of view. She'd said to him during one of their phone conversations through the summer that she sensed he was feeling guilty about their friendship, that it was getting too deep and he was about to run and hide behind Suzanne's memory once again; she'd called it his 'get out clause.' to avoid making any commitment.

Turning over he watched her sleeping, listened to her breathing. Quiet breaths taken slowly held for a moment then released, she seemed so calm and peaceful. Her back was to him, he moved closer forming his body around hers. She stirred ever so slightly shuffling to complete the shape and nestled back into him, he froze holding his breath he didn't want her to wake just yet. When her breathing had slowed again he slipped an arm under the quilt and discovered that her full-length nightie had ridden up her thighs. Gently he stroked the soft smooth skin following the shape of her thigh up to her hip. He slid the palm of his hand across her abdomen, his fingers gently catching the neat triangle of hair, she sighed still asleep and moved slightly. Tracing his index finger down through the tight curls of hair, he found her soft warm lips, she turned away from him a little and uttered something he couldn't understand, he kissed her shoulder tenderly she sighed in response.

'Mmm, that's so nice what a lovely way to be woken up.'

She reached an arm round behind her to pulling him closer and felt him pressing against her back.

'I want to make love to you again.' he said against her shoulder.

She wanted him too 'Wait...' she said pulling away from him and onto her knees.

'I want you too... from behind Stephen, from behind... now!' she said urgently.

He moved closer to her, throwing the duvet to one side, she slipped her nightie off and reached for him. He responded pushing himself hard against her buttocks.

'Ugh, Yes!' She almost spat the words out. 'Harder!' she demanded.

'Is that good?'

'Oh so good... don't you stop now!' moments later with the pitch of her voice rising she gasped, 'Oh, I'm coming... Oh!'

She squealed as she had done the previous night, her hands grasped at the sheet on the bed and pulling a pillow towards her she buried her head in it letting out a full bloodied scream as her orgasm took control of her body. Stephen too was at the point of no return, finally collapsing on her back. As he recovered his composure he became aware that Nita was shaking, not in the convulsive way she had when experiencing an orgasm, this was different. He moved to lie beside her and went to take her in his arms but she resisted.

'Nita are you okay? Did I hurt you?'

She shook her head, he realised she was actually crying. Again he went to cradle her but she continued to resist.

'Nita, what's wrong why the tears?'

Clearly very distressed the only thing he felt he could do was to hold her. This time he took a firm hold of her and drew her into a tight embrace. It was a good ten minutes before she lay quietly in his arms sobbing occasionally. The sobs, the tears reminded him of the times Emma would come to him for a cuddle when her life and her world had simply collapsed again after Suzanne had died. Quite suddenly she disengaged herself from him, sat up on the edge of the bed and said abruptly.

'Can I have a Shower?'

Somewhat confused by her behaviour he replied.

'Sure, of course you can, are you okay?'

She didn't look at him but answered.

'I'm fine, honestly.'

With that she stood up and walked into the en-suite shower closing the door behind her. He lay on the bed for some time listening to the shower pump working trying to fathom out just what had happened in the last half an hour. Eventually he sat up shook his head in disbelief and grabbing some clothes went through the galley to the other shower.

Sometime later Nita emerged from the cabin dressed in jeans and a warm top, her face was all made up her hair pulled back and loosely platted. Stephen was seated at the galley table with a mug of coffee and a plate of toast, he looked at her.

'Tea?'

She nodded. 'Please.' sliding into a seat opposite him.

'Toast?'

She shook her head, he poured her a mug of tea and pushed it across the table. Their eyes met, they held each other's gaze for a while. He realised now wasn't the time for twenty questions. Finishing his toast he stood up refilled his mug from the cafetiere and turned to leave. Nita reached across the table and took hold of his hand. He glanced down at their hands then at Nita, her face was sad, she spoke quietly.

'I'm sorry… I need to explain, but just now I can't I'm sorry.'

He nodded, giving her hand a squeeze.

'We need to be on our way.'

Turning he went up to the saloon, moments later *Finbar* vibrated slightly as one of her engines fired up. She heard the patio doors open and felt the boat rock slightly as Stephen stepped onto the tow path to release the mooring lines. Moments later he returned and the engine note increased; looking out of the galley windows she saw that they were moving. Slipping out of her seat she watched through a porthole for a while as they slipped past the pub and a couple of barges then went back to the cabin. Straightening the duvet, she packed her bag returning to the galley and dropping it on one of the seats then refilled the kettle. As she waited for it to boil a growing feeling of anger welled up inside her, she owed Stephen an explanation but wasn't quite sure how to go about it. Going into the saloon she put one mug down on a flat surface by his side.

'Why are you steering from here today?'

'It's a bit grey and chilly to be up top, could even rain. Anyway we're only an hour or so away from the boat yard.'

She stood at his shoulder sipping her tea thinking how to begin explaining her behaviour this morning.

'Stephen' she began. 'I want to ex…'

'Nita, its fine you don't need to explain anything!'

He said firmly.

'No listen.'

She got no further. Without looking up at her he cut her off again.

'Nita I said its okay, if it was something I did or said then I'm sorry.'

She tried to say what she wanted to for the third time.

'Stephen please,'

He ignored her plea.

'Will you stop the boat… please? I want to explain something to you.'

No response, he just carried on steering the boat. She did a little pirouette, put her mug down on the low coffee table by the long settee then turned back to face him again. She shouted at him this time.

'Will you stop this sodding boat NOW! I want to explain and I can't if you're driving. I need you to look at me.'

He continued to ignore her. This time she just exploded in frustration.

'Bloody hell Stephen! Stop for christ's sake!'

He threw her a quick glance. 'Okay, okay. Calm down, I'll stop.'

'Ohh!'

She clenched her fists to suppress her anger and frustration. Steering towards the tow path he brought *Finbar* to a stop allowing her to settle gently by the side of the canal then turned his seat round to face her.

'Thank you.'

He shrugged and began to say.

'I don't know what's wrong Nita, but...is'

'Shut up and listen sod you!'

He held his hands up, palms towards her in a gesture of surrender. She sat down on the edge of the long settee, taking a deep breath she began to explain.

'Six months ago my life was simple, it was organised and structured I was content with my lot. Then in the course of my job I was part of a team investigating a series of particularly vicious assaults and met a man, one of the victims who'd got involved by accident. I had to get to know this man to build up one of the profiles needed to solve the case.' She paused, taking another breath, and collecting her thoughts. 'He was a widower, he was a parent, he had a boat; It was because he was sailing down river that he'd become involved. To provide for his family he worked hard spending weeks at a time working abroad. I had a huge amount of respect for this man, his efforts and achievements.' Another pause. 'Although still suffering from his injuries, he insisted on continuing his journey down the river to the marina. I should have realised then that he could be pig headed at times.' She glanced at him for a moment, 'I asked him to keep in touch because I wanted to know he was all right. I had the feeling… no, I felt we could be friends. Well we did keep in touch through the summer, by phone Skype or e-mail.'

Watching her he realised what she was saying was from the heart and she was finding it very difficult to control her emotions, she continued.

'Through the summer we talked, talked about our working day, our down time, how we felt about all sorts of silly pointless things in life, the world good or bad, everything. When he said he was bringing the boat back up river for the winter and wondered if I would like to join him for the last bit from Portbridge I jumped at the idea, I mean what girl wouldn't, just think how your street cred would balloon! A weekend on a boat it's a no-brainer!'

She fell silent, her eyes were wide and moist with tears; she held his gaze saying quietly.

'Do you remember that evening in April before you left Portbridge? We had that meal at the Duchess.' he nodded. 'Remember I told you about a guy I'd met in New England when I was working for the State Police there?'

'Yeah.' He replied.

'He meant a lot to me, we had something special but it wasn't meant to be in the end so when I came back here it just fizzled out. Oh I've had one or two flings since but they've been just that, flings.'

Rising from the settee she walked towards him, wiping a tear from her cheek with the back of her hand.

'Thirty-six hours or so ago I met man, this friend with a boat for a weekend jaunt. Twenty-six hours ago we became more than friends. This morning my organised and structured world simply disintegrated into mush… chaos, I can't think I feel sick, I'm…'

Standing in front of him now her arms by her side eyes brim full of tears, voice full of emotion, almost whispering she said.

'I'm lost and I don't know what to do anymore.'

He stood up and put his hands on her shoulders drawing her into his chest. More than anything it was to support her and comfort her;

her voice muffled against his chest she said.

'This man who became a friend and now a lover, who I spent endless hours trying to re-assure that it was time to move his life forward and not to use the memory of his wife to hide behind, this man...' she hesitated, loosely encircling her arms around his waist, and with her voice finally cracking simply said. 'I think I have fallen in love with him!'

With that she dissolved into tears. He held her for some time gently stroking her back to calm her. Softly he said.

'Nita love I can't tell you how I feel right now because I don't know to be honest.'

She gave his waist a squeeze in response as he added.

'I can tell you that I have never felt so content so satisfied, so at peace. It's you who've made me feel all these emotions this weekend. You've given me so much of my life back, so much pleasure emotionally, sexually, I feel on top of the world, you've woken me up to living again and it feels so good.'

Her head still on his chest she said.

'We are good together, I have enjoyed every minute of being around you and, yes I guess I sort of feel complete in a way too. I've never had an orgasm like the one you gave me this morning. It was indescribable, truly.'

Finbar bumped against the tow path two or three times as a narrow boat passed them.

'I'm sorry' he said, 'but we need to move.'

He felt her nod against his chest. Stepping away from him she sniffed and gave him a half smile.

'I bet I look a right mess, yeah?'

'No,' he shook his head, 'no, you look wonderful.'

Nita smiled at him again. 'Yeah, right.'

They kissed briefly before he sat back down on the helm seat. Turning back to the control panel he pushed the control lever forward and making a quarter turn of the wheel drawing the boat away from the bank out into the centre of the canal. Nita stood by his shoulder, putting an arm around him, stooped and kissed his neck whispering.

'Thank you.'

He glanced up at her briefly. 'For what?'

'For being the lovely man I had the good fortune to meet six months ago. For giving me so much pleasure this weekend, for making it something special. Wait until I tell the girls at work tomorrow I spent a weekend on a boat with a drop-dead gorgeous sailor.'

She giggled adding,

'Right I'm going to try and rescue my face, okay?'

He glanced at her and nodded.

Through the morning they motored up the canal passing through a mixture of scenery, heavily tree'd areas then open farmland with cattle and sheep grazing. Nita leant on the shelf opposite Stephen that held the radar VDU screen watching the changing scenery passing by. She felt calm and relaxed after this morning's moment of emotional trauma.

'We're coming up to a swing bridge.' Stephen said quietly. 'Do you feel confident to take *Finbar* through if I work the bridge?'

She threw him a slightly horrified glance.

'It's just the same as yesterday.' He said reassuringly. 'Remember, line her up on something ahead and keep her on course. You can always stop if you're not sure.'

She thought for a moment. 'Okay.' She replied.

'Good, come on then take over and get the feel of her again.'

Ten minutes later they'd worked through the bridge without any disasters. Nita remained at the wheel feeling more confident and enjoying the experience this time. Some time later as she steered the boat around a long bend a collection of buildings appeared in the distance. She turned briefly to Stephen.

'Stephen look.'

Getting up from the settee where he'd been sitting watching, ready to help if she got into a mess, he moved to her side looking ahead through the cabin windows. Grinning broadly he said quietly.

'We're home.'

Going down to the galley he returned moments later slipping into a long-sleeved jacket.

'The end of another year cruising,' he said sighing. 'Sad when you think about it that that's nearly another year gone.'

Taking her by the shoulders he guided her off the helms seat.

'True,' she said thoughtfully, 'but what a year, just think what has happened since you left here six months ago.'

He smiled at her.

'Put a jacket on it'll be chilly now.'

Sitting down and taking the wheel he started the second engine and settled down to approach the group of buildings nestled around the canal side. Nita could see more clearly now that this was the marina. There were neat rows of different types of boats, some tied up to pontoons. Others on trolleys parked in what looked like a large car park by a slipway.

'Wow!'

'Surprised?' he said watching her face.

'Yeah, you don't expect to see so many boats in one place in the countryside.'

Slowing *Finbar* until they only had steerage way he brought her up alongside one of the pontoons near the slipway. Nita went to fetch her jacket returning to the saloon to stand by his shoulder. Out of one of the sheds a slim, elderly looking man appeared dressed in a navy boiler suit wiping his hands on a piece of rag. He was followed by a young lad, likewise dressed in a boiler suit. As the older man walked down to the pontoon by *Finbar* he took a pipe from the breast pocket of his overalls. Putting the pipe in his mouth, he reached onto the foredeck pulling a mooring line through the stanchion rails securing it to one of the bollards on the pontoon. Nita followed Stephen through the saloon onto the sun deck where he took the stern mooring line and stepping onto the pontoon secured it to another bollard at the boat's stern. Taking her hand he steadied her as she stepped onto the pontoon, together they stood and watched as the elderly man came towards them. Taking the pipe from his mouth he stopped short of where they were standing and looked at the pair for a moment then in a thick, north east dialect said.

'Whey, Stephen Leigh-Grace as I live and breathe son it's good to see ya back.'

He held his hand out to Stephen as he spoke, Stephen shook his hand.

'Mr Graham, good to see you too. How are you doing?'

'Ah well son. Could be better but I'm still in the ring fighting ya na.'

He turned to the young lad who was standing near the bow.

'Come on Jamie make yer 'sel useful son, away and shut the engines down.'

The lad moved past the three of them and sprang onto *Finbar*.

'How's Mrs G?' Stephen asked.

Relative silence fell on the yard as the engines stopped.

'Oh she's grand thanks for asking son. She'll be waiting for us up at the hoose when she sees *Finbar*.'

Stephen and Nita followed Mr Graham as he turned and set off back along the pontoon filling his pipe from a leather pouch he'd taken from his pocket. Reaching the steps up to the hard standing of the yard, he turned and called back to the young lad.

'Jamie, tea in ten minutes, okay.'

The lad waved, turning the three of them set off across the yard Mr Graham lighting his pipe as they walked.

'Robert.' Stephen began. 'This is Nita, Nita meet Mr Robert Graham known to his friends as Mr G and that young lad was Jamie, one of his apprentices.'

Taking the pipe from his mouth and letting the cloud of smoke that shrouded his face clear, he said to Nita.

'Hello pet, good to meet you. Where did he press-gang you from then?'

He winked at her as he held his hand out, she took his hand and grinned at the gesture.

'Hi, it's good to meet you.'

Stephen began to explain to Mr G. 'Nita was one of the detectives involved in sorting out the trouble I got into back in April. We got talking and, well... here we are.'

Robert Graham simply nodded puffing on his pipe. They made their way towards a house set back from the yard.

'Go on then son tell us what happened, from what ah heard you were very lucky. Ya na you shouldn't get involved in other folks' fights.'

Stephen went through the events that led up to him being attacked and meeting Nita. Taking the pipe from his mouth, Mr G asked.

'And what did your Emma have to say aboot you being a hero eh?' Stephen gave a little chuckle as Mr G continued. 'Ah bet she gave you hell eh, a right ear full, yes?'

He had known Stephens's daughter for more than eight years, had watched her grow up and commented in the past that if she had something to say she came right out with it, looking at Nita he said.

'Have you met our Emma yet pet?'

She shook her head. 'No, not yet, I've heard a lot about her though.'

He continued, 'She's growing up to be grand lass despite all she's been through. She's full of confidence and I guess very bright.' He glanced at Stephen momentarily then back to Nita winking again. 'Ah div'en nah where she gets that from mind, certainly not from her Da, guess she must be just like her mother.'

Nita couldn't help grinning as they both looked at Stephen who feigned surprise. Opening his mouth to protest. Robert's face was expressionless however, he couldn't help himself, finally breaking into a broad grin.

'Ha'way up to the hoose yous two for some tea and you can meet the missus.'

Putting his arm through Nita's he guided her off towards the house.

'It's about time someone took him in hand pet, ah think he's a bit useless on his own and ma Maggie thinks so too.' He glanced over his shoulder at Stephen walking behind them.

Approaching the house through the maze of boats, trailers and discarded bits and pieces of sailing equipment lying about, a dog began to bark from the direction of the house. Stephen stepped up to Nita's other side taking her hand in his.

'Get ready, we're about to be welcomed.'

She tensed, sensing that perhaps the barking was a warning. Nervously she looked at him.

'Large or small?'

He thought for a moment then replied. 'Oh about average I'd say.'

At this point, a black and white ball of fur cleared the wall by the gate hurtling towards the three of them barking excitedly. Nita froze momentarily falling half a step behind Stephen gripping his hand more tightly. Removing the pipe from his mouth Mr G said firmly.

'Sally, down!'

Nita heard the authority in his voice, the dog slithered to a halt some four feet in front of them the last three feet of its headlong charge on its belly. Stephen looked at Nita.

'This is Sally, she greets everyone the same way, right Robert?'

'Way-aye, daft dog.' then to the dog he said. 'Ha'way then girl, gahn.'

The dog circled around them her tail wagging like a windmill as she fell in between Mr G and Stephen. Continuing up the path towards the house Sally walked between them occasionally nuzzling their hands in an attempt to get some attention. Nearing the gate she retraced her original headlong charge leaping back over the wall ready to greet them again by the door to the house. Mr G gave a quiet command.

'In yer bed girl.'

Obediently the dog turned and led the way into the house going to her bed by the side of an Aga cooking range set into a large old open fireplace. Mr G called as they entered the combined kitchen parlour and living room.

'Maggie love, visitors.'

Looking around the room they'd entered Nita thought how quaint it was, she felt she'd just stepped back in time to another century. Old wooden beams stretched across the ceiling, a long refectory table stood in the centre of the room surrounded by an assortment of dining chairs. Off to one side was an old, almost threadbare, settee adorned with an array of rugs and different cushions, various easy chairs were placed around the room and against one wall was a tall dresser with a set of plates and other crockery set on the shelves. The small windows completed the overall effect of another era, dimly lighting the room. From an adjoining room a woman's voice answered him, it was soft and gentle with just a hint of a Scottish dialect.

'Robert, can a woman not finish tidying round the house before you come tramping into it again?'

Grinning he glanced at Stephen and Nita as he replied.

'Well ah thought you'd want to say hello to these two people.'

A tall slender middle-aged woman emerged from the room. Dressed in trousers, a blouse and cardigan, a floral apron covered her clothes; her greying hair framing the soft features of her face. She continued speaking to her husband as she came into the kitchen parlour.

'Robert apart from our Josie and the children who...'

She stopped in her tracks, falling silent looking at Stephen then slowly moved towards him. As she got within a couple of paces she held her arms out as a mother would to a child, Stephen stepped into the embrace and just for a moment nothing, or no one in the world mattered. Nita watched, touched by the sensitivity of the moment, she saw Maggie's hand gently stroking his back reassuringly. Eventually she pushed him away a little and studied his face closely, nodded then said tenderly.

'How are you Stephen? Recovered now? We were so worried when the news reached us about the assault, they say you were very brave.'

'I'm fine now Mrs G, fully fit and back on the road again.'

Without taking her eyes from his face she reached out taking Nita's hand and drew her closer to her side.

'Good, good, now are you not going to introduce this beautiful young lady to me?'

She turned to look at Nita, still holding her hand.

Stephen smiled, 'This is Nita Patel Mrs G.'

Maggie Graham lifted Nita's hand a little and covered it with her other hand as Stephen said to Nita.

'Meet Mrs Maggie Graham.'

Mrs G looked deeply into her eyes, smiling.

'Welcome my dear, welcome.'

Nita returned her smile. 'Thank you.'

'Nita was one of the detectives investigating the attacks.' he began to explain.

Mrs G turned back to him.

'Aye,' she said. 'Well you can tell me all about it over a cup of tea and some cake.'

Letting go of Nita's hand she turned and moved across the kitchen to the Aga. Taking a large kettle that was sitting to one side of the hot plates she filled it returning it to the cooker placing it directly on one of the hot plates. Speaking to Stephen again she said without looking at him.

'Come on Stephen. You know the drill, make yourselves at home.'

Looking across to Nita she said smiling.

'Oh men, do you not find they get under your feet if you let them stand about? I like to put them where I can see them then I can get on.'

Nita glanced at Stephen and grinned. Mr G had moved quietly to sit in one of the old armchairs. Sally came from her bed to sit at his feet as he motioned Stephen and Nita to sit on the settee. Stephen put his head close to Nita's ear as they made themselves comfortable, whispering.

'She makes the most amazing cakes and her fruit scones are... mmm, just yum.'

Nita chuckled.

In a matter of minutes the tea was made and as if by magic an array of pies, cakes and scones accompanied by pots of jam appeared on the table. Gesturing to Stephen and Nita to come to the table, she sat and began to pour the tea into delicately decorated China cups, Mr G joined them just as young Jamie walked through the door. Mrs Graham looked at the young lad.

'I've made you up some sandwiches Jamie, they're in the fridge, fetch a mug and pour yourself a drink.'

The lad collected his food and a drink and left them. More than an hour flashed by as Stephen and Nita talked to both Robert and Maggie Graham telling them about the assault and how they'd then begun to form this friendship. Stephen related this summer's holiday to them and how he'd explained the events in April to Emma and his in-laws Mary and Richard, acknowledging that Nita had been right when she'd told him that telling the story as it happened was the best way. Emma, although angry that her dad had got involved at all soon calmed down when she heard the rest of the story; Mr G eventually stirred and stood up.

'Right, yous and me'd best get on son, your mate brought your car on Friday night.'

Pulling open a drawer in an old bureau in the corner of the room, he took out a set of car keys handing them to Stephen.

'What are we doing with *Finbar* this winter, do you want her out?'

'Yes, she needs cleaning and anti-fouling and can we repaint the hull whilst she's out. The starboard prop needs some attention as well, I think I probably chipped or bent a blade when I beached her on the riverbank, she vibrates quite a bit at cruising speed.'

Mr G nodded, mentally noting everything he was saying. Stephen and Nita stood up together to follow Robert Graham out of the house.

'Right son, I'll lift her in the next two or three weeks depends where I can put her. When are you home again?'

Stephen thought for a moment.

'Mm… Four maybe five weeks, no longer. I have a reason to be here now.'

He glanced at Nita as he replied.

Maggie Graham reached out and squeezed Nita's hand.

'I never thought I'd hear him say that; except for wee Emma nothing keeps him here in the winter. You've obviously had an effect on him my dear.'

Stephen smiled and before the conversation got too mushy said to Nita.

'We need to get our stuff off *Finbar* and get on our way home.'

She nodded and turned to Mrs G who enveloped her in a tight embrace before gently pushing her away, saying quietly.

'Be firm with him my dear or he'll do his own thing. He's like my Robert, pig headed sometimes!'

Nita chuckled clearly remembering the incident at the hospital when he discharged himself against everyone's advice. Throwing Stephen a quick glance she replied.

'I'll try but that's not easy when he's away so much. Hopefully, we can change things little by little but I am going to miss him if he's away for too long.'

Smiling at her Mrs G moved across the room to Stephen and just as when they had arrived held out her arms to him and hugged him. Looking him in the eyes she said quietly but firmly.

'You be good Stephen Leigh-Grace, I sense this young lady is special and you ought to be glad you've met her. Do you hear me?' She kissed him on each cheek.

He nodded. 'I'll do my best… promise.'

With Robert Graham bringing up the rear they left the house and walked back down to pontoons. Gathering all their bags and bits of stuff they needed, Nita built a small heap of kit on the pontoon, Stephen meanwhile opened one of the sundeck lockers taking out a cover. Climbing up to the flying bridge he spread it over the bridge fitting it neatly over the screen at the front, then he moulded it around the seats. Returning to deck level he secured the edges of the sheet around the whole bridge structure pulling it tight before fastening a rope that ran around the cover edge to a series of clips set into the superstructure until the entire bridge area was protected from the weather. Returning to the galley he saw Nita had taken it upon herself to clear the fridge part filling a black bag with stuff to throw away. Taking her in his arms he kissed her.

'We'll make a sailor of you yet.'

He parried a swipe from her in response adding.

'I'm going to fetch the car down to the pontoon so we can throw all our gear into it, okay?'

'Okay.' she answered.

Forty minutes later they were driving down the narrow lane that led from the boatyard to the main road heading back towards Portbridge. They sat in silence for some time, Nita casually resting her hand on Stephen's thigh watching him as he drove. Eventually she asked quietly.

'How do we end this weekend?'

He glanced at her.

'I was just thinking the same.' he replied.

She gave a little smirk. 'We met as friends just for a weekend on a boat, your boat. Here we are forty-something hours later very much more than friends. Odd isn't it; if we'd planned a romantic, passionate weekend it probably wouldn't have worked out. However, because we've just let things happen it's been amazing, magical!'

He just nodded and smiled, concentrating on the road.

'I just feel so relaxed,' he said.

She continued. 'Is this what it's like after a week or two on the boat?'

He smiled.

'There's something special about sailing, whether on a cruiser like *Finbar* or a yacht. You've got the fresh air bit and okay, the salt and sun. I find the whole experience completely relaxing. There's something else that makes it different too. Take Scarborough or Whitby, Brid even. Most people come to these towns from the land, by road.'

He glanced at her briefly.

'Like you said yesterday, you're travelling at fifty or sixty miles an hour. You never get chance to see what's around you or you're nose to tail in traffic, stressing out of your head and so are the kids too if you've got them with you. But come at the same place by sea and the whole thing is different. As you come into the harbour, instead of streets with houses or shops and hotels all around you, you see the whole of the harbour and the town laid out in front of you. Instead of parking your car and just wondering around following the crowd, you find people will stand on the quayside watching you. You see it in their eyes, the question, I wonder where they've come from?' He chuckled softly, 'If you're good at handling the boat you can show off a bit... you know, lots of revs going astern to stop and mooring up to the quay, it's very impressive sometimes.'

She was smiling at him, there was a passion in his voice she'd not heard before, she squeezed his thigh.

'Wow that is the first time I've heard you speak with such feeling, such love. This is the real Stephen the real you who's been hiding for goodness knows how long.'

Giving him another squeeze she leant across and kissed his cheek, adding.

'I love the Stephen Leigh-Grace I've found this weekend, just as much as the lover I've found in him.'

Taking his hand off the steering wheel he covered hers that was still resting on his thigh.

'So, just how are we going to end this weekend then?' he said.

Cheekily she slipped her hand from under his, sliding it down the side of his groin.

'Ermm...Tell me if this wouldn't work,' she said gently rubbing her hand over his thigh.

He sensed a sexual tone in her voice; glancing at her briefly he smiled. She was definitely getting to him.

'Go on.'

'What time are you working tomorrow?'

He shuffled in his seat slightly as she continued to gently slide her up and down his groin.

'Mid-afternoon, I'm taking a trailer to Sheffield loading out of there then across to Hull for the ferry. This trips going to be around four week's maybe.'

Still sounding sexy and very seductive she continued.

'I don't think I can go cold turkey tonight, having had you all this weekend. Sooo, and this is just a suggestion,' she couldn't help a little giggle at her boldness, 'how's about we get something to eat on the way home now then we have the rest of the evening and night to talk about you and me... hhmm?'

Taking hold of her hand he placed it back on his thigh holding it there, giving himself time to regain some self-control.

'Sounds good to me, where are we going then your place or mine?'

For the first time today she sounded a little reticent.

'It's going to have to be yours if that's alright, the two girls I share with will be home and right now I don't want any distractions, you're mine tonight. I mean we do need to talk about where you and I are going now, yes?'

He was a bit surprised at her sudden boldness. Thinking for a moment he replied.

'Lady, had you even hinted at such a thing on Friday night or yesterday for that matter, then I'd either have curled up in a heap in a corner or jumped overboard and swum to the bank! Today however,' he shrugged his shoulders slightly, 'I think it's a brilliant idea.'

They chuckled together, but at the same time experienced a tingle of excitement and anticipation at the thought of one more night of shared passion. He felt a shiver run down his spine at the thought of holding her one more time and making love to her before he ventured away again.

In the late evening, in the amber glow of a streetlight on the opposite side of the road from his house, they lay entwined together in bed just as they had on *Finbar*. Each time they'd made love over the past forty-odd hours they'd become more relaxed with one another, especially Stephen. He lay quietly, Nita resting her head on his chest casually stroking her side in long slow caresses. Neither of them wanted to break this moment, yet both knew they were going to have to talk about tomorrow and face whatever happened after the morning. Eventually driven to breaking the silence he said quietly.

'What time are you at work tomorrow?'

'I have to be in by nine.'

'Have you got a car?'

'Mmm no, I left it at work, Alan Syms brought me to the wharf on Friday.'

'I'll take you in then.'

'Thanks.' she replied squeezing him gently.

Silence again but this time there was a palpable tension in the room, she began to say.

'I'm going to have a bit of a problem if this weekend is going to just fade into history. Are you going to simply drive off into the sunset in your truck leaving me on the pavement this time instead of the wharf as you did back in April?'

He thought carefully, he felt the same as her; would it be him in the end left wondering what had happened to this weekend. He moved to unwind himself from their embrace and sitting up moved her around until she was lying on her back her head resting in his lap.

'Remember when I sailed off into the sunset in April, you gave me your card and said keep in touch, mmm?' She nodded watching his face. 'I have a small corkboard fastened to one of the locker doors in my cab with important cards, notes and messages pinned to it that are special. I've got a picture of Emma and Suzanne and yes one of *Finbar* also. Along with those pictures of my three loves, your card takes pride of place.'

He put his hand on her stomach and stroked it gently. She squirmed and uttered a little giggle.

'That tickles.' She said covering his hand with hers to keep it still.

He smiled. 'I began to look forward to our chats on Skype or the messenger board at the end of each day if I was parked up for the night. I'd have a wash and my dinner then I'd wait for you to call. If we went more than two days without speaking I could feel myself becoming low but now its age's, years probably, since I've felt this good. I'm buzzing inside Nita, I feel on top of the world, that's down to you to what you've said to me over the past six months and how you've taken me by the hand and led through this weekend. I told you back in April that after just one meal together, one evening, you'd made me realise that I needed to move on from living in the past. Look at me now, in my home in my bed with a woman, with you.'

Impulsively he scooped her up in his arms bringing her up to his face in a passionate embrace, he kissed her once, twice and the third time deeply, searchingly. She responded curling her arms around him, one hand holding the back of his head so the kiss couldn't be broken. When they came up for air they remained nose to nose and Stephen finished what he'd set out to say.

'So in answer to your question my sweet sweet lady yes, I am going to drive off into the sunset but I'll be back soon with headlights blazing.'

Struggling out of their embrace, she turned to face him, straddling his thighs. Taking his hands she placed them on her breasts and holding them there leaned towards him and kissed him in another deep kiss. She circled her arms around his shoulders as he gently caressed her breasts. Slowly their passion grew until she could feel him hard and erect. Moving ever so slightly without breaking the kiss, she raised herself a little then sank down on him until he was deep inside her. They moved together until the inevitable ending rushed at them. Finally lying together spent, they slept.

~~~~~~~~~~~~~~~~~~~~~~~~~~~~~~~~~~~~~
~~~~~~~~~~~~~~~~~~~~~~~~~~~~~~~~~~~~~

MONDAY

'What time is it?'

A blurry-eyed Nita stood by the kitchen door wrapped in Stephen's dressing gown. She waited for the answer.

'Just gone seven, did you sleep?'

'Mmm...' she stretched, 'not long enough. What time did you get up?'

'Oh just before six, my body clock got me up.'

She watched him moving round his small kitchen putting tins, cartons and things into some boxes. He had a cool box by the fridge that had packs of cheese and meats in it. She sensed his pre-occupation in getting things ready to take away in his truck, it was obvious he had a routine when he was going away. 'Breakfast?' he asked suddenly.

She shook herself, brought back to the here and now by his question.

'Err... toast please... just toast and a coffee.'

He stopped and looked at her.

'Coffee? You don't do coffee do you?' he said surprised.

'I do sometimes and I fancy a coffee now, problem?'

He shrugged, 'No... How do you like it?'

'Black, two sugars please.'

Looking at her again he reached over one of the boxes on the worktop and clicked the kettle on.

'There's some bread in the bin there.'

He said pointing to the corner of the work surface as he took a box to the front door. She half blocked the doorway as he came back to the kitchen.

'Good morning, can I have a shower?'

She said kissing him.

'Morning, sorry sugar I've got my work head on.'

He said returning her kiss.

'Mmm... I can see that, I'll be down in ten minutes.'

As she got halfway up the stairs, he called after her.

'There are towels in the cupboard on the landing. Take the bottom one's, they'll be warm from the tank.'

Ten minutes later she was back downstairs dressed, made up and ready to face the day. Dropping her travel bag by the front door along with all Stephens' stuff she went back to the kitchen to see all the worktops were clear and two bar stools stood by the worktop. Two places were set for breakfast, there was orange juice, toast, jams and two steaming mugs of tea and coffee. Sitting on one of the stools she said.

'I hope you don't mind but I used the hair dryer from, I guess Emma's room.'

'Yep that's fine.'

For a while they sat in silence eating toast and drinking their tea and coffee, Stephen was looking through the contents of a zip briefcase, sorting papers documents and his passport.

'Do you always take all this stuff with you when you're on the road?'

'Yeah, it's mainly the basics in case I end up in some dead-end place where there are no shops or cafes. Most times it's okay as I'm in cities or big towns but I've been caught out in the past.'

After another brief silence she said quietly.

'Are we going to make this work...?'

He looked up at her smiled and reached for her hand.

'I want nothing more in the world right now than to go away and in two or three weeks, or however long, come home to you. I said it last night and I'll say it again now, you've opened a door in my life that I couldn't find where the handle was. I feel so different today, so alive and that's down to you. It 'aint going to be easy sugar but I really do want to make this work, honestly.'

Lifting her hand, he kissed it. Breakfast finished and everything tided away, they loaded his car with all his stuff and Nita's bag, checked round the house, locked it all up and together drove off towards Portbridge. Their goodbye, when they reached her office was a little strained and a tear was shed as they kissed. Standing alone on the pavement she waved as he drove away for the next four weeks or more.

Quietly to herself she said.

'Take care Stephen, I never told you I love you.'

Turning, she keyed her pass number into the electronic lock and ascended the three flights of stairs to her office, Stephen meanwhile drove the ten miles to his depot.

Elsewhere Monday had dawned grey and damp, a classic autumn morning. At a small harbour on the Norfolk coast a converted fishing boat had docked in the early morning in the sanctuary of the inner harbour. Having tied up two men left the boat and made their way to the harbour masters office to report their arrival and complete the necessary paperwork. Both looked fit and athletic, both sported an array of tattoos on their arms. They spoke to each other in their native tongue that had an Eastern European dialect to it. In the office they explained that they had developed an engine problem that had forced them to make a land fall here in Norfolk. One of them, who appeared to be the captain of the boat and spoke the best English explained that the engine was not a common one used in many Western European boats and the part that needed replacing was on its way to them from Northern Russia and should be here within the next twenty four to thirty six hours. They should be on their way then within five to six hours depending on how long it took to get the engine running properly again. Having filed the necessary forms with the harbour office regarding the boats name the origin for this voyage, destination, number of crew, their names and, any cargo they were carrying, they returned to the boat. Periodically throughout the next day and a half various members of the crew spent some time wandering around the small town. Refuelling was arranged, some fresh supplies were delivered to them by two of the local businesses in the town. During the afternoon of the second day a blue Mercedes van arrived at the harbour. Its registration plate showed that it had come from Georgia. Boxes of parts were unloaded and carried onto the boat, the hatches above the engine room were opened and the boxes were lowered into the engine space using the boats crane. Through the last rays of daylight and with deck lights ablaze work began to repair the engine. Just before eleven `o'clock the deck crane lifted a couple of boxes back out of the engine room and they were manhandled quite delicately into the van. The hatches were closed, lights shut down and moments later the boats engine fired into life.

The captain and another man from the van made their way to the harbour office that was closed now. Using the telephone by the side of the office door he contacted the nearest manned customs office, explained what had happened and they were ready to continue their voyage. The custom officer they were speaking to said they'd had been updated by the local office and if the tide was right for them they were clear to depart. They returned to the boat and the captain shook hands with the van driver and went back aboard the MFV. He gave a command to a crewman on the wharf to cast them off. He quickly moved to release the bow line and coiling it up stepping off the wharf onto the bow as the gap between them and the land widened. As in Belgium five nights earlier the fishing boat sailed quietly away leaving the town to rest peacefully for the rest of the night.

~~~~~~~~~~~~~~~~~~~~~~~~~~~~~~~~~~~~~~
~~~~~~~~~~~~~~~~~~~~~~~~~~~~~~~~~~~~~~

Back in Portbridge Monday morning began as it had for years with the various teams gathering together for a report and briefing session. By ten am everyone was in the office holding mugs of tea or coffee, some nibbling on sandwiches that had been brought in by a couple of the detectives. Everyone was chatting quite animatedly about their weekend or collating a last-minute report to present to the boss. Quite a few of the detectives quizzed Nita about her weekend, especially the three women officers there. It was impossible for her to hide how much she had enjoyed the whole weekend, her face and eyes gave it away. Another colleague Linda came and sat with her before the briefing started. Putting her mug down on Nita's desk she looked her straight in the eyes.

'Well...?'

Nita shrugged a little embarrassed. 'Great...'

'Go on then... spill?'

'Hmm... It was just... magic.'

'So you got your leg over then?'

Nita coloured up and went to punch Linda playfully.

'Well, either you did or didn't you? Come on Patel spill,' she said, rotating her wrists to hurry her up with more details, her eyes wide and bright willing her to speak.

'Once or twice.' Nita replied hesitantly.

'Ohh... Nita Patel you tramp...!'

She exclaimed in a stage whisper then after a moment's hesitation said.

'Only once or twice?' She sounded disappointed. 'Come off it girl... how many times?'

Nita leaned in close to Linda.

'Well, most of the weekend actually.'

Linda drew back from her, her mouth open in feigned shock.

'Nita Patel you wicked girl! Taking advantage of some poor innocent man like that, you should be ashamed.' then added quickly, 'Was it good?'

Nita nodded again, 'Oh yes...' she answered firmly, 'it was good, a perfect weekend, like I said… magic.'

Inspector Allen's door opened and he walked into the main office. Nita touched Linda's knee to hold her attention a moment longer.

'Don't say anything… please?'

Linda drew her fingers across her lips to seal them. They exchanged knowing smiles as the Inspector began to speak to them all.

'Morning everyone a good weekend was had by all I hope, good to see everyone's made it in.'

He paused very briefly as he said this, his eyes focusing on Nita. She couldn't help squirming a little in her seat. The Inspector, smiling briefly, carried on with his introduction to the mornings briefing. Later DI Allen dismissed the meeting telling them to get on with their enquiries and 'get results'. He looked across the desks.

'DC Patel, can I see you in my office please.'

'Sir.' Nita replied getting up from her desk and picking up a notepad wove her way across the office to the Inspectors door.

'Come in Nita, sit down.'

He reached for a file from the top of a low cupboard. He studied the attached note clipped to the cover and handed it to her.

'Good weekend? How is Mr Leigh-Grace, fully recovered now?'

He was looking straight at her.

'Yes sir thank you it was a great weekend and he has fully recovered from the assault.'

'Good good, now as you perhaps know I gave Alan Syms a file on Friday, it was passed down from uniform last week. He's away looking into the available evidence just now, it looks like there could be some involvement for you too as there is a partner and some children involved. Take a look at the domestic situation will you and when he gets back from the local nick have a word; see if you can do a visit with him, okay.'

Getting up from her seat she nodded.

'Yes that's okay sir, I'll sort this out now.'

Sitting at her desk she began to sort through the information in the file. Some of it she could disregard as it wasn't within her remit as a community liaison officer. That would be down to social services. Her mobile buzzed in her jacket at the same time as the phone rang on her desk. She answered the phone first, it was Alan Syms.

'Has the boss had a word?'

'He has, what do you want to do?'

'I'm on my way back in now. If you want a sandwich bringing in we can have a look at what I've got so far then maybe go and see the partner later this afternoon.'

'Yep, sounds good to me.' Nita replied.

'Right, Barry's Baps suit you, what do you want?'

'Fine, I'll have a tuna salad on granary please, no onion and get me a banana too will you?'

'Okay,' Alan said, 'ten minutes or so.'

Putting the phone down, she reached for her mobile from her jacket pocket and scanned through the menu to her messages.

'If you'd said a week ago I'd be sending slushy messages to a woman, to you, I'd have said you were way off the mark... But here I am doing just that. What can I say but thank you for an amazing W/E, I really do feel a different person, a new man, thank you XXXXXXX

P.S. I hope you had a good time too?'

She smiled and sent a message back.

'What do you think... silly man. I told you on Sunday morning, in less than 36 hours you managed to turn my world upside down. I said then that I think I've fallen... again! Yes I had a magical weekend with someone who has hidden his passion away for far too long. Guess what... I found it...Wohoo! Take care, I want my knight of the road back again ASAP. Love you. X

Twenty minutes later Alan Syms walked into the office carrying some paper bags. Dropping them on their desk he walked over to the free vend drinks machine in the corner of the office.

'Tea?' he called.

'Fine.' She replied.

Sitting together they munched through their sandwiches while sorting through all the evidence they had so far from the files to hand. Added to this evidence was the additional information Alan had put together today from talking to the uniform officers at the local station. He'd also managed to have a meeting with the pathologist to review the report on the victim's injuries and eventual cause of death. In just over an hour the two of them had built up a picture of their victim and begun to answer some of the questions regarding his last hours. All they needed now was a name and more information about the person, their habits hobbies and work. Putting everything together in the file Alan pushed his chair back.

'Right I'll have a word with the DI and if you're fit we'll go and visit his partner.'

Nita nodded, 'Were uniforms able to tell you anything about the family?'

Alan puffed his lips out a little. 'Not really, they live on the Wooldridge estate, Mum and two kids. The flat's in a bit of a state by all accounts.'

'Okay.'

He moved across the office and knocked on the Detective Inspectors door. Nita heard him call. 'Yeah, come...'

While Alan was updating DI Allen on the investigation, Nita gathered together her family liaison file adding in some forms and pamphlets to give to the family that would possibly be helpful in getting immediate assistance from an assortment of agencies. A quarter of an hour later the two detectives were driving through Portbridge in the direction of the Wooldridge estate. Parking in between the burned-out shells of some car and two skips overflowing with all sorts of household rubbish they stood by their car surveying their surroundings. Locking the car they walked carefully across a paved square towards the entrance to the block of flats where the family lived.

'Christ, it looks like there's been a war, just look at the mess.' Alan said.

All around the area there was debris and rubbish, broken glass, bits of buggies, old bikes, even a supermarket trolley.

'Mm, it's really deprived round here.' Nita said, 'I was involved in another suspicious death last year. Turned out to be father, son and step-Mum. The son was having it away with the woman. Dad threw him off their balcony, claimed he was drunk at the time and couldn't remember a thing. He got nine years.'

'Oh yeah,' Alan said, 'That was another one our lord and master cleared up in double quick time. Don't you think he rushes at a job sometimes and just anyone who fits the MO will do?'

Nita screwed her face up a little.

'No, surely not, I mean when I've worked with him he's always seemed professional and thorough. I think he's learned to see through all the crap and smoke screens to be honest. I mean ten years as a redcap with a load of squaddies, you're going to hear some fairly stupid excuses... yes?'

Alan had to agree, he nodded. 'Suppose.'

Reaching the entrance to the flats, they were overcome with the mixture of smells that greeted them as they walked through the door into the foyer. The smell of ammonia stale urine gives off, stale beer, even a pool of stagnant water in the stair well, all these aromas invaded their senses. Pressing the lift call button they waited, somewhere above them on one of the upper floors they could hear someone having a real argument. There were raised voices, lots of shouting and swearing, a door slammed and they heard someone shout.

'Screw you, you old cow!'

Seconds later a door opened and a woman screamed.

'Go on then, go and see your mates. We've got no money `cause you've drunk it all so don't expect any dinner tonight.'

The lift had arrived, the doors squealed opened slowly and both detectives recoiled instantly at the strong acrid smell of urine that hit them from such confined space.

'Stairs?' Alan said.

'Definitely.'

At the top of the first flight of steps an over-weight, scruffily dressed middle aged man shuffled past them chuntering to himself under his breath.

'We've got no money... stupid cow, what am I supposed to do...'

He lifted his eyes from the floor, threw the two detectives a cursory glance as he passed them to descend the last flight of steps to the ground floor. Two flights further up they passed a group of young people huddled together at the end of one of the balcony's which ran the length of that floor giving access to all the apartments on that level.

'Truants most of them I'll bet.'

Alan commented as they ascended another flight. Nita agreed, adding.

'What chance have they got today Alan? You know fifteen years ago there were two pits working plus all the engineering back-up that kept everyone in work, all gone now, hopeless.'

'They ought to get out, right away, to Leeds or Sheffield. They might have a chance there.' Alan commented.

'But what are they going to do there? The girls on the streets... all of them prime for crime. I know it sounds trite but it has to start here with the parents and school. They have to work together to make the system work to get the start they need.'

'Okay, yeah, I agree but that's easy for us Nita, we've done alright. This lot have no role models that are going point them in that direction... you know upwards. Most of the parents are too engrossed with their own issues to notice, look at the guy we passed on the stairs, it's so easy to follow the gang, not so easy to resist it, easier to aim low. You could end up with no friends otherwise or even in an unconscious heap in a stair-well. The gang is often the only real family for some of these kids.'

On level four now they walked along the balcony to 409. Alan knocked on the door, moments later it was opened by a small girl who stood and looked at them she was joined by a toddler, a little boy, who stood behind her peering around her to see who was at the door.

'You two get back inside now, do you hear!'

A woman's voice shouted the order from somewhere inside the dark hallway. Her dialect was hard, tone menacing. The woman appeared at the door, took one look at the two detectives and snapped at the children once more.

'You two... I'll not tell you again. Get inside!'

The two children turned and ran back into the flat passing the woman on the way. She cuffed the girl on the back of her head as she ran by her.

'Don't open the bloody door 'til we know who it is. How many times do you have to be sodding well told, Aye?' she shouted at her.

Coming to the door she stood, arms folded.

'Well you're either DHSS, council or police so which one and what do you want?'

Both detectives produced their warrant cards as Alan said.

'I'm detective constable Syms, and my colleague is DC Patel. Can we have a word with you?'

The woman slouched against the scuffed and finger marked wall by the front door studying the two officers.

'If it's about that cheating bastard I've just kicked out you can go screw yer'selves. I've told your mates in uniform what happened.'

With that she went to close the door on them. Alan put his hand up and held the door open.

'It is about your partner yes and we really would like a word with you.'

Something in Alan's voice seemed to stop her, she looked from one to the other then opened the door properly turned and just walked back into the flat. They followed her, Nita closing the door behind them, she followed Alan along the dark corridor into a small living room. As they passed a bedroom and the bathroom Nita had a quick glance into. They were untidy, clothes scattered everywhere and the bathroom needed a thorough clean, it smelled. Standing in the living room now, it appeared to Nita that almost every flat surface seemed to be sporting dirty dishes or mugs. There was unfinished food on discarded plates, broken biscuits, empty crisp packets and drink cartons littering the floor. She noticed the two children who'd opened the door to them now, were sitting squat on the floor by a grubby, finger marked brown faux leather settee that sported a few cuts and burn marks in the plasticised fabric. They were watching a children's cartoon show on a wide screen television. The girl seemed to Nita to be about four, five perhaps. She looked pale and under nourished, her shoulder length hair needed a wash and a good brush to remove all the knots. She was dressed in faded blue jeans, a grubby jumper that originally may have been white. Her brother, only a toddler had an action man top on, no trousers just baggy under-pants, he too looked pale and very thin. Turning to their mother she was able to see her in a better light. She guessed she was around her early twenties. Her face was pale and drawn, she looked tired in need of a good night's sleep. Like the children she too was pale and under-nourished, her brown hair unkempt and dull. She was stick thin and the jeans and jumper she was wearing seemed two sizes too big for her.

'Do you want to sit down?'

The woman asked, at the same time rounding on the two children.

'Yous two, shift yer'selves and let these two people sit and turn that tele down!' she snapped at them.

The children shuffled sideways over the dirty matted carpet to sit to one side of the settee still glued to the programme on the television. The woman reached over the settee back picking up some magazines and un-opened post and threw them across the room where they landed on another heap of papers and post on an armchair in the corner of the room. Nita and Alan carefully sat down, the woman sat on the arm of the chair where all the papers were.

'Well, what do you want to know now?'

Alan opened the file he'd been carrying.

'Are you Vivienne Watson?'

'Yes.' She replied curtly, 'What's this about anyway?'

Alan continued in a calm and level voice.

'Vivienne, what was the name of your partner?'

'Patrick... Patrick Doyle,' she replied, 'and he's my ex-partner the cheating bastard! Why has something happened to him?'

Suddenly there was concern in her voice.

'You don't have a picture of him by any chance do you?' Alan Syms asked.

'Yes, why?'

'Could you get it for us please?' Nita said.

Vivienne stood up and left the room, returning moments later handing a picture frame to Nita. It showed the two of them together possibly taken on holiday, Nita guessed it was before the children were around. Vivienne confirmed that, saying.

'That was when we first met, he gave me all the blarney and I fell for it... stupid cow.' She added quietly.

Alan continued. 'Vivienne can I borrow this please. Were you aware if Patrick was in any sort of trouble?'

'Trouble... he was always in bloody trouble, it followed him around. If he thought he could make a fast buck he'd go for it. He was a useless shit a lot of the time, money was wasted on him, it ran through his fingers like water. He... we, owed on everything, he was a selfish bastard everything was always for himself look at this lot.'

She pointed at the pile of post on the armchair all un-opened.

'Bills, court orders you name it! Listen, are you going to tell me what this is all about you're scaring me.'

'In a minute,' Alan said. 'Tell me when you last saw Patrick.'

'Oh bloody hell, has something happened to the stupid pillock?'

'Vivienne,' Alan repeated himself, 'When was the last time you saw Patrick?'

The woman seemed to be losing concentration, her breathing was becoming heavier a clear signs of stress. Nita spoke quietly to her.

'Vivienne it's important that you remember the last time you saw Patrick.'

She thought for a moment then answered, vacantly.

'Pearl had just had her birthday, it was two weeks after that so, July.' Nita took over asking the questions, her softer tones seemed to calm the young woman.

'Without getting too up-set Vivienne can you tell me what happened after Pearls birthday?'

She looked blankly at Nita for some time until she prompted her again. 'Vivienne?' Still looking at Nita she began to explain quietly.

'I'd had a feeling he was into someone else it was driving me mad. Anyway he got a call one day on his mobile, he was in the bog so I answered it. It was some foreign bird said she had to see him and to meet him at the usual place. Well I went off on one, I told him to get out and take that bloody dog with him. It was his anyway the smelly mingy thing. Oh he tried on the charm, swore on his mother's grave that nowt was going on but that was a load of bollocks,'

She continued answering Nita's question but the pitch of her voice began to rise as she clearly started to become angry.

'He was a real charmer when he had to be, full of the blarney... bastard! Just look at us now, no money, nothing!'

She was beginning to get really agitated.

'Nothing...sod all, Jack shit! and where is he? Off with some slag somewhere leaving me here with all this... bastard!'

She spat the words out, her face flushed with anger as her imagination worked overtime picturing this man with someone else. Alan Syms tried to get her to focus more on their questions hoping it would calm her, he asked.

'Vivienne can you tell us where Patrick worked and what he did?'

She was silent for some time, thinking about what Alan had asked her.

'He was a sort of odd job man, driver and general dogsbody for some club in Leeds.' She smirked adding. 'Dogsbody just about says it all, I guess that's where he's met this slapper. I hate him! Listen why all these questions? I still don't know what all this is about are you going to tell me or what.'

Nita threw Alan a look, he nodded and she said slowly but firmly.

'Vivienne, there's no easy way to say this but the body of a man has been discovered and the circumstances surrounding his death lead us to believe it might, just might be Patrick, I'm sorry Vivienne.'

The woman stared blankly at Nita.

'Oh my god...' she mouthed quietly at first and then, 'Oh my god!' she repeated herself louder this time. 'Oh no, no... How do you know it's Pat?'

Alan intervened. 'We received a report recently from the local police station, two months ago a vet had to put a dog to sleep that was badly injured. It had a micro-chip fitted and that led to the uniform lads paying you a visit, remember?'

She nodded, Alan continued relating the events of the past two months to her. Vivienne just stared blankly at him seemingly numbed by what she was hearing, Nita quietly got up and ventured into the kitchen. Despite feeling a little sick at the smell and general state of the place, she put the kettle on, washed some mugs and made a considered judgement that coffee was Vivienne's drink. Returning to the lounge with the drinks she offered the woman one, passed one to Alan and sat down with hers as Alan finished explaining where the police enquiry was at the moment. Clearly shocked and upset by all she'd just been told, Vivienne just sat on the arm of the chair staring into space as though Alan had just put her into a trance. Nita asked gently.

'Is there any one we can call to help you, or take the children to them perhaps?'

Vacantly Vivienne replied. 'My sister lives at 516, she'll help.'

'Do you want me to go for her?' Nita said.

'No... No,' she looked at Nita. 'I'll get the kids dressed and go up to hers.'

'Are you sure Vivienne, I don't mind taking them to her if you get them ready.' Nita said calmly, quietly. The woman shook her head. Opening her file Nita took some of the leaflets from it and showed

Vivienne them.

'Listen to me Vivienne. I know this is difficult to take in just now but my role in all this is that of a family liaison officer. Here are some leaflets from various agencies that can and will help you right now. Here is my card with my direct number. Call them and get them to get in touch with me if you're having any problems.'

She waited for a moment watching the woman's face to see she'd understood what she had just told her.

'Vivienne,' she said holding her arm, 'listen to me, this is important we're not the enemy here, we are all here to help. Do you understand?'

She said trying to reinforce what she was telling the woman, she nodded then asked.

'Will I have to see him? You know, identify him like they do on telly?'

Alan answered her. 'Not at the moment, the pathologists are still trying to find out how it all happened.

Nita asked Vivienne once again.

'Now are you sure that you don't want me to get your sister for you?'

The woman shook her head. 'No, I'll get us sorted and go and see her now.'

The two detectives were standing now moving down the corridor to the door, the woman followed them. Alan Syms said as they got to the door.

'DC Patel will keep you Informed as we sort through everything, all right?'

'Yes.' she replied.

Just before they left Nita turned to the young women.

'Vivienne, you have my number any problem you call me okay, I'm here to help you sort things out that's my job okay?'

The woman looked directly at Nita and nodded. Outside the flat the air felt fresh and smelled clean as they walked back to their car each with their own thoughts. Alan radioed control that they'd finished their enquiries, asking for any relevant up-dates for them. There was just one, from DI Allen.

'You know,' Alan said as they drove back to the office, 'the uniform lads said they wiped their feet after they left that flat because their boots were sticky from the carpet. It's like we said when we arrived, what chance have those two littlun's got in the future.'

Nita agreed with him. 'They could all do with some proper food, when I was making the drinks I noticed there was hardly anything to eat in the place, some milk in the fridge and just frozen bits, fish fingers, pizzas and burgers.'

It was never easy meeting a family to give them such dreadful news. It took a very hard-hearted policeman or detective not to feel for the relatives particularly if there were young children in the equation no matter what their circumstances or background were. Back in the office they wrote up their files and just before the end of the day were called in to see DI Allen.

'Well, have you got anywhere?' he asked Alan Syms directly.

'I think, in fact we're fairly certain that the deceased could be one Patrick Doyle sir.'

'Have you got some background on him?'

'Sir, his partner, ex-partner has given us a fair bit of detail about his work and daily movements and a bit of detail on another woman he appears to have been involved with. We have a photograph of him now albeit taken six years ago, but it does give us some idea what he looked like before someone smashed his face in.'

The Detective Inspector shifted his gaze to Nita.

'Have you got what you need? Can you do anything to help the family?'

'For the present yes sir, but I get the feeling she sees us as the opposition. I think she's afraid were going to march in with Social Services and take the children away. I've done my best, I'll keep her regularly up dated with what's going on and try to get her to relax.'

'Any family around to help?' the inspector asked.

'A sister lives in the same block of flats sir.'

'Good, right let's see how it all pans out this week, Alan if you need more bodies to help talk to me okay.'

'Sir, thank you.'

'Okay that's all.'

The inspector said abruptly and returned to the paperwork on his desk. Alan and Nita returned to their desks just as the church clock was striking five. Alan sat down and began to sift through all the papers he'd collated since the weekend, putting them into some sort of date order to create a time line. Nita cleared her desk of files locking them into the drawers.

'Right I'm going home having a soak and getting an early night I'm knackered.'

Alan looked up from the file in front of him and grinned.

'Strenuous weekend then was it?'

There was a knowing look in his eyes as he said this, she knew she'd flushed a little and tried to hide her secret weekend experience by answering tritely.

'It was very physical actually. You know working some of the locks really takes it out of you.'

Alan just gazed at her grinning. 'Really...' was all he said.

She studied him for a moment seeing that look again. Resigned to the fact that he knew only too well how the weekend had gone she picked up her bag and holdall, walked across the office taking her jacket from the coat stand. Calling to those still at their desks, 'Tomorrow folks.' she left.

~~~~~~
~~~~~~

LIFE APART

'Hello you, this is really weird. Most nights through the summer we just talked but tonight is so different. I know you now, I mean I really know who you are and what makes you tick, anyway how's your day been where are you tonight?' Nita asked.

Sitting cross legged on her bed looking at her laptop and the image of Stephen's head and shoulders filling the screen. She'd been home just over an hour, time enough to rustle up some dinner change out of her work clothes into some baggy trousers and a loose top. She'd waited until the arranged time before trying to Skype him.

'Hello you too, yeah I'm good just waiting to run onto the ferry and then get my head down. Good day really, got loaded okay got across here a couple of hours ago, got all the paperwork done and now I'm just waiting. There are a couple of other drivers I know in the queue so we might have a half when we get on board. What about you, okay?'

'I'm all right, busy day, well not busy just a bit involved. I'm helping Alan Syms on a case, we're trying to find some sort of lead there are too many loose ends at the moment and missing bits.'

'Anything said at work this morning?' he asked.

'Hmm... Linda, another DC was all over me this morning wanting to know how it had gone. I tried to be as discreet as possible but I think my face gave it away! Anyway I don't care, like I said last night the whole weekend was just magical.'

The tone of her voice changed now, becoming sultry.

'You're a very passionate man you know, you made me tingle all over it's a long time since anyone has done that.'

'Oh anyone is it, so I'm just another one of your conquests then,

I see. Well now I know where I stand and I thought it was special...'

'I didn't mean it like that... I.'

'Oh don't worry about me I'll manage, get drunk on the boat and mope, tell my mates how it is.'

'Don't...' Nita said sharply, 'You're not here so I can't show you how good you are!'

Instantly he picked up the sudden change of mood.

'No, I'm not there and yes it is hard tonight `cause I wish I was there too.'

Looking at his image on the laptop screen she reached out and touched it. She just stared at it for a while eventually replying quietly.

'From nothing but a vague, casual friendship; in just three days I've fallen in love with you, only to find myself on my own tonight with just an image to talk to. I'm missing you, how am I going to manage for four weeks for god's sake?'

'Nita... sugar, you knew before this weekend how much time I'm over here and not there.'

'Yes yes I know, but we were just friends then and just talked, it's so different now, like I said earlier... I want you now, tonight.' She heard him sigh.

'I don't think we thought beyond the weekend did we?' he said, 'about what would happen if the friendship became something else; so here we are facing it now. Nita you said last night that you didn't feel you could go cold turkey, well for the next week or two we're both going to have to learn to get used to it.'

He looked at his laptop screen and the image of a very forlorn Nita staring back at him. Smiling at the picture he added.

'On the upside, think what it'll be like when I come home.'

A brief smile flashed across her face.

'You'd better not be tired, because I'm going to wear you out, mark my words Ferryman.'

He grinned back at her, relieved that he'd managed to break her mood.

'If that's a challenge lady, you've lost already.'

Something distracted him and he glanced away from the screen.

'Okay in ten minutes, right thanks.' Turning back he said. 'Got to go sugar we're loading.'

Nita reached out and touched the screen again.

'Love you, be safe speak tomorrow.'

He touched where her fingers were on his screen.

'Night sugar hope you sleep okay and we'll speak tomorrow. Nita...'

'Yes...' He saw her nod.

'Night... bye.' And he was gone from her screen.

She sat for some time the laptop on her lap with just a blank screen. A tap on her door brought her out of her thoughts.

'Yeah, come in.'

Louise, Alan Syms's sister opened the door and put her head round the door.

'Do you want to come and join me and Moira for a glass of red, we'd like to hear about your weekend as a galley slave and deck hand.'

She couldn't help breaking into a giggly grin as she spoke. Shaking herself out of her melancholy, she smiled back at Lou.

'Yeah, two minutes okay?'

For a few minutes more she sat lost in her thoughts then taking a deep breath got off the bed, ran a brush through her long hair and went downstairs to join her house mates. The three girls sat for ages talking and laughing at Nita's reflections on the weekend's adventures and misadventures, such as the first big lock. They were in tears one minute laughing at the lock exploits and the next they were overcome by the romance of the pub dinner and starlit walk back to the boat. By the time they all padded off to bed Nita was at peace once again. She fell asleep thinking happy thoughts of Stephen and their weekend. On the ferry Stephen fell asleep with similar thoughts of Nita as the ship sailed further away from home. During the night, somewhere in the North Sea, two ships passed in the dark visible only by their navigation lights and an eerie green blip on a radar screen.

One a converted fishing boat with an odd cargo the other, a large North Sea ferry carrying Stephen and other truckers to Rotterdam.

The next morning, Tuesday, saw Nita at her desk in Portbridge and Stephen in Holland at the Euro-port each beginning a determined effort to learn to live with their new relationship that for the foreseeable future would be a long distance one highlighted by periods of intense passion. At some point through their long morning they both reflected on the old adage, 'Absence makes the heart grow fond.' For Stephen it was about learning that for the past eight years, his habit of hiding behind the memory of his dear Suzanne when he felt things appeared to be getting away from him were in the past. The challenge facing him now was adjusting to this new freedom he felt in this relationship with Nita; begun as just a long-distance friendship and now lovers. They had spent almost the entire weekend locked in an intensely powerful vacuum that excluded the real world. They had absented themselves for the whole weekend and now he felt invigorated, glad to be alive and feeling like a new man. He smiled to himself briefly re-calling some of high points from the weekend and realised he was becoming quite aroused by them, his body was tingling all over. As if to emphasize how distracted he was, he'd only been in Holland four hours and had already been pulled by customs over an administration issue regarding his manifest, plus he'd made two wrong turns since leaving the Euro-port, this was so out of character for him; ordinarily he was so focused and organised. His CB radio burst into life bringing him back to reality.

'Hey, heads up Ferryman I thought you were going to Enscheda.'

'Shit!' Stephen thought as he saw signs for the auto-route to Luxembourg. Picking up the mic, he replied to the caller.

'Thanks for that Rory. My mind was somewhere else.'

'Channel thirty-three Ferryman.'

The caller immediately came back at him. Switching the selector to the channel he heard the caller say.

'Come on Stephen man get a grip mate stay on track, you can't afford to make mistakes you know that.'

'I know Trev,' he replied. 'I'll be okay now. I'll do a loop before the toll bar. Thanks for that see you around.'

'Yeah, no probs mate, stay safe, speak later, I'm out.'

He travelled the ten kilometres to the next junction and looped round heading back North West towards the Dutch-German border. By the time he was en-route his head was in gear and he was fully focused on the busy auto-route.

Nita too was struggling to adjust, to thinking about another person after so long on her own albeit it for a totally different set of circumstances. It was almost five years since she'd returned from her two-year stint in America with the New England police. When she'd left she'd walked away from a relationship that seemed to be as intense and as passionate as the past forty-eight hours had been with Stephen.

'Nita... hello, are you in there or are the lights on just for show?'

It was Linda speaking to her, startled momentarily she reacted to the question appearing a little flustered.

'Are you okay lovie?' Linda asked again.

'No, I mean yes I'm all right honestly, I was a bit lost in my thoughts about the weekend.'

Linda rested her hand on her shoulder sympathetically.

'Mmm... Going cold turkey after the weekend you've just had `aint going to be easy girl. When's he back?'

Nita hunched her shoulders, 'Three, four weeks.'

'Oh... tough love.' Leaning close to Nita's ear she whispered, 'I've got something you could borrow if it gets really hard.' She couldn't help chuckling at her unfortunate quip. 'You'll have to get some batteries for it though.'

Nita looked at her friend bewildered trying to comprehend what she was saying, then the penny dropped. Surprised and a little shocked at what Linda was offering her she exclaimed quietly to her.

'Linda...! I wouldn't, I mean, I never thought you'd...'

'Hey come on needs must you know, we're all in need of some relief if the real thing isn't available. I bet he's got some top shelf literature in that cab?'

She raised her eyebrows in a knowing look nodding, Nita playfully pushed her away, Linda grinned at her.

'Know what I mean…' she added and touched Nita's shoulder. Walking across the office to the vending machine, she said. 'Want one?'

Nita nodded, 'Please, tea.'

She brought the two cups across the office and put one on her desk.

'You okay now?'

'Yeah… I'm fine now thanks.'

'Good, the offer still stands if you want to borrow it…'

Linda said over her shoulder and wandered back to her own desk.

Through the rest of the day they toiled on with their respective jobs, Stephen in his cab Nita at her desk. After what seemed like an age the day ended with Stephen parked up in a German truck stop and Nita driving home to her house through the rush hour traffic, at times vacantly studying the illuminated array of red tail lights and orange, flashing indicators as she made her way slowly out of town. What a difference she thought compared to the canal the countryside and the peace she'd discovered over the weekend.

Observed from space the two of them could have been mirror images as almost in unison they showered cooked and ate dinner, except for the fact they were separated by 450 miles. Finally she settled cross-legged on her bed again with her laptop in front of her, at the same time Stephen was settled in his cab his laptop on waiting for the tone of an incoming call. They talked for a long time, firstly about their respective day then their thoughts about each other and finally lots of nonsense stuff. Tonight was a little easier, more in keeping with the conversations they used to have over the summer when they were just friends. Ending the conversation became the stuff of a TV comedy sketch. They said their goodbyes and then began the comical palaver of who was going to disconnect first.

'Go on then,' Stephen said 'Goodbye, sleep well... love you sugar.'

'Yeah, love you too, miss you.' Nita replied.

'Go on then, switch off.' he said.

'No you switch off.' Nita answered.

'Okay... bye.'

'Bye, love you.'

A moment or two passed as they both watched their respective screens.

'Go on then,' Nita said, 'turn off.'

'No, you turn off.'

'After three then.' She compromised.

'Okay, after three. One two...'

Nita joined in, 'Three...'

Nothing happened, neither of them ended the connection. Laughing at each other, Nita said.

'Cheat, you should have switched off!'

'I wanted to see if you would.' he answered.

'This could go on all night. I'm tired and want to go to bed.' Nita said.

'Well you close down then.'

'No... I don't want to be first, you go!'

'All right, night night speak tomorrow.'

He blew her a kiss and touched the screen, she responded and just as her fingers reached for the screen, it went blank, for a terrible moment she felt alone completely isolated. 'Stupid woman' she thought closing the screen. Separated by the North Sea they readied themselves for bed, Stephen settled himself on his bunk and fell asleep with the sounds of other trucks arriving and leaving at the night halt, but with thoughts of Nita at home. Tucking herself into her bed and wishing he was by her side, she snuggled into her duvet reached for the polar bear; she'd had it since her childhood, it went everywhere with her whenever she travelled. Giving it a hug sighed, 'Night Stephen, take care.' She turned onto her side, shuffled to get comfy and wished she could feel Stephen's warm body nestled around her back, and fell asleep.

~~~~~~~~~~~~~~~~~~~~~~~~~~~~~~~~~

Day by day and night after night the first week passed and just as through the summer they spoke to each other every night. Their first weekend apart found Stephen in Sweden. He parked up on the Saturday near the place he was to deliver to on the Monday morning. Nita meanwhile opted to work the Saturday morning to keep herself occupied then met her house mates and did the supermarket shop for the week. The two flat mates were very conscious that she was distracted as they wandered around the aisles of the market and suggested they all went for a meal at one of the restaurants in Portbridge. They had a great evening and returned home with three bottles of wine, quite fresh and squiffy from what they'd already consumed.

The Skype connection tonight started off well enough, they told each other what they'd done through the day but as time went on an element of melancholy began to slip into the conversation. The animated chatter that had filled every night's connection through the week was gone, they just looked at the others image on their screens. Both lovesick and in need of wanting to hold the other to make the pain go away. Finally they surrendered to their mood and said their goodbyes.

In the confined space of his cab he found it hard to pull himself out of the overwhelming feeling of homesickness, an experience that was new to him. When Suzanne had died, he'd coped helping Emma to grieve and begin to put her life back in order, as well as being there for his dad and Mary and Richard. He'd found the isolation of being away on the road for weeks at a time helped him deal with his own grief. The cab had become a sanctuary for him over the past years, he'd grown used to the security it offered. If he ever found that things were getting out of his control with people, or relationships, then this
~~~~~~~~~~~~~~~~~~~~~~~~~~~~~~~~~

was a place he could retreat to. When he'd first met Nita and they'd had dinner together at the Duchess just before he continued that journey down to the Marina,she'd quickly identified this trait. Tonight though he just wanted to be with her, to go out somewhere have fun and then make love to her. Right now this isolation was hurting him, for the first time in years he didn't want to be here. Standing in the cab he rummaged about among the contents lying on the second bunk, the top one. Finding a bottle of whisky he settled back opened the bottle inhaling the aroma of the spirit and poured himself a good measure of the tan liquid, adding a splash of water he turned on the TV and slowly drank his way through half the bottle before climbing into his bunk and falling into a restless sleep.

Back in Portbridge Nita closed the lid of her laptop crying silently. Pushing it to one side she lay across her bed and reaching for her bear drew it tightly into a hug. She wept into it until the fur was wet with tears. Not since the breakup of her relationship with the American police officer had she felt so wretched, so alone and miserable. Only now did she grasp how much last weekend's jaunt with Stephen had affected her, how much the intense passion of those hours had drawn her into the painful clutches of this new relationship. Okay they'd talked about his work and the weeks he spent away but not for one minute had she imagined just how hard it was going to be. She felt sick, she didn't want to do anything. 'How am I going to survive three or four weeks of this for god's sake if after only a week I feel this bad,' she asked herself. After half an hour she had pulled herself together, applied a bit of makeup, ran a brush through her hair then slipped downstairs to join the girls for the rest of the evening. Just after midnight she crawled into bed definitely suffering the effects of overindulging the juice of the grape and fell into an alcohol induced stupor.

~~~~~~
~~~~~~

Stephen spent Sunday morning wandering around the town, shopped for essentials had a meal in a local bar chatting to half a dozen other drivers from all over England and the Low Countries who, like himself, were here ready to unload on Monday morning. As he walked back to his truck on the industrial estate it never ceased to surprise him that in all the years he'd done this job whether in Southern Europe, Germany or anywhere, every industrial estate was the same, deserted except for the odd security car or police patrol, oh and the usual procession of 'working girls'. The exception was the UK where you met the same people yes, but many sites were working twenty-four seven. Strange he thought we work hardest, more than many other country in the EU but we're well down the table of leading industrial nations despite the hours worked.

Arriving back at his truck he sided all his purchases, cleaned his cab changed his duvet cover bagging it up with other stuff he'd wash somewhere when he got chance. He checked his e-mails answering those from his depot and set about working on routes and loads into next week. Later he called Mary, Richard and Emma and spent an hour speaking to them. Looking at the digital clock on the cab bulkhead he saw it was almost time to Skype Nita. She wasn't online the first time so he waited until later in the evening and called again. Tonight's connection was less emotional than Saturdays, they both seemed to have rationalised their current situation through the day getting it into some sort of proportion. They talked to each other as they had through most of last week, they were honest about how they felt and just how difficult this first weekend apart had been. Surprisingly, both the same things seemed to have affected them, how they really would have wanted to go out to eat somewhere and come home to make love for the rest of the night. When they finally ended tonight's connection it was in the same silly fashion as nearly every other evening through the week. He sat for a while feeling easier after tonight's conversation, he smiled to himself remembering the fact that they'd both had similar feelings yesterday but couldn't be honest enough to actually speak about it. He sighed, switched on his TV found a channel covering a motor GP race and lounged back on the passenger seat to watch it. As darkness fell he turned in, tomorrow was going to be a long day. In Portbridge Nita bagged the bathroom, took a shower then spent the rest of the evening pampering herself with creams and oils before slipping under the duvet and falling into a peaceful asleep.

Somewhere between Stephen asleep in his cab in Sweden and Nita in Portbridge, the familiar outline of a, converted fishing boat left the Europort just as darkness was falling and set a course across the North Sea. No one noticed its departure or would have been particularly bothered if they had, it was en-passage to a small harbour somewhere between the Wash on the Norfolk coast and the Humber. Before the boat had slipped away there had been a riotous party on board with some young girls and a group of very smartly dressed young men having fun eating and drinking and dancing the night away. Around midnight things had quietened down just before all the guys had left the boat and driven away. Of the young ladies, they apeared to be spending the night on board going to wherever the boat made land fall.

A CONNECTION.

The second week of separation passed much as the first, they both had to focus on their own work. However, every evening became an almost religious routine. Supper, domestic stuff then thirty minutes or more talking to each other and so began week three. Monday six thirty in the morning Stephen had been up since five had breakfast and was now backed onto the dock of a factory near to where he'd spent the weekend. While he was being unloaded he checked the instructions as to where his next consignment was to be collected then the destination, delivery day and time. He looked at his European route map working out a plan, he did use his sat-nav to get from A to B but never totally relied on it. Over the years he'd heard too many disaster stories about drivers who, following the sat-nav had found themselves stranded unable to extricate their units from narrow lanes or tiny villages.

Back in Portbridge Nita arrived at her office and like every Monday it began with the briefing with DI Allen. When the detectives eventually broke away, DI Allen asked Nita and Alan Syms to join him in his office. Sitting around his desk he reached for a report sheet from the top of an adjacent cupboard handing it to Alan Syms who glanced over it before passing it to Nita, while she looked at the report the DI continued.

'This has been sent over by Wharf-street station this morning. A young woman, definitely not English was found beaten up in a snicket early hours of Sunday morning. No ID no cards, no phone or money. Her injuries are not life threatening but pretty nasty. No sign of rape or robbery, drugs or alcohol. She's in the PCH at the moment, the local lads say they can't find a reason for the attack and wondered if we'd have a look. I know you're busy with your suspicious death but I wondered if you'd go to the hospital and see if you can get anything from her that's going to help us find out who she is.'

'Foreign.' Alan asked.

'Yep, more than likely.'

'Do we know where from?'

'Nope, she's not said a word since she was admitted.'

'Nothing?' Nita said looking up at the DI, handing the report back to him.

'Not a peep, the medics had their work cut out just sorting her injuries out.'

Nita and Alan exchanged glances then looking at the Inspector Alan said.

'We'll nip over there now boss, ok.'

DI Allen held his hand up.

'Fine by me.' then as they left his office he added. 'Let me know if you need an interpreter, ok.'

'Boss.' Alan acknowledged him.

Alan and Nita duly arrived at the hospital parking in one of the few spaces available. He lowered the passenger sun visor to reveal the crest and laurels of the county insignia. Glancing around the car park he commented,

'You know at this rate trying to park here to visit someone is going to be as bad as parking at a concert. We'll end up walking a couple of miles just to get in.'

Nita looked at him. 'You know you can sound like a right grumpy old man sometimes.'

They both laughed briefly as they walked into the foyer. Showing their warrant cards to the young girl on the desk, Alan said.

'We're looking for a young woman who was admitted late Sunday night.'

'Name.' The receptionist asked abruptly.

'Sorry, no name I'm afraid.' Nita said, 'She was brought in last night.'

The girl searched the files, after a couple of minutes she looked up from the screen.

I've got an unknown admission at 0200 this morning, she's on Jasmine ward, that's high dependency.'

Handing him a printed sheet of the hospitals floor plan she hi-lighted the route to Jasmine ward.

'If you go through that door, turn right and take the second corridor you'll see the signs for ITU and the HD ward.'

Alan nodded, Nita thanked the girl. Arriving at the ward they pressed the access bell, cleansing their hands with some anti-septic gel as they waited. A nurse eventually came to the door, they showed her their warrant cards and she let them enter then seemed to just disappear. Walking to the nurse's station they stood by the desk looking down the different corridors waiting for someone to come and see them.

Seeing a ward plan on the wall Nita studied it for a moment then touched Alan Sym's arm.

'This way, she's in F3 a side room.'

As they went down one corridor, a voice called out behind them.

'Excuse me, can I help you?'

Nita didn't have to turn around as she recognised the soft Welsh tones of the person challenging them. Turning, she looked straight at Sian Morgan.

'Staff nurse Morgan, DCs Patel and Syms.' she introduced herself and Alan. 'We've come to talk to your unknown patient if she's up to visitors.'

Sian stood for a moment. 'Patel,' she said thoughtfully, 'weren't you one of those detectives dealing with that series of river assaults earlier this year? The young couple and that truck driver off the boat.'

Nita nodded. 'Yes, we were both on that case.'

'She's in F3.' Sian said and led the way to the room. 'How did things pan out with everyone then?' the nurse asked, 'the man that was attacked along with his girlfriend; he was here for almost three months. Did he recover in the end?'

Nita replied. 'Yes, he and the young Asian girl left Portbridge three months later.'

'And what of the sailor guy?' Sian asked.

Alan chuckled, Nita cuffed him across the shoulder as she replied.

'Oh he's just fine, made a full recovery and he's driving and sailing again.'

Alan looked at Nita and then at Sian and in a stage whisper said.

'Ask her how she knows... go on, ask her.'

Nita swiped at him again, Sian looked at her and kind of guessing the answer said.

'Let me guess. 'You're an item?'

Nita broke into a huge grin, 'Sort of.'

Alan gave a stifled choked laugh, collecting yet another back hander from Nita. Sian continued.

'He was a tough one that one, pig headed too. Have you tamed him?'

Nita pulled a face.

'Sort of... work in progress you could say, he's better for knowing. He was very introvert but I'm bringing him out of himself.'

They were standing outside a room now, Sian opened the door and they followed her into the dimly lit room. Lying in the bed was a young woman whose age Nita put to be mid to late twenties. It was difficult to judge really as her face was quite heavily bandaged and what they could see was bruised and grazed in places. Her right arm was resting on top of the covers, plastered up to the elbow. They stood looking at her, she watched them her eyes full of suspicion even fear, Sian said quietly.

'This is the young lady who came up to us from A&E in the early hours of this morning. Your beat crews found her not far from the Woolridge estate she'd been attacked and dumped in a ginnel. She's in a bit of a state but she'll mend.'

Sian added quietly.

'Hasn't said much since she came up to us.'

She turned to leave saying to the young woman before she let the door close behind her.

'Sweetheart these two police officers are here to help you. Don't worry my love, you'll be alright. Press your buzzer if you want anything all right?'

The young woman watched Sian leave the room and as the door closed slowly turned her attention back to the two detectives standing at the foot of her bed studying them. Nita spoke first quietly but firmly.

'My name is Nita Patel I'm a community liaison officer, do you understand me?'

The woman just looked at Nita, she continued.

'This is detective Alan Syms, he's a colleague who works with me.'

They both waited for some response from the woman, none came.

'Can you tell us anything about what happened last night? Who did this to you? How you came to be attacked?'

Still getting no response, Nita looked at Alan and gave a slight nod, a hint that he should leave them alone.

'I'll go and get a drink for us, okay?' he turned and left the room.

Nita pulled a chair to the bedside and sat down. Both women studied each other for some time, Nita eventually said gently.

'I want to help you but it's a bit difficult if I don't know your name.'

There was no response, nothing.

'I could always invent one I suppose... mmm, how does Jane Doe sound?'

The woman's eyes never left her face but there was a hint of a smile. Nita waited for a moment before saying.

'Okay so Jane then, so can you tell...'

The woman spoke quietly.

'My name is Katterine, Katterine Worzinski. If you call me Kate it is easier, yes?'

Her accent sounded Eastern European taking Katterine's free

hand in hers she looked into her eyes.

'Listen to me Kate I don't know why you've been beaten so badly. I don't know what the reason was for you to deserve this. I do know that no one should have to suffer something like this, it's just not right or fair. I want to help you, I want to keep you safe from any more harm or violence. Do you understand what I'm saying? Do you speak much English?'

The woman was still watching at her. She let go of her hand and sat back on the chair and waited. Minutes passed, they sat in silence once more, Nita racking her brain how to get the woman to speak, just one word a sentence.

'Where are you from Kate, do you have family here or friends I can contact for you? They must be worried if you haven't been home or called them.'

The young woman had completely closed down. Sian came into the room to run an Obs check, pulse, BP, temperature. Completing the report sheet on the clip board she looked at the woman then Nita. Sitting on the edge of the bed she smiled at Katterine saying gently.

'This lady here is very special bach, earlier this year she helped a young couple who'd been attacked just like you. She made sure they were safe and in no more danger. She got the people who'd attacked them too and now they're locked away for a long time. I'm sure she can help you in the same way alright, you need to trust her though do you understand what I'm saying my love?'

The woman was watching Sian and when she'd finished speaking she slid off the bed to leave the room. As she got to the door the woman suddenly said.

'Can I have some coffee please?'

Sian stopped turned throwing Nita a quick glance and replied.

'How do you like it?'

'Black please.'

'Sugar?'

The woman shook her head, Sian left the two women alone.

Nita sat and waited, reluctant to say anything that might upset any tenuous link Sian and herself just might have formed with this young woman. Katterine was watching Nita again, nothing was said. Sian brought the cup of coffee into the room and placed it on the bedside cabinet.

'I've brought a straw bach, it will help if your lips are tender. You should be able to manage to drink it one way or the other alright.'

Turning to leave the room she gave Nita a little smile and let her hand rest briefly on her shoulder. Nita stood and walked around the bed picking up the cup and straw.

'This could be difficult with one hand, let me help.'

Putting the straw in the drink she offered it to the young woman. Gingerly she took it between her lips and sucked, she winced at the first mouthful as the hot liquid stung her tender lips then drank half of the black liquid in one go. Nita put the cup back on the cabinet and sat on the bed beside Kate who had settled back against the stack of pillows supporting her. Sighing she closed her eyes and a few moments later began to shake, it became quite exaggerated. At first Nita thought she was having some sort of a fit then realised she was crying silently, there were tears streaming down her bruised face. Taking her free hand once more she held it tightly, Kate opened eyes looking directly at her.

'Help me...' she whispered, 'Please... I'm so frightened...'

Nita moved slightly to make it easier to take the woman in her arms. As soon as she felt the safety of Nita's arms around her she began to wail uncontrollably. Her crying brought Sian and Alan Syms to the room in a rush. Nita looked at them both shaking her head, Sian knew there was no emergency and touched Alans arm for him to leave. Just before the door closed Nita said quietly to him.

'Go talk to the uniforms that found her okay.' he nodded and left.

Quite some time passed before Kate calmed down, Nita sat with her holding her the whole time. Once, Sian came to the door and looked through the window and seeing that all was well left the two women alone. Reaching for some tissues on the bedside cabinet Nita first dabbed the young woman's tears away then gave her a tissue of her own to dry her tears properly. She moved off the bed and sat down again. After a while she spoke calmly and quietly.

'Do you want to share what happened to you? It needn't go any further if you don't want it to. I'm happy just to listen, do you understand what I'm saying?'

Kate studied her deeply for some time. Sitting patiently she waited to see if she was going to get any conversation out of the woman.

'He said he would help us get away.'

'Who did Kate?'

'Our friend... he said he could get us away maybe home.'

Nita waited for more.

'He was kind man. We would see him sometimes when he came bringing things. Then they knew somehow and they took him away.'

Nita sat waiting for the woman to continue.

'Kate,' she said eventually, 'this is all a bit mixed up. Would you mind if I took some notes to help me understand would that be okay?'

The woman suddenly looked anxious.

'You said we could talk only okay and you would say nothing.'

Nita nodded and to reassure her added.

'That's right, this is for me only. When we've finished and I know who's who I'll give you my notes all right.'

She nodded, 'Da, yes okay.'

Still not sure of Nita the young woman laid quietly for some time.

'Okay Kate, so tell me what has happened to you in the last few days. You said this man was going to help you. How many of you was he going to help?'

'There are five of us in this house. We have to work in this club and then sometimes there are men who come back to the house and we had to have sex and do things for them. It was not nice, they were not nice.'

'Kate, was this in Portbridge?'

She shook her head.

'No Hull, that's where we have to live and work.'

Looking directly at Nita her eyes filled tears again as she said, her voice full of emotion.

'Just because we are from Poland or Russia or Lithuania, or somewhere another country, why do these men feel we are different from English girls? Why do they think we are only here for sex with them? We are good girls, we know what is right and not, just the same as your English girls. I am catholic girl I go to church, I work and I want what they want, a husband, home and children.'

'Kate, I know about prejudice and abuse, it's happened to me but this is more serious, do you understand? My job is to help you and the best way I can get that result is for you to tell me all you can about how you came here. Who brought you, where from and the conditions you've been exposed to, all right?'

Kate nodded.

'How have you come to be here in Portbridge, where were you trying to go?'

The woman pointed to the bedside cabinet, Nita opened the door and saw some clothes muddied with traces of blood on some of them, she glanced at Kate who nodded. She took the pair of muddy damp jeans from the cupboard passing them to the woman. She tried to take a piece of paper out of one pocket but fumbled only being able to use one hand. Nita moved to help her until they found the paper.

'This man said he would help us, I came to find him I have this paper with his phone number. I took some money from one of the men who came to my room for sex and got out of the house at night. I took bus to Leeds and then here next day but my bosses found me.'

Taking the screwed-up paper from the woman Nita studied it for a moment.

'Now this is the hard bit, you're going to have to trust me, okay.'

Kate nodded again, Nita continued.

'My guess is you've been told that going to the police would be a very bad idea, yes?' A nod from Kate. 'Also, that if you say anything they will get you, even though you are protected. Am I right?'

Kate gave Nita a shocked look.

'Da, yes. They say it make no difference they will kill us if we talk to authorities.'

'Kate, in England we are bigger than these gang masters. If we are going to make you safe, then that will happen and you stay safe, they won't be able to get near you. Help me, help us catch them and get them off the streets so that other girls are safe. We will put them away for a long time, trust me Kate let me help you.'

Nita paused for a moment to let her words sink in.

'Now, from the beginning, who have you been living with and if you can remember where in Hull? Who was this man that was going to help you, do you know what happened to him?'

Kate began to tell Nita about how she'd seen an advert in Latvia offering women jobs in the UK. She'd called the contact number and then met some people who offered her a good job, earning good money living and working in England. Two other girls were at the same meeting and offered the same deal. From someone who a short while ago was too frightened to say anything, it was as though a door had been opened and all the pent-up fear and stress just poured out of her. She spoke of a party on a boat where the three girls were joined by some young men and the owner of the boat and her husband. If there had been any doubts in Kate's mind about the offer of good work in England, then the lifestyle she and the other girls were promised disappeared altogether that night on the boat.

Sian interrupted their conversation a little later, bringing another coffee in for Katterine and a tea for Nita. For another hour she talked while Nita tried to keep up, making notes and asking questions. At times some very searching questions attempting to get the fullest possible picture of this woman's experiences at the hands these people who were clearly running organised trafficking of young impressionable girls and women for the sex trade. At this point Kate became quite agitated and distressed again, dissolving into tears as she recalled some of the more frightening experiences. It took all Nita's skills as an experienced support officer to calm her down, all the time striving to keep her focused. She quickly realised there was a distinct possibility that reliving these events might cause Kate to become too frightened to continue and withdraw into herself again. Right now anything Kate could tell her was vital; Nita calmly encouraged her to continue giving as much information as possible. As Kate told her more about what she and her friends had had to submit to they began to speak of a man who the girls would see from time to time. He would bring boxes of things to the dingy club, the boxes looked like wine or spirits and cigarettes. If one of the managers saw him talking to the girls they would be hustled out of the way and told the man was a bad man and wasn't very nice to girls. She'd seen him pushed up against a wall once by two of the door men when they'd caught the girls talking to him. One of them had hit him again and again until he collapsed to the floor. One night he'd come to the club through the back door and hid until everyone had gone then came to her room. Kate said she was frightened that he was going to force her to do something because they'd been told he wasn't nice to women. He told her his name was Patrick, he had a funny accent and when she asked about it he said he was from Ireland. Stunned by this bit of information Nita looked quickly at Kate.

'Kate,' she said, 'Kate… stop for a moment. You're sure this man was called Patrick?'

'Da, yes I'm sure.' she replied, 'Patrick.'

'Could you describe him for me?'

She thought for a moment and then proceeded to describe exactly the person in the picture that Vivienne had given them. Shocked at how accurate her description was, Nita stopped her again. Sitting for some time assimilating in her head what she ought to do now, she reached for the bedside buzzer and pressed it. She waited for someone to come to the room. Eventually hearing footsteps on the corridor she looked at the door where Sian stood with a junior nurse behind her.

'Problem?'

'Hmm big problem, I think!'

Handing her one of her cards she said.

'Will you call this number and ask for DI Allen. Tell him he needs to come here and bring some uniforms with him. Tell him it's in connection with our suspicious death and it's urgent!'

Kate looked at Nita then Sian, they both saw the fear appear in her eyes again.

Nita followed her to the door saying quietly.

'Sian... not a word, no-one comes in here without a pass or some ID okay! Can you get one of your security guys up here until my boss arrives? If they asks just say you've got an unruly patient and you might need them.'

The nurse nodded and left with her colleague. Alone with Kate again who was looking decidedly panicky, Nita took hold of her hand and squeezed it.

'Kate, did you ever notice if Patrick had a dog with him?'

She nodded.

'Da a black and white one, it guarded the van, but it was nice when it was with him.'

Still holding her hand Nita continued.

'I'm not certain, but I think the managers you were working for are very violent people. I don't want to upset you but I have to tell you that my partner and I are investigating a suspicious death and from the description you've just given me, I think it is the same person... Patrick.'

Kate let out an ear-splitting scream pulling away from Nita. In a moment there was the sound of running on the corridor. Alan Syms, Sian and an overweight guy in a uniform burst through the door to Kate's room. The shock of their sudden arrival set Kate off again and she let out another scream.

'YOU, out!' Nita shouted at the security guy over Kate's hysterical screaming.

He spun round and left immediately!

'Alan get down to the entrance and bring the boss up here when he arrives. Sian we need a doctor, a sedative… something, I think!'

The security guy stopped Alan Syms as he went past him in the corridor.

'What the bloody hell just happened in there mate that was proper scary I tell you.'

Through the door they could still hear the woman crying hysterically. Alan looked at the guy saying briefly.

'Sorry, can't say right now, but stay here, stay alert okay, no-one in there who isn't staff or has a warrant card, right.'

The man nodded firmly without question, Alan continued on his way to meet the boss.

In room F3 meanwhile, Sian reached behind the bed and pressed the crash button at the same time saying to Nita.

'What the hell's going on Nita, we need to know what it's all about if she needs sedating.'

While both of them tried to calm Kate, Nita briefly explained the build up to Kate becoming hysterical. From all over the hospital the crash team responded to their bleepers descending on Jasmine ward. By the time DI Allen arrived along with two uniformed officers, one a woman Nita had left Katterine resting in the care of the medical team. She briefed them on the information Kate had given her about how she had ended up here in Portbridge hospital, plus the details she'd given regarding Patrick. DI Allen slouched on one of the settees in the family room listening to Nita until she'd completed her report. Thinking for some time he eventually leaned closer to her studying her for a moment; finally reaching a decision he said.

'Right, I think I need to escalate this to Division and the Regional team.' Glancing at Alan and at Nita he added. 'I've got a feeling that this isn't just an isolated event in Hull or our area. I reckon this could be the tip of a very large iceberg that may well be national or even wider reaching than that. I've got a meeting next week at one of the inter-regional forums, I'll see if any other divisions have had any similar cases.'

Standing, he moved towards the door the two detectives followed him. Turning to the two uniformed officers there he said.

'Follow DC Patel's instructions for the moment, I'm going back to the station to have a word with your Inspector to set up a team here for the next few days. I'll get you relieved shortly, okay?'

The two officers nodded, responding in unison, 'Sir.'

'You all right hanging on here for the moment detective?' he said to Nita, 'This woman appears to trust you, I need you to get as much info as you can, whilst you can. Introduce her to this officer,' he said gesturing towards the policewoman standing by them. 'Reassure her she's safe okay?'

To Alan he said. 'This might just be the breakthrough you need to get some sense and motive out of your case, yes!'

'Possibly sir, yes.'

'Right, get what you need from DC Patel, go back to the office and review what you already have and see if it makes any sense. I need something to take with me to the forum next Tuesday. Can you manage that lad?'

'Sir.' Alan replied.

'Good.' To the uniformed woman officer he said, 'You know what you're doing,'

She nodded, then to her colleague he added.

'You're on the door, all right. A big lad like you ought to deter anyone, yes?'

The male officer grinned, 'Sir.' he replied.

'Right let's get about this and solve both incidents, okay!'

DI Allen turned and walked off down the corridor, saying over his shoulder. 'Two for one possibly aye, I like those sort of special deals.'

With Alan Syms and the two uniform officers following, Nita walked up to the nurses' station.

'Sian are we okay to use that family room as a base for a day or so. Kate's going to need round the clock guarding and we need somewhere for the uniform guys to rest and take breaks?'

Nodding Sian replying, 'I see no reason why not. I'll need to run it past the nursing manager first. If you come with me and explain we can sort that out now, all right?'

'Fine,' Nita answered.

Turning to the woman police officer she said.

'The woman is called Katterine, Kate for ease OK? Before you go into the room take your tunic off it'll be less official. This woman is on the edge, volatile and terrified. Make notes of anything she says, I'll be back pronto okay?' To her colleague she said. 'You're on the door okay. Be alert to anyone wanting to see the woman! Make sure they have some ID, don't be fooled by a white coat, stethoscope or a clip board or any other excuse got it!

The officer nodded, replying. 'Absolutely.'

Nita sent the two of them down to room F3, telling the WPC once more that a softly-softly approach was needed; most importantly she had to gain her trust and keep her calm.

Sitting on one of the easy chairs in the family room Nita let out a long sigh releasing all the pent-up tension she'd suddenly become aware of; her shoulders felt as though she'd been carrying a 50-kilo bag of coal. Resting her head on the back of the chair and closing her eyes she re-ran the last two hours through her mind trying to find a common link between what Kate had told her and what she and Alan Syms knew of Patrick Doyle and his death. Similarly Alan on his was on his way back to their office in Portbridge, began to try and create some mental trail to add to what they'd already gathered about their mysterious death. In his mind he searched to see if something leapt out at him linking the two cases. Hopefully there would be enough pieces of this case to start building a proper timeline, a more complete picture of their victim's last movements. Sian peered around the door of the family room nodding to Nita.

'Come on, she wants a word.'

The two of them walked down the corridor to the nursing managers office where Nita explained the situation that they'd found themselves faced with. The answer when it came was, that providing everything remained calm and the general running of the unit wasn't disrupted, she would agree until Katterine could be moved.

Throughout the rest of the day Nita joined the woman officer from time to time at Kate's bedside as they built a connection with her; she was conscious of not pushing her too much for information. As time went on Kate began to relax filtering more bits of information to them about how the clubs ran and how the girl's friendship with Patrick Doyle had developed. Later with Sian's help they encouraged Kate to have some food and then rest, Nita told her she was going to leave but would be back the following morning. The woman looked momentarily frightened but relaxed when Nita explained again that she wouldn't be alone and through the night there would be police officers by her room all the time. After calling back at the office and up-dating both Alan Syms and DI Allen with the latest pieces of information, she travelled back to her house. Later showered and fed she sat in her room computer open waiting for Stephen to come online. It suddenly chimed, she opened her screen to see Stephen grinning at her.

'Ohh I am missing you so much.' She blurted out touching the screen.

'Same here sugar.' he echoed, 'How's your day gone then?'

'Hellish!' she replied, it was as though Stephens question released some safety valve and for the next twenty minutes she downloaded so much news and chatter almost without taking a breath. At some point she noticed he was smiling at her and stopped speaking momentarily.

'What...?

'Nothing you're like an answer machine and I've just pressed replay. I don't think you've taken more than three breaths the whole time you've been talking.'

She shrivelled her nose up at his image on the screen.

'Go on then tell me about your day.'

'Oh you know, it started off much as any other day.' he ran through where he'd been and where he was parked this evening. 'Look on your map,' he said, 'I'm just into Denmark on my home run now. If I look to my right I can see this amazing view of some sort of stately home or palace. I saw the Northern lights last night, they were amazing! All greens, blues and purples swirling around like someone was waving a cloak in the sky. Sometime if you can get the holiday and I'm doing this run I'd love to bring you up here with me, you'd be blown away by the sights.'

'Could I come with you sometime, is that allowed?' she said fidgeting excitedly.

'Yeah, some of the lads take their wives or partners to Italy or Spain. We just have to arrange it with the boss to cover you on the permit and insurance.'

'What a thought,' she began, 'I'd love seeing all these places with you. I follow you on the map but it's not the same, plus I can keep you entertained at night.' she giggled briefly adding, 'I'm getting quite excited at the thought of making love to you in your bunk...'

He laughed, 'Have you any idea how little room there is in my bunk, hmmm?'

'Well we don't take up a lot of room when we are... you know... together!'

'True,' he replied, 'but could we stay like that all night? I don't think you could keep still for that long and I know I certainly couldn't.' Giving a little smirk he said, 'Your muscles do funny things to me and I can't stop myself from moving; know what I mean?'

She laughed. 'Well you make me quiver when you're inside me I can't help it, I just want all the time.'

'Listen sugar, I've been thinking this trip.' he started to say.

'Sounds serious.' she said noticing a more serious look on his face.

He continued, 'Until now I've never thought too much about being away for weeks on end mainly because Emma's at school or with her grandparents at the weekends and there's been no-one there for me to come back for. This time though I'm finding being away hard because of you!' He paused for a moment. 'I know it's going to hit my pocket but I've decided to ask the boss to bring me home and just do the UK runs. It still means I'll be away through the week but home every weekend.'

Falling silent he looked at Nita on his screen.

'Wow… I didn't expect that, I know I'm struggling a litt…'

He interrupted her. 'I'm homesick Nita! I've never been homesick, I don't do homesick! I don't want to be away from you. It's your fault you've stirred me up and now you're going to have to live with the consequences!'

'Hey, don't blame me Ferryman, it takes two to tango you know!'

He grinned, 'Oh I know and don't we make a good partnership, perfectly matched wouldn't you say?'

'Hmm, yeah we are good together, you give me so many rushes when we make love, I haven't felt anything like it with anyone before.'

'Sugar, it's not just the sex, but that is truly mind blowing I have to say, no, it's just about being with you. For over seven years I've avoided meeting anyone, let alone thinking about any sort of relationship. Then out of nowhere you appear at my bedside like some vision.' Pausing he added thoughtfully. 'I suppose it could have been the morphine that screwed my sense of reason you know!'

'Hey, don't spoil it.' Nita cautioned him. 'I feel a lot the same you know. I come back from the States to what…! There's been no-one I've met that I'd ever have considered settling with… until now. Stephen this is your first trip since we moved things up a level. I want you in my life, in me, in everything but don't make hasty decisions based on this one trip. Think about what you're doing my lovely man, let's talk about it when you're home.' She paused smiling at him watching his face for some reaction. 'Speaking of home, did you say you are coming back?'

'Yep, should be back in good old Portbridge a week on Friday.'

'How long for?'

'Probably out again mid-week the following week, Wednesday say but I do plan to have a word with the boss.'

'Stephen, have you heard a word of what I've been saying?'

'Yes sugar, but I want to test the water. It isn't going to happen overnight trust me. Not all the lads want Europe. Out of fifteen units there are only five of us that do long haul. It's going to take some time.'

'Okay,' she nodded at the screen. 'So next Friday home… yes?' he nodded. 'Right I'm going to book some time off then, I've got loads they owe me 'cause I've worked rest days since you've been gone just to keep myself busy. See I've missed you too!'

He grinned at her bright face on his screen.

'Right, bed-time I think pretty lady. I love you and I'm missing you.'

'Missing you too soooo much Ferryman,' she replied, 'I'm aching already at the thought of having you! Oh I can't wait. I'll sleep tonight, watch out teddy you're in for some serious hugging!'

Reaching across the bed she pulled her teddy to her and showed it to Stephen.

'Night Sugar' he said waving at the screen.

'Night Stephen, take care tomorrow, love you.' She blew him a kiss and waved one of her teddy bears paws.

Closing her laptop she slipped off the bed and went downstairs. Skipping into the living room where her house mates were watching television she dropped into an armchair.

'Guess who's coming home…' she said excitedly.

Louise and Moira exchanged glances, 'O lord, she's going to be hell to live with.' Moira muttered.

'When?' Louise asked.

'Week on Friday… Wahoo.' Nita replied.

'You're going to be un-live-able with for the next two weeks.' Louise added.

Moira giggled, 'Sorry Lo, I'm staying at Riks parents this weekend, you've got her all to yourself… Ha!'

Louise pushed across the settee at Moira, 'Cow!' she said.

Shrugging a little Moira replied in a guilty voice. 'Sorry sweetie… not!' and laughed again. Quietly Louise said.

'Wonder what our kids doing this weekend and if he fancies

getting wrecked somewhere.'

'Come on you two,' Nita said appealingly, 'he'll have been away for four weeks! Can't you be happy for me?'

The two girls looked at one another before Moira said.

'Yes, only if you promise not to make our lives a misery counting the hours down.'

They both fixed Nita with a stare.

'I Promise… I promise, okay!'

'Okay then,' Louise said, 'shopping Saturday morning.'

Nita shook her head, 'Can't, I'm working but the afternoon's okay!'

'Regardless, I'll still see what Alan's doing and if he wants to meet us. I haven't seen him for a while,' Louise quickly added before Nita could speak. 'No shop talk though okay, I don't like trying to eat when you two start on about corpses and killings!'

Moira nodded in agreement. 'It puts you right off a good steak when blood and guts are part of the table talk.'

Nita shrugged, 'Sorry, I'll try and remember next time we're all round the table.'

Louise disappeared into the kitchen returning minutes later with a tray of drinks and nibbles. Looking at Nita she said.

'Will you staying at his then or keeping us awake all night as you two make up for those lost weeks?'

Calmly Moira added, 'Looks like I could be at Riks for two weekends on the trot… hope they don't mind.'

Nita giggled, 'Probably his, we won't want to be disturbed either.'

Louise and Moira exchanged glances and tutted in unison. Later, they tidied up and went off to bed.

For the rest of the week Stephen travelled south through Scandinavia heading in the general direction of the Euro-port in Holland all the time delivering loads and collecting other consignments for delivery further south. Nita meanwhile spent each day working through her own cases or with Alan on their suspicious death. As promised and as part of her roll she visited Vivienne,

Patrick Doyle's partner keeping her updated on how the enquiries were progressing. In all honesty gathering evidence regarding his death was proving difficult, it seemed that this group of criminals appeared very good at covering their tracks. There were very few clues or links to help the team build a time line regarding Patricks last known movements, where he had been living, who he might have been associating with. The information Kate had initially given them helped which DI Allen took to the regional meeting. Returning later in the day he briefed the two officers and they formed a small team to sift through what was known about Patrick Doyle and where he'd possibly been. The most encouraging outcome from the meeting was that the Humberside team would look at all the information Kate had told them about the club and if they could identify any of the other girls she'd mentioned. If anything came from that then they were prepared to operate a silent watch on the premises. Also other divisions with coastal boundaries would look for any events with similar patterns of small harbours being used by the gang. Nita visited Vivienne later to update her; returning to the office she dropped her file on her desk. Alan looked up at her.

'Everything okay?'

'Yeah… a bit surprising actually!' she replied.

Intrigued by her answer he said.

'Go on, tell me more.'

'Remember the day we had to tell Vivienne that we thought it was Patrick who'd died, what a

pigsty the flat was?' he nodded, 'Well I knocked on the door and I have to say I was surprised when Vivienne answered it, I actually thought I'd gone to the wrong flat. I didn't recognise her, she looked clean, kind of smart you know.' Glancing at Alan for a moment, she continued. 'Remember how… well, scruffy they all looked? Like they needed a good wash and their hair needed a comb or brush? It was just the same the last time I went to see her. Today! A total make-over, she looked really well. Face on, clean jeans and a top, even the two littlies were smartened up. She made me a coffee and I noticed the kitchen had been sorted too, there was even food in the fridge in fact the whole place looked clean and tidy.'

'Bloody hell has she come into some money or something?'

'Not exactly, it seems Patrick was paying his NI so she's got some death benefit plus her sister seems to have her head screwed on and she's been able to get her a shed load of other benefits. She's helped her clean the place up too. I tell you I was really surprised.'

'Did you stick to the carpet?' Alan asked.

'No, that seemed to have been well-and-truly cleaned. You know Alan I really hope we can nail this lot just for the satisfaction of saying to Vivienne we got the bastards! It would be a real bonus to tell her we'd got them!'

By the end of the day she had all her reports written up and as she travelled home felt today had turned out well.

~~~~~~

Three weeks after initially interviewing Katterine in the Cottage Hospital she was released and went to a safe house, a refuge. The focus now was where she could stay safely until fully recovered and a decision made where she could go to begin to rebuild her life. There was an option where-by she might qualify for assisted repatriation home because of the circumstances surrounding the abuse she'd been subjected to; having been effectively trafficked as a sex slave. Being placed in a safe house meant that the operation to keep her safe could be scaled down, it also meant some of the immediate pressure could be taken off Nita, Alan and the team in their efforts to find evidence and build the case to present to the CPS.

Nita was living on a high in anticipation of Stephen's return this weekend, to the point that her house mates had given up trying to have sensible conversations with her. Things at work weren't much different either, Alan Syms was finding it difficult to get any sense out of her at times. Ruth, Nita's sergeant had got involved at one point
~~~~~~

trying to get her to focus on the various cases she was working on. The regular evening contacts were on a different plane too. Stephen, not usually known to get excited by anything couldn't hide the fact that in six days he would be back in Portbridge, while Nita sat on her bed unable to sit still fidgeting all through their conversation. By Thursday night he was parked in the queue at the Euro port terminal waiting to board, their contact tonight was short and sweet. As they said their goodbye he said simply.

'Home tomorrow afternoon sugar everything being equal.'

'Ohh god Stephen I can't wait! Be safe Ferryman, love you.'

'Me neither, I will; night… love you too.'

Finally boarded and all secured, Stephen was leaning on a railing on one of the ferry's decks casually chatting to a couple of other drivers. Without paying too much attention he watched a small, brightly painted fishing boat tied up not far away from where the ferry was berthed. It sounded as though there was something of party going on, there was loud music and the people on its deck seemed to be having a great time. Parked on the quayside by the boat were some very expensive cars. One of the drivers Stephen was standing with commented.

'That's the life aye, parties on the poop deck no expense spared, look at those motors someone's got some brass.'

'Another life eh, if only.' Stephen commented,

The other driver added.

'Too right, we do all the bloody work and they just live off the profits we make for them. All right for some wouldn't you say?'

All three men murmured in agreement. The massive ferry doors started to close as the PA system began to make a series of announcements.

'Bar?' One of the drivers said.

'Aye, bar.' Stephen and the other driver agreed, turning to make their way down to the ferry's lounge and bar Stephen took one more look around the port area as he walked to the stairs, his eyes falling momentarily on the fishing boat. Then turning he followed the other two drivers into the warmth of the lounge. An hour later the ferry was into the North Sea at full speed heading for Hull and home for Stephen, whilst back in the Euro port the expensive cars were all gone and the converted fishing boat was also slipping away into the North Sea all peaceful after the evening's wild party heading towards the English coast.

Docking in Hull before six in the morning Stephen had cleared customs and was on his way to the M62 to run to Sheffield, deliver this consignment before travelling back to the yard and then home for four days. He was excited wanting to push this last job on quickly without problems. The CB radio burst into life.

'Heads up fellers any of you off last night's ferry and west bound M62, sorry guys but there's been a coming together west of gate 37 just before the bridge. Two HGVs and three or more cars, nothing's moving they're all running with square wheels. Blues n twos en-route, you could be there for a while. Keep the dirty side down and the shiny side up Humpty Dumpty east bound down on the side.'

Swearing quietly to himself he thought this is just 'sod's law,' and reached for the mic to acknowledge the drivers warning. However a number of other drivers were already on air. Junction 38 was a mile in front so thinking quickly he decided to exit there do a loop and head back towards Hull then cross the Humber Bridge and join the M180 and run into Sheffield that way. He made the delivery an hour and a half late which meant after he'd unloaded he had to take his statutory rest break. Those accumulated delays plus the heavier traffic meant it was well into the afternoon before he finally dropped his trailer at the depot and left his unit with the mechanics. Handing all the paperwork to the office he arranged a time in the next five days to come in and speak to the boss about changing his work schedule. Finally he loaded his car with all his gear, heaved a huge sigh thinking 'Home, here I come!' as drove away from the depot.

Nita's mobile buzzed frantically, she picked it up and quickly read the message.

Hi Sugar, back at the yard now, should be away by 4 ish, see you at home... out of breath at the thought. Love you xxx S

She grinned and felt her stomach do a somersault at the thought he was so near. Crossing the office to her sergeant's desk, she dropped into the seat opposite and leaning on the desk said softly.

'Sarge.'

'Hmmm.' her colleague answered without looking up from the file she was reading.

'Ruth,' Nita continued.

Something in her tone made the sergeant look up.

'Oh god... I know that look,' she said, adding quickly. 'The answer's no... now the question was?'

Nita held her colleagues look, 'Do you think I can take back an hour?' she paused for a moment. 'I am owed some time?'

Over the top of her glasses Ruth studied her and after a little thought replied.

'Let me think about this okay. When would you want to take it?'

'Now!' Nita almost exploded with her answer.

'Mmm, let me see,' Ruth began to say, 'the only reason you'd want an early finish is because someone's home tonight, am I right?'

Nita was fidgeting excitedly, like a child willing Ruth to agree to her request.

'Oh pretty please sarge!'

Ruth hesitated deep thought, putting her pen down she sat back in her chair looking directly at Nita bobbing about in front of her.

'Ohh go on who am I to stand in the way of true love. Don't let it be said that I ever stopped anyone getting their leg over. I want you back in here first thing tomorrow mind... do you hear!'

The sergeant was talking to an empty chair as Nita had returned to her desk, cleared it and was at the door sorting her coat out from the over-laden stand. She called as she opened the office door.

'I'll buy the cakes on Saturday, promise.'

The door banged shut just as the penny dropped in Ruth's head.

'Hang on, it's my weekend off monkey,' then added, 'hey, just a minute you've booked it off too, you sod Patel!' she shouted after Nita.

From somewhere in the room someone said.

'If she comes in with cakes, can I have yours sarge?'

Ruth replied sharply, 'No you bloody can't! I might come in just to hold her to it.'

Someone else chirped up in a stage whisper. 'Grumpy old cow.'

Ruth stood up looking round the office but no-one made eye contact with her. All she could see were the backs or tops of heads. 'I heard that!' she said to the room at large. A titter started that quickly spread round the room until everyone was laughing at the childish banter.

Nita was at Stephen's house in less than twenty minutes, she couldn't have bettered it even with blue lights and sirens. Checking that he wasn't home she drove down to the little shop at the end of the street, bought some flowers a bottle of wine and some cakes and other essentials for tomorrow's breakfast then rushed back to the house. Letting herself in she switched on the heating and some of the lights to make it homely then quickly looked round all the rooms to see if anything needed tidying before he arrived home. Arranging the flowers in the only suitable vessel she could find, a wine carafe, she put them on the coffee table making a mental note to herself to buy a couple of vases for the future. Switching on the wood burner effect electric fire she put the bottle of wine by it to warm. Searching through her bag she found her mobile and sent Stephen a text.

'What's your ETA home? xxx'

A few minutes elapsed before the reply pinged on her phone.

'30 mins +, can't wait!!!xxx.'

Satisfied that she'd done everything to greet Stephen when he arrived home she rushed upstairs to the bedroom and tried to sort something out to wear from the few clothes she'd brought here over the past few months. Twenty minutes later she'd showered and was back down stairs feeling refreshed ready for Stephen coming through the front door. A quick glance at the clock, that's thirty minutes she noticed. Excited at thought of seeing him again, her tummy felt tight and knotted, she ached low down in her abdomen almost like a period pain. Trying to calm herself she made some tea put some music on the hi-fi and sat down to wait. Why does the clock go so slowly sometimes, that's forty minutes she thought. Neither the music nor the tea worked and she found herself pacing round the lounge, dining area and the kitchen. Hearing a car outside she set off to the front door then hesitated. Should she meet him at the door or wait here in the lounge, or the hall? Oh hell, she walked out of the lounge just as the front door opened and they stood facing each other.

'Hello.' Stephen said framed in the doorway.

'Hi you're home.'

Stephen looked behind onto the street and then around the hallway.

'Err yes, this is my house I think, at least it was four weeks ago.'

Dropping his holdall by the door he closed it and walked towards Nita saying.

'Either you're a figment of my imagination of someone I know or I've got squatters!'

'I'm not a figment of your imagination Ferryman.'

She said taking a step towards him putting her arms around his neck and just before their lips met, added.

'This might convince you that I'm real and I want you so much... now!'

The kiss was passionate and full of pent up love and lust and it went on and on, neither of them wanting to break this moment. Finally they had to part to breathe but stayed in the embrace, Nita resting her head on his shoulder. He took a deep breath, nuzzling his face into her neck and hair breathing in her scent.

'I have missed you so much,' he said into her neck and began to give her little kisses, moving up to her cheek, and running his fingers through her hair. She threw her head back a little, pleasuring at his touch her eyes closed and sighed.

'Mmmm'

Nuzzling her neck once more, he said.

'Your scent your smell your skin, how it feels and your body. Oh god it's so good to hold you again.'

By now he'd kissed his way around to her lips again and they fell into another deeply passionate kiss. Pushing him away, out of the embrace she took his hand and set off up the stairs almost dragging him behind her. In the bedroom they tore at their clothes before tumbling onto the bed. Sighs of pleasurable passion along with words of encouragement not to stop, drove the two of them quickly to a shattering, noisy climax.

Quite some time later Stephen said quietly.

'I have missed you so much this trip, I thought it might get better as time went on and we got used to me being away but that's not happening. It was all right before I met you because Emma was my focus and she was at school so I could work away and be back for term breaks, but now! Now, I'm beginning to resent the job, oh the money's good I mean let's be straight, without that sort of money I doubt I could have done what I have over the past seven years with the boat and holidays you know.' Giving her a hug he concluded. 'Now there's you in the equation, what am I to do with you?'

She chuckled and lithely slithered on top of him, kissing his lips.

'Hmm,' she answered thoughtfully, 'I have an idea for just now.'

She kissed his shoulders chest and stomach then worked her way down his body slipping under the duvet. She nipped him gently with her teeth as she travelled down his torso. Each nip aroused him that little bit more, from under the quilt he heard her say softly, caressing him.

'Got you Ferryman, got you.'

Emerging from under the covers, she straddled him, sighing at the sensations coursing through her body. She leaned forward a hand on each of his shoulders, her long hair trailing like curtains to cover their two faces. He lifted his head from the pillow and kissed her, he caressed her breasts playing with her hard nipples making her squeal with pleasure. Unable to remain still any longer she began to move, slowly deliberately revelling in the waves of pleasure she was experiencing and knew from his face he was feeling them too. He slipped his hands from her breast to hold her hips. The sensations became more powerful beginning to dominate their rhythm and with the same violent intensity they'd both felt earlier they surged towards that inevitable shattering orgasm, Nita crying out as before. A little later, lying across his chest her head resting on the pillow by his, she said softly.

'From that first night at the wharf when we made love I've not been able to get enough of you Ferryman do you know that?'

He gave her a gentle squeeze.

'You being away so much is hell to be honest, the nights and weekends are the worst. Okay I go out with the girls but part of me wants you here so that we can do things together and I can come home and just screw the arse off you all the time.'

He moved his head a little so he could look at her as she gave a little chuckle adding.

'Do you think that's tarty of me? I'm sorry but I want so much I ache.'

Closing the gap between their faces he kissed her quickly.

'No, I want you just as much, like I've said I'm not enjoying being away on these European runs anymore.'

Moving into a more comfortable position they lay together propped up on pillows.

'I need another shower,' she said giving him a sideways glance. 'You certainly make up for it when your home.' Nudging him she added, giggling 'Know what I mean gov… nudge nudge, wink wink, aye… know what I mean aye!'

He looked at her for a moment but couldn't help himself and laughed at her very Indian inflection as she tried to sound like one of the Monty Python characters, then in his best 'Monty Python' tone replied.

'Don't know what you mean gov!'

They laughed together, the laughter descending into mild hysterics until Nita, with tears running down her cheeks and holding her tummy cried.

'Stop it, I can't breathe and I hurt.'

Slipping out of bed she crossed the landing to the bathroom. He lay in the bed his thoughts centring on the two of them together and how he'd changed so much since falling into this relationship and into love with this wonderful woman.

'Stephen can you get me a couple of towels from the cupboard please.'

Rolling out of bed he walked across the little landing taking two towels from the airing cupboard into the bathroom.

'Can I join you in there, I need a shower too?'

'Not really, there's not much room.'

Peering around the screen on the edge of the bath he said.

'Oh I don't know, could be cosy!' and went to climb into the bath.

'Stephen... no!' she exclaimed in protest.

Ignoring her he moved under the shower head, sliding his arms around her wet slippery body, stroking her stomach with one hand while caressing her breasts with the other.

Sighing a little she relaxed back against him her head resting back on his shoulder water cascading on both of them.

'Have you ever made love in a shower?' she said softly.

'Not recently,' he said, 'have you?'

She reached a hand behind her and gently caressed him as the warm water ran down their bodies.

'Once a long time ago, it's very sexy.' She replied and turned to face him.

They held each other for a while pleasuring in the warmth of the water on them and the sensation of their hands sliding over the others skin. Suddenly she broke away from him.

'Right I'm clean, I'm out and it's all yours my lovely man.'

She kissed him quickly, manoeuvred herself past him out of the bath. Taking a bath sheet from the towel rail she wrapped herself in it, patted her legs dry with another towel before gathering up her long hair in a bun and wrapping the towel around her head in a turban. Leaving the bathroom for a moment she returned with another bath sheet for him.

'I'll cook something up for tea, any requests?'

From the other side of the steamy screen he replied. 'Not especially, you decide.'

Ten minutes later as faint aromas of cooking wafted up the stairs he realised he was really very hungry. Making his way downstairs he walked into the kitchen; she pushed his favourite mug across the bar towards him.

'Oh tea... just as I like it thanks. What are we having?'

'A sort of curry risotto all right?'

'Fine, I'm starving.'

She smiled at him, 'Me too, maybe it's all that exercise hmm!'

She raised an eyebrow giving him a cheeky look.

'Could be,' he replied with a grin and sorted out mats and cutlery in the cupboards laying then out on the breakfast bar.

They spent the rest of the evening curled up together on the settee drinking wine with some quiet music on in the background. They talked about all sorts of things, catching up on what had happened to eachother while they'd been apart and making plans for the weekend and for the rest of the week ahead until he had to set off again. In the small hours Stephen made them a hot drink and once that was finished they padded off to bed. Snuggling together, arms and legs entwined they slipped into a deep restful sleep.

From a deep sleep Stephen stirred, stretched his arm out and swept the other side of the bed. Meeting no resistance he surfaced quickly, looked across the bed to see he was alone. Sitting up he stretched yawned and gathered his thoughts. Glancing at the clock he saw it was past nine, his senses also told him something was cooking and he could smell coffee. Dragging on some pyjamas he wandered downstairs to see Nita at the cooker dressed and busying herself.

'Hey, I could get used to this you know, if I come back on UK work am I going to get this treatment all the time?'

Turning to face him she waved a spatula at him. 'Don't push it Ferryman.'

He wandered over to a cupboard and taking a mug from it poured himself some of the coffee. Passing behind Nita he kissed the nape of her neck.

'I didn't think we had anything in for breakfast.'

'We didn't.' she replied returning his kiss quickly, 'I went to Habibie's, it's ready so park yourself and I'll serve up.'

He sat on one of the bar stools at the breakfast bar where moments later a full English breakfast was set before him. She came around the bar and sat next to him.

'Thank you.'

She smiled at him, 'Not a problem I enjoyed making it. It kind of felt sort of right, a bit happy families if that doesn't sound too odd... you know?'

'Hmm,' he replied, 'Just what I was thinking watching you at the cooker, you seemed so relaxed, like we've been together for ages.'

Breakfast finished they sat for some time until Nita said thoughtfully.

'It did feel comfortable, odd really I didn't feel like a stranger, a visitor, do you understand?' she said looking at him.

He stood and began clearing their plates putting them on the drainer. What she'd just said started him thinking.

'Wait I'll do those,' she said, 'you go put some clothes on and we'll see what the days going to do for us.'

'I need to go up to the boat really and see what Mr G has done,' he hesitated for a moment then reached for Nita pulling her towards him, 'We could always go back to bed and decide what we're going to do a bit later...'

'Hmm and that'll be the morning gone.' she responded kissing him quickly then gently pushing him away. 'No, you go get dressed and we'll see what then!'

He pulled a hung dog face turned and went to leave the kitchen muttering as he went.

'Spoil sport...'

Nita chuckled.

Twenty minutes later he reappeared dressed to see the kitchen tidy and Nita in the lounge looking through a trucking magazine.

'You ok?'

She looked up from the journal and smiled.

'Fine, but if I'm going to be here more often you need some different reading matter.' she said, holding up the copy of Truck and Driver she'd been reading.

'I'll get some copies of 'On the Beat'

Stephen looked at her surprised. 'Joking... Yes!'

She waited before replying, then nodded, 'Mmm Joking!'

'Phew... you had me going then. So are we going up to the yard then shop and do whatever after that?'

'Ok, yep I'm fine with that.'

In just over an hour they were driving down the narrow lane to the Marina where Nita was surprised to see so many people milling around the boats. As they walked down to the yard they saw Finbar out of the water on a cradle.

'Wow! I hadn't thought of her being so big,' she said, 'she looks so different out of the water.'

'Yeah, you don't realise how much is in the water.' he replied casually.

Skirting around the boats greenish discoloured, shell encrusted hull, he made mental notes about her general condition noticing that the right side, the starboard propeller was off.

'Hello son.'

They both turned to see Robert Graham watching them.

'Robert.' Stephen said, 'How are you?'

'Aye just fine just fine, busy ya nah but if ah weren't now ah'd be worried mind.' He looked at Nita. 'Hello pet, my you're a sight for sore eyes, you've not had enough of him yet then?'

She smiled throwing Stephen a quick glance.

'Not yet no but time will tell.'

Robert grinned.

'Aye too true, right yous,' he said to Nita, 'gahn up the hoose and tell ma Maggie we'll be up for some tea in ten minutes or so. We're just going to sort out a couple of things forst all right pet?'

She looked at Stephen, mainly for reassurance he nodded, she kissed him on the cheek and set off for the house, Stephen and Mr G turned to look at *Finbar*.

'What's the dog's name again?' they heard her shout.

In unison they replied 'Sally.'

As they briefly discussed how the work was progressing on the boat they heard Sally barking, Stephen paused mid-sentence and looked towards the house.

'She'll be all right with Sally won't she?'

'Wye aye man, Sally's just wind she'll be na botha.'

The two men eventually walked up to the house still discussing work to be done on *Finbar*. As they entered the house they saw Nita sitting on the old settee with Sally quietly lying by her feet while she stroked her. The dog lifted her head as they walked into the room, and satisfied they weren't a problem, dropped her head back onto Nita's foot again. Mrs G emerged from a small room off the kitchen carrying two plates of assorted cakes and scones. Placing them on the table among an array of other delicacies and teacups she turned her attention to Stephen giving him a look, a general inspection then crossed the room offering her cheek to him, he stooped slightly and kissed her.

'Mmm I hear you're behaving yourself good good, now wash up both of you and go and ring the bell someone.'

Stephen went to the door as Robert washed his hands and rang a bell hanging from the wall. Having returned and washed his hands, he came and sat beside Nita.

'What's the bell for?'

'It's the tea-time bell, any of the boat owners who fancy a brew will come up and join us.'

A matter of minutes elapsed before two other couples came into the room. Before long the room was filled with chatter as everyone tucked into the array of food on the table. An hour or so passed and people began to drift away back to their boats.

Nita stood beginning to clear some of the crockery to the drainer by two very old deep sinks.

'And just what are you doing young lady?'

She turned and faced Mrs Graham who also had her hands full of plates and things.

'I was just going to help clear away.' she replied.

'Well thank you Nita that's kind but I think you'll be on your way shortly.'

Mrs G finally shooed her away to the yard, giving her a hug as she left. She found Stephen draped in a heavy apron, big heavy waders and a long-handled brush in hand, at his feet there was a big bucket. As she walked towards him she could see where he'd cleaned the hull so far.

'Don't come too near sugar, you don't want this stuff on your clothes it's very caustic.

'Okay, what can I do?'

He thought for a moment.

'See if you can get a waterproof suit from the shed and then you can hose the hull down where I've scrubbed it.'

A few minutes later she reappeared wearing a grubby one-piece suit that at one time had been orange, now it was a pale apricot, she wore some clumpy boots and to finish off the ensemble heavy-duty gauntlets and she was carrying a length of reeled up hose. Dropping the coils on the floor she shouted in the direction of the shed.

'Turn on!'

Moments later the hose nozzle started to spit and splutter until a steady stream of water flowed from it. Directing the jet onto the hull she washed down where Stephen had brushed. Between them they managed to clean all the hull before the failing autumn light started to make things difficult to see. Clearing away the bits and pieces, they changed out of the protective clothing then stood together viewing their handy work. Stephen put his arm around Nita.

'We've done well today crew, this job usually takes me two or three weekends. Just needs the anti-fouling now and she'll be good for another couple of years and another two knots.'

'Does it make that much difference cleaning the hull?'

Nodding he answered, 'Oh yeah, neglected boats that have sat on moorings for ages, particularly sea moorings, grow beards. That'll take five or six knots off their designed speed even more off yachts, makes them very slow.

Together they sought out Mr G, said their farewells and left the yard in almost total darkness.

Nita shuffled herself into her seat and rested her hand on Stephens's thigh.

'This boat maintenance thing is tiring, I'm knackered!'

'Fresh air and exercise sugar you're just out of condition.'

Giving Stephens's thigh a gentle slap she replied.

'I've exerted myself in other ways... yes?'

Stephen chuckled, 'Okay, yes I'll give you that.'

'Mmmm.' She responded.

They'd only travelled a few miles when Stephen noticed her breathing had changed. He glanced at her and realised she was fast asleep. She slept for most of the journey home only waking as they came into the outskirts of Portbridge.

'Have I slept all the way back?'

'Yep,' he replied, 'driving them home you were, driving them home.'

Giving his leg a slap.

'Ohh, that's a lie I don't snore!' she protested.

He glanced at her and smirked.

'Don't like these dark nights.' She muttered as they drew up outside Stephen's house. She feigned a shiver to emphasise her displeasure. He chuckled.

'Does that mean we are staying home tonight then?'

'Oh definitely!'

The house felt warm as they went through the front door. She switched on the lounge gas fire then followed Stephen into the kitchen. 'Hungry?' he said to her over his shoulder.

'Mmmm, not starving after the tea at the Grahams.'

'Ok, snacks later then.'

'Yeah…' she nodded, 'What are your plans tomorrow then?'

He thought for a moment.

'I've got to sort some bills out, need to get the car MOT'd but work will do that if I arrange it with the service guys. It's cheaper them doing it, oh and I've got a lunch date… I think and then I'm free in the afternoon.'

Having made a pot of tea they went back into the lounge and settled down.

'Hang on,' Nita said as she followed him. 'Lunch date… should I know about this?'

He smiled at her, 'Only if you can't make it.'

'Oh… oh, I'm not sure if I'm free, I'll have to check my diary…' she responded playfully, 'seriously though I will if I can but it all depends on the morning briefing and how we are doing with my enquiry.'

'Okay, but I'd like to meet you if you can.'

The rest of evening was spent relaxing, watching television and snacking. Around ten-thirty they locked up and went to bed.

~~~~~~

A truly grey, damp autumnal morning greeted them as Stephen pulled the curtains open. They sat together at the bar eating breakfast listening to the local FM channel news updates between a selection of 80s hits. Stephen studied Nita for a while, she looked different this morning to the last few days. He saw the professional Nita now, the no nonsense detective, as opposed to the sexy seductress he'd spent
~~~~~~

the weekend with. A shiver ran down his spine as he felt the spark of passion remembering Friday night when he'd walked through the door.

'Something wrong?'

Her question brought him back from his thoughts, he focused on her smiling.

'No I was just thinking we're sitting here like we've been together for years,' pausing mid- sentence, he eventually said, 'it just feels so... normal.'

She reached across the bar and held his hand.

'Been there, thought that earlier. I've had a great weekend thank you. I do miss you so much when you're away but wow! It's worth it when you come home!'

'Funny I was just thinking the same, I'm still going to speak to the boss about coming back onto UK only. Four weeks or more away from you is too long.'

Slipping from her stool she gathered her bags and things and started to make her way to the door.

'Got to go Ferryman, villains to bring to book you know.'

Following her to the door he reached out taking hold of her hips spinning her round encircling her with his arms. Face to face they kissed.

'By the way we're out for dinner tonight sugar, okay?'

'Mmmm.' she kissed him again quickly, turned opened the door and glancing over her shoulder mouthed, 'Love you.'

He watched her into her car and waited for her to drive away. Returning to the kitchen something made him look into the lounge, his gaze fell on a picture collage of himself, Suzanne and Emma standing on an occasional table beside the stone fireplace. Going into the lounge he picked it up and sat down studying it. There were pictures of just the two of them before Emma was born then a series of pics with all three of them as Em grew from a babe in arms to a toddler and then a young girl. He rested his head on the back of the chair and hugged the frame to his chest. At some point he was aware that his cheeks were wet and with a start realised he was actually crying, this was the first time in years that any sort of emotion had touched him. Wiping the tears away he rested his head on the chair back once more but the tears still flowed. Silent words came but only in his head at first until through the tears he said aloud.

'I miss you Suz so much, I know Em does too.'

Then he recalled something she'd said to both of them before she'd passed away.

'Listen, life doesn't stand still, it goes on, so miss me sometimes but don't you dare stand still, move on both of you move on!'

He looked at the pictures again recalling where and when they'd been taken and the times they'd all been together, quietly he said.

'I hope you're okay with what's happening in my life sweetness. I've met this lady and she's moved my life on... Why am I telling you this, you're probably aware of my life and Emma's without me saying anything.'

Replacing the frame on the nest of tables he went to the kitchen and cleared away the breakfast things, set a wash programme to clean all his work stuff then spent couple of hours cleaning round the house. Chores completed he sat at the breakfast bar sorting through the pile of post that had accumulated during his last trip. Mid-morning his mobile buzzed on the work surface, he saw from the screen it was Nita calling.

'My favourite person.' He said answering it.

'This is quick okay, yes to lunch but only because you asked so nicely! It is going have to be quick though!'

'Surely, where and when?'

'Mmm, how about Andrews's bakery at the bottom of the high street, I'll try and be there just before one all right?'

'Fine, I'll be there, everything okay?'

'Fine but busy following up some stuff, got to go love you.'

'You too, bye.' The line clicked off.

Frustratingly he couldn't find his car keys when it was time to leave. Eventually finding them on the floor of the bedroom he smiled, 'must have fallen out of my pocket' he thought in the rush to get his trousers off on Friday! He finally set off into Portbridge to meet Nita for their quick lunch then spent the afternoon at his depot talking to the boss exploring the possibility of coming home to run UK routes only. Their meeting ended with the boss promising to look at the options, adding that any changes wouldn't happen overnight, in the meantime he'd have to continue the Scan-Euro runs until another driver could be found.

Arriving back home late afternoon he unpacked some shopping, some for himself and Nita the remainder for his next trip away in two days' time, then set about cooking dinner for the two of them. Nita finally crashed through the front door just before six thirty, dropped her bag kicked off her shoes in the hallway before padding into the kitchen and coming right up behind him standing by the cooker. Sliding her arms around his waist and gently squeezing him she said into his back.

'Hello.'

'Hello yourself,' he replied.

'So did you see your boss about coming home?'

'Pardon... what did you just say?'

'You heard. Did you see your boss?'

'I did yes. Look, you set up for dinner and we can talk then.'

'Thought we were going out to eat?'

'We were and I think we'll still go to the Duchess later. I just fancied cooking for us instead of going out.'

She kissed him on the neck.

'Don't mind, it's been a hellish day.' and began putting out the cutlery on the bar.

They sat and ate dinner talking about their respective day before clearing away and taking themselves off to the Duchess for a drink; sitting quietly in a corner of the bar until quite late.

Arriving home a little after eleven they parked on the street, he walked round to the passenger door which Nita had opened but was having some difficulty getting herself out of the car, giggling at herself.

Eventually out and standing or rather leaning against Stephen, she draped an arm around his shoulder staring closely into his eyes and said, her words a little slurred.

'The perrrfect gentleman, this just goes to prove my theory… the age of churv…chi… chivalry is not dear, dead! Are you going to escort me to the door hmmm?'

She began to giggle again, Stephen looked at her and chuckled.

'Oh you are going to hate yourself in the morning lady. Come on let's get you into the house.'

'Are you going to take me to bed?'

She said struggling to focus on his face under the dim streetlights. He didn't reply but with an arm round her slim waist, guided her to the front door. Still trying to focus on his face she said.

'Would you like to come in for…?'

Hesitating for a moment trying to remember what she'd intended to say, she ended up saying.

'You can make mad passionate love to me you know, if you play your cards right… hmmm.'

She began giggling again as he gently propelled her through the door. What followed was copybook comedy that even had Stephen struggling to keep control. To lock the door he needed both hands because being old, it needed some gentle persuasion sometimes to close properly. He uncoupled himself from Nita expecting her to stay where she was, big mistake! Turning she set off upstairs, misjudged the first step falling forward so she was lying face down up the first five steps. Hearing the thud he turned quickly to see her flat out on the stairs. Going to help her up he asked anxiously.

'Christ Nita! Are you okay sugar?'

She turned over to lie on her back beginning to laugh. He tried to help her up but she put her arms round his neck and pulled him on top of her.

'Have you ever made love on a staircase Ferryman?'

'No!'

Planting a soft wet kiss on his lips she said.

'Should we give it a go then?'

She giggled while he struggled to free himself from her embrace.

'Stay there Nita whilst I go and turn the lights off.'

By the time he came back to the foot of the stairs, she'd slithered down them to sit on the bottom step resting her head on the next one up. He stood looking at her for a moment.

'Wasted... well there's only one way we're going to get you to bed tonight. Come on!'

Bending down he scooped her up in his arms and set off up the stairs. Unfortunately, he'd only gone two steps when he bumped her head on the wall.

'Owww!'

'Sorry sugar.'

Turning her slightly he put her over his shoulder in a fireman's lift and proceeded up the remainder of the staircase Nita protesting and slapping his bottom.

'Put me down... do you hear, put me down, now...Stephen!'

Finally they got into his room where he deposited her full length, on the bed.

'I need the loo!' she slurred.

Stephen sighed, 'Shit!'

'No weeeeee,' came the reply.

Helping her off the bed he went to assist her to the bathroom. Pushing him away with some force he sat back on the bed as she said.

'I don't need any help thank you, I'm a big girl now, and I can manage on my own thank you!' Weaving her way across the landing she tottered to the bathroom, returning some minutes later the same wayward route. Coming up to him she kissed him and turning her back said.

'Can you unzip me please?'

Obliging he pulled the zipper down before beginning to remove his own clothes. She remained standing.

'Well take it off then!'

He did as he was asked.

'And the rest'

'Nita It's late, you're wasted and…'

She unfastened her bra letting it drop to the floor, turned and embraced him pressing herself against his bare chest.

'When you caress my breasts like you do you make my legs all go to Jelly and lobbly… I mean wobbly and I just want you inside me,' resting her head on his chest she added, 'I want you to screw me stupid tonight Ferryman… I just want you!'

Sighing he picked her up and carried her to the bed laying her on the covers. He gently took off her remaining clothes, pulled the covers from under her and manoeuvred her into bed before covering her up, he finished undressing himself and went to the bathroom. Returning minutes later he climbed into bed and switched off the light. Turning he put his arm over her body drawing her close.

He heard her say quietly. 'Mmm that was so good, I love you.'

Lifting his head off the pillow he looked at her.

'Good, did the earth move sugar?'

'Mmm oh yes, go to sleep now, I'm tired!'

Lying back on his pillow he laughed quietly. 'Priceless.'

With Nita gently snoring like a purring cat he soon slipped into a calm slumber.

Sitting at the breakfast bar in the morning eating toast with a mug of tea Stephen heard the stairs creak a little and looking towards the door leading to the short hall, watched as Nita came into the kitchen. Reaching across the bar he clicked the kettle on.

'Oh I feel rubbish, my heads pounding.'

She sat on the other side of the bar resting her head on her arms and moaned again. He stood up poured the hot water from the kettle into the mug recoiling a little at the sudden pungent aroma of strong coffee then sliding the steaming mug towards to her said.

'Paracetamol or something stronger?'

'One of each please and some toast too, Thank you.'

They sat in silence until the toaster threw up the lightly browned bread. Buttering it he slid the plate across the bar to sit beside the mug of coffee and put two tablets on the plate.

'I was naked when I woke up, Did we…'

Stephen was nodding his head when she looked up at him, struggling to focus on his face.

'No… we didn't… did we!'

'No sugar we didn't although you were definitely up for it, in fact you said I was very good and you felt the earth move, remember?

'Did I?'

'Mmm.'

'I didn't… you're winding me up!'

'Nope, you'd already said how chivalrous I was and invited me into your house would you believe, to… how did you put it… Ah yes, screw me stupid.'

'NO!' She exclaimed then held her head as she responded. 'Oww!'

'Oh yes, and just before you finally passed out told me it was soooo good!'

'Really!'

He nodded. She drank some of her coffee, took her tablets and began to eat her toast.

'I can't remember the last time I couldn't remember last night, it must be years ago. Why did you let me drink so much? And why weren't you drunk… Oh yeah someone had to drive us home.' Answering her own question. Draining her mug she slid it back across the bar.

'Please can I have another one? Thank you.'

With her mug replenished she got off the bar stool heading for the stairs.

'Can I have a shower it should help.'

'Surely.'

A few minutes later he heard the shower running and whilst she was in the bathroom he went and threw on some jeans a T-shirt and hoody top. As he got to the top of the stairs to return to the kitchen, the bathroom door opened.

'Better?'

'Yeah, I feel fine now… apart from some gremlins trying to burrow into my skull.'

She passed him going into their bedroom and finished drying herself. He could see her hunting around searching for something. Pulling her bra from under the occasional chair by the dressing table, she waved it at him.

'If you are going to undress me, put my clothes where I can find them!' then with her foot closed the door.

He smiled and continued downstairs and put the TV on to a news channel. Fifteen minutes later a very different Nita appeared through the living room door looking more human than a while ago and ready for another day chasing villains. Dropping down beside him on the settee she shuffled herself closer.

'I'll have to set off in a few minutes, what are your plans today.'

'I'm nipping up to the yard to see how things are going with the boat.'

'Oh okay,' she paused then said, 'Did I make a pillock of myself then?'

Slipping his arm round her shoulders he drew her closer kissing the top of her head breathing in that smell that was just Nita her scent, her hair, then said.

'No, only when we got home and the cool air hit you, then it got silly it was like something out of the two Ronnie's.'

She gently punched him in the side, he repeated himself.

'It was really… just like the two Ronnie's. I left you standing at the bottom of the stairs whilst I locked the door, you tried to go upstairs missed the step and just fell flat on your face up the first five steps and laid there giggling. I stood you up, went to turn the lights off down here, came back and you were in a heap on the bottom step.'

He could feel her giggling against his side.

'I picked you up and set off upstairs but banged your head on the wall so put you over my shoulder and carried you fireman style.'

Nita rubbed the side of her head for a moment.

'I thought my head hurt when I was in the shower!'

He held his free hand up in a conciliatory gesture.

'Sorry, anyway how do you feel now?'

'Okay, still got a bit of a head but okay.'

They sat watching the news for some time without speaking just enjoying being together. The programme ended and the channel went to a commercial break. Disengaging himself from her he stood and went into the kitchen. 'Brew?'

'I wish but no I need to go, I feel rubbish and parched too, I need coffee,' she grinned adding, 'a bucket full ideally. Just how much did I drink?'

'Ohh eight, nine maybe.'

She heard Stephen laugh in the kitchen before replying.

'HOW many?'

'You heard.'

'Bloody hell Stephen why did you let me drink so much?'

'You've got to admit, it was a good night though, we met some locals and had a laugh didn't we?'

'How would I know, I can't remember a bloody thing!'

She waited until he came back into the lounge then picked up her bags and kissing him walked towards the front door.

'No, there's nothing wrong with a good night out but please don't let me drink so much again, I don't like myself in the morning.'

He shrugged and nodded, 'Okay, understand.'

'Right, see you tonight.'

Getting to the door she looked back at him briefly, smiled affectionately and blew a kiss then left.

Nita was at her desk accompanied by a mug of hot strong black coffee when Alan Syms arrived followed by their Sergeant.

'Morning all, everyone well I hope?' she said as she passed through the general office into her own room.

DI Allen came in a few minutes later and indicated to Nita and Alan to join him. Passing the sergeants' office he motioned for her to join them as well. Squashed into his office the two women sat, Alan remained standing leaning against a filing cabinet. Having removed his jacket the DI dropped into his chair pulled a few sheets of paper out of his briefcase then scanned the faces of the little group for a moment.

'Right, you know that brick wall we've run into regarding our Mr Doyles suspicious death and our mysterious young lady who's somewhere in the mix?. Well I think the walls cracked a little. Glancing at the group and his notes he continued. 'The local nick got a three nines call on Thursday from a very distressed woman to say she'd been threatened by two foreign people. Considering the location we eventually responded expecting to find it had been a domestic, you know how it goes? However when our lads got there one of them remembered that the last time he was at that address was to inform the woman that her partner... a certain Mr Patrick Doyle no less, had unfortunately been found dead.'

He paused for a moment to allow them to catch up.

'What they actually found was a very frightened and distressed woman hanging onto her kids for grim death. She'd just had a visit from two people, a woman and man from Russia she thought who had literally barged their way into her flat demanding answers to questions about our Mr Doyle. Apparently it was becoming quite ugly with threats being made when this woman's sister arrived on the scene. It appears a neighbour had heard the row and went and fetched her. She waded in all guns blazing and quite simply told the pair to 'Foxtrot Oscar.' She watched them drive away from the flats balcony in what she told the local lads looked like a posh, black mini bus with black windows. Now CCTV is sparse on the estate as most of it has been vandalized...

No surprise there! but at the edge of the estate on the roundabout onto Sheffield Road we've got that vehicle heading into town.'

Nita and Alan Syms started to ask questions but the DI held his hand up.

'Wait... there's more! This isn't the first time these two people have been asking questions. Three days after you moved Katterine to the safe house these two arrived at the Cottage Hospital asking about a friend who they thought might be there having been attacked in the town three weeks earlier. The woman claimed she was the sister and had just arrived from Poland. They were sent up to Jasmine ward.' he glanced briefly at Nita, 'was that the ward she was on?' Nita nodded. 'Right, well when they couldn't get any information it all began get nasty. Security were called and escorted them out of the hospital. They made a note of the vehicle and its reg and guess what?' The DI nodded to the three of them, 'A Merc people carrier with Bulgarian plates. CCTV has them heading out of Portbridge towards the M62.'

Looking at the sergeant he said. 'Ruth, if we need to let's put a civvie with these two to do the paper work that'll free them up to get deeper into it.'

The sergeant nodded, to Nita and Alan he said.

'You two go and interview Ms Doyle again, Nita go to the PCH and have a word with whoever was on ward duty the day they were visited by these two reprobates, have a word with the security guys if you can as well. Let's see where this puts us now in finding whoever did for our Mr Doyle. Right, get to it and hope we've got enough to get a result, this one's been hanging on too long for my liking.'

They left his office returning to their own desk, Ruth followed them.

'I'll give you Linda as well as the civvie, if we get enough info from this latest development then you may well need her Okay?'

They both nodded before Ruth added finally.

'Right listen I'm in the 'need to know camp' now alright?'

'Sarge, they said in unison.

Meanwhile Stephen had travelled up to the boat yard where he spent most of the day doing jobs on Finbar he'd promised himself had needed doing for ages but always seemed to get forgotten. He had lunch with the Grahams where Mrs G grilled him about Nita and how Emma and the rest of the family were taking to this 'lovely young lady, this breath of fresh air in his life' as she put it. Before returning to Portbridge he went up to the house to say goodbye to Mrs G. She took him in her arms and hugged him briefly.

'Just so you know Stephen Leigh-Grace and you can tell Emma and the family, Robert and I approve of this young lady of yours we like her a lot and she's been good for you, it's changed you... for the better. I think your Suzanne would be pleased do you hear?'

He nodded, 'Thank you that means a lot.' he said returning her hug.

As he walked to his car Robert Graham intercepted him and shaking his hand said.

'Has my Maggie had a word son?' Stephen nodded. 'Good good we think a lot of you son you're a grand family. We've watched your Emma grow up, whey we're nearly as proud of her as you are man, she's family you nah! Now you hang onto this young lass you've met do you hear, she just grand for you son, just grand, alright!'

Stephen put his arm round Robert Grahams' shoulder giving it a squeeze, his voice cracked slightly with emotion as he replied.

'I intend to Robert, thank you.'

'Good... away son and be safe! We'll have the boat back in the water when you're next home.'

He stood and watched Stephen walk the last few yards to his car and waved as he drove out of the small car park.

Stephen found the drive home quite emotional, all the talk about Emma and the family seemed to resurrect memories he'd locked away for years as he'd tried to avoid the pain of loss, of grieving for Suzanne. There were demons here that he'd never really faced and surprisingly, anger too, something he hadn't felt after she'd passed away. He realised now just what a huge influence meeting Nita last Easter had had on his life. From the beginning after that initial contact of her Nita interviewing him and learning of his loss, then spending time with her, someone of the opposite sex, that it wasn't cheating on Suzanne; an excuse he often used to avoid becoming close to someone. She'd patiently shown him that talking to them, letting them see who he really was wasn't being unfaithful. Turning into his street he parked outside his house. Brewing a mug of tea he put the cd-player on and sat in the lounge. He realised that whilst he was in weekly contact Emma, Richard and Mary, it had been some time since he'd spoken to, or seen his own father who was a lot nearer in York. He decided that a visit was necessary before he went away this next week, plus he could introduce Nita to him. He dialled Nita's number, it went to answer phone.

'Hi just me, do you fancy fish 'n chips tonight? If so will you call at Frank's fishery at West Fording on your way home? Love you sugar.'

It was ten minutes before his phone vibrated in his pocket, he saw it was Nita,

'Sorry,' she said, 'I was away from my phone, sounds like a plan, just one of each?'

'Yes fine, if you're not hungry get a special and we'll split it, up to you.'

She responded, 'Okay, I'll call as I leave, TTFN' and blew kisses down the phone.

Just after five his phone buzzed. *'Leaving now, home in thirty minutes with dinner, warm some plates! xxx'*

It was a bit more than thirty minutes before she burst through the front door carrying her bags and two white paper packages. Handing them over to Stephen she went back into the hall dropped her bags hung her coat up and kicked off her shoes. Returning to the dinning kitchen she sat on one of the bar stools watching him serve up their dinner. Very little was said until they'd both eaten.

'So come on Ferryman out with it 'cause something's wrong! You got to the yard I take it so is there a problem?'

'No the boat's coming on fine, it was something Mrs G and Robert said brought up a lot of pain and anger actually that I thought I'd got past.'

Picking up her tea she inclined her head.

'Come on let's get comfortable,' and walked to the lounge. They sat together.

'Okay so where has this come from now?'

He smiled, 'I had lunch with them and Mrs G said how she and Robert thought you were lovely and how I'd changed since we'd met, for the better she said! Then just as I was leaving Robert spoke to me saying basically the same thing.'

He shrugged his shoulders and looked directly at her. She sat for a while before reaching for his hand.

'When we first met and you told me bits about your life both with Suzanne and afterwards, I kind of got the feeling then that you hadn't really gone through the whole pain and the grieving bit on account of how quickly she'd become ill and died. You didn't have the time for either you or Emma to come to terms with her illness, to face up to it together, hmm?' She held his eyes with hers, 'Afterwards, well Em was so young you had to be there for her and I guess you were there for everyone else too. I think that was your self defence system kicking in. By keeping yourself busy you could avoid coping with your own grief. Am I making sense here Ferryman?'

He nodded, she continued.

'We both know that another part of your defence has been to hide behind what was special between you and Suzanne to avoid anything or anyone getting close to the real you, yes?'

Again he nodded giving another shrug.

'I can't explain why it was me you chose to trust last Easter, but something grew between us through the summer whilst you were away, so in September when we met at the wharf we were friends but in those forty odd hours it changed. Okay I encouraged it somewhat but it was you! You decided to let things go to the next level. I saw your inner turmoil that Friday night Ferryman, how troubled you were when your emotions began to take over, when you began to get excited and lose control. All you wanted to do was to run, to escape, to use Suzanne to hide behind. That said I also saw the passion in you begin to surface, you were aroused by the moment. Listen can you remember years ago how excited you'd get when you realised you wanted that person so much? You had that rush of passion, lust, whatever you want to call it. By the end of our weekend you'd come through your own battle and dropped me right in the middle of mine… thanks a bunch!'

She chuckled briefly and stroked his arm, he grinned at her.

'How long have we been together now, seven months, any regrets?'

He shook his head.

'No not one,' he said, 'by that Monday morning I understood what you'd been trying to explain all through the summer. I felt different, a new man, I said that to you that I didn't feel guilty.'

She smiled at him, 'Told you as much, it doesn't diminish or disrespect Suzanne at all, you're not cheating you're moving on! Didn't you say that in that brief time you all had together after she'd been diagnosed you were to move on and not dwell on things.?'

He nodded saying, 'Yes.'

'Okay so what did the Grahams say today that stirred up the murky waters that threw you right back. It may be a bit late my lovely man but today has allowed you to face up to and deal with some of that hidden grief you didn't face up to at the time. I hope sharing it now and not having to handle it on your own has made it easier. Stephen I'm here I'm not going anywhere… at least I not planning to. Look, if anything else troubles you talk to me, share whatever it is alright?'

Looking at her he nodded, she shuffled closer and hugged him for some time before changing the subject.

'Right, with you off again on Thursday, I've booked Wednesday afternoon as holiday so is there anything in particular you'd like to do?'

'I would like to go and see Dad if that's all right, I missed him last time I was home.'

'Okay I don't mind, do you want me to come with you? I'm going to have to meet him one- day why not tomorrow?'

He sat quietly, she could see he was mulling over what she'd just suggest, eventually he said.

'Funny, I was thinking that earlier so yeah why not, now's as good time as any.'

Getting up from the settee she said.

'Okay, that's sorted then, now do you fancy a nip of one of your whiskies?'

'Yeah that'd be lovely thanks just on ice please, there's some in the fridge tray I think.'

While Nita was getting the drinks Stephen picked up the picture frame of the family and stroked his finger over Suzanne's image replacing it as Nita returned with two glass tumblers of the soft amber liquid. Stephen said quietly as they savoured the whisky.

'You are such a lovely person do you know that? So patient and sensitive, you seem to sense a person's mood and just know the right things to say. I do love you for that and all your other special qualities... and the passion too!'

She smiled at him gently stroking his thigh. For the rest of the evening they watched a film sitting together. Later snuggling close together in bed, she kissed his cheek.

'Are you okay, Ferryman?'

Pulling her into a tighter embrace he replied.

'Yeah fine, thank you for helping me understand what I'm feeling and why. I need to learn to keep it in perspective and not work myself into a decline.'

They hugged and kissed one another shuffled around until they were spooned together and slipped into a restful sleep.
Nita arrived back at Stephens Wednesday lunch time, they had a snack then she went and changed while Stephen tidied up.

'Crikey Nita, you look as good as that first night at the Duchess.' He crossed the room and embraced her. 'You've got that perfume on again, it's lovely.'

She nodded at him.

'Yes I like wearing it for you. I thought I should make the effort for your dad.'

He laughed. 'I'm in jeans and a zipper jacket, there's no comparison.'

Shrugging she grinned.

'Well he knows you so you can look scruffy! He's never met me and I want to make a good impression.'

Driving to York where Stephens' dad lived in a small warden managed housing complex he told her a little about his dad, Harold. He chuckled as he said that he could be quite feisty at times, that he was an independent man and whilst he was losing some of his mobility still managed to go shopping, cook, and keep his bungalow tidy and how he and Emma had always been very close.

'Thick as thieves at times.' he said.

She asked about his mum, he was quiet for a while then told her about Janet who'd passed away two years before Suzanne adding how his dad had still been coming to terms with that loss when Suz died. He and Emma had become much closer since her granny and Suzanne had passed away. Being so young and traumatised by both losses in such a short time, things were initially very difficult but eventually settled down into some sort of routine. It was almost a year before, with his dad, Mary and Richard had got together to talked about what was going to be best for Emma. Always a practical man his dad realised that he wasn't getting any younger so taking on full time care for Emma, a lively young girl, wasn't really an option but he wanted to provide as much support as he could, to be involved in her life as much as possible. All he could do was offer what he could afford towards supporting them financially in whatever was decided. They'd all sat with Emma and explained the options asking her what she would like to happen. In the end it was decided that she would go to Poole and live with Mary and Richard and that's how it's been for the past eight years. He recalled how upset his dad had been the weekend Emma moved to Poole, the two of them hugged one another and cried. Emma promised she'd speak to him every week and come to see him whenever she was home; and to be fair she's kept that promise and today they still have this special relationship. Nita listened as he related how good he was with his hands and some stories about his days as a carpenter, not a joiner,' he emphasized, 'a carpenter! There's a difference you know!' he pointed out.

Her first impression of the little houses was how lovely they were as they drew into the courtyard car park, Stephen said,

'They were modelled on the style of the old alms houses, the old man just fell in love with them when he saw the plans. I know it's quite a way away from where he lived but he was up for a new start after mum and then Suzanne had died. He was so depressed by all the memories that he almost just gave up.'

Out of the car they walked towards the ornate entrance, Stephen added.

'He changed when he got here and settled in, got his get-up-and-go back, he's easy to get on with and made friends with the other ressies quite quickly. In fact he's got a lady friend now.'

Nita looked at him, mouth open, eyes wide, 'Really!'

'Yep, Sylvia, she's a couple of years older than dad, they spend a lot of time together either at his or hers.'

'Aw that's so sweet.'

Inside the entrance hall he filled in the visitors' book then nodded for Nita to follow him, they walked to the day room where he had a quick look around but couldn't see his dad. He acknowledged a carer and a couple of the residents before walking out to the car park again and along a canopied path that ran around all the house frontages. Stopping at number eleven, he knocked on the brown door. A couple of minutes elapsed before it opened and Nita saw Stephens' double looking at them. Same features but older, a little shorter with white hair around the sides but still a spitting image. He was wearing cord trousers a lumberjacks check shirt with a well-worn cardigan over that. It took a moment for him to recognise Stephen but when the penny dropped his face lit up and he grinned broadly.

'By heck lad it's good to see you, come on in I'll put kettle on.'

Stephen went through the door, Nita followed. Inside the little entrance lobby the two men embraced.

'Aye Stephen lad I'm right glad to see you, how've you been son. Still trucking in't Northern hemisphere?'

Stephen nodded, 'I am but looking at coming back onto UK runs as soon as possible, I want to be nearer to home and everybody.'

Moving his gaze from his son he looked at Nita.

'Hello love, have you got anything to do with this?'

Stephen interrupted.

'Dad this is Nita, Nita Patel. Sugar this is my dad, Harold.'

The old man held his hand out, she took it shaking it. Still holding it he said.

'Lovely to meet you, come on in and I'll make us all some tea.'

She allowed herself to be led into the small living room where he indicated for her to sit on the little settee. In a few minutes there was a tray of tea and a plate of assorted fancy cakes on the occasional table. The three of them sat and talked about what had been happening in their lives since Stephen had last been to see his dad. It was mainly the two men talking but when it came to the attack and how he'd met Nita, she was drawn into the conversation. When Harold found out she was a detective he asked her lots of questions about her work and about Stephen's incident. There was a knock at his door which opened straight away and a woman's voice called.

'Hello Harry, just me.'

Quite a plump lady appeared in the room, same height as Harold, jet black hair which Nita thought wasn't her natural colour, just helped along a bit! She was wearing trousers, a floral blouse tucked into the waistband and a shawl draped over her shoulders.

'Oh sorry love I didn't know you had visitors I'll come back.'

Harold stood up.

'No no Sylvie come on in love it's our Stephen and a friend, you remember Stephen?'

The lady looked at them both for a moment.

'Of course, sorry love it's been a while and my eyes aren't as good as they were. How are you, and how's that lovely daughter of yours? My she's very pretty, I reckon she'll break a few hearts before she settles down. You know your dads so made up when she comes to see him.'

Looking at Nita she added.

'He takes her over to the day room and introduces her to everyone; "this is my granddaughter" he says, he's right proud of her.'

Stephen stood up, 'Hello Sylvia good to see you again, I see you're keeping him in line.'

This remark brought a little chuckle which they all shared, he turned to Nita.

'This is Nita Patel Sylvia, she's a friend of mine.'

'She's a detective.' Harold said quietly.

Sylvia looked at him and then back at Nita.

'Eee you look too young to be a detective love, how old are you? No don't answer that I'm sorry that was rude of me, no offence love.'

Nita shook Sylvia's hand and smiled at her, 'None taken.'

Harold had disappeared into the kitchenette and returned with another mug and topped up the teapot. He poured one for Sylvia then topped up everyone else's. Over the next hour there were so many questions about where Stephen, Emma and the family had been in the summer, how were Mary and Richard. Conversely, he asked how Harold had been over the last couple of months and so it went on until Stephen looked at the clock on the mantle over the gas fire.

Nudging Nita who followed his gaze to the clock as he stood up saying.

'Dad sorry but we need to be away.'

Harold got to his feet. '

'Nay I wanted to take you over t' lounge, are you sure?'

Stephen nodded, 'Next time dad, okay?'

'Aye suppose but don't leave it so long next time. Any roads I want this beautiful young lady to come again she makes me feel right grand, just like our Emma does.'

As he said this he reached out for Nita's hand and squeezed it. Sylvia looked up at Nita and winked.

'What did I tell you, jewel of his eye Emma is.'

Nita giggled softly. They made their way to the door, the two men embraced one another.

'Take care and be safe son!'

'I will dad, promise.'

He turned to Nita, 'Don't be a stranger love, if he's coming over you come too.'

'I will.' she gave him a gentle hug, 'and thanks for the tea.' turning back she called, 'Bye Sylvia, see you another time.'

'Bye love,' came the reply from inside the room.

The old man watched them walk back through the arch to the car park turned and closed the door. As they drove away from York Stephen apologised for his father's behaviour, Nita looked at him. He'd been the perfect host and she hadn't taken any offence with anything he'd said, or Sylvia and she'd like to go and see him again soon and learn more about his life. They called for fish and chips nearing home as they hadn't planned anything for their evening meal.

As the evening drew on they began to get silly together, winding each other up about another three or four weeks apart and what they thought the other would get up to. At some point the mood switched from funny to passionate. The joking stopped as did the chores with Stephen finally chasing Nita up the stairs, she squealed as she tried to escape him. Breathlessly they fell onto the bed kissing and caressing one another helping the other undress before climbing under the duvet. They wound their arms and legs around each other and gently made love.

Stephen was up early to complete the last of his packing, concentrating on the essential supplies he needed with him. Nita stayed out of his way as much as possible getting herself sorted and ready to go to work. She'd learnt conversation was pointless as he had his working head on and acted and behaved like a robot, putting things in a particular order and in a specific box or container. Occasionally she'd hear him swear under his breath when he realised there was something he'd forgotten to get or an item needed replacing.

'Stephen, I'm ready I'll get off.'

Leaving what he was doing he came to her in the hall taking her in his arms.

'Love you so much sugar.'

She completed the embrace putting her arms around him.

'You too Ferryman, you know what's coming next hmm.'

Leaning back from her for a moment he looked her in the face.

'Take care, be careful… oh and no heroics! Does that cover it?'

She grinned, 'Pretty much, don't forget I love you… massively!'

They kissed and hugged again. Picking her bags up she turned unlocked the door and looked back.

'Bye, speak tonight?'

Blowing him a kiss she walked to her car, he waved, closed the door and went back to the kitchen. Quite a bit later with all his stuff packed and the house tidied he set off for his depot stopping en-route at the supermarket to get the things he'd run short of. Booking on at work he was briefed by the transport team and given a mountain of paperwork, before transferring all his kit into the wagon. Driving round the yard he picked up the trailer he'd been allocated and left the yard two hours later. Travelling to Goole he loaded out of a warehouse near the harbour then left the town, crossed the Humber Bridge to the ferry port and waited to board the night ferry to Rotterdam. There was even time to speak to Nita who was back at her house with the girls again, and so began another four weeks away.

CHRISTMAS

On his homeward run they talked about plans for Christmas. Separately they'd both given some thought about what it would be like to live together, maybe now was the right time. Sitting at the bar in the kitchen after dinner he reached for her hand, studying her. Glancing at his hand holding hers she looked at him.

'Errr, what's all this, should I be worried?'

He smiled, 'I hope not, but I've been thinking about this over the last two runs… I don't quite know how to put it.'

'Come on Ferryman out with it, just say what's going on!'

He gave her a little smirk.

'You mean just like you told me about telling Em after the assault?'

She nodded. 'Just like I told you!'

Still holding her hand, he took a breath.

'Well, last time we were here you said it felt like we'd together for years, remember?' she nodded, he continued, 'I get that feeling too, I've said so many times how you've given me so much of my life back since that run up to the Grahams' yard with *Finbar* in September. Well now I can't imagine you not being here, so it's quite simple really, but trying to say it out loud is the difficult bit!'

He looked into her eyes searching for the next sentence. She couldn't help smiling at him sensing his awkwardness. Gently squeezing his hands she said softly.

'What are you trying to tell me Stephen?'

He watched her for a few moments longer, then said.

'I wonder if you've con… no, have you thought; look I'd like you to come here permanently, move in here with me… okay that's it! I want you to come and live here, with me!'

He stared at her waiting for a response. She returned his stare but said nothing. As she didn't answer for some time he said.

'Sorry, perhaps I said that the wrong way?'

Shaking her head slowly she eventually replied.

'No, that was fine, a surprise but fine. I have to be honest I wasn't expecting that.'

'Well how do feel about it, I mean has it crossed your mind at all? Nita say something... please, or am I going too fast?'

'Hmm, going too fast, no! We've both gone at this relationship at full speed haven't we?' She paused before adding thoughtfully. 'Come here and stay, now that's something I've not thought about. However I have thought about the future and wondered where it might lead. I've never lived with anyone before, I mean a man... in a relationship, as a partner you know? Okay I live with the girls, that's a convenience, plus we all get on so there's never any trouble, we rub along I suppose.'

'So is that a no then?'

'No! I mean no it's not a no, I don't know. I love you, I love loving you, the sex you know, being with you is truly amazing, I think I said that after that first weekend it was magical, but coming to live with you is a big step. Do you think we'd get on?'

She looked to see how he was taking what she was saying. He shrugged.

'I don't know, I mean there's been no-one since Suzanne died until you.' Thinking briefly he added, 'Could this be a delayed sort of thing and I'm sort of on the rebound and just wanting someone to live with me, not wanting to be on my own... perhaps?'

She stared at him a little surprised by his answer.

'Whoa where's this going, I'm confused now! What are you saying? I didn't say I wouldn't want to come and live with you! I do love you to bits Stephen I need to think about it, come on you've just dropped this on me!'

He shrugged again.

'I thought you'd say yes straight away but yes you're right, maybe I haven't thought everything through. I'm sorry if I've upset you.'

'Stephen I'm not upset, a bit surprised... definitely! Part of me wants to say yes.'

He interrupted before she could finish. 'And the other part?'

'The other part is panicking right now, is this how you felt that Friday night on the boat?'

He grinned, 'Sounds about right but you knew what you were doing and I trusted you. Maybe you need to trust me now, I mean I have lived with someone before. Look sugar when I'm home you pretty much live here, moving in full time isn't going to be much different. If I'm away either in the UK or Europe will be the only difference and you can always get one of the girls to come round and keep you company or go there.'

Leaving the kitchen he walked into the living room and brought the bottle of whisky and two glasses with him setting them on the breakfast bar, then reaching into the freezer and taking some ice-cubes from the freezer box poured the pale tan liquid over the ice, passing one to Nita, he raised his.

'Cheers, here's to us and our future'

She smiled and raised her glass in response, taking a mouthful she shuddered briefly then said.

'Hang on I haven't said yes!'

He smiled at her, 'No, but you're trusting me this time and I'll lead you, it'll be alright trust me!'

They spent the rest of the evening discussing the finer points of living together and the logistics if she were to come here permanently. Two days later Stephen left for Germany and Denmark but only for three weeks this time, his last run before Christmas. The morning of his departure, just before Nita went off to her office, she gave him her answer as they said their goodbyes. Holding one another in the little hallway she said as she kissed him one more time.

'What you asked me last night, well I've thought about it and the answers... yes! I'm tired of this too-ing and fro-ing every time you go away. Let's make it simple and permanent... happy?'

'Yes... oh yes very happy.

He was beaming; she stopped at the door looking back at him.

'Will you wait until you're home before we go public please, I'd like get used to the idea first before all the questions start... alright?'

'Surely, not a problem.' he said still beaming at her.

Unfortunately, this plan didn't take into consideration any outside interference, namely work! Having just come back from his Denmark run, he was focusing on Nitas' move and plans for Christmas, an urgent job came in from one of the company's biggest customer's suppyling some leading Supermarkets. As Stephen was the only 'continental' driver home it fell to him to do the run. Despite his protests his boss, while full of apologies said.

'Stephen lad you have to understand this is a priority job for a hugely valued customer, I'm not risking losing this contract, I'm sorry.'

That was the end of the discussion. Stephen left the office a little aggrieved that he was having to do the run so near to the Christmas break. Trying to see an upside he thought, 'Oh well, it'll help my case for coming back to UK runs later on.' This was the basis of his argument that evening when he tackled Nita about rearranging their plans to meet her parents. In the end she reluctantly accepted his point making it clear that he was on a warning that...

'Come hell or high water, he was back in the five days!'

The following morning he left for a flying run to France promising on his life he'd be back.

Finally homeward bound for the Christmas break he'd crossed from Cherbourg but had to take his night break at the first services on the motorway. He'd been a bit concerned that any delay in getting back to Portbridge would affect their plans for the coming ten-day break.

'I'm so glad it's worked out,' Nita said when he called her, 'you had me worried when work said it was just four days.'

'Yes, I was panicking a bit I'll tell you, any way all's well.'

'I can relax a bit now you'll be here tomorrow.'

'Bank on it sugar.'

She giggled. 'Oh I am, believe me...'

'Bedtime,' he said, 'until tomorrow my love. Sleep tight, bed bugs and all that.'

'Night Ferryman.' she responded touching his image on the screen, 'Love you.'

'You too Sugar.'

Her screen went blank, sliding off the settee she went around the house clearing a few things away and locking the doors. Slipping under the duvet she snuggled down and lay there thinking about Stephen, their relationship, his house, this house and how comfortable she felt here now. Only two weeks ago she'd moved most of her personal things in, then set about subtly introducing a little feminine influence into the place, so far it had been painless the house felt more homely now.

The following evening they virtually arrived home at the same time, Stephen with two bunches of flowers, bottle of wine and a small, gift-wrapped box, Nita with three bags.

As they made their way through to the kitchen-diner she looked at him a little suspiciously. Dropping her bags by the breakfast bar she turned to him.

'Okay what's up? Is this a guilt offering or peace offering?'

He smiled, 'Hello yourself... no nothing like that.' Handing her one of the floral bunches, 'these are for you, as is this,' he said handing her the bottle of wine. 'And this is an early Christmas present.' He said passing her the small box.

Putting the flowers and the bottle down she studied him as she carefully undid the yellow ribbon around the box. Opening the wrapping paper she removed the lid of the box, studied the contents for a moment and then stared at him wide eyed.

'Stephen!' she exclaimed, gently lifting a snake linked silver chain with five little ruby coloured cut stones, the centre one being the largest of the five each separated by a little ornate silver link. She held it up for a moment, again just staring at him, this time though there were tears in her eyes. Replacing it back in the box she came to him.

'It's beautiful but why, I mean thank you but why what have I done to deserve it?'

Slipping his arms around her, he shrugged.

'Because you're you and I need you to know that you are just so very special to me. I needed to show you how special.

Wiping a tear from her cheek with the back of her hand, she said almost in a whisper.

'I don't know what to say… just thank you, it's gorgeous I've never seen anything so beautiful.'

She offered her lips up to him and he kissed them gently. When they parted the tears were flowing freely now which she tried to wipe them away with the backs of her hands. He reached across the breakfast bar, tore off two sheets of kitchen roll handing them to her. She giggled at him, dabbing her eyes repeatedly until she'd managed to stem the flow.

'I bet I look a mess now… runny mascara and puffy eyes…Yes?'

Shedding her coat she picked up the necklace and handing it to him said.

'Put it on please,'

Turning her back to him and lifting her ponytail to expose her neck.

'My eyes are blind to you as anything other than beautiful!' he patted her shoulder. 'There now let's have a look?'

She turned smiling showing of her neck.

'Very nice!' he said.

She went through to the lounge and peered into the large mirror.

'Oh Stephen it's so beautiful, thank you.'

Turning to face him again, she saw he was nodding gently.

'I thought it would suit you, I'd seen one in the shop on the ferry some time ago and thought it was just you but I was sort of shy about buying it as I didn't really know you at the time and I didn't want to give the wrong impression. This was in a jewellers in France where I've just been.' He laughed briefly.

'What?'

'Oh nothing, only I caused a bit of a traffic jam when I went to buy it. I parked the whole unit on the main road in the town and created a bit of a gridlock. The local gendarme weren't too happy!' He chuckled again.

'Didn't you tell him it was for your sweetheart back in England?'

'That wouldn't have helped, he threatened me with prison... at least I think that's what he was saying... who knows!'

'Well it's gorgeous, I love it.' She put her arms round his neck and kissed him.

'I thought it would look great on you when you wear those trousers and top, it'll show off your beautiful neck.'

'Shalwar Kameez,' she said, turning to look in the mirror once more, 'yes it will look great.'

He nodded 'I love it when you wear your traditional clothes, you have such a lovely neck and being tall and slim you look a million dollars... edible even! I just want to kiss you all over and nibble your neck.'

She gave him a strange look, chuckling as she undid the clasp.

'You worry me sometimes Ferryman, I get the feeling your family were cannibals years back. I have this picture in my head of the family sitting in a cave around a huge cooking pot, stacking wood on a fire and adding vegetables into the pot before cooking somebody up for dinner.'

Punching the air he declared, 'Shucks I hadn't realised I was so transparent!'

She playfully pushed him. 'Idiot!' they both laughed and walked back to the kitchen.

Replacing the necklace in its box she looked at him.

'I haven't bought you anything as special as this, I'm sorry I feel guilty now.'

He smiled at her as he stroked her arm.

'Don't, it's not a competition. I saw this and could see you wearing it and it's a way of not just saying how much I love you, it's a way of showing it too.'

'Well thank you.'

'Okay, now food, should we go out 'cause unless it's from the freezer there's nothing to eat!'

'Out then I suppose.'

They went back into Portbridge to their favourite Indian restaurant, enjoyed their meal and returned home at a reasonable time ready as Nita put it for 'tomorrow's challenge.' Meeting her family!' They both laughed a little at the prospect, deep down though she felt quite apprehensive, while Stephen felt decidedly nervous. They had a 'nip' of whisky and went to bed

~~~~~~

Breakfast was a rather subdued affair, both were feeling the same reservations they'd had last night. Telling both families meant that if either one wasn't happy then they'd know what they were up against from the start. That said, it wasn't going to make any difference to either of them, they were adults, mature and certain in how they felt about each other. The first hurdle was introducing Stephen to her parents and family, she smiled; fed to the lions more like she thought! She felt he'd drawn the short straw really.

Later at her parents' house she felt her family had welcomed him more out of politeness than as a possible suitor for their daughter. Two of her aunts subsequently told her they liked him, her cousins asked if he had any brothers or cousins who were single. They were instantly reprimanded by Nita's father and mother, even the aunties spoke to the girls reminding them how they should behave and respect their visitor. Nita's mother asked him directly how he felt about mixed-race relationships and how would he deal with the possible stigma and anti-race bigots he would undoubtedly come across. She was proud of him as he answered every challenge her mother threw at him. When they found out that he was a widower
~~~~~~

however, with a teenage daughter. Her mother turned on Nita launching into a tirade which went on for some time until her father stepped in stopping it and reminding her mother, as they'd previously done to her cousins, that Stephen was a guest in their house. He apologised to Stephen and taking him by the elbow led him into another room. Once out of the room with the door closed Stephen heard raised voices again as Nita's mother begin to challenge her once more.

In the relative peace of a living room he asked Stephen about his wife and daughter and how he managed. Stephen told him most of the history of events back to Suzanne's death. Her father told him about Nita and her determination to follow her own dream carving out the career in life she wanted, how her rebellious attitude could be a little abrasive at times. Stephen smiled agreeing with him, adding that in the time they'd been together he'd found this out to his own cost. Her father smiled and continued saying there had been a times when he'd felt disappointed that she'd let her family down by turning her back on their culture and traditions, adding that he thought his attempts to persuade her to follow family traditions had ultimately led her to almost rejecting him and the family by making the decision to go abroad to pursue her career. However, in time he'd come to realise she was very much part of the growing new British Asian culture where daughters wanted the same freedoms as their brothers to pursue careers, even relationships that seemed wrong to him and the older generation; the more traditional thinking parents. Having returned from two years in the States she'd found a position with the police CID branch in Portbridge and he had to admit now that he was actually really proud of her, the way she was able to work with people from the wider community of social and cultural backgrounds mainly because she always came across as being impartial.

They re-joined the rest of the family where an uneasy peace settled on the gathering. Nita's mother and her aunts had prepared a huge array of dishes which everyone enjoyed. There were moments of hilarity that had everyone near to tears as Stephen sampled some of the dishes that were a little spicy for him. The aunts and cousins talked to him about his adventures driving through Europe, the places he'd visited and sights he'd seen. Time passed through the afternoon with everyone trying to avoid any tetchy subjects. When they were leaving, Nita's father shook his hand warmly, Nita embraced her father and he kissed her forehead, she took his hands and bowed her head as she kissed them, she then went to embrace her mother but her response wasn't as forgiving. Stephen went to shake her hand but the look on her face changed his mind and he left it by saying. 'Good-bye Mrs Patel and thank you.'

The drive home was just as eventful as Stephens's time alone with her father. Nita was quiet at first, then asked what her dad had said to him when they'd left the room. He related their chat to her and she couldn't avoid smiling at how her father had described some of her mannerisms. He reached for her hand glancing across at her, there were tears in her eyes. Squeezing her hand reassuringly, he said.

'Talk to me sugar.'

For a while she sat quietly then began relating her 'chat' as she put it with her mother, using her fingers to emphasize 'chat' with inverted comers. She told him that her mother had asked how she could be involved with a man many years older than her, with the added complication of a child, how! Yet again she was bringing disgrace on the family, just as she'd done at university when she'd told them she wanted a career and not a marriage and turned her back on them by going to America. She said all her attempts to explain how they'd met just seemed to go over her head, she didn't want to know she didn't listen to a word Nita said. Had it not been for one of her aunties, her mother's sister intervening, then Nita's efforts to explain that 'you and I' just happened then she'd never have heard the end of how! She went quiet again and they travelled home in almost complete silence.

One thing the events of the day had done however, was to focus them both on their future. They spent the evening sitting in front of an open fire talking about where they were going in this relationship. Nita wanted to know if, after today, he felt differently about her. He tried to lift the atmosphere by winding her up about her apparent abrasiveness and coping with her feisty quest to be independent; quickly though he realised she wasn't having any of it. They had a Chinese for supper, some wine and cuddled together on the couch cosy and warm listening to cd's content to be in each other's arms. Going to bed early they made love, gently, tenderly. It was different tonight, they showed it with tenderness. Finally in a gentle embrace they slept, the trauma of the day behind them. Nita turned over pulling the duvet around her neck and just before falling asleep wondered how she would be welcomed by Stephen's family.

~~~~~~~~~~~~~~~~~~~~~~~~~~~~~~~~~~~~~~~

Richard and Mary lived near Poole in Dorset with Emma, he'd told them all about meeting Nita in hospital while they were on their summer cruise. He'd also told Richard and Mary that they were in a relationship and asked how they thought Emma would take this latest news. Replying, as Nita had earlier they said.

'Just tell her the truth. If you try and flower it up or make some sort of a story up, she'll smell a rat Stephen, Em's not stupid, Mary added, you know she does know about boys and things, Stephen she's coming up seventeen this year.'

By the time they arrived in Poole the introductions were just a formality, Nita felt welcome straight away although she was aware that Emma was studying her when she thought she was distracted. The run up to Christmas day was fun, they'd all gone food shopping and had a laugh about individual likes and dis-likes. She'd helped Emma decorate the tree with lights, streamers, and tinsel, Stephen stayed out of their way as Nita had asked, she wanted to get to know Emma on her terms and allow Emma to form her own opinion of her without him acting as a go-between; she'd then spent time with Mary
~~~~~~~~~~~~~~~~~~~~~~~~~~~~~~~~~~~~~~~

preparing food for the following day. She found that for once in her life she was excited by the thought of Christmas and how much of a new experience it was going to be for her. Year on year she would go home for her family's celebrations for their festivals then listen to her colleagues relate there Christmas to all and sundry at the office. How much they'd eaten or drunk, what presents they'd been given and how useless some of them were! This year she was going to experience it for real. She joined them on Christmas Eve when they'd strolled into the village to gather with others around a huge Christmas tree brightly adorned with a huge array of lights and streamers and joined in singing carols. They'd gone to visit some friends of Mary and Richard's then and had hot punch, sausage rolls and mince pies finally returning home just after mid-night, Christmas Day. Emma wanted to open some presents then but had to be dissuaded and told to wait until the morning. Pouting like a small child, she'd reluctantly gone to bed.

Christmas Day itself was amazing. Thanksgiving had been the nearest thing she'd experienced when in America spending the day with the family of the guy she was seeing there, so long ago now she thought. During the afternoon she'd phoned her parents to wish them a Happy Christmas and whilst her sister was all bubbly on the phone, her mother and father seemed very cool, although her father did ask her to wish Stephen and his family all the best.

On the thirtieth they left Poole aiming to be home for New Year's Eve, Nita felt she'd put pounds on with all the food she'd eaten. All the way home she interrogated Stephen about how they all felt about her, what they'd said, how were they about the two of them being together, especially Emma. Time and time again he told her that she'd been a great success, they all liked you.

'Yes but what about Emma, what did she say?' she asked.

'She likes you, how many more times have I to tell you sugar... they like you! Now be quiet or I'll drop you on the motorway and you can thumb it home.'

She leaned across and kissed his cheek then playfully punched his thigh.

'Hey! What was that for?' he exclaimed.

Grinning she replied, 'You're mean, you wouldn't tell me even if they didn't like me.'

He glanced quickly at her.

'Wrong, you know I would. That said, it wouldn't make any difference because I just love everything about you, even down to your little toes.'

Responding she said. 'What's wrong with my toes?'

'Nothing, I was just saying I love every bit of you, every bit. Tell you what, just to prove it I'll kiss your little toes tonight how's that?'

Laughing she replied. 'You're mad!'

'I know... mad for you.'

She kissed his cheek once more. The journey back to Portbridge seemed to take for ever, but they were pleased to finally walk through their front door and just drop.

They spent New Year's Eve out with Louise, Moira, Moira's feller, Louise's brother Alan Syms, and a couple of other friends of the girls, returning home in the early hours happy and a little 'tiddly'. As Stephen was away to Germany in two days, Nita had opted for the first shift of the New Year. It seemed pointless her mopping around the house with him gone.

~~~~~~~~~~~~~~~~~~~~~~~~~~~~~~~~~~~

Standing on the doorstep they said their goodbyes with all the promises and instructions to each other to 'Take care,' and 'Not to worry,' before she drove off to work. An hour later he packed his car secured the house and went to the depot. Transferring all his kit into his unit, he checked that everything he'd left in it before Christmas was still there. Going to the office he collected the load manifest and number of the trailer he was taking to Hull for the night ferry. As he was leaving the transport desk his boss called him to one side.
~~~~~~~~~~~~~~~~~~~~~~~~~~~~~~~~~~~

'Right, I've put the word out about you coming back onto UK only runs, have you thought about it over the break, what a difference it'll make to your salary just to begin with?'

'I know but now I need to be home more often, you know things have changed since Easter. Listen boss you were there eight years ago when I needed to be away from here and the memories. I needed to work myself to death just to get through today or tomorrow, now I want to come home!'

'All right, there are a couple of guys who could be interested, I've asked them to come back to me asap okay. Right, have a safe run I'll see in three weeks or so. Take care Steve.'

The boss patted his shoulder. Driving round the yard he found his trailer, checked the seals on the rear doors before reversing under it and hooking up the lines. Leaving the yard he made his way to the M62 and travelled to Hull, parked up and waited for the ferry. Sometime later there was a knock on his cab door making him start, opening the door he saw two men standing there.

'Aye-up Steve we thought it was you, straight back into it then after the break, where're you off to up north again?'

'Yep, Germany first then Sweden and it's anybody's guess after that, depends on the weather, it's been a mild winter really, a bit of snow further north but not too bad, the main routes have been open so we'll see what happens. It can come in late and then it's heavy, where are you two going?'

The heavier of the two drivers replied.

'Same as you Germany first then south into France and two weeks shuttling trailers back and forth out of Calais. How long you away this time?'

'Four weeks I think, you, where are you going?'

He said to the other driver, adding before he could reply.

'Let me guess, off to the sun again?'

The thinner man grinned.

'Of course, Veggies and soft fruits out of Spain and Portugal, only ten days though then back from Bilbao... bonus!'

Looking at the heavier of the two, Stephen said.

'We need some of his work don't you think?'

The chunky guy agreed adding,

'He'd kill anyone if they tried to take his run off him.'

All three of them laughed, 'Drinks in the bar later lads?' the slim driver said. Stephen and the other man agreed.

'Sounds like a plan, have you got cabins or couchettes?'

Before they could answer, his laptop began buzzing, 'Sorry guys got to go, see you on board.'

The two men walked away as Stephen turned to his computer to see Nita's smiling face light up his screen. They only had fifteen minutes or so to talk as the rows of cars and trucks began to move. Saying their farewells he joined the column moving into the cavernous hold of the ferry. Making his way up numerous flights of stairs, he emerged out onto one of the open decks and stood surveying the port around him, he was surprised how busy it appeared so soon after Christmas and New Year. Studying the scene for a few minutes he breathed in the cool night air, that pungent mix of diesel fumes from the boats exhaust mixing with the aroma of sea air, the smell of stale fish catching in the back of his throat. Turning to make his way to the bar to meet the other drivers, he stopped as something caught his attention. Three wharves away was the familiar outline of that converted fishing boat he kept coming across. Come to think of it, he recalled he'd seen it in Cherbourg just before Christmas but then wasn't sure. Oh well, never mind he thought and went to join his friends in the warmth of the bar.

Between Christmas and the end of March, Stephens's runs into Northern Europe seemed to settle into a four-weekly cycle. He'd leave between the first and seventh and be home again as the month end approached. With each passing month he began to think about the long Easter break. This year he was actually looking forward to it, it would be the first anniversary of meeting Nita. Likewise, back in Portbridge, Nita found concentrating on her case work increasingly difficult as she reflected on the fact it had been a year since Stephen

Leigh-Grace had made a dramatic entry into her life and almost seven months since their friendship had become a deeply intense love affair.

'God I want you so much Nita, I ache to make love to you.'

Stephen had said last night, he was just one day away from the Euro-port and the night crossing to Felixstowe. 'It's like, as a kid when I slipped off the saddle of my bike onto the cross bar and crushed my balls, the ache is that bad.'

She gave a little squeal shuffling on the bed at the thought, giggled a little and replied sternly, but in a joking way.

'You'd better be fully functioning when you get back Ferryman. We've got three weeks to make up for.'

He grinned at her face on his laptop screen.

'Don't you worry sugar, just you make sure the front door isn't locked 'cause I won't have time to unlock it... trust me.'

Giggling again, she replied. 'Promises... I'll hold you to that Ferryman.'

'Listen sugar, Mr G has *Finbar* all set up to move. I'm back in the UK tomorrow. I should be clear and back at the yard and all done by teatime. What time have you booked off?'

'Thursday to Tuesday... problem?' she asked.

'No, no,' he said, then thinking allowed said, 'Say Thursday lunch time at the yard, Thursday night at Portbridge, Friday at the branch and Friday night in York.'

Nita joined in now. 'Emma, Richard and Mary are hoping to be there Friday afternoon depending on traffic.'

'Mmm, Easter can be a nightmare if the weather's going to be good. It can be almost as bad on the river as on the roads. Anyway if we're moored up, they can arrive whenever.'

'We can shop whilst we wait for them,' she said, 'I've got some necessities, I thought the rest we could get together when you're back.'

She saw him lounge back on his bunk.

'I'm really looking forward to this,' he said, 'ten whole days with you sweetie. This will be the first time since Suz died that there will be someone with us for me.'

He sounded a little distant.

'It was only after Suzanne died and I needed to earn proper money to pay my share in bringing Emma up that I started to spend the term time over here. Since we've been together I've found this so hard.' Looking directly into the screen he added, 'So much of what you said last Easter makes sense now. Then I was running away now I want to stay because you're there.'

Watching his face on the screen for a moment she agreed.

'Same for me too, this time last year I was living an organised life I knew where I was going, thought I knew where my career was going too... mmm, maybe I was in ignorant bliss of my own needs, until you sailed into it... literally! Since the States there hadn't been anyone special I'd wanted to spend time with, until you!'

They sat in silence watching their respective screens each recalling moments from the past eight months. Nita spoke first.

'Ferryman,' she said. 'I love you, come home safe... yes.'

'I will, see you tomorrow night...can't wait! I'll sign off now, love sugar'

He blew kisses at the screen. She responded likewise until her laptop screen went blank.

Changing into her jim-jams she padded downstairs to the kitchen, made herself a drink and took it back to her room. The house seemed lifeless with her two-house mates already away for the Easter break. 'Still in 24 hours I'll be away too.' she thought. Settling under her duvet she finished her drink, pulled her bear into a tight hug switched her light off and slept.

In Holland, Stephen sat in his cab in the queue of trucks and vans watching the cars loading willing them to 'get a move on'. Finally the coach's and vans then trucks were loaded. Just before mid-night the ships PA announced that they were leaving the port instructing everyone to attend the pursers' desk to have their documents checked. About one thirty along with three other English drivers he'd met, they got themselves settled in a quiet area of the ferry on couchettes and were all soon asleep.

~~~~~~
~~~~~~

EASTER

Since January every time he was home he enquired from his boss if he was any nearer to bringing him back onto home runs; each time the answer was the same, it was in hand. During the times he was home and had the time, he went up to the Grahams to finish the last jobs on *Finbar*. Robert had completed the engine services, refitted the straightened propeller and at the beginning of March put *Finbar* back in the water ready to move her down to the estuary Marina. The task of taking her all the way round to Poole would take six weeks, a week at a time when he was between work trips. This year he talked to Nita about bringing the boat down early so all the family could spend Easter in York using her as a base. 'Do the tourist thing around the city.' he'd said. She jumped at the idea becoming excited at the prospect of being on the boat again, with the added bonus of spending time with his family.

Thursday, Maundy Thursday, he said bye to Nita as she went off to work and he left to go to the boat yard.

'See you at the wharf tonight sugar.'

'Okay, but please, without the drama of last year, just ignore everyone okay?' she kissed him and left.

Driving up to the Grahams he parked as near as he could to the pontoon where *Finbar* was moored, transferred the essential bedding and clothes and sufficient supplies to see them to York for Friday. Leaving his car in the car park he made his way up to the house acknowledging some other people around the yard also making ready to leave and travel down the river. Robert was sitting at a really antique roll-topped desk with various piles of paperwork around him. He greeted Stephen as he walked into the room.

'All set son, happy with everything.'

'Of course Robert, as ever a perfect job. What's the damage then?'

Handing him a bill from one or the piles of paper, he said. 'That's the total, if you want to see it itemised then there's the pile of bills.' He pointed to one stack of paperwork on his desk.

Stephen shook his head, 'No need Robert it'll be right.'

Taking a pen from the desk he wrote out a cheque and handed it over.

'Right son, that's the business bit done, now for the lecture all-rite? Ah divant want to hear that yous been playing the hero again this year. There are too many people who worry about you 'cause they love you, do you hear Stephen son? Ahve known you for eight years, from the grief of losing your Suzanne and just holding it together, to this new you since this young lady's come into your life. You need to concentrate on this new family now.'

Stephen shook his hand, 'Thank you, I feel I've been fortunate, okay the circumstances perhaps weren't exactly the best way to meet, but the outcome Robert has been amazing.'

The man patted his shoulder and grinned at him. As he went to leave the house Maggie Roberts met him at the door, holding her arms out to him she hugged him saying in her soft Scots dialect.

'I guess you've had the hard word so I'm not going to say anything else except you look after that young lady of yours, she's just lovely, perfect for you. Take heed what she says Stephen, you hear!'

Smiling he replied, 'Oh yes, I had my instructions this morning and from Robert just now.'

'Good, well say hello to Emma from us and have a lovely summer all of you.'

'I intend to Maggie, I'm looking forward to showing Nita some wonderful bays and harbours.'

Giving him a gentle smack she said, 'Go on get away with you now.'

He left the house and walked down to the pontoons. *Finbar*

was moored on one quite a way down the bank in slightly deeper water. It took him another hour clearing and stowing the bridge cover before he was ready to get under way. Sitting at the helms seat on the flying bridge he turned off the isolator switch and waited for the battery lights to go green. Turning the two keys, he heard the pumps whir as they primed the engines. When everything fell silent he turned the key for the port engine. The starter turned over four or five times before the engine fired into life. *Finbar* shuddered for a moment or two until the engine settled into a steady rhythm. Repeating the process he started the starboard engine waiting for it to settle. Listening to the steady beat, he stroked the top of the control panel, 'Hello old girl, good to have you back, are you ready for another year?' Leaving the bridge he stepped onto the pontoon and slipped the bow line, throwing it onto the foredeck then pushed the bow away from the pontoon before making his way to the stern, he slipped that line taking it with him as he climbed back into *Finbar's* sun deck. Settled again at the helms seat and all the dials showing green and normal temperatures he pushed both throttle levers to slow ahead. *Finbar* pulled away from the pontoon. Looking back over his shoulder he saw Mr G standing by one of the shed doors, giving two short blasts on *Finbar's* claxon he lifted his arm. Moments later he saw Robert Graham wave back. 'Here we go.' He thought and sighed happy to be back on the boat.

Later in the afternoon when he was about hour away from the coal wharf at Porbridge he switched the CB radio on.

'This is motor cruiser *Finbar II* calling NCB wharf Portbridge, receiving, over?'

He waited for a couple of minutes for a reply and then repeated the call. This time he got a response.

'*Finbar* this is NCB Portbridge, that you Steve? Over.'

'Yes Mick, any chance I can moor up tonight I'm on my way down to the Marina. Over.'

'Don't see why not mate, when you due?'

'Forty-five minutes, to an hour maybe.'

'Okay, lower end of the wharf remember.'

'Thanks, see you later.'

'Aye, no heroics this time okay, my heart won't stand another episode like last year! Over'

'My god Mick everyone's on my case! It's like I'm being tracked all the way down the canal.'

Mick laughed, 'Out to you Steve.'

Just before five he sounded the claxon to announce his arrival. A couple of minutes later he saw Mick emerge from his office and walk briskly across the wharf. The river was quite high this year and flowing quickly as there'd been a fair amount of rain over the past two weeks. Using both engines he brought *Finbar* as smoothly as he could alongside the wharf, he'd put some fenders out earlier so as they bumped along the wharf timbers Mick reached onto the foredeck to take the bow line and secured it to a nearby bollard then went back to the stern to get that line and tie the boat up there. Stephen played the throttles to keep the boat alongside until Mick had finished securing her. Stopping the engines he left the bridge and moments later stepped from the sun deck onto the wharf and shook Mick's hand.

'Good to see you Michael, how have you been?'

Mick smiled and shrugged.

'Oh you know, keeping the wolf from the door. You look well mate, better than this time last year. Still seeing that detective?'

Stephen nodded, 'I am, she's coming here at five.'

'I put the kettle on when you sounded off, want a brew?' Mick asked.

'Yeah, perfect, I'll be in in a Jiffy, I'm just going to put some spring lines on her as the rivers fast.'

'Right, you get the lines I'll give you a hand.'

Boarding *Finbar* again he fished two more strong ropes from one of the lockers, securing one to a cleat at the stern, he threw it to Mick standing beyond the boats bow where he secured it to a bollard. Making his way to the bow Stephen tied the second rope to a cleat there and threw that one to Mick who'd walked down to the stern. Catching it he fastened that one to a bollard further away. Walking over to the office, Stephen looked back at the boat and nodded, she was secure now and unlikely to bump and crash against the wharf in the strong current. A few minutes later they sat in the office enjoying mugs of tea and dunking ginger biscuits.

'You know you drink far too much tea Mick.'

'So I've been told, but it's that or graze all day and then I'd not get thro' door,' grinning he patted his large girth, 'tea's the lesser of two evils mate'

'Listen Mick if you want to get off I can wait for Nita on the boat.'

'No it's not a problem, anyway I want to see her again. I'll side this lot then when she gets here I'll lock up and get off.'

It was another fifteen minutes before they heard a siren close by and moments later a marked police car pulled onto the wharf with flashing blue lights stopping outside the office. Nita got out dragging a bag with her, speaking briefly to the crew she waved as they drove off back onto the road.

Stephen and Mick went out to meet her, she hugged Stephen briefly, kissed him and then hugged Mick.

'They didn't use blue lights did they?' Stephen said.

Nita chuckled, 'and sirens too,' she said.

'You're joking!'

She laughed, 'Yes... they only put them on as we turned into the wharf, I said it'd surprise you.'

Stephen laughed and exhaling said, 'Certainly did that.'

Nita turned to Mick, 'Hello Mick, how're you doing, I see the diet's working.' she giggled.

He responded with a chuckle, 'Yeah I know, I said in September I was going to start one... lasted all of, oh three days.'

She hugged him again. 'Right are we ready?' she looked at Stephen.

He nodded, 'I thought we'd lay over here tonight, it's safe and *Finbar's* secure, Micks okay with that.'

She glanced at Mick, he nodded.

'Will you two be down at the Duchess later?' he asked.

'No not tonight Mick, we'll get some food sorted and get an early night, I want to pinch an hour in the morning if I can before too many people clutter up the locks, ideally I want to be in York tonight and hopefully get a good berth.'

'Right well, I'll see you in September then if not before.'

'Thanks Mick.' Stephen shock his hand and Nita kissed his cheek hugging him. He turned and went back to the office, saying over his shoulder.

'I could get used to all this affection you know.' all three of them laughed.

Stephen and Nita walked hand in hand towards *Finbar.* He offered her a hand to board but she just stepped onto the gunnel and down into the sun deck on her own. They turned as they heard the tinkle of Mick's bicycle bell and waved as he left the yard.

'Hello how's your day been?' He said kissing her briefly.

'Okay, found it hard to stay focused though, it's almost a year since...'

'I know,' he interrupted her smiling cheekily 'where's it gone, so much has happened. Can you believe it's a year since we met but only eight months since you seduced me!'

Nita chuckled and replied nonchalantly.

'You didn't take much seducing, I think I'd worn you down by then, didn't you realise that was my strategy all through the summer with those long chats?'

Settled around the table in the galley, Stephen asked.

'What do you fancy for dinner?'

'I'm easy, something simple. You made spag-bol last year, told me you had Keith Floyd stashed in a cupboard.'

'I did yes I remember, well the simplest thing would be a jacket spud with beans or cheese.'

'Sounds good, yeah that'll do, with wine yes.'

In half an hour they were eating this simple meal accompanied with a very nice red wine left over from the summer jaunt. Stephen began to say.

'When you think back to what has happened in the last year, well since last Easter. We sat round this table, you, me and Shamir and spoke about the pain and hurt we were going through. What did you feel about us then?'

She studied his face for a while then replied,

'To be honest I don't know, I mean what you'd got involved in intrigued me. Out of concern you'd put yourself in harm's way to help Shamir and David, I'm not sure everyone would have done that! Then getting to know you, your background your own loss all those years ago, then learning about Emma and the way the whole family had worked together. I guess I felt a wave of sympathy for you, you made me cross though when you insisted on continuing down river so soon. I thought you were foolish and unreasonable, particularly when you consider all the effort the medics and hospital had put in to fixing you.' she chuckled, 'Sian was spitting fur and feathers when I arrived that morning, she was so mad at you!'

Stephen shrugged, 'Yeah I know but I needed to be gone, I only had until the Monday to get *Finbar* down to the Marina, I just could...'

'I know, you just couldn't waste any more time.' He shrugged as she continued, 'I guess I developed a grudging respect for you that out of pure guts and determination you were going to complete the trip come what may. That's why I gave you my details, I truly wanted to know that you'd got to the Marina safely.'

He smiled, 'When you gave me that little hug and kissed my cheek as you and Shamir were leaving, I got this shiver through my body, I hadn't felt that since Suzanne and I first started our relationship. I felt good you know!'

'Good,' Nita said, 'to be honest I was actually very surprised that you got in touch later and then, well it just grew. The more we talked the more I got to know the real Stephen and not the man who hid behind the memory of his wife when he couldn't keep control of things. You were self-limiting yourself from moving on with your own life Stephen, I mean come on you'd helped everyone else to live and get on with their lives except you.'

'I did didn't I? well you just wore me down then talking about the fact that to meet someone or spend time with them, wasn't cheating on Suz.' He gave a little smirk, 'You know I even felt guilty just talking to you in the beginning! Do you remember saying honesty was the best advice when it came to telling Em about the attack?'

'I do and I remember you saying after you'd told her that she was okay with it, she just told you to walk away in future.'

He poured the last of the wine into their glasses.

'What did you think when in September I said I was bringing the boat up to her moorings and wondered how you felt doing the last bit of the trip with me?'

She smiled, 'I didn't have a problem with that, I was happy enough that I knew you well enough that nothing was expected of the other. If anything happened then... it happened! You know we could actually have been incompatible!'

'I know, in fact when you said yes, I thought oh shit and regretted saying anything to you at all. I mean I have my ways of doing things that I've learned over the years either by experience or by mistakes, they've proved costly at times!' The thought of having to explain why and how I was doing something this way, or that... nightmare!'

She laughed aloud.

'Tell me about it... that big lock... my god! I thought you were an absolute bastard putting me through that so soon. If all locks were going to be like that then I was going home, and you were doing the rest of the trip solo.'

They sat quietly for a while sipping the wine.

'So here we are,' Stephen said, 'a year on a new season beginning, cruising to wherever who knows but this time you're with us, with me.'

'And?' that questioning look again. 'Listen Ferryman, you asked me what I thought about us then. Well a year ago you were a closed person, hurting, still grieving and stuck somewhere way back.' She gestured with her arm. 'Now there's this lovely, settled content man enjoying something of lifes pleasures for himself, pleasures he's given his family for the past seven, eight years and never fully appreciated for himself. For me, there's this man who'd turned my world upside down in just thirty six hours, who changed my ordered world into something special.'

He shuffled on his seat a little embraced at her directness, no-one since Suzanne had spoken to him like this saying to his face about how they felt. For a moment he was lost for words, Nita's eyes studied his face waiting for a response.

'Wow!' he said, 'I ought to be used to you saying just how it is by now, you're always so direct about everything. When it comes to everyday stuff I'm okay with that, but when it's about you and me then that's still difficult.'

She reached across the table and gently gripped his arm.

'All I'm doing is holding up the mirror.' she said softly.

'Hmm I know, but what I hear when you say it like that, is a bit of a shock!'

'Why... am I wrong?'

Hesitating for a moment he said.

'No, that's the difficult bit! When...' he took a breath, 'When I asked you last September if you fancied coming on the last bit of the trip, I hadn't a clue what might happen. Like you said we were just friends meeting up, now here we are virtually inseparable wouldn't you say? It's just amazing.'

Sliding out from the table he cleared everything away. She watched him for a moment and saw from his body language that any further conversation about them were out of the question, 'the door' was closed. 'Mmmm' she said under her breath. Later all tidied up they sat snuggled together on the long settee in the saloon watching the television. He kissed the top of her head resting on his shoulder.

'If someone had said a year ago we'd be here tonight like this I'd have died laughing at the prospect.'

Into his shoulder she asked, 'Why, was that so impossible for you to consider that it could be an actual possibility?'

'At that time yes, I think it was. There I was laid up in a hospital bed having had the brown stuff kicked out of me and the boat trashed. Everything looked a mess and then like a modern-day Florence Nightingale you walked into my life and despite my best efforts to run away, here I am even more involved than ever.'

'And?'

'And...erm I wouldn't wish it any other way.'

She hugged him tightly. 'Me neither Ferryman, me neither.'

Around eleven Stephen secured the saloon patio doors and taking Nita by the hand led her to the main cabin, said.

'Do you remember this time last year when you led me through the boat and seduced me?'

Nita dropped on the bed, swung her legs round and draped herself across the covers. Removing the clip from her hair she let it cascade down around her shoulders and resting her chin on a hand she said in a low sexy voice.

'As I recall it went something like, do I get to fraternise with the crew Captain? To which you replied, no they're dirty and smelly, they live in the bilges or something like that.' Sliding off the bed she came and stood directly in front of him putting her arms around his neck and drawing him into a deep searching passionate kiss, saying as their lips met, 'but this was the best moment!' Softly she added. 'Make love to me Ferryman!'

They helped each other undress, their caresses becoming more urgent. Nita slid her hand between them sighing as she felt him becoming erect. She moved her hands to his hips and gently pulled him towards her, they collapsed onto the bed giggling. Gently he took hold of her hips then in one swift movement flipped her onto her tummy pulling her onto her knees, she squealed as he manhandled her. Kneeling behind her he caressed her buttocks sliding his hands up her sides to caress her breasts, teasing her nipples until they were hard. Her breathing changed, becoming harsh and rasping. Gathering her hair in his hands he pulled it back to lift her head and lying across her back said softly against her ear.

'Do you want this?'

So aroused now, she could hardly speak.

'Ohh god please Stephen… now!'

Guiding himself into her, she emitted one long low moan dropping her head onto the bed but he pulled gently again.

'Come up, come up now!' he commanded her.

Obediently she obeyed him but that simple act of changing her position sent her into one of her mini orgasms. Crying out in ecstasy she tried to drop her head again but he pulled her back.

'Tell me what you want… tell me Nita!'

'Oh shit… I want you, oh god finish it now, pleeease!'

That last word rose to a crescendo as she orgasmed again. He let go of her hair now and grasped her hips unable to hold himself back any longer.

Burying her head in the bedding, gripping the covers tightly making two fists she let go a full-blooded scream into the covers as she orgasmed once more

Dropping flat onto the bed under his weight they lay together locked in the tight embrace of a sated couple. Stroking his face a little later, she kissed him tenderly.

'If you ever thought why you met me when you did and having got to know me wondered why I wanted to be in your life? Just remember this last half an hour… pure magic, truly! I do love you Ferryman, so much!'

She rolled away from him disappearing into the shower room returning some minutes later. Together they sorted out their discarded clothes before pulling back the covers and settling for the night snuggled together. A little while later she said quietly.

'When you're home, the best part of the day is when we come to bed 'cause I get to snuggle up real close and I sleep soundly, you make me feel safe. When you're away I have to rely on my bear for comfort.' She giggled momentarily.

He chuckled and kissed her cheek, nibbling her ear.

'I'd forgotten how lovely it is to be this close to someone at bedtime. It makes me feel complete, you have a smell that's just you your skin, your hair. I close my eyes wherever I am and feel, no sense you beside me. I knew Suzanne's smell too but I wasn't away so much then, now I'm away too much. I want to come home to the UK.'

Finally, they drifted off into a peaceful slumber.

~~~~~~~~~~~~~~~~~~~~~~~~~~~~~~~~~~~~~~

They were up early in the morning, ate a good breakfast sharing a joke about last night's exertions. Shuffling out from the table and kissing her head Stephen left the galley to release the spring lines. Returning he started the engines while Nita stood ready to release the bow line then the stern line quickly jumping the gap between the wharf and the boat. As soon as *Finbar* was free the strong current took them away to the middle of the river. Stephen set the throttles giving them steerage way but let the current take them down-river. They passed through two manned commercial locks with no dramas.

'You handled that like you'd been doing it for years!' he said grinning at her.

She grinned back at him pleased with herself. During the mid-afternoon he asked her to take the helm as he wanted to check something; returning a few minutes later he said.

'We need to look for a left turn soon that'll take us up to York.'

Later, exiting another lock Nita suddenly giggled. Stephen glanced at her.

'What?'

'Look, there's a signpost,' she said pointing, 'that's so funny.' laughing again.

Following her gaze he saw a finger post on the riverbank that read York, he laughed now.

'You know I've been up and down this river so often and never noticed that before.'
~~~~~~~~~~~~~~~~~~~~~~~~~~~~~~~~~~~~~~

They both laughed as he brought the boat around into the cut increasing the revs giving them more steerage way against the current.

Nita chipped in, 'Observant then... hmm?'

The rest of the day they motored up towards York, the towers of the Minster clearly visible as a landmark long before they came into the outskirts of the city. It was late afternoon when they finally got moored up within the city itself. Weary from the days travelling they crashed into bed quite early and slept soundly.

~~~~~~~~~~~~~~~~~~~~~~~~~~~~~~~~~~~

Next morning they shopped for essentials to cater for everyone after their long journey then sat on the flying bridge watching the world pass by observing a true cross section of society wandering beside the river. Just after lunch Stephens's phone rang announcing the family's arrival in the city. He gave Richard directions where they were moored and forty minutes later the boat was alive with chatter and activity as everyone sorted out who was sleeping where and where their bags were going. Once everything was cleared away they sat around enjoying some light refreshments discussing the plans for the next three days. After an early dinner they decided it would be a good idea to go for a little exercise and explore some of the city's sights and night lights. Calling at a local pub near the river they had a few drinks before returning to *Finbar*. It wasn't long before all the berths were made up and everybody had turned in intending to be well rested for the following day.

Being moored near the city centre meant by the time the rest of the world had made the trip to York, found somewhere to park and set off to wander around the streets to see the sights, they were all sitting at a street cafe watching the ever growing crowds roaming around the quaint streets enjoying the spring day. Returning to the boat later in the afternoon it was decided that as it was so busy
~~~~~~~~~~~~~~~~~~~~~~~~~~~~~~~~~~~

they'd stay on the boat for the rest of the day. Just after eleven having consumed a Chinese take away they locked up and retired for the night.

Stirring from her deep sleep Nita hadn't realised that wondering around York looking at the Minster, Shambles, museums, could be so tiring. On top of that they'd all pigged out on that Chinese banquet. She and Stephen had sat up on the bridge until silly-o-clock drinking wine and talking about things. Sliding her hand behind her expecting to feel Stephen there she was surprised to find an empty space. For another five minutes she allowed herself to snuggle under the duvet enjoying the comfort and warmth, finally her inquisitiveness got the better of her. Slipping from under the covers she pulled on jogging trousers, a t-shirt and her hoodie then worming her feet into her trainers had a quick look in the mirror running a brush through her hair and pulling it back into a ponytail. Opening the door she slipped quietly past Richard and Mary asleep on the double galley berth then through the saloon, quietly padding past the sleeping Emma and Rachel.

Seeing Stephen wasn't in the sun deck area she climbed up the steps to the flying bridge. He was legged out on one of the long seats running around the bridge. Kneeling by his side she offered her face up to his for a kiss. Slipping an arm around her shoulders he drew her up to his level kissing her gently, but passionately, she sighed.

'Mmm... I do love waking up to you in the morning. You're just so gentle and cuddly I wish we could be like this every day. I miss you so much when you're away you know.'

He looked into her brown eyes for a moment, drew her into another embrace and kissed her again.

'I know, it's lovely I never thought I would ever feel like this again.

'Mmm I love you Stephen Leigh-Grace...lots.'

Standing, she stretched and glanced around where they were moored taking in some of the other boats tied up near them. The river was wide here and there were a good number of barges and cruisers all moored neatly on both sides of the river. This Easter, the weather had been kind and for most of the time they'd been here the sun had shone. All in all she thought it did feel very spring like. Tomorrow they would have to move further down river as they'd stayed the allowed 72 hours. Tapping his feet for him to move them she sat next to him and slid up towards his chest pulling his legs up across her thighs.

'Anyway, why are you up so early? It's only...' lifting his wrist and taking a quick glance at his watch. 'Just gone seven, what are you writing?'

He hesitated for a moment.

'See that boat across there.'

He nodded in the direction he wanted her to look.

'Which one?' she asked.

'The biggish one, that looks a bit like a fishing boat... there.'

Looking across the river again, she answered.

'Oh yes, that one. What about it?'

'I'm certain I've seen it before, in fact I've seen it a few times. It was in Rotterdam only two weeks ago and I've seen it in Calais and at Euro-port as well on other occasions.'

She looked at him quizzically.

'So, what are you saying? That it shouldn't be there? Could it not be a coincidence that it ends up in the same port as you do? Do you think they're smuggling stuff on it?'

She sounded a little sinister, almost mocking, but she was smiling as she said it. He knew she was teasing him, but her tone became serious as she added.

'Come on Stephen, if you think there's something wrong, odd even then you've got to be sure of your facts before you go throwing accusations around. If there was anything in it, surely HMC and E would be on to them. Look the same could be said of you, you visit all these channel ports supposedly en-route somewhere. How do we know, how do they know that you're legit and not running drugs or fags?'

'Listen,' he replied, 'when I've seen it before, there's always been a van delivering stuff to it and it always sails at night. It just slips away.'

She studied the boat for a while.

'There's something else too.' he began to say. 'A couple of months ago it was in Felixstowe. I was on my way back from that trip to Sweden and I saw it on the morning we docked. The odd thing was the same van I'd seen in the Euro-port in Holland was on our ferry as well.'

She glanced at him briefly, 'Really?'

He nodded. 'I'm not joking sugar, it just seems odd that's all I'm saying.'

Both of them sat in silence for some time watching the boat lost in their own thoughts. Sounds and movement from below eventually disturbed them, shortly followed by the wonderful aroma of cooking bacon.

'Mmm... Breakfast, come on let's go eat.' he said.

Over breakfast plans were made for their last day in York. So far they'd done the Minster, rail museum; even the girls had found bits of that interesting, particularly the Royal train display.

They'd enjoyed some excellent cuisine from a selection of different hostelries. Lazed around on *Finbar* in the evenings snacking on junk and some superb wines left over from the holiday in Northern France. So all that remained to do really was to walk the walls.

'If you don't mind I need half an hour to myself there's something I would like to do.' Nita interjected.

'Okay,' Stephen said, 'you go and do whatever and we'll meet up for lunch say one'ish outside M and S. How does that suit?

Within the hour the galley was cleared, all the sleeping stuff stowed and Stephen, Nita, Richard, Mary, Emma and her friend Rachel were standing by the side of *Finbar* on the wide pathway which ran for miles alongside the River Ouse. On nearby boats people were up and about too, getting on with their day. It was obvious some were due to leave during the morning by the ever-increasing mountain of rubbish bags stacked around a couple of overflowing skips near the water and sanitation building. There were joggers out and about and cyclist all using the pathways as a route into the centre of York. They set off towards the nearest access point that allowed them onto the battlements to start the walk around part of the city. They'd covered about a mile when Nita left them; kissing Stephen before she descended one of the stairways back to street level.

At one 'o'clock, foot sore and weary they met up with Nita. She had a number of shopping bags with her and seemed pleased with her purchases. Over lunch she listened as they talked about the history they'd learned from their tour of the battlements. She shared with them her shopping spree, periodically rummaging through one of her bags to give one of the assembled family a gift. A bracelet for Mary, a baseball hat for Richard, adorned with a captain's crest. For Rachel, a brightly coloured top featuring one of her favourite groups and for Emma a Victorian blouse and a pashmina. Finally Stephen, firstly some aftershave that she liked him wearing and knew he was out of, then a pair of cord chino jeans. They thanked her for their individual presents but Nita sensed reservation in their voices. Glancing around the table a little perplexed by their expressions, it was Stephen who asked the question for them all.

'What's all this for sugar, I mean, thank you but it wasn't necessary.'

Her explanation why she was playing the 'gift fairy' was.

'Since meeting you all for the first time this Christmas and being made so welcome, this is the first time we've all been together. Over the past three months whilst Stephen and I have been learning to live with each other, getting to know the others little foibles you know? this weekend has just been magical, I'm sure that Rachel would agree, yes?'

Rachel nodded. 'Definitely yes, thank you for asking me.'

Nita glanced at her briefly and continued.

'Stephen's told me how great the summer cruises are and if I get the chance I'd love to come with you. The main thing is you're a very close family, for obvious reasons and I feel very privileged that you've let me in.'

Stephen watched her while she explained her reasons. When she'd finished he took her hand then kissed her affectionately. Emma and Rachel both pulled faces, Emma saying.

'Dad, not here not in public, that's gross.'

They looked at her then at each other smiled and kissed again, Stephen enfolding her in an exaggerated hug.

'DAD!' Emma exclaimed in a horrified stage whisper at this public display of affection. Richard leant across the table tapping Emma's shoulder.

'We were all young once Em, even Nan and I kissed in public you know.'

He raised his eyebrows giving Emma a nod and a knowing look as he spoke.

Emma looked at him stunned. 'Granddad...!' she said.

Mary started to speak.

'Nita, for long enough we, Richard and I, hoped that Stephen would meet someone who would bring him out of his self-imposed isolation. Suzanne was a special daughter, together they were such a lovely couple, then with Emma a wonderful family. When she died he helped everyone move on with their lives, Emma, us and Harold, everyone except himself. If things got difficult for anyone he was there. However if things got awkward for him, he'd hide behind Suzanne's memory using it as a shield to avoid facing up to whatever it was. It has never been about finding someone to replace Suzanne that just wouldn't happen, it's about companionship, he needed that, he needs that. *Finbar* was a safe place for him like his cab, but they were poor substitutes.'

Reaching over the table taking Nita's hand in hers.

'I wouldn't wish the circumstances surrounding how you two met on anyone but out of the trauma and pain came some good, you! Since you two met you've made such a difference to him and a new Stephen has immerged the Stephen we knew a long time ago, Richard and I are happy for you both.'

Emma had gone quiet listening to her Nan. When she'd finished speaking she reached out for Mary's hand and squeezed it glancing at Stephen her eyes full of tears and said quietly.

'Nan's right dad, you did use mum and *Finbar* as a shield. I know you'd never set out to replace mum, I didn't know who Nita was only she was a detective who'd you'd met when you were attacked. I didn't know how or if we'd get on when we met. I know now from talking to her you'd thought up all sorts of stories about the attack and about you two but like Nita said and does now, be honest dad that's what you've always said to me. I love you more than anything and no I won't ever accept a substitute for mum but I understand that you need someone special in your life and I can't think of anyone better than Nita.'

Everyone around the table was focused on Emma, Mary smiled and squeezed her granddaughter's hand, Emma smiled back at her then finished off by saying.

'If you ever think of dumping her dad, you'd better have a bloody good reason 'cause I think she's special, just like Nan said.'

The mood around the table had become a little sombre and looking at everyone for a moment Nita said.

'Well it wasn't my intention to dampen our spirits, I just wanted to say thank you for a great weekend, well for everything really.'

Firmly and quite loudly Stephen picked up the pepper grinder from the table and using it as a microphone said.

'Okay folks, we've run out of time, so that's the end of this week's episode of family truths.

Tune in and join us again next week, when we learn who can't cook boiled eggs and toast for breakfast on another episode of family truths!'

Emma tried to swipe him across the table protesting.

'That was ages ago Dad...'

Laughing he dodged her swinging arm saying.

'Back to the boat then for cream cakes and special coffees.' He winked at Richard. 'I think I know where there is a particularly good bottle of Cognac.'

Richard insisted on settling the bill for lunch and they all trooped off back to the river through the narrow streets of the old part of York, stopping off on the way to buy a large box of assorted cream cakes from a patisserie. Returning to *Finbar* the aroma of freshly brewed coffee soon permeated throughout the boat. Moments later some glass coffee tumblers appeared on the saloon table suitably laced with cognac for the adults. Short work was made of consuming the box of cakes. The rest of the afternoon was spent relaxing. Richard and Mary retired to the main cabin for an afternoon nap after the route march around the city walls. Emma and Rachel watched a film, Stephen and Nita cuddled up together sitting on the sun deck enjoying the heat of a very warm sunny, spring afternoon.

'Thank you for the prezzies sugar, there was no need to do that you know.'

She looked at him thoughtfully for a moment.

'My shopping spree was a smoke screen actually. You got me thinking about our fellow sailors over there this morning,' she said nodding towards the brightly painted fishing boat, 'so I thought I'd make some enquiries from the waterway's guys. It seems they've come up from the coast but have developed some sort of engine problem which requires a special part that can only be supplied from somewhere in Holland or Germany. The van turned up with it yesterday and they should be off later today.'

Stephen nodded glancing across to the fishing boat on the other bank. The explanation was quite plausible, believable even but something still didn't ring true in his mind. Anyway, now wasn't the time to play amateur sleuth. Having eaten so well at lunch time after their 'do it yourself' guided tour of the walls and the old part of York using an old street map Richard had found. The rest of the day was spent around the boat just enjoying the mild spring weather and talking to other boat owners moored around them. Some people, tourists like themselves, stopped and chatted to Stephen and Richard from time to time asking about *Finbar* or about things to do with the rivers and canals. Nita even found herself drawn into a conversation with two women who wanted to know about cooking and how food was stored and kept on board.

Later Mary prepared Emma's favourite treat for tea, a bits and pieces platter. Cold meats, cheese chunks, carrot sticks, fruit and crisps, fresh baked bread and butter. They all sat in the saloon around the long table and picked at what they wanted. As the afternoon turned into evening the walkway by the side of the river fell quiet but on the bridge over the river the traffic was nose-to-tail as day trippers set off to their homes. Stephen and Richard shared the view that the only way into some cities and towns was by boat, it invariably avoided traffic jams and the associated stress that goes with queuing and finding somewhere to park!

After seven 'o'clock Nita noticed that the converted MFV had gone further upriver, turned and was headed down river in the direction the coast and Hull. Evening fell and the girls wandered off into the city to taste the night life. The others sat in the saloon talking the night away sharing a bottle of wine and some cheese and biscuits. They listened to Nita talk about her time with the New England police fascinated by some of her stories. By midnight everyone was back on board all tucked up for the night. Tomorrow after Mary, Richard and the girls would leave. Stephen and Nita would continue down to a marina between Goole and Hull where the boat would stay until he could begin the next stage of moving her all the way to Poole ready for the summer cruise.

Finbar was a hive of activity in the morning until eventually standing together on the walkway, they embraced, hugged and kissed saying their goodbyes. Stephen and Nita watched them walk away before turning to Nita.

'Stand to crew, prepare to slip the lines.'

She glanced at him shaking her head, 'Aye aye cap'n.' she tugged her fringe and as she turned away he heard her add, 'What are you like?'

He went to chase her but she ran off giggling at him.

Back on board he started the engines and looking over the bridge screen waved to her. She slipped the bow line, roughly coiled it and deftly threw it onto the bow, went to the stern and slipped that line stepping onto the gunnel and into the sun deck, calling to Stephen,

'All clear.'

She heard the engine pitch change as they pulled away from the paved side waving briefly to a woman and two young children who were waving frantically at them. Climbing the stairs she looked around where they'd been moored for the past three nights, beautiful she thought with the flowering cherry trees lining the bank some already in bloom. The whole scene was perfect just as the whole weekend had been. The passage down to the branch then into the estuary passed without any dramas, they worked through the locks like old hands. Late in the afternoon they moored up at the North shore marina, returning to Portbridge by taxi, train and bus arriving back at Stephens early evening.

~~~~~~~~~~~~~~~~~~~~~~~~~~~~~~~~~~~~~~~
~~~~~~~~~~~~~~~~~~~~~~~~~~~~~~~~~~~~~~~

INVOLVED AGAIN

First thing in the morning Stephen went to find where his car was parked after his friend had brought it back from the Graham's yard. He packed all his stuff for this next trip, locked the house up drove Nita into work then travelled to the transport yard. An hour later, having collected his paper work he left for Lincolnshire to load before travelling down to Felixstowe for the night ferry to Holland. This evening was one of the very few occasions that the two of them were unable to hook-up and speak to one another but he messaged her telling her all about his day. Twice through May he saw the brightly painted fishing boat, the first time in Rotterdam where there was the usual wild party in full swing, the second time was during a day-light passage between Calais and Dover. The rest of May and June seemed to fly by as they made plans with the family for the long summer holiday on *Finbar*. This year would be different as Nita would be joining them for the final two weeks. She was excited at the prospect of actually sailing at sea for the first time in her life, although a little worried she might get sea-sick.

At the end of June Stephen set off again for what he hoped would be the last run before the long summer break. The plan this year was to sail over to Northern France and explore some of the smaller ports until it was time to meet up with Nita on Jersey. Just as Stephen got on with the job in hand in Sweden and Denmark so Nita turned into her office to deal with the piles of 'work in process files' that were stacked up on the edge of her desk. She sometimes wondered if she would ever reduce it or even clear it. The one outstanding case making little or no progress was the murder of Patrick Doyle. They'd had something of a breakthrough when the Latvian woman

Katterine had dropped into their laps following her assault and the subsequent link they'd been able to establish between her and his death. Although the DI had escalated their information to other forces at the regular regional meetings they'd so far drawn a blank.

Nita decided to report Stephen's concerns about the number of sightings he'd told her about regarding the converted fishing boat, the fact that there always seemed to be a wild party just before it would sail that night; she added her own feelings about the circumstances too. When DI Allen asked her for her gut feeling she'd said it all seemed a bit odd. Having listened to her suspicions and considered the facts he told her later that on the strength of her own feelings he'd escalate it to Region and the HMC and see if anything came back. As she left his office he'd said to her.

'Nita it may well be nothing but anything that might help us break this case open has to be worth a punt because we've hit a wall so far.'

By the end of the day she'd forgotten about the mysterious boat. She'd actually managed to clear some community cases and left the office feeling quite pleased with herself.

Every day was pretty much the same for the two of them until things changed dramatically when he suffered a major breakdown and found he was unable to complete the run. Parking the trailer up at a container base for someone else to complete the deliveries, he waited three days for his unit to be repaired before picking up an empty curtain-sider and begin the run back home. Arriving Thursday night at the Euro Port for the night ferry to Felixstowe he waited to board. On his own this trip he found a quiet corner on the ferry, bagged a couchette, had something to eat and curled up for the night.

Disembarking before eight in the morning he was surprised to be channelled into one of the inspection bays. It happened now and again but with more countries joining the EU and with the removal of a lot of border controls, this seldom happened. However this being Felixstowe and one of the biggest and busiest UK ports, he supposed there were more spot checks. Stopping in the bay he was approached by two customs officers and two men in suits. The customs officers asked him for his passport and manifest, he explained he was empty and the circumstances regarding the breakdown, one of the customs officers handed his passport to the other two men who studied it for a while. One of them compared his passport picture against his face and after another brief exchange with his companion said to him.

'Morning driver could you come with us please.'

Worried that something was wrong he climbed down from his cab. One of the customs men said quietly to him.

'Don't worry drive there's nothing wrong, these two gents would just like to talk to you.' Trying to reassure him he added, 'Lock your cab, it'll be okay here.'

Stephen was really concerned, he'd never had this happen before. The little group walked towards the main office block, Stephen between the two men with the customs officers bringing up the rear. Entering the building they made their way up to the third floor where he was shown into an office suite. Two more men and a woman were waiting for him. He was invited to sit at a large table and offered a drink. Of the group sitting around the table an older man, who appeared senior, spoke.

'Mr Leigh-Grace, may I call you Stephen it makes everything easier and less formal or intimidating for you. My name is Mathew Hawks, I'm a principal officer with the Immigration Department. These other gentlemen are either Special branch, Interpol or customs, the young lady is here to take notes, are you all right with that?'

Stephen was struck dumb for a moment finding it difficult to comprehend what was happening. He looked around the room wondering if there'd been some mistaken identity mix up somewhere or he'd wandered into some reality spy documentary. Mathew Hawks watched him for a moment before continuing.

'We'd like to talk to you about a boat, to be exact a converted fishing boat named I believe, *Caspian Blue*. My information is that you've observed her,' he glanced at his notes momentarily then said, 'in your own words, acting strangely, yes?' Stephen nodded. 'You spoke about it to your girlfriend I believe, a detective constable Patel, yes?' Again he nodded. 'We, that is to say, a number of agencies here in the UK and Europe have become interested in this boats movements and are concerned that all is not what it seems. Are you following me?' Another nod from Stephen. 'Good, so can you tell us where and when you've seen this boat and if you can remember dates that would be helpful too and anything else you may feel could be connected with it? I believe you've also seen a van on occasions associated with the vessel, if you can give us any details about that vehicle that would be most helpful too.'

Over the next hour Stephen told the group all he could about the boat. The group quizzed him about the parties he'd observed, the people he'd seen, could he possibly describe them. And so it went on. Throughout the whole time the woman took notes of every question and answer. During a moment of silence Mathew Hawks looked around the table before saying.

'Gentlemen, I think we've detained Stephen long enough, any further delay might cause him to be asked some difficult questions, hmm?'

The group nodded, then addressing Stephen directly he said.

'This is most important Stephen; it's paramount at this stage of our enquiries that you say nothing to anyone, most importantly those closest to you. I cannot emphasize that strongly enough, no-one has to know anything, do you understand?'

Stephen nodded, 'Yes no-one, absolutely.'

'I'm sorry but that must include DC Patel also, we know she has certain security clearance, but this is at the highest level.' Stephen acknowledged him with nod. 'Finally, we would hope that you will continue to observe and report future sightings of the *Caspian Blue*. We are going to give you some contact details that will allow you to report any sightings to this team only, here in the UK, or through our Interpol colleagues if you are abroad. Now risk wise, if at any time you feel your position has been compromised, or your family is in danger, there will be a panic procedure that you can activate whereby all of your close family will be put under passive security. Do you understand and are you happy with this arrangement?'

Nodding Stephen said, 'Thank you, as you were asking me to continue reporting to you, it did cross my mind that if I got myself into a sticky situation how I would keep my daughter and DC Patel safe, along with the rest of my family.'

Standing at the door of the office suite Mathew Hawks offered him his hand.

'We'll see that you are all safe.' As the two men shook hands he ended saying, 'We are indebted to you for noticing this boat in the first place and the people involved and for bringing it to our, that is the authorities attention. If on further investigation we discover that this group of people are breaking British and International law, then you will have been instrumental in bringing them to account. Thank you again. Goodbye.'

Returning to his wagon he sat in the cab for some time thinking about what he'd just got himself into. Eventually exiting the port area he travelled home towards Portbridge.

Since their Easter weekend in York, each time Stephen was home he tried to move *Finbar* further round the coast towards her final mooring in the Poole. This year was taking much longer than expected because of the time both he and Nita wanted to spend together. He finally had to accept that with less than two months remaining before this year's cruise, the family would probably have to begin the holiday from Dover. For these two days while Nita continued to work on her remaining cases in Portbridge, he'd arranged for Richard to come and meet him. The aim was to get the boat south of the wash, he'd learnt that this part of coastline was notoriously difficult to navigate and was keen to cover a considerable distance to avoid having problems finding a suitable anchorage. With Richard on board they would be able to work watch-and-watch about and keep running south even through the night.

Thirty six hours later with his aim achieved. *Finbar* was safely moored in a small marina on the North Foreshore. They closed her down and went to find a pub where they shared lunch to celebrate their success. Bidding one another goodbye they caught trains back to their respective homes. Nita met him at Portbridge and they went on to the Duchess, had supper while he told her about the last thirty-six hours and how the passage had gone. They'd just finished their meal when Mick Holmes ambled in, bought a pint and seeing the two of them in the corner came and joined them. They caught up with each other's news and were surprised when he told them that the coaling business run from the wharf was likely end in the next six months as part of a cost cutting review. The owners of the former NCB site needed to make savings and the likelihood was that when Stephen brought the boat back up the river in autumn, the wharf wouldn't be there anymore.

'Thirty-two years there 'Man and boy!' as he put it.

It was a subdued trio that stood on the steps of the pub saying goodnight and promising to stay in touch.

'That's hard to face after thirty odd years,' Nita said as she drove them back home, 'What do you do, I mean he's in his late forties that's all he's known since leaving school. It's going to be so hard.'

'He'll get redundancy though, they might even offer him another job in the company.'

Stephen said.

'Mmmm, I think the owners will take the opportunity to prune any long service staff, which means Mick, so sad, so sad.'

Later, tucked up in bed, Nita resting her head on his chest, she said.

'What time you off tomorrow?'

'Mmm I'd like to be away by mid-day for the night ferry. I think I'm shipping out of Felixstowe so it's quite a run down there.'

'How long this time?'

'Three weeks I think.'

'Going to miss you!!' She said moulding herself against his body saying sleepily, 'And then holidays… can't wait. I'm really excited you know.'

He tightened his arm around her shoulder momentarily.

'Night night sugar.'

'Mmmm… you too,' came a drowsy reply.

She woke to an empty bed with sounds from the kitchen as Stephen put the usual collection of supplies together for his trip. Dressed and ready for work she made her way to the kitchen where they had breakfast together before she gathered her stuff to leave for work. Standing in the short hallway they hugged, kissed saying their goodbyes, Nita telling him quite forcefully to stay well clear of any trouble. To drive the point home she held his face in her hands repeating herself.

'Yes… okay, yes I promise, alright!' he replied.

'Good, I love you just as you are, in one piece okay!'

Given the number of times he'd criss-crossed the North Sea or the Channel over the past eight years, it was inevitable he would get the occasional bad crossing. Seasickness seldom affected him on the big ferries or even on *Finbar*. This crossing though was one of those exceptions. Lying on his couchette feeling like death he surveyed the other drivers and passengers around him. Hardly anyone was able to move, laid low by 'mal-de-mer,' unable to carry out even simple tasks like walking about!

Once ashore in Holland standing beside his unit on 'terra-firma,' he inhaled lungs full of fresh air to clear his senses of the terrible smell that goes with the condition. Being delayed by the night crossing and the time it had taken for his body and balance to recover, he failed to make his first delivery. Parked up at the factory ready for the first available bay in the morning he Skyped Nita telling her his story of the crossing and how he'd suffered. She listened to his tale of woe sympathetically saying how sorry she was before relating what she'd done through the day. After saying goodnight to Nita, he was settling for the night only for Emma to call him. She'd been given a week's study leave to complete course work ready for assessment prior to her 'A' level exams. While she could stay at Mary and Richard's, she wanted to come home and work there feeling there would be less distractions in Portbridge from her friends encouraging her to 'bunk off' for a night out, also she could see Nita.

'Sweetheart, your timing's way off I'll still be in Germany, I'll' be back that weekend though if that helps, we can all get together then.'

'Please Dad! Can I still come, ask Nita she can keep an eye on me? I'll be at home the whole time, I'm going to be working and I'm okay in the house on my own. I can make stuff to eat so I'll be alright, please dad?'

She was putting him under pressure asking him this now. Thinking how to refuse her request without upsetting her too much he replied trying to buy himself some time.

'Let me have a word with Nita love, let's see if we can work something out is that okay?'

He heard the disappointment in her voice that he hadn't said yes immediately.

She replied. 'Suppose... but I won't be a nuisance dad honestly.'

'Emma, I'll speak to Nita and we'll see okay, I promise. Now is everything else okay, how are you doing are you ready. When do the mocks start?'

'Yeah, my teachers reckon I'm on track, I just want to get them done it seems to have taken forever to get to this point. I have my two projects to complete but I can do those after the mains, Dad ask Nita please!'

'I will love, sorry but I'll have to go work stuff! Love you Em never forget that! Seven weeks and we're off to France... can't wait. Bye sweetheart.'

'Yeah me too, Rachel is so excited. Be safe dad, I love you loads, Bye.'

There was a click and then a dial tone. Replacing the phone on its rest he sat back contemplating the conversation he'd just had. Making a coffee and lacing it with whisky to settle his stomach which still felt delicate he climbed back into his bunk.

Six thirty in the morning and he was being unloaded in the factory yard which was unusual and very awkward. It took two frustrating hours to complete the task as the fork-lift driver kept being called away to other jobs. Finally parked in a lay-by on the approach to the autobahn he called the office asking to re-schedule the next two days work. It took thirty minutes before they came back to him with a revised schedule. For the rest of the day he tramped north up towards Denmark and having crossed the border parked up at the next halt for the night. Skyping Nita, she asked how he was and had he recovered.

'Yeah, much better today. You forget how long it takes to get over something like that.'

Later in the conversation he talked to her about what Emma was wanting to do. She thought briefly then said.

'I don't mind going over to yours for the week, I'll have to work some of it but I'm sure Emma will be okay on those days, plus I can spend a bit of 'us' time with her and get to know her better. Yeah, I'd quite like that actually.'

'Okay if you're sure you don't mind, I'm alright with that if you are.'

Before they ended the days contact Nita asked him where he was and his expected time to run back home.

'I'm just into Denmark tonight, tomorrow reload about a hundred K's further north and then into Sweden Wednesday. I've got a week or so there and then begin the home run ending up in Rotterdam at Euro port to reload for the Thursday night ferry back to Felixstowe, Friday tip near Ipswich and then home Friday night; that's always assuming there are no hold ups! So another fifteen days I think.'

'Okay, so am I booking that Saturday morning off then?'

'Fine, I'm sure we can find things to do, don't you?'

Nita giggled, 'Oh I'm sure we can find things to do Ferryman, be safe love you.'

'You too sugar, night night bed bugs and all that. Bye.'

Alone again in his cab, Nita at the shared house with the girls, they readied themselves for bed, once settled they slept soundly until their alarms woke them to face a new day. Stephen at six, Nita at seven thirty. As she rolled out of her bed, he was already backed onto a factory loading-bay being vigorously shaken about every now and again when the electric rider truck ran on and off his trailer unloading him. Two hours behind him Nita logged on at her office around nine, by this time Stephen was back on the autobahns heading to his next destination. Today, as every day when he was away, their respective timetables seemed to chase each other's playing catch-up all the time, until with Nita at home and Stephen parked at a truck-stop they could speak to one another again. Before he spoke to Nita he called Emma's school, eventually she came to the phone and he told her that, yes she could come up for the weeks study leave.

Twelve days after explaining his timetable to Nita, he arrived at the ferry terminal with more than two hours to spare to clear his documentation then join the waiting queue of trucks. He wandered around the parking area to stretch his legs, exchanging the odd comment with other drivers. He stood beside some railings at the edge of the dock looking at the different boats moored there comparing how yacht and cruiser designs were changing. He often found himself comparing new designs against *Finbar,* usually ending up deciding that she was still a prettier looking boat than these new, often radically designed craft. A slight commotion on the dockside brought his attention to the boats moored nearer. Looking down he was surprised to see the converted fishing boat tied up against the dock side, its name, *Caspian Blue* clearly visible across its stern. A cold shiver ran down his spine, this was the first time he'd actually seen the boat so close. He reached for his phone intending to take a couple of pictures of the boat to send to the investigation team. Then the thought came to him that would be too obvious, so he videoed the dock basin showing all the boats including *Caspian Blue.*

He was suddenly aware that someone had come to stand beside him, glancing towards them, he saw a smartly dressed man he guessed in his late twenties, a head taller than himself, broad shoulders and a strong square jaw, definitely very fit and he guessed well able to take care of himself, not someone you'd want to get on the wrong side of. He nodded at him, the man studied Stephen momentarily, then said.

'You take picture of boat?' He pointed to the fishing boat, his accent was definitely eastern European, his English enunciation very Russian sounding.

Stephen nodded, 'Yeah, I have a boat at home and I like to take videos of boats I see in other places, why do you ask?'

He was struggling to appear casual and calm. Setting his phone on replay he showed the man the video clip he'd just taken, ending with the camera sweeping along this dock side showing the *Caspian Blue* for the last fifteen seconds.

'Quite good I think, there are lot of boats here don't you think?'

'Da...yes but please you take no more film here, okay!'

Stephen shrugged, 'Sure, not a problem,' stuffing his phone back into his trouser pocket he nodded to the man then turned and walked slowly back to his truck, aware that standing some distance away was another guy also suited and booted watching him as he went back to his unit. Climbing back into his cab he sat for some time breathing heavily trying to calm himself, feeling he'd just had a close call. Then the questions started in his head, why should I feel like this, after all I'm just a driver looking at some boats. Those guys hadn't a clue who he was, he'd never seen them up close before they weren't to know that he was in fact reporting sightings of their boat. Calming down he began to realise that all his fears were in his head, he smiled thinking.

'I'm not wearing a sign that says hey I'm watching your boat.'

At the same time though he was still learning to adjust to this alter-ego person, the informant for the police, HMC and the immigration people. Over the past ten weeks he'd only seen the fishing boat three or four times and as requested he'd fed the information to the investigation team. Up until now he'd always observed the boat from some distance, across two or three wharves or moored in some inner harbour. Reaching for his laptop he logged on to his contact at the Interpol centre, reported the boat forwarding the video clip, then Skyped Nita for twenty minutes. By the time they signed off for the night, he felt happier in himself and quite at ease. An hour later boarded on the ferry and talking to three other English drivers he'd forgotten the experience. Of the fishing boat, had he bothered to look she'd also gone, spirited away in the night once again.

~~~~~~~~~~~~~~~~~~~~~~~~~~~~~~~~~~

Having made his delivery just outside Ipswich, he continued up to the depot at Portbridge arriving back mid-afternoon. Handing all the paperwork from this trip to the transport team and checking his pigeonhole for messages he finally signed off for four full days. Just after six Nita crashed through the front door, dropped bags and coat, kicked off her shoes and made her way towards him finally enveloping him in a bear like embrace smothering him in kisses.

'Missed you… missed you… missed you!' she said between each kiss.

'Hey! Put me down woman, you don't know where I've been.'

'Don't care, you're here now and I've missed you!

Wrapping her in his arms in an effort to end this onslaught, he returned her kisses as she tried to struggle free.

'I've missed you too sugar.'

Calm now he released her and stepped back to look at her, she squirmed under his gaze feeling embarrassed, 'What?' she said.

'I try to keep this image of you in my head when I'm away. You've just walked through the door and your scent is just so lovely, I wanted to add that smell to the image in my head. Sorry if that sounds a bit odd!'

She came back to hold him again, 'I think that's lovely, thank you.'

Sniffing the air she looked round the kitchen, went to the oven
~~~~~~~~~~~~~~~~~~~~~~~~~~~~~~~~~~

and opened it a blast of hot air hit her face making her step back, closing the door she turned to him.

'Lasagne nice, I'm hungry now so let's eat and talk later.'

'Fine by me, I'll get the plates, you lay up.'

After dinner they sat in the small lounge, the TV was on and they half watched it and talked.

'You said last night that you thought you might have to work tomorrow?'

Nita nodded, 'Yep sorry, something's come up that's connected to an important case I've been working on with Alan. It's the first real break we've had so the DI wants us in, sorry.'

'No not a problem, remember Emma's here tomorrow for the week, are you still okay with that.'

Nodding, she replied.

'Sure, like I said I can get to know her better without you around.'

Later, all warm and snuggled together. Stephen said quietly.

'This is so what I miss, my bunk was always welcoming but here now with you is just so much nicer. This is why I'm nattering to come home.'

She smiled, kissed his chest and gently hugged him.

~~~~~~

She was off to work early, hoping to get all her case work finished in time to meet Emma with Stephen. Alan turned up a little later as did DI Allen.

'Morning team.' he said as he came in.

'Morning sir.' They both replied surprised to see him in the office.

'Sort some drinks out and bring them into my office, mines coffee please.' he said.

The three of them eventually settled round the DI's desk.

Opening a file he shuffled the papers around for a moment then glancing at them said.
~~~~~~

'Right, reference your Patrick Doyle case and this mystery woman Katterine. The Regional Crime Team have come back to us. There have been two developments, firstly, they've found the club that our lady told us about in Hull and are interested enough to put a silent operation in place. Their intention is to work with immigration as they feel something is off here which involves people, girls that is. Secondly and connected to the same place, Humberside traffic recently pulled a van just off the M62, heading towards Hull. The vehicle check came back as registered to guess where?' he looked at them both briefly, 'Yep the club! From our point of view it fits perfectly to the one this Katterine of yours described. The other interesting thing was it had some engine parts in it and some boxes of wine and spirits. Some switched on bright spark officer appears to have paid attention at the briefings and let it carry on. Now as I recall Nita when you told me about the boat In York, you mentioned it had kind of engine problem?'

She nodded, 'Yes sir, it needed special parts that were only available from Eastern Europe, something to do with where it was built and fitted out.'

'Okay, sensibly again, someone has had the foresight to download some pictures of said van from the camera in the traffic car.'

Handing her some prints he added.

'Go and show them to this Katterine and see if she recognises the van. Alan see if the regional team have anything else on the club.'

He wrote something down on his jotter handing it to him. As he studied the note the DI continued.

'Sergeant Mason, he's the officer co-ordinating the operation, speak to him see what you can glean about the club and see if there's anything that might help us get a clearer picture of our Mr Doyle. Right I'm off, do what you need to do but don't burn the night oil, it's the weekend okay?'

He stood up, pulled his jacket from the back of his chair and followed Nita and Alan out into the general office. 'See you two Monday for briefings, bye!' and walked out of the door.

The two spent the rest of the morning collating and cross-referencing this new information adding it to what they already had in connection with Patrick's death. Just as they were tidying their desks Nita's phone pinged in her bag, taking a quick look at it she smiled. Alan glanced at her.

'That will be his lordship asking where his lunch is.'

Nita giggled, 'No he's just picked Emma up from Leeds she's coming to stay for the week to study.'

'He's home is he?'

'Mmm, until Tuesday and then I'm in charge!'

'Ho ho… oh I'd love to be a fly-on-the-wall with you two, I reckon that could be very interesting.'

'Could be, I'm hoping just being the two of us I can get to know this young lady better. She's been on her own with Stephen since mum passed so there's only ever been the two of them for eight years. My guess is she's going to be super protective of her dad.'

'Where does she live when he's away then, school?'

'I wondered at first, but no, she lives with her Grand-parents in Poole.'

'Poole… as in Dorset, Poole?'

'Yep.'

'Bloody hell Nita, that's the other end of the country, isn't there anybody nearer?'

She smiled, 'There's his dad but he couldn't cope, anyway he's in a management home now. Harold, he's lovely but he couldn't manage a hormone fuelled teenage granddaughter.'

Studying her for a moment Alan said, 'So what's the plan then?'

'She's here on study leave so that's the day filled. The rest of the time we'll see how it pans out but we'll do alright I think, girlie talk, clothes shopping, pictures, normal stuff. Maybe a night out with your sister and Moira?' Nita shrugged.

Alan gave a choked guffaw, 'Yeah right, I'll ask you again next week.'

Nita gave him a look and finished tidying her desk and files. The two of them walked out and down the stairs to the car park. 'Monday then?' Alan said getting into his car.

Nita nodded, 'Monday, enjoy the rest of the weekend.'

Sitting in her car she checked her messages, sending one to Stephen letting him know she was on her way home. She waved to Alan as he drove past her, moments later following him.

Stephen and Emma were carrying bags into the house when she pulled into the street. As she walked into the house Emma was coming down the stairs, they stood looking at one another. Nita smiled at her.

'Hello, you're here then, good journey?'

Emma replied hesitantly.

'Err yes okay, it just seemed to take for ever though.'

Stephen came down the stairs behind Emma.

'Come on move yourself or are you just going to look at each other sizing one another up?'

Emma came down the last few steps to stand next to Nita.

'You know something,' Nita began to say, 'I think you've grown since Easter.'

Emma grinned.

'That's what dad said at the station.' Turning to look at him she added, 'I am growing out of some of my clothes to be sure,' then glancing quickly at Nita added, 'Can we go shopping before I go back?'

Nita looked at Stephen saying.

'Can't see why not. Just depends if the bank of dad will finance it.'

She smiled at him, raising an eyebrow waiting for a response. Emitting a long sigh and shaking his head slightly, he said.

'I just knew this was a bad idea and would end up costing me!'

Emma smirked trying not to laugh and put her arm through his.

'Thank you daddy, I only need a few bits,' glancing at Nita again, she added. 'I'm sure Nita will see that I don't spend too much.'

Looking directly at his daughter he couldn't help smiling at the 'angelic' face looking back at him. 'Mmmm.' was all he could say. Emma put her arms around him hugging him.

'Oh I do love you dad!'

The remainder of Saturday was spent quietly while Emma sorted her room out. They decided on a fish supper for dinner. Tomorrow they'd go to York to see Harold and take him out to a carvery for a Sunday roast.

Harolds face lit up when he opened the door to see the three of them standing there. After a while Harold spirited Emma away to the day room to show her off to the other residents, something he took the opportunity to do whenever she went to see him. In his absence Nita helped Stephen change his dads' bed, run a wash programme, then while he straightened round the apartment, Nita sorted through the old mans' fridge discarding a few things that were beyond their use-by date. A good hour passed before the pair returned and almost as soon as they'd walked through the door Harold stood in the centre of his small lounge, hands on hips.

'You've been at it again haven't you,' he said, 'tidying round? I know you know, suppose I'll not be able to find owt I want now.'

Emma giggled putting her arm through his and kissing his cheek, Nita linked the other arm.

'Sorry Harold,' she said, 'I've been through your fridge too and chucked some out of date stuff away.'

He glanced at her, shook his head and tutted then looking at Stephen grinned broadly,

'Aye lad, look at me, a girl on each arm! Can't remember last time this happened, maybe end o' war 'appen.'

They all had a laugh as the old man turned, still linked to the girls and walked towards his front door calling back over his shoulder.

'Be a gent son and get us mi coat, I've got mi 'ands full here.'

Picking up everyone's coats and jackets Stephen followed them out of the house to the car park. He heard Harold say to Nita as they approached the car.

'By 'eck our lass'd've give me hell if she could see me now.'

Stephen called to the three of them.

'You'd better believe it dad, she always said you were a massive flirt!'

They drove the few miles to a pub that served a Sunday roast carvery. Harold attacked his Sunday dinner with relish. They were all a little surprised at how much food he put away. It looked like he'd not had a good meal for ages. Much later in the afternoon, after visiting a garden centre, they returned home. Seeing Harold into his house they said their farewells. Harold slipped a five-pound note into Emma's hand as he hugged her goodbye. She tried to give it back to him but he just folded her fingers around the note, took her in his arms and kissed her again. Emma glanced at Stephen and saw him shrug slightly, putting her arms round her grandpa once more she hugged him tightly.

'Thank you grandpa.'

Smiling he gently pushed her away and winked. He watched them walked back to the car park and waved them off.

~~~~~~

Everyone was down for breakfast in good time to sort out the day's plan, Nita left for work just for today before taking half days off to spend time with Emma. Stephen set off to his depot for a meeting with his boss while Emma brought a stack of books downstairs into the lounge to work on. Walking into the depot office at nine thirty, he acknowledged the welcome from the two secretaries and the transport team. The only time he ever really got to talk to any of them was at the Christmas party or on guest days the company held occasionally. The office manager came to the desk,

'Morning Stephen nice morning, everything alright with you?'

'Fine thanks Chris, what's this about do you know?'

Chris, Christine shook her head and shrugged.

'How would I know, I'm just the manager... I know nothing!'

Stephen gave her a look, 'Yeah right... as if!'

The office manager and traffic supervisor, Chris had been at the
~~~~~~

depot since the business began almost twenty years ago. She'd been married to one of the first drivers, until he'd died from a heart attack, they had two children and until he'd passed away she'd worked part time. In her fifties, petite, stick thin from living on her nerves while trying to keep the boss in line and everyone else; customer's drivers and office staff alike all singing from the same songbook. She was considered by everyone to be the font of all knowledge when it came to matters transport related. All the drivers were of the opinion the business would fold without Chris. She was always nicely turned out with short jet-black hair cut into a bob that suited her face. Her make-up skilfully applied giving her a youthful appearance that belied her fifty plus years. From another room they heard a man call.

'Chris, let me know when yer man gets here and can I have a tea please!'

Glancing at Stephen she grinned and was about to answer when Stephen interjected.

'He's here, been here for ages… waiting as usual!'

'Cheeky git!' came the response, 'get yer backside in here.'

Chris raised an eyebrow, 'Do you want tea as well?'

Stephen nodded, walking through the desks to the other office. As he went into the boss's office, he said.

'Shut the door. You're making a draft.'

As the door closed Chris said to a young man at the back of the room.

'Take two teas in will you, the boss you know, Stephen's is with milk no sugar.'

The lad got up from his desk and duly delivered the drinks.

Emerging after three-quarters of an hour he walked back across the office, stopping briefly responding to a shout from the boss, 'Door!' He stopped, grinning turned and closed the door.

Chris looked at him, 'Well… important?'

'Might be later, after the hols, we'll see.'

Giving him an odd look she continued.

'Mmm, we'll see. Right you're off again Tuesday, Yes?'

He nodded as she studied the scheduling board.

'Just the Low Countries this time ending with a drop in Northern France then back from Calais. Fifteen days, give or take that alright?'

'Yes, I suppose, but if you've anything after that it's got to be short 'cause I'm away with the family remember.'

Smiling she replied, 'As if you'd let me forget. Err is your lady accompanying you?'

'The last two weeks,' he said grinning. 'Right I'm off, see you tomorrow, you will you have all the paperwork done won't you?'

He ducked instinctively as a screwed-up piece of paper flew over his head then keeping low slipped out of the main door calling.

'Bye darling see you anon!'

Walking into the house an hour later he was taken aback to see almost every flat surface strewn with an array of books and seated at the kitchen bar like a librarian Emma, hair roughly caught up and a pencil sticking out of it totally engrossed in some great tomb. Looking up from the book she smiled.

'Hi dad, okay?'

'Err yes love,' he replied looking around the kitchen and lounge. 'Emma, is all this necessary?' He swept his arm round in an arc encompassing the room. She looked round both rooms.

'There's so many relevant bits in various books dad I've got to put them somewhere, that's why I wanted to come here for the week because I can spread out. There's not enough space in my bedroom at nans, sorry.'

Glancing at both rooms again he said.

'Okay but tidy up every day when you've finished love, it's not fair on Nita to live in all this, I mean there's nowhere to sit even!'

'Okay yeah I'll clear up, promise.'

'Right lunch, what do you fancy?'

She looked at him, thoughtfully then said.

'One of your floppy fish finger sandwiches… with ketchup,' pausing mid-sentence she added thoughtfully, 'you'd make those when we were struggling after mum remember, god I loved them they were like soul food.'

'Okay, floppy fish finger sandwiches it is.'

By the time he'd made them, Emma had cleared the breakfast bar. Sitting at the bar he watched her tuck into the sandwiches making small noises as she ate them.

'Alright for you?'

'Mmmm awesome, I'd forgotten how good they are, thank you dad.'

'My pleasure love.'

In the evening they took Emma to the Duchess, somewhere she'd never been. Over dinner Stephen and Nita gave Emma a potted history of their first date here and how their relationship had grown right up to Christmas when met Nita for the first time.

In the morning Stephen said goodbye to Nita watching her drive off to work. Returning to the kitchen as a blurry eyed Emma came down, he passed her a note from Nita with her contact details. Just before he left the house he went through a list of 'do's and 'don'ts emphasizing the importance that she looked after the house and behaved herself; not winding Nita up. She crossed her heart promising she'd be an 'angel' for the rest of the week. It felt very odd as he packed all his gear into his car knowing he wouldn't be locking the house but leaving it for the two most important women in his life to look after. Before he said goodbye to Emma, he stood on the street looking at the house. Smiling to himself he wondered if this was going to be a new beginning for them all. Emma stood at the front door looking at her dad.

'Bye sweetheart, I love the socks off you, I don't need to say...'

'No dad you don't, it'll still be here when you get back, so will Nita and me... okay!'

'Yeah, have a great week, hope the study goes okay. Take care Em, I love you!'

'You too dad, you be safe, okay!'

He turned and walked towards his car glancing back at her and gave her a wave. Parking his car at the depot he transferred all the gear he'd brought for the trip, collected his paperwork and left Portbridge forty minutes later running tractor only to Boston in Lincolnshire collecting a loaded trailer there he drove to Hull for the night ferry to Holland. That evening he had a brief conversation with Nita and Emma whilst waiting to run onto the ferry.

~~~~~~~~~~~~~~~~~~~~~~~~~~~~~~~~~~~~

While Stephen began to criss-cross northern Germany through the first week running back through Holland and down to Strasbourg before eventually turning for home via Calais; Emma spent each day studying until Nita returned home around lunch time. They spent time talking about their lives, aims and ambitions. The second night Nita took Emma over to the house she shared with Louise and Moira and had an entertaining evening talking and laughing, hysterically at times, as they shared stories about work, holidays and even relationships. Emma listened intently, surprised how candid they were as they spoke about past relationships. In the end it was decided that they would stay over for the night. In no time two bottles of wine were opened and a take-away ordered. Nita kept an eye on what Emma drank for the rest of the evening. Finally retiring for the night she shared Nita's bed; not ideal for Nita as Em shuffled around all through the night. In the morning she phoned the office asking to take the whole day off. Saying bye to Louise and Moira the two of them went off to Leeds shopping. Returning to Portbridge during the afternoon laden with bags. Nita took them to a café in West Fording just outside town called 'CU at 2', finding a small table they sat down.

'They do the best hot chocolate with marshmallows you will ever taste!' Nita said ordering one for Emma and a cafetiere of coffee for herself.

'This is the nearest blend I can get to the coffee I drank in the States, that's one thing I really do miss, the coffee.'

'Could you have stayed if you'd wanted?' Emma asked.
~~~~~~~~~~~~~~~~~~~~~~~~~~~~~~~~~~~~

'Not really, it would have meant lots of paperwork, permits and so on, citizenship even, and I wasn't sure then whether I wanted to stay. Mind you some of the stuff I worked on was really good. There was always lots of action over there, they certainly don't do things by halves!'

'Did you come back and just start here then?'

'Pretty well, I was upset at leaving the guy I told you about last night and I wasn't sure the police force was for me you know. My family are around here so I spent a bit of time with them that said I'd really pee'd them off by going to the States in the first place, so they weren't very forgiving. My dad said I was too head strong... a rebel!'

She smiled, half to herself reflecting back to the three months she'd just swanned around.

'I kind of went walk about for a while, caught up on old friends you know,'

Emma nodded.

'They were nearly all married with kids or busy with their own careers and jobs. I got bored in the end saw they were recruiting for officers, applied and was sent forward for CID. They said it was because of my time and experience in the States and, well here I am now.'

'Yeah, funny isn't it, kind of fate you could say otherwise you wouldn't have met dad.'

'Mmm yes... bit of a surprise really!'

'Yeah but I'm glad though, you've changed him so much, he's like the old dad ten years ago. Even Nan and Granddad have said as much, like the Stephen they knew when mum was alive.'

Nita watched her for a moment then reached for her hand.

'You're so grown up Em, when you talk about your mum you're so mature about how you faced such a loss. You're a credit to dad and nan and granddad you really are.'

Emma grinned and shuffling on her seat a little embarrassed.

'Grandpa Harold was the best, he just had a way of saying how it was without making it sad, you know? I mean everyone was fussing over me, but Grandpa Harold was ace. He just wrapped me in his arms and told me how much mum loved me. I always try to see him when I'm home, his hugs are still the best!' she smiled and shrugged. Nita listened to her, smiling.

All the time the two of them had been talking she hadn't really taken any notice of the comings and goings in the café, it was always busy so was quite shocked when a woman suddenly came to their table and sat down. They both looked at her, Nita looked round the room and then back at the woman.

'Can I help you?'

Leaning forward closer the woman said.

'I know you are involved with a friend of mine. She has run away from where she works and come here, I am worried for her I think something has happened.'

Alarm bells started to sound in Nita's mind, who was this woman. From her accent she was Polish or from some other eastern bloc country. How did she know Nita? With Emma here, her first concern was her safety, thinking quickly she looked at the woman.

'I'm sorry, I don't know who you are, and I haven't a clue what you're talking about, sorry.'

'My name's Olga I know Katterine, she is a friend. We come to UK together and work, now she has disappeared! A friend Patrick was going to meet us but he has gone too.'

Nita really began to panic now, wanting to get Emma away.

'I sorry but right now I can't help you.'

Reaching for her bag she took a small card case out and taking a card she passed it to her,

'There's my direct line, call me tomorrow and I'll try to help you, but right now we are leaving, okay'

She hoped the firmness of that statement would make this stranger leave. However the women persisted reaching out and holding Nita's arm.

'Please, I need your help now, if they find us we are in so much danger you have to help.'

Emma stood up saying to Nita,

'Just off to the loo, okay!'

Nita nodded and turned her attention back to the woman.

'Listen, if you are in so much danger then go to the nearest police station and ask to see a detective and explain, alright!'

The woman began to protest again but Nita stopped her.

'No! You're not listening... right now I cannot help you. You have my number speak to me tomorrow.'

A commotion at the back of the café distracted Nita, turning she saw Emma being confronted by a rough looking man. Instantly she was up on her feet and across the café.

'YOU stand away from that woman NOW!' she commanded the man.

He looked at her, held his hands up and took a step back.

'Sorry, sorry I just say hello, please I meant no problem.'

The woman, Olga, called across the café to him in what Nita thought was perhaps Polish, the man nodded apologising again. Nita walked back to their table with Emma where the woman said.

'I'm sorry, he was only being friendly, sorry.'

'Finish your drink Em we're leaving now.'

They both drained their mugs and turned to leave. Olga held Nita's arm again then released it when she saw the look on her face, again Nita said firmly.

'Tomorrow I told you, call that number.'

The two of them walked out of the cafe to where she'd parked the car.

'Em I'm so sorry that was very awkward. Getting you involved in my work stuff is not a good idea.'

Emma giggled, 'No, but it was exciting in a way, that Olga was really upset about her friend. Will you be able to help her?'

Nita shrugged, 'We'll see tomorrow.' Changing the subject she continued, 'So what are we doing for dinner tonight?'

They continued to the end of the terrace of shops turning down the side street towards Nita's car. Emma suddenly stumbled grabbing hold of Nita to steady herself.

'Big feet!' Emma laughed.

A few minutes later they were standing by Nita's car, Emma leant against the wing of her car.

'I feel really funny, lightheaded and a bit dizzy, like when you feel you might fa....'

She slumped down the wing a little, Nita made a grab for her.

'Em... Emma what's the matter love?'

Nita could clearly see that she was having trouble focusing.

'I feel really very strange, I think I'm going to be sick.'

Trying to hold her upright she struggled to open the passenger door of the car. Two young guys who were walking past them stopped, one of them said.

'You alright love, do you need some help?'

Nita glanced at them, 'Oh please my friend doesn't feel well.'

Taking hold of Emma's arm one of the men held her up while Nita opened the door wide.

'She needs to take more water with it in future.' the guy said.

Nita gave a little laugh and taking Emma's other arm started to help her into the front passenger seat. As she stood up she staggered a little, the other man reached to hold her steady as his friend said.

'You don't look too clever either love, are you going to be okay to drive?'

Nita tried to reply but her mouth didn't work and she definitely felt odd only she couldn't explain, then she couldn't remember.

~~~~~~~~~~~~~~~~~~~~~~~~~~~~~~~~~~~~~
~~~~~~~~~~~~~~~~~~~~~~~~~~~~~~~~~~~~~

WARNED OFF

At the end of a very long and tiring day Stephen eventually pulled into the truck stop at the side of the autobahn, checking in at the security cabin he paid the fee then drove into the park to find a space among the other trucks parked up for the night. Too tired to make anything for his dinner he grabbed some snacks from his supplies, made a drink and climbed onto his bunk.

Bang bang! on the cab door… It seemed as though he'd just fallen asleep when the loud banging on his cab door woke him.

'Driver… achtung driver raus, bitte schon, kompt!'

Collecting his thoughts he replied, 'Yeah, okay give me a minute.'

Looking at the clock on the bulkhead he saw it was 02-30. Slipping into his trousers and pulling a T-shirt on and his hi-vis jacket he opened the cab door to see someone standing by his truck shining a torch in his face.

The man repeated himself in a mixture of German and English.

'Bitte kompt your doors are…are urfnet… open,' he hesitated searching for the right word, 'raus raus hurry!'

Looking down the length of his trailer he could see one of his trailer doors was swinging open, alarmed he said to the man.

'Okay, let me put my boots on.'

Quickly he slipped his feet into his boots tied them and climbed down to the ground anxious to see if his load had been pilfered. The security guy had already walked towards the rear of the trailer. Ducking under the swinging door he joined the man who was shining his torch into the trailer.

'Good ya?' he said.

Stephen went to reply when something hit him on the back of his head and neck. Stunned his knees buckled at the force of the blow cannoning him into the body of the trailer. His face hit the back plate of the trailer at floor height. A second heavy blow caught him again this time knocking him to the ground. Dazed he rolled onto his back trying to see who was attacking him. Yet another blow landed on his stomach this time. Winded he instinctively curled into a ball holding his mid-riff gasping for breath, another blow, this time to his side and ribs. Somewhere close by a driver must have been disturbed by the noise. Suddenly the whole area was bathed in bright light as the driver switched on all his lights.

Stephen heard someone say urgently!

'Go! Schnell schnell... go!'

He was aware of feet scuffling on the rough surface he guessed belonging to people who'd been hitting him. A truck horn started to sound to add to the confusion and light. Stephen reached out for the under-run bar of his trailer to help himself up but someone knocked him back to the ground. He heard a woman's' voice, they must have been close to him as he was aware of their scent, sweet but intense invading his senses. They spoke with a thick Eastern European accent.

'Mr Leigh-Grace, you and your detective friend in Englandt are a big thorn in my side causing me great trouble. If you value their lives and yours for that matter take this as a warning to stop meddling... now! Versten zie!' They stood up to leave adding, 'And if you are in any doubt as how serious I am, your girlfriend has been warned as well!'

Stephen lay still for some time until he got his breath back, reaching for the trailer bar he gingerly pulled himself upright to sit against it, breathing hard. Still lit by the lights of the adjacent truck he saw two people approaching him.

One of them with a German accent said.

'Yo drive you okay my friend, what was that all about?'

'Come on let's get you up and take a look at you.' a second person added.

Leaving Stephen resting against the trailer side the two men secured first the trailer doors then his cab before carefully walking him across to the service centre. Once inside the brightly lit area some of the staff, seeing that he was bleeding from where his head had collided with the back of the trailer and covered in mud, came to help. Carefully they removed his jacket and T-shirt to reveal other cuts and bruises. There were abrasions around his shoulders and arms and bruising to the rest of his upper body. Obviously in considerable pain and discomfort, the German driver who'd helped him to the centre had a brief conversation with the staff, then said to Stephen.

'We feel that you need proper medical attention and want you to go to emergency! We also think you should call the police, this was a serious attempt to hijack you or your trailer!'

Everyone turned to look at the main entrance as two sets of blue lights pulled up to the front of the building. Four policemen appeared in the main area and made their way towards the group of people gathered around Stephen. The officers asked the staff questions and then one officer sat with him and in his best English asked him some questions. Between them both speaking in broken English and Stephen's limited German, the officer was eventually satisfied that he'd got the essence of what had happened. He asked him to write down all that had happened so he could complete his report and statement. As they were finishing the questioning another set of blue lights appeared and moments later two paramedics came into the building. Again following another discussion the police officer said to him.

'My... er colleagues think you should attend the clinic for check over. They believe you may have other injuries that need treatment. Have you people to speak to in England, your company perhaps?'

Stephen's mind began to work more clearly as the officer asked him the question.

'Yes there are people I need to get hold of, thank you.'

'I will see you at the medical centre then,' the officer said, 'and you can make your calls after your checks, ya?'

As the medics helped him to the ambulance he turned to the

gathered group of people in the reception area.

'Thank you everyone, danke shon, thank you.'

~~~~~~~~~~~~~~~~~~~~~~~~~~~~~~~~~~~~~~

Three hundred miles away Erik Van Dijk was approaching the outskirts of Portbridge en-route to catch the midday ferry back to Holland. He'd delivered his trailer load of machine tools the previous afternoon, reloaded empty pallets and having got all his paperwork signed off and took his daily rest break. In the early hours of the morning he left Sheffield for the docks and as he'd anticipated, the roads were quiet; he'd only seen a handful of vehicles mainly trucks. His truck was running well, the cab was warm, he was listening to his favourite music occasionally singing along to the track. Negotiating the roundabout at the start of the Portbridge bypass, he pressed the cruise control resume button on the steering column leaving the truck to accelerate up to its cruising speed by itself. About three or four miles along the unlit bypass, his headlights picked out a sequence of black and white chevrons as the road curved quite sharply to the right following the contours of the river which ran alongside the road. His headlights on main beam suddenly picked up quite a large cylindrical object in the nearside lane. Erik, fully alert focused on what was in his way. 'Hooligans' he thought to himself realising it was a bin from the layby he was just passing. Touching the brake pedal he disengaged the cruise control, a quick check of his offside mirror he moved into the second lane. At the same time though he thought he saw a brief flash of red through the gaps in the Armco on the central reservation. Moments later he was horrified to see, parked against the central reservation, a car, with no lights on. Instinctively he swerved left, back to the nearside to avoid colliding with the car. Unfortunately, before he could straighten up again the rear wheels of his trailer hit and ran over the obstruction he'd tried to avoid. The effect of hitting it caused his truck and trailer to lurch onto his offside to such an angle that he
~~~~~~~~~~~~~~~~~~~~~~~~~~~~~~~~~~~~~~

was powerless to stop it falling onto its side.

Although in real time it was only seconds before the truck came to rest. It seemed that the motion, the sound of breaking glass screeching and grinding metal as the side of the unit and trailer slid along the tarmac went on for ever. All his belongings on his bunk or the shelf above, added to the horrendous noise as they crashed across the cab, to lie in a heap below him. Finally there was silence, except for his music playing. Erik reached to turn it off and sat or rather hung in his seat restrained only by his seat belt. He swore under his breath, asking himself. 'Shit... what the hell do I do now?'

From the trailer he heard a crash and guessed some of the pallets had slipped and fallen over.

Talking to himself again he said.

'Better get some help.'

Reaching up he turned on the cab lights and looking around saw that everything that wasn't in a locker lay in a heap at the other side of his cab. Duvet, pillows, towels, holdall, all sorts. Looking through the windscreen, he saw, in the headlight beams, the verge of the road and bushes, the dashboard in front of him was lit up like a Christmas tree as every warning light had come up. He realised also that the engine had stalled. He could smell diesel, that pungent, sickly oily smell, it had always reminded him of harbours and ferries. However more importantly there was a risk of fire. He reached and turned the headlights off leaving the sidelights on and switched on the hazard lights. His mobile phone had fallen to the other side of the cab to lie somewhere amongst all the gear there.

Reaching up he dialled 999 on the cab phone and waited for an answer. A woman's voice said.

'Emergency, which service do you require?'

'Police and fire.' Erik replied.

'Connecting you to the police.' she said.

Erik heard her give the police operator his phone details

'Police emergency, how can I help?'

'My name is Erik Van Dijk. I'm a truck driver, my lorry has turned over on the Portbridge bypass, I'm blocking the road.'

'Which carriageway is blocked, sir?' the police operator asked.

'Erm... I'm going to the docks, so that would be the East one I think.'

'Right, thank you for that sir. We are on our way to you now. Are you on your own?'

Erik replied, 'Yes.'

'Are you injured, do you require an ambulance?'

'No,' Erik replied, 'I'm stuck in my seat and can't get out of the lorry.'

'Okay, thank you sir,' the operator said, 'I need you to stay safe and move away from the vehicle and off the carriageway. If you have any pets with you will you keep them under control?'

'Right, thank you.' Erik said. 'Stupid idiot' he thought, how can I stay safe. Why don't you listen dummy, I'm stuck.'

The operator continued to speak to Erik and he guessed that he was probably working from some sort of a script.

'The fire service has been informed and they are en-route to you as well.'

'Thank you.' Erik said again.

'Goodbye.' The operator said.

Erik replied, 'Yes, goodbye.'

Pressing the 'end call' button, he just hung there in his seat belt for a moment.

Thinking it was time to try and work out how to get out of his cab, he was suddenly surprised to see a face appear at the windscreen and look into the cab.

'Bloody hell mate,' they shouted through the screen, 'you alright in there?'

Erik nodded and acknowledged the person with a thumbs up. The stranger called out again.

'Just hang on driver I've got a ladder on my cab then we can get you out.'

The man disappeared, Erik sat and waited. After a few minutes he saw the reflection of flashing blue lights all around him and noticed some more blue lights were coming towards him on the opposite carriageway. The knowledge that help was finally arriving he found comforting making him feel less isolated. There was a bang at his side of the cab which made him start, at the same time someone wearing a yellow hi-vis jacket appeared at the front of the truck and peered in. They waved and shouted.

'We're going to get you out now, okay?'

Erik waved back, and the man disappeared. A minute later the door above him opened and two faces peered into the cab. One of them was the policeman he'd just seen through the windscreen, the other Erik assumed was the other driver who'd first spoken to him.

'Right, come on mate, let's get you out of here.' the driver said.

'Are you hurt anywhere?' the policeman asked.

'No,' Erik replied, 'but I'll be glad to be out.'

With a certain amount of pulling, some tugging and lifting and with Erik hanging onto the cab sides where possible and using the steering column as a makeshift step he eventually arrived back on terra-firma, albeit a little shaky and quite a bit shocked. Someone draped a hi-vis jacket around his shoulders. A few minutes later a paramedic came to check him over. He asked a series of question to assess whether he'd possibly suffered a concussion in the accident. The medic eventually turned to the policeman.

'He's okay, suffering from some residual shock most likely. There will be some stiffness over the next day or two, but he's been lucky today.' Looking at Erik he added, 'If you begin to experience headaches or start to feel nauseous or unwell you'll need to contact your hospital or GP. Otherwise I suggest you start on some anti-inflammatory tablets and pain killers if the stiffness begins to trouble you.'

Erik listened to the paramedic. 'Thank you.' he said.

'Not a problem, you take care now.' He said and returned to his ambulance.

Erik listened as the policeman briefly asked the other driver if he'd witnessed the accident. Shaking his head he said simply.

'Nah, it was all over when I got here. I'm just glad you're okay mate.' The driver glancing at Erik.

'Right, I've got your details drive so you're okay to carry on and thanks for your help.'

The driver nodded then shook Erik's hand.

'Good luck mate, take care aye.'

'You too and thanks.' he replied.

Collecting his ladder the driver made his way to the Armco, climbed over it and returned to his truck on the other carriage way. Quite a few vehicles had stopped to gawp at the scene, some offering help. Eventually all were sent on their way by the police.

Erik was sitting on the grass verge looking at his truck on its side. He'd never seen its belly before and was quite surprised at just how long the tractor and trailer appeared to be from this angle.

'Okay,' the officer said, 'if you'd like to come and sit in my car I'll get some details from you as to what happened.'

Together they started to walk to the nearest police car when Erik suddenly stopped and looked around.

'Where's the other motor car?'

He said to the police officer.

'What other car, there was only your truck...'

Erik repeated himself again.

'No, there was a car... here!'

He gestured towards the central reservation.

'It was here... with no lights on. I'd swerved to avoid a bin or something in the road and then saw the car in my lights. I turned the other way but the trailer hit the container and I turned...' Erik was becoming agitated now. 'I turned over!'

He was sure in his mind that there had been a car here. He looked at the policeman then back at the Armco thinking. 'Where was the...' Then penny suddenly dropped. 'Ohh god! Ohh shit... bloody hell!' Erik exclaimed in horror. Quickly, with the police officer in pursuit he skirted around the up-turned trailer to the back doors. Struggling he eventually released the door fastenings shouting at the policeman.

'STAND BACK!'

Taking a step back himself, he pulled the heavy door open letting it slam down on the road. Both men stepped onto the door and crouching peered into the gloom of the trailer. They could just make out the mishmash of pallets that had been thrown around. Erik ducked under the other door into the trailer and stood upright. As his eyes adjusted to the low light he began to make out the shapes of the scattered pallets then to his horror he saw the clear outline of a car among the debris. It was partially hidden under some pallets and the shredded remains of the trailers curtain side, through which the car had burst as the trailer landed on it, calling to the police officer outside he said.

'The car's here get help quickly! And some lights.'

'Right!' The officer replied.

Erik heard him calling to some of the fire crew on the scene, moments later half a dozen heads appeared at the trailer door. Erik climbed out and began to release the locking bars on the other door. Using two salvage poles one of the firemen had collected they managed to push the door up and over so that it rested on what was now the top side of the trailer. That done the group made their way into the trailer adequately lit now with their lights and the strengthening morning light. Some other firemen joined them and they formed a chain passing out the empty pallets and stacking on the road. Gradually the car was uncovered revealing two people inside, both unconscious. A white helmeted sub-fire officer called towards the back of the trailer.

'Get some medics in here, we've got two casualties.'

As the medics arrived the policeman took Erik by the elbow.

'Will you come to my car sir the medics can do their job now, and we can start to sort out just what happened.'

'Sure.' Erik replied.

As they walked across the carriageway to one of the patrol cars the police officer introduced himself.

'I'm Sergeant Sam Bentley by the way.'

Settling in the front seats the officer reached for a clip board. Turning the chattering radio down low he switched on the interior light instantly flooding the car in a bright light, looking at Erik he said.

'Are you sure you're fit to answer these questions or do you require any further medical assistance?'

Erik shook his head. 'No, I am quite alright thank you.'

'Right, because of the nature of this accident I'm going to caution you.'

Erik nodded as the officer cautioned him.

'Can we start with your driving licences please?'

Over the next half an hour Erik took a breath test and answered the officers' questions while the fire crews and medics worked to release the two people from the car. As an ambulance left the scene lights flashing followed by one of the rapid response units a police officer made his way over to the patrol car. It was obvious to both Erik and the traffic officer something wasn't right. As he got to the side of the car he opened the driver's door and crouching by his colleague's side said quietly to him.

'You'd best get the Inspector down here Sam, there's a problem.'

'They're not...?' Sam asked.

'No, no... Both alive, if a little the worse for wear, looks like they've made a day of it though the back seats full of shopping bags...' he smiled, 'No naked lights, the car reeks of booze.'

'So the problem is?'

'The problem is sarge the car's registered to a Nita Patel, and she's one of ours, a DC in Portbridge.'

Sam exclaimed, 'Shit... seriously?'

Erik looked from one officer to the other.

'This is a joke, yes?'

The policeman crouching at the side of the car shook his head.

'Fraid not mate. The passenger is a teenager, an Emma Leigh-Grace according to a credit card and student card.'

It was Erik who was visibly shaken with this bit of news.

'Leigh-Grace did you say?'

The officer nodded adding.

'She has an address here in Portbridge and one down south. Looks like the parents could be separated and she lives with both parents from time to time.'

Erik shook his head.

'No, no, I know this man, he is from here, he is like me a driver from here. He is called Leigh-Grace. We travel the ferry together often from the Channel ports. He is a... what is the English word? His wife is dead.'

Both policemen stared at him.

'A widower, you're saying he's a widower?'

'Ya, a widower, he has a daughter named Emma.'

'Oh sodding hell, this just gets better.'

Picking up the handset by the side of the centre console Sam said.

'Tango sierra one zero to control, priority over.'

In a moment his call was answered.

'Control, tango sierra one zero, go ahead, over.'

Sam began to explain the situation at the scene giving an update of what was happening and confirming the identities of the two women now en-route to hospital, he ended the message by requesting the duty Inspector attend the scene urgently.

Almost an hour elapsed before the Inspector arrived accompanied by another man. It was full daylight now and the true horror of just how bad the accident had been could be clearly seen. Heavy lifting equipment had been called in to get the lorry and its trailer upright and moved away for inspection and to reveal the car. The by-pass had been closed both ways to avoid the possibility of another accident because the sight of Erik's unit on its side would distract drivers.

Sam had completed his preliminary enquiries when they saw the Inspectors car arrive. The officers stood to attention as the Inspector and his companion approached them.

'Morning Sam.' the Inspector said.

'Sir.' Sam replied.

'This is DI Allen, he's Nita Patel's boss.'

Sam responded, acknowledging DI Allen.

'Morning sir.'

Allen nodded to him as the Inspector drew Sam away from the gathered group.

DI Allen asked. 'Do we know what happened yet?'

'Only what the driver has said in his statement. Sir, do we know how the two women are yet?'

He offered DI Allen his clip board with Erik's statement attached.

'No,' the inspector replied, 'they're still being assessed at the hospital. We've got two officers down there with them.'

DI Allen handed the board back to Sam, briefly glanced over towards Erik.

'Do you believe him? Has he blown a test yet?'

He studied Sam waiting for his answer. Searching through the papers he found the entry he wanted showing it to DI Allen and pointing out the relevant place.

'It was clear sir here's the reading.' then added, 'In his statement he says he swerved to avoid some sort of drum on the carriageway and then saw the car by the Armco without lights. I've sent couple of the lads down the carriage to see if they can find the drum. They've found a rubbish bin from the lay-by wedged in the central reservation badly crushed. We're going to compare the tyre marks on it to the trucks.'

Allen glanced towards the trailer then nodded. 'Mmm.'

The Inspector asked. 'Have you been able to check his Tachograph or taken a look at the unit yet?'

'No sir, until we can get it standing up again we can't get into the cab to have a proper look.'

'Fair enough.'

'You're going to impound it, yes?'

The Detective Inspector said. The Inspector responded this time turning to DI Allen.

'Of course, look there's nothing we can do here should we get up to the hospital and have a word with the two women?'

'Yes,' Allen replied, 'Good idea.'

Turning to Sam, DI Allen added.

'I want a word with the driver later at the station, understand?'

'Yes sir.' Sam answered.

The two officers made their way to their car and were driven away. Sam walked back to the group saying.

'Bloody hell I'm glad he's not our boss, I don't think much of his people skills he'd never make traffic in a month of Sundays with that attitude.'

The officers with him nodded in agreement.

The heavy recovery vehicle and mobile crane eventually turned up to begin the recovery operation. It was almost mid-day by the time the car from inside the trailer had been pulled out and Erik's lorry and trailer were righted. Both vehicles were removed to a commercial garage where they could be thoroughly checked over. As Nita's car appeared from inside the trailer slowly being winched out, it looked to everyone that it had been exposed to a giant hailstorm with stones the size of crown green balls hitting it. All over the body work there were huge dents from where the pallets had landed on it. The by-pass reopened shortly after that and traffic started to flow again some nine hours after the accident had happened. As the truck and trailer were towed away Sam followed the recovery vehicles to the commercial garage where he checked the lorry's tachograph and Erik retrieved his mobile phone and personal belongings before the two of them returned to the police station where Erik called his company.

'Well how are you getting home then?'

Sam asked as they walked out of the traffic office, Erik replied,

'There is a driver from my company in Newcastle on the Tyne they are going to get him to come here for me to go home together. So I have to wait for him here.'

Sam nodded. 'Fancy something proper to eat then?'

Erik's eyes lit up, his last meal had been nearly fifteen hours ago. Together they made their way to the station canteen, where Erik ate his way through a banquet of pie, chips, vegetables, and a huge portion of currant sponge and custard. 'Spotted Dick' he was informed by the canteen manager which he found very amusing, laughing uncontrollably as he returned to the table with the pudding. Later in the afternoon as the shifts changed Sam came up to the canteen to say good-bye. Around four in the afternoon a smartly dressed young man came up to Erik, who was sitting in the corner of the canteen dozing.

'Erik Van Dijk?'

Erik sat up. 'Ya.'

'Hello, I'm DC Syms would you mind coming with me sir? My boss would like a word with you about this morning's accident.'

Erik stood up. 'Certainly,' he replied and followed Alan out of the canteen along a labyrinth of corridors until they arrived at the door of Detective Inspector Allan. Alan knocked.

'Come in.'

He opened the door, DI Allan looked up from his desk.

'Mr Van Dijk come in please, take a seat.'

Erik moved into the office and sat opposite DI Allen.

Three quarters of an hour passed before Erik came out of DI Allen's office. At the door they shook hands and Alan heard the DI say.

'Don't worry about it unduly. It's unlikely that any further action will be taken that would involve you, you understand?' Erik nodded.

DI Allen turned to look for Alan.

'Syms,' he said, 'when transport arrives for Mr Van Dijk, he's free to go, okay?'

'Sir.' Alan replied.

Giving Erik a curt nod he turned on his heels and returned to his office. Alan walked back to the canteen with Erik.

'So back to Holland tonight once your mate gets here?'

Erik replied, 'Ya, but I don't think we can make tonight's sailing. Ve vill have to get the morning boat perhaps.'

Back in the canteen Alan bought two mugs of tea sitting together Alan asked.

'What happens to your wagon and trailer now?'

'Oh it vill be repaired and I come back when it is finished. The trailer is borrowed... hired, so there is a company here in England also, they will take this and make it good again.'

Alan nodded, 'Have you got all the gear you need out of it?'

Erik nodded. 'Oh ja, I took out from the truck what is mine at the garage. So I wait now for my friend to come for me.'

'Right, well excuse me but I've finished for the day so as long as you're okay I'll get off.'

'Thank you for the tea, goot'n tag, err, good night.'

A couple of hours passed before Erik's ride home arrived. He could relax a little now relieved that today was over and in twelve hours possibly he would be back in Holland and amongst friends. Only now did he realise how tired he was from the shock of the day's events.

~~~~~~

As the time passed for Erik waiting at the police station, for Nita and Emma it was lost in the hospital. They'd been rushed from the scene with an escort to Portbridge hospital where their injuries could be assessed then depending on how life threatening they were, could be transferred to either York or Leeds where more intensive treatment was available. On arrival at A & E their condition was assessed as not critical, so it was decided that they could be treated here. Over two hours had passed since they'd been admitted to the IC unit and neither of them showed any signs of waking from the unconscious state they'd been found in. At one end of the unit Emma lay comatose, she was breathing steadily for herself but had been hooked up to a number of monitors to warn staff if her condition worsened. A uniformed policewoman sat by her bed to make notes of
~~~~~~

anything she said. At the opposite end of the unit, Nita was also being monitored for any changes in her condition, a detective sat with her.

On admission special attention was paid to the possibility that the accident had happened because Nita had been drinking then driven her car and crashed into the Armco. Although smelling strongly of alcohol at the scene, her blood test results showed she was actually below the legal limit. The implication now, to both the medics and police, was that she'd been force fed the alcohol after falling unconscious. The fact that someone deliberately wanted to give such an impression was very worrying however, until she regained consciousness they were in the dark as to the events leading up to what could have been a tragic, even fatal accident.

From what felt like a long tunnel Nita began to hear voices that appeared to be coming from the other end of it. She felt she was floating it was such a strange sensation, almost how she imagined being kept in a state of suspended animation would feel like. The voices she could hear at the end of the tunnel were strange enough, but what was more worrying was the fact she couldn't move her arms or legs yet could feel them being moved by someone else from time to time. It felt really odd she felt like a puppet, but had no idea how she was being controlled. As the floating sensation continued to wear off she found she was able to focus more on the sounds of her current surroundings and began to make sense of the different noises and smells around her. She tried to get her head in gear to assimilate where she was and why, what had happened to her, when and how long ago? Her last clear memory was sitting in a cafe` bar in West Fording with Emma chatting and having a bit of a girlie day as Emma's study week was coming to an end. They were writing up a shopping list for a blitz of international food for this weekend before Nita put her back on the train to Richard and Mary's. Where was Emma was she okay, what had happened to her? She moaned, unable to clear her thoughts enough to remember, turning her head she looked to see if Emma was here. Someone was sitting by her bedside albeit a blurry silhouette.

'Em are you all right?'

The person looked up from the folder they were reading as Nita reached out for their hand.

'What happened, how did I end up here?'

The person replied.

'It's Ruth lovie, how do you feel?'

'Ruth... Sarge.' Nita's confused state just scrambled itself again. 'Ruth,' she repeated herself, 'what's going on, how did I get here? Emma... do you know what's happened to Em Ruth, is she all right?'

Taking her hand firmly Ruth smiled.

'It's all right love, Emma's here. She's okay honestly but like you ko'd and has been for some time. Don't worry lovie she's going to be okay, just needs to sleep off whatever it is you two have had.'

Nita replied, 'What do you mean, what we've had?'

She was finding everything really confusing, each time she asked a question the answer she received wasn't the one she was expecting and because she couldn't remember anything it just added to her general state of confusion.

'We were hoping you could tell us what you've been up to?' Ruth said. 'Right now you're in something of a pickle lovie and we need to sort it out ASAP. Can you remember anything that could help explain the last twelve hours?'

Shaking her head, Nita replied.

'Not really, we were at the cafe` at West Fording, CU at 2, you know the one?'

Ruth nodded and began to write down what Nita was saying.

'We were just having a coffee,' she said trying to sit up in her bed. 'Oh shit... ow! That hurts.' She exclaimed as her head seemed to exploded, she slid back down the bed again. 'I feel like I've been on a right bender... What's wrong with me?'

Sitting on the bed beside her, Ruth said.

'Nita love, you and Emma are both lucky to be alive. As it stands right now you appear to have had a right skin full and then driven from who knows where, lost control on the by-pass and stuffed your car into the Armco. Had it not been for a very alert truck driver you could have both been killed. He missed you... just... but still ended up crashing into you. Trust me it was scary, the photos the traffic guys took at the scene are not pretty.'

Speechless, Nita tried to focus on Ruth as she told her what had happened. She lay still for some time digesting all she'd just heard. Feeling near to tears, she threw her hands up in desperation at not being able to remember and just blurted out.

'Ruth, I wouldn't... I don't.'

Ruth held her hand up to stop her.

'I know, I know lovie and I know you that's why this just isn't right, it's too disjointed. I need you to tell me as much of what you can remember so we can get a proper handle on what happened and who might be involved.'

Taking a deep breath she began to explain again.

'We were at the café, we didn't go to a bar or pub. I wouldn't not with Em!'

She began to get emotional again because she couldn't recall anything that made sense moreover, she'd begun to understand the implications the last twelve hours could have on her career. There was also the matter of how Stephen would react when he heard about all this. Ruth shuffled a little further up the bed putting her arms around her. Feeling that sense of security at that moment she burst into tears. Stroking her shoulder Ruth said quietly.

'Nita love, we don't know for sure you were drunk. Yes you smelled of booze, but your bloods came back clear, so let's wait and see what the results of the other tests are okay?'

Reaching for some tissues on the bed side cabinet, Ruth gave them to her, she dabbed her eyes and blew her nose. Calming herself she nodded to Ruth.

'Is Emma in the same state as me?'

Ruth nodded. 'Yes, but no trace of alcohol.'

For quite a while they sat in silence, all the time Nita tried to work through the sequence of events since her last clear memory, trying to find something she was sure of. Half to herself she said absentmindedly.

'It was about two, two thirty-ish Emma and I were having a coffee this woman came over to our table. Erm... Olivia or something, No Olga, yes Olga. She'd come into the café with some guy, I didn't really clock him at all, she came straight to our table.'

Repeating herself she glanced at Ruth.

'She just came up to our table, she even knew my name!'

Becoming increasingly animated explaining the events she could remember, she was almost babbling now.

'Whoa, whoa! Slow down lovie, take your time okay!' Ruth said firmly reaching out and squeezing Nita's wrist. More controlled now she continued.

'Yes...yes, I told her I was off duty and I couldn't discuss any police matter with her. Then she said she knew Katterine and what had happened to her. Obviously, I was interested but told her she'd have to see me tomorrow at the office, or I'd meet her somewhere. She just kept on saying that she was in danger if anyone saw her talking to me. She said this was one of the safest places to meet, as it was out of the town centre.'

Nita paused collecting her thoughts.

'It was really chuffing awkward with Em there. I think she sensed it too 'cause she went off to the loo at one point. I gave this Olga woman my card and asked her when the best time to meet up was? She said tomorrow morning at the café.'

Giving a cynical 'huh, she added, 'I guess tomorrow is today. Yes?'

Ruth nodded. 'Spot on lovie.'

'What time is it?'

'Oh, nearly twelve.' Ruth replied.

Calmly Nita continued relating the events of yesterday, to her sergeant who was making notes.

'There was a bit of a commotion at the back of the café. I turned and saw this guy who'd come in with this Olga trying to talk to Emma. She wasn't having any of it. I called out to him to move away, got up to go across to him and he stepped away to let Emma come back to the table.'

Ruth put her hand on Nita's wrist to stop her.

'You've been drugged lovie,' she said, 'While you were distracted by all the fuss with Emma, she's slipped something into your drinks.'

Nita stared at Ruth for just a moment, struck dumb.

'Bastards!' she spat out! 'Emma as well, do you think?'

Ruth nodded. ''fraid so.'

'Bastards,' Nita said again, 'chuffing, slimy rotten bastards!'

For some time Nita lay quietly, angry that she had got herself and Emma into a situation that had put their own safety at serious risk. She felt guilty that she hadn't been more vigilant at the café. Her training should have told her that something wasn't right, despite the fact that she was off duty. She'd let her guard down and felt bad about it. However, on the plus side she was so angry that come what may she was determined to find this Olga woman and see her arrested. After a while Ruth said quietly.

'After the commotion, what happened next?'

'I told this Olga woman that the meeting was over, she had my card and I'd see her tomorrow as planned... today now I suppose. I told Em to finish her drink we were leaving. That's what we did, Emma finished her chocolate I finished my cafetiere and we left.'

'Did they follow you?' Ruth asked.

'Don't think so,' Nita said thoughtfully, 'we were only parked down the side of the cafe` on the Close. We'd just got to the car when Emma stumbled. She said she felt queasy and floaty, I managed to get her to sit on the passenger seat and then she just went limp. She was trying to talk but it sounded like gobbledy-gook.' Nita paused for a moment then added, 'I must admit I was feeling a bit odd myself. I remember asking two guys if they could help me get Emma into the car, and then I was gone myself.'

She paused glancing at her sergeant.

'It's not that you're unconscious, it's more like an out-of-body experience. You're aware of what's going on around you but you can't do anything about it, to influence it I mean. It's... well I can't explain, do you understand?' Ruth nodded.

She tried another way of explaining how she'd felt.

'Say you were in an immersion tank, just floating. You hear sounds, sense movement but you're helpless to do anything about it. You've got no sensation of touch no feeling... it's really very weird.'

Ruth glanced up from her notebook. 'I'd say you've both been slipped a 'micky-finn' something like Rhino.'

'Sarge go and find out how Em is please... now.'

'Okay lovie, back in a mo.'

Ruth walked up to the other end of the IC unit. Whilst she was away from Nita's bed her nurse took the opportunity to run a set of checks. As she was writing up her chart Nita asked.

'Do you know when the rest of the test results will be back?'

Without looking up from the chart she replied.

'Difficult to say, the easy ones we have now and you're okay in all those. The difficult ones can take some time to track.'

Replacing the chart board on the end of the bed, she looked directly at Nita and smiled.

'Don't worry love, you and your friend are going to be all right, you see.'

She walked off passing Ruth on the way.

'How is she?' Nita asked anxiously.

'Fine, she's good.' Ruth smiled, adding. 'A bit groggy and confused but coming round all the time, she's asked for you.'

Sitting by the bedside again, Ruth tried to get Nita to recall more of yesterday's events that led up to the two of them ending up on the Portbridge by-pass in the middle of the night stuck against the central reservation.

'Sweetie, can you remember anything of what happened after you went down?'

'You know, those two young guys I asked for help must have been involved too... I think. They helped me up from the pavement and then I somehow ended up in a big people carrier. It had widows but was dark inside, must have been privacy glass. I remember Emma was there too, I think I tried to resist, well in my head I did but nothing worked. We were driven around then until … who knows.' she sighed slumping back into her pillows. 'I feel like shit sarge and my head's banging, sorry.'

She massaged her temples with her knuckles trying and ease the pain. Ruth realised that the effort of recalling what had happened had exhausted Nita. Turning to the nurse she said.

'Can you give her something for the headache?'

Smiling she replied, 'Not a problem, I'll write something up now.'

Stroking Nita's arm gently, Ruth said.

'Enough now lovie, you've been brilliant. Just relax and get some sleep.'

Nita's eyes were closed but she nodded saying absentmindedly.

'Need to call Stephen, he'll be worried.' with that she fell asleep.

Ruth sat by her for a while longer then walked to Emma's bed. She looked at the girl and then the police officer by her bedside.

'Keep your eyes and ears open, make notes of anything she says, anything, you understand. I'm going to phone the boss, okay?'

The woman officer nodded, replying. 'Sarge,'

~~~~~~

Nita and Emma slept off the effects of whatever they had been given for most of the afternoon. Both were eventually considered well enough to be moved from the IC unit to a general ward, where for the first time they could see each other. Nita carefully slipped out of her bed, trying not to do anything that would set off the terrible pounding in her head, gingerly she slid up onto Emma's bed and they gently hugged each other. They talked through everything they could remember the previous afternoon however, Emma's recollections pretty well ended at the café. She became quite emotional because she couldn't remember anything and that scared her. As her tears
~~~~~~

became sobs Nita took her in her arms and she cried into Nita's shoulder. Eventually her tears stopped and she calmed down drifting off to sleep. Lying her gently back on her pillows she returned to her own bed settling back into her pillows. With her eyes closed she started again to recall anything that might shed some light on what had happened to the two of them after they had been put into the other vehicle.

'Nita... Nita lovie, it's Ruth.'

In a sudden panic she sat up in her bed opening her eyes putting her arms up defensively and quickly looking around her surroundings. She realised she was still in hospital then held her head in her hands trying and ease the thumping pain. 'What...?' she said.

'It's me lovie, Ruth it's okay you were asleep, come on calm down.'

As she spoke she gently stroked her shoulder. Nita noticed the curtains around her bed had been drawn and there was a man in a white coat standing at the other side of her bed. He seemed very tall and slim from where Nita lay, his dark almost black skin was such a contrast against his brilliant white coat.

'Nita this is the doctor who's been running the tests on you and Emma.'

He grinned broadly showing teeth almost as white as his coat, when he spoke it was with a hint of a South African accent.

'Miss Patel,' he began, 'I have good news and not so good news I'm afraid.'

Nita threw Ruth a look that said, what the hell's wrong. The doctor, grinning again continued.

'The good news is you and your friend are going to be all right in a little while. All the tests have come back to me clear, except for one. That is the bad news, there are definite traces of I think Rohipnol in this one. Do not worry there are no long-term after-effects, I would think that in the next twenty-four hours or so it will be completely out of your system. I want to observe you both for the rest of the day then repeat one of the tests and I think you can go home tomorrow.

Are you all right with that?'

He waited for Nita to absorb all the information he'd just given her, she glanced at Ruth and then the doctor and nodded.

'Yes,' she said, 'I think so thank you.'

He grinned at her again, 'Excellent not a problem, I'll get some bloods from you both later and have the results before I leave this evening.'

Nodding to Nita and then Ruth he turned, opening the curtains and strode off down the ward the open white coat flapping like some wings on a big bird. Before he'd got to the door of the ward Nita dissolved into tears. Ruth realised that all the tension and stress of the last hours had finally got to her. Shuffling onto the bed she put an arm round her shoulders.

'Shush lovie, it's all right now you heard the Doc you and Emma are going to be okay.'

Nita nodded but continued to cry releasing all the pent-up stress and frustration she was feeling, plus the guilt she felt that Emma had got involved too. In the next bed Emma heard Nita catch her breath as she sobbed. Carefully she eased herself out of the bed and went to sit on Nita's bed. Nita sensed Emma next to her reached for her hand and then looked at her, her eyes full of tears.

'I'm so sorry Em,' she said, 'you shouldn't have got mixed up in this it's all my fault. The job caught up with me and I put you at risk. I'm sorry.'

Emma squeezed her hand reassuringly.

'Not your fault, you weren't to know that woman was going to find us at the café.'

The two women stayed beside Nita until she calmed down and fell asleep. As Emma moved back to her own bed, Ruth said quietly.

'I'm just going to phone the office with the test results, okay?'

'Fine.' Emma replied.

Apart from someone coming to take some bloods later in the afternoon, they were left on their own now. After the supper trolley had been round, the two of them pulled their chairs round to face each other sat and talked, they held hands sharing the occasional hug. Quite a bit later, as the light was fading outside the night staff came on duty. True to his word the South African doctor came down the ward towards them. As before his open coat flowed by his side like a cape. Approaching their beds he broke into one of his broad grins showing off his teeth. Nita wondered if he always looked this happy.

'Good news this time,' he said as he got to their bed side, 'you're both all clear so tomorrow morning you should be able to leave.'

Nita and Emma grinned almost as broadly as the doctor.

'Thank you, that's really great news, thank you.'

Emma echoed her. 'Yes thank you.'

'Excellent,' the doctor said, 'not a problem. Now I'm going home, goodnight ladies.'

He sort of bowed to them and, as before walked briskly out of the ward coat tails flapping.

Passing one of the night nurses at the door, she walked down the ward towards them.

'Does a Stephen Leigh-Grace mean anything to either of you two ladies?' she said trying very hard not to grin at Nita.

'Dad!' Emma said loudly.

Nita sighed, 'Thank God.' she said, 'Go on Em you talk to him first.'

Emma half grabbed the phone from the nurse and sitting cross legged on her bed launched into a verbal download about all that had happened, gabbling away so much that she hardly took a breath. The nurse giggled a little saying to Nita.

'Children aye, sometimes you can't keep them quiet. Love them.'

As she left them alone, Nita heard Emma say to Stephen.

'Do you want to speak to Nita now?'

He replied to her and just before she passed the phone to her she said.

'Love you Dad! See you soon.' Blowing kisses down the phone.

Taking the phone from Emma, she heard him say, 'Hello sugar.'

'Oh Stephen, I'm so sorry that Em has got mixed up in something that's to do with work.'

She blurted the words out without hearing what Stephen was trying to say to her.

'You know I wouldn't do anything to put either of you at risk or in danger, I'm sorry.'

She repeated herself again, then heard him telling her to be quiet and listen.

'Nita stop... Listen to me! None of this is your fault my wonderful lady, do you hear! It's not your fault? This is so much bigger than you can imagine sugar, it should be me saying sorry to you and Emma for what's happened. Listen for a mo, I'm on my way back home now on the Euro-link. I've phoned the boss and told him some of what has happened, he's letting me come back tonight. I've parked the unit up in Frankfurt and all things being equal I'll be home tomorrow afternoon. Nita my love stop worrying I'm on my way home okay? I love you, nothing has changed have you got that?'

A little confused by what he was saying, she simply answered, 'Mmm... yes.'

'Wrong answer... it should be yes Stephen and then, I love you too.'

She half smiled. 'Yes Stephen, I love you too.'

'Good, got to go sugar got a train to catch, see you tomorrow.'

Nita spoke urgently, wanting to ask him.

'How do you mean it's much bigger than I could imagine?'

'Explain tomorrow, I'm going... love you and Em too, Bye'

'Bye.' She answered, but the line was dead. She looked at Emma sitting on the other bed, she'd visibly perked up since speaking to Stephen.

'Did he just say he'd be back tomorrow?' Emma asked.

Nita absently nodded in response to her question still very confused wondering what he'd meant by; 'This is much bigger than she could imagine.'

'Brill, do you think they'll let us out then?' she said.

'Oh I think so,' Nita answered vaguely, 'these last tests were all good so we should get our marching orders in the morning.'

'Yeah... get in!'

Emma exclaimed punching and air then settling back into her bed. Nita shuffled into a more comfortable position relieved Stephen didn't blame her for all that had happened. Shortly after the phone call the night staff did their final rounds, settling everyone down for the night and dimming the main lights. A sense of calm and tranquillity settled on the ward and everyone slept.

~~~~~~~~~~~~~~~~~~~~~~~~~~~~~~~~~~~

Mid-morning the following day saw Nita and Emma brought back to Stephen's house by Alan Syms and Ruth; repeating the instructions from the hospital to take things easy for the next twenty-four hours. After a light lunch they heard a car pull up outside, Emma peered through the window then set off rushing to the front door exclaiming as she passed Nita.

'It's Dad!'

Throwing open the front door she went to hug Stephen but he put his hands up to ward her off, she stopped then and took a step back.

'Easy sweetheart, I'm a little bit sore just now.'

Reaching out she touched his face, he had cuts and bruises over one eye, his cheek bones showed a little proudly through his skin. There was a graze on one side of his chin and he sported a fat lip that had obviously been split but was healing.

'Oh my god Dad what happened?' Emma squealed.

Nita pushed passed her on hearing her exclamation. She stood shocked at his appearance then threw her arms around him bursting into tears.

'Hey steady on sugar the ribs have taken a beating again. Come on let's get into the house.'
~~~~~~~~~~~~~~~~~~~~~~~~~~~~~~~~~~~

With his arm round Nita's waist he guided her into the house, taking Emma's hand too as he passed her in the doorway. Neither of them had noticed that Nita's sergeant and DI Allen were waiting patiently behind him on the street, they followed them into the house. Stephen lowered himself carefully into one of the easy chairs with arms that he could use for support. Nita realised now that DI Allen and Ruth were standing in the hallway.

'Sorry sir,' she said, at the same acknowledging her colleague, 'Sarge.'

'That's alright detective,' the DI said.

'Come in, please.' Nita added.

They filed through into the lounge and she indicated for them to sit on the settee. Turning to Emma she said.

'Emma this is my boss Detective Inspector Allen, and my sergeant you know already.'

Emma nodded towards the detective inspector.

'Emma.' He responded courteously.

'Can I get you something sir, tea coffee?' Nita asked.

'Coffee, black...'

Nita finished off his sentence. 'Three sugars.'

He nodded and smiled. 'Please.'

Turning to Ruth, 'Tea please lovie.'

Emma left the room while Nita went over to Stephen and slid onto the floor beside him resting her arm on the edge of the seat cushion.

With the four of them settled DI Allen spoke first.

'This goes no further than this room for the moment but seeing as you are all involved; action needs to be taken now to secure your safety. Do you understand?'

He paused looking at each of them.

'For the past few months Mr Leigh-Grace has noticed a particular vessel working out of some of the ports he uses crossing the channel.'

Nita nodded. 'You mean the one we saw in York at Easter that converted fishing boat?'

'Yes.' Stephen said.

DI Allen glanced at Nita.

'Yes that's the one, now you flagged this up to Special Branch back in April and following a brief investigation they escalated it up to the Serious Crime boys and HMCE, particularly the immigration people.'

Emma brought the drinks into the lounge and passed them around.

'I guess you wanted tea Dad?'

'Thanks love, that's grand.'

Continuing the DI said. 'It seems that this boat belongs to a group of very unpleasant people mainly from the former Eastern bloc. They move anything from people to cigarettes, wine, even drugs. They are movement facilitators for anyone prepared to pay the going rate. For some reason, this little group of reprobates seem to have managed to stay below the radar of organised gangs. It's just possible that because they don't specialize in one facet of crime but spread it about, they've not hit any of the markers. Anyway, up until now no-one has had a clue who they were and where their operating base was. Their MO seems to be to use small coastal ports, satellite ones that don't have a permanent harbour master or customs office. They put into the harbour claiming their boat has developed some technical problem that requires spares which can only be sourced from obscure places in the old Eastern part of Europe. In two or three days a van arrives with the replacement bits and the boat is repaired and off it goes. Immigration have tried all sorts of ways to track what is happening but so far have failed to find any evidence to at least take out the UK element.'

Pausing he took a mouthful of his drink.

'The times the van has been stopped by customs have drawn a blank. All the paperwork has been in order, whether it's been coming into the UK or leaving. Somewhere though there's been a switch made.'

Ruth spoke now. 'When you and DC Syms followed up on the

murder of Patrick Doyle and the assault on the Lithuanian girl, Kate was it?'

'Katterine, Kate, yes.' Nita interjected, DI Allen nodded and Ruth continued.

'Kate then, well it seems you inadvertently came close to getting to this group through the back door so as to speak. However, after what has happened to all of you in the last two days is potentially very worrying regarding your safety. With the bits of information Kate has given us we've managed to get a couple more girls into safe houses and they've told us more about these 'linesmen' as they call them who run the operation here.

DI Allen, speaking directly to Nita said.

'Listen, Division feel that as a direct result of the two incidents at the flats and the hospital a few weeks ago the gang have been watching both places and appear to have identified you as a common link. It appears that once they connected you to Ms Doyle and Katterine they've been following you. Have you been aware of a vehicle tailing you around?

Nita shook her head, 'Not so I've noticed sir, no.'

'Our techy guys have been reviewing CCTV over the last four weeks from all cameras around Portbridge and a black Merc people-carrier crops up fairly regularly. There is footage of that vehicle in West Fording on the day you and Emma were attacked. We think that you and this house allowed them to link your enquiries to here and Mr Leigh-Grace.'

Glancing across to Stephen he added.

'Your brush with the heavy weights at the port recently probably gave them the confirmation they wanted. We've asked the Port authorities at Hull, Felixstowe and Rotterdam to look at their CCTV footage, we are still waiting on them to get back to us on that. Now what has happened to all of you over the past forty-eight hours clearly shows that you need protection. Serious Crimes have instructed me to tell you Mr Leigh-Grace that you are to cease immediately reporting any of the group's movements, do you understand?'

Stephen nodded. Then too Nita he said.

'DC Patel, as of now you are off the enquiry into Mr Doyle's death and the ongoing work with Katterine, do you understand?'

'Sir' Nita replied a little surprised.

'I know this seems like a belt and braces reaction, I'm sure you particularly believe Mr Leigh-Grace that the odd phone call reporting a sighting of the boat appears unimportant. The thing is they know who your daughter is now and that poses a serious risk to her safety. Be under no illusion, this lot are absolutely ruthless. We know that from the evidence we've been able to gather so far.'

Stephen shuffled in his chair and grimaced as a sharp pain shot through his body.

'Inspector, how are you going to keep an eye on Emma? She's only here for this study break. Next week she goes back to her grandparents in Poole. What am I going to do about her safety then?'

The DI held his hand up.

'I'll come to that in a minute okay. I believe you were informed by the senior immigration manager when they interviewed you that if the panic button was pressed then you and all your family would come under a passive security watch. That is happening now however, with Emma going back to Poole she is in a way removing herself from this situation. We're fairly confident that they've only observed her here around Portbridge and have no notion of her life in Poole. The regional crime unit in Dorset are being briefed this weekend by the National Crime Unit. They will be tasked with keeping an eye on her when she's back in Poole and school.'

The inspector turned to Emma.

'A female DC will be in direct contact with you when you get back to your grandparents. Now this is very important Emma, as far as they are concerned and your school friends, she is someone you've known from around here who has just moved to Poole. She is young and originally from Sheffield so her dialect will be local to this area. Do you think you can handle this until we can close the case?'

Before Emma could reply, the Inspector added firmly.

'Emma, this really is important we need you to work with us on this. You cannot tell anyone anything, not your grandparents and particularly your school friends, you understand? They would then be as much at risk as your dad and DC Patel are now.'

Unusually for Emma, her reply when it came was quiet and very timid. She'd obviously realised the gravity of the whole situation.

'Err yes, I think I can cope with it. I am going to be okay aren't I?'

She glanced at Stephen, he saw the anxiety in her eyes, reaching out he took her hand holding it firmly. It was Ruth who answered this time.

'Yes lovie, you'll be fine.'

'The hard part is going to be not saying anything to your Nan and Granddad.'

Emma said, 'we don't have secrets.'

Ruth smiled, 'I'm sure you can keep this secret Emma, I bet there are things you don't tell them or your dad... you know.'

'Emma.' Stephen said flashing her a quizzical look. She flushed a little and giggled glancing at the Inspector and then Ruth.

Stephen asked, 'What about me?'

'Right,' the Inspector began, 'we've spoken to your boss and informed him that for the moment we need you to remain here in the UK to help us with some enquiries.'

Stephen wondered just how that could be arranged without revealing this on-going situation, DI Allen continued.

'Do you recall that there was a trailer theft at Felixstowe three months ago?'

'Oh yes,' Stephen replied, 'it belonged to a company running out of Newcastle. A lot of us knew the driver. Didn't he get done for that... accessory or something?'

The inspector nodded, 'That's right it turns out he wasn't actually involved but his brother was. We've told your boss that he's going to call you as a character witness at his appeal hearing.'

'When's that likely to be?'

The inspector shrugged his shoulders. 'Who knows, these appeal cases can take ages to put together. Probably around the time we put our case to bed if you get my drift…'

'Ah yes.' The plan suddenly clicked in Stephens head.

'But it gives us the necessary smoke screen to keep you local for the moment.'

Ruth reached out touching Nita's shoulder.

'Nita, you'll be back in the office,' she added quickly, 'but don't worry lovie it'll be interesting, you won't be filing, promise!'

She smiled relieved to hear that she wasn't to become a clerk. Getting to his feet DI Allen moved towards the door and the hallway, Ruth followed him. At the front door he turned back to the three of them.

'The DC in Poole will contact Emma as soon as she arrives back at her grandparents all right?'

To Nita he said, 'See how you feel on Monday, work with the sergeant and let her know if you feel you can come in, okay?'

She nodded, then said. 'Let the others know I'm ok Sarge, please.'

Ruth replied, 'I will. You get fit first, right?'

Touching Stephens arm the Inspector said quietly, 'Mr Leigh-Grace, can I have a quick word?'

Opening the front door he stepped out onto the street, Stephen followed him. Standing side by side DI Allen said.

'I wasn't going to make an issue of it in front of your daughter but two plain clothes officers will be on the train with her just to see that she travels safely. I thought that would put your mind at rest.'

Stephen looked at the detective. 'Thank you, that's a massive relief for sure.'

As a gesture of reassurance DI Allen put his hand on Stephen's shoulder.

'Think nothing of it, you've been invaluable in helping with this case so far, we'll finish it off now but we need you to be safe.'

Turning to their car, he opened the front passenger door and sat next to the detective sergeant. Stephen stood on the pavement watching them car drive away down the street and went back into his house.

~~~~~~

watching them car drive away down the street and went back into his house.
~~~~~~

CONSEQUENCES

The three of them sat in the living room and talked about the last forty odd hours. They all had questions to ask, Nita and Emma wanted to know how he'd come to have been attacked at almost the same time as they'd been left on the Portbridge by-pass. He told them what had happened at the truck stop. How a couple of drivers nearby helped until the police turned up and an ambulance. He'd tried to call them but getting no reply he'd called the contact number the Special Branch people had given him to use in an emergency. Shortly after that police and some security people who seemed to know what was going on turned up. Having been given the all-clear at the medical centre he'd taken a shower then re-joined the security people. By now the police and security team had found out what had happened here in Portbridge and arranged to get him home as soon as possible. Having got his unit and trailer moved to a secured park they'd taken him to the train station putting him onto the next Euro link home. Sitting back carefully he looked at both women sitting on the settee.

'The rest, well you know as much as I do now.'

Nita watched intently as his story unfolded.

'Why didn't I know about this, why didn't you share it with me Stephen?'

Sensing a tone of anger in her voice he said.

'I'd been specifically told not to say anything sugar, not even to you. After you'd made the possible connection between what you and I saw in York, plus the other times I'd seen the boat. Someone made a connection between the enquiry you were involved with; remember your boss took it to a regional meeting and it appears to have escalated from there. I was stopped in Felixstowe by immigration, HMC&E and two detectives from the Serious Crime team and asked to notify them whenever I saw the boat, since then I've reported about a dozen sightings.'

Thinking about his explanation leading up to the events of the past twenty-four hours, she asked.

'How have they linked you to us and our enquiries... do you know?'

'No idea... but in recent weeks I have noticed a people carrier that's been around when I've been coming and going through Holland and the Low Countries. It even travelled on the same ferry a month ago but I just thought it was a coincidence.'

'Didn't you think to report it?' Nita asked.

'I didn't, no. I didn't make the connection.'

He could see from her body language that she was not a happy person. Emma must have sensed that too. Getting up, she collected the selection of mugs that were dotted around the room and went off to the kitchen.

Fixing Stephen in a cold stare Nita said quietly. 'Bastard...!'

Stunned Stephen looked at her. 'What.'

'Bastard!' she repeated, 'I've just gone through thirty odd hours of pain and guilt thinking all of this was because of me. Have you any idea how bloody wretched I've been feeling? How I got Emma involved in god knows what through my job, wondering how you're going to react when you found out! No I suppose you haven't. Now I find out it's because of you and okay, some of what I'm involved in as well. Suddenly now I find out you are part of a bigger operation that even I'm not to know about. I'm sorry but it stinks! Why the bloody hell couldn't you talk to me... aye? Come on Stephen... this is my job, I deal with secure details and confidences every day.'

She sat looking at him, waiting for a reply.

'I'm sorry, I was only doing what I was told to do. I wanted...'

Nita held her hand up.

'Sorry... SORRY!... NO, sorry doesn't cut it Stephen!'

Reaching for her bag she fumbled through it until she found her phone.

'What are you doing?'

'Phoning Alan, I want to go home.'

'Nita wait, you're not well enough.'

She glared at him holding the phone close to her ear.

'Alan its Nita, where are you?' he must have replied to her as she continued, 'Can you come and pick me up from Stephens place please and take me home.'

He must have begun to make some objection to her because she snapped back at him.

'Sod you then, I'll get a bloody taxi!'

There was another pause and Nita finished by saying. 'Thank you.' snapping the flip top of her phone shut.

Stephen started to protest again.

'Nita stop! I, we need to sort this out, I was only…'

'I'm going home, I need some space to think about everything, okay… end of!'

Going into the hall she came face to face with Emma. There were tears in her eyes.

'Nita.' She started to say.

Nita put her arms around her saying quietly into her ear.

'Emma, this isn't your fault, you've got involved by accident my lovely. I need space to think and I want to be on my own all right; it's not your fault okay.'

She held her at arm's length looking directly into her eyes before drawing her back into the embrace holding her for a few moments longer. Kissing her on the forehead she went up the stairs.

By the time she returned down stairs with her holdall Stephen was standing by the door with Emma by his shoulder. Again he began to plead with her to stay.

'Nita stay, please, let's try and sort this out.'

She just stared at him as coldly as earlier. There was a knock on the door, she went to open it but Stephen, watching her face, put his hand on the doorknob. After a moment's hesitation he opened the door for her. Alan Syms was standing on the pavement, he looked at Nita then Stephen. Nita edged past all of them opened the rear door and throwing her bag onto the back seat stood waiting for Alan.

'Nita…' Emma called, her voice cracking with emotion. Nita looked at her and gave her a sad smile. Alan, acknowledging Stephen shrugged his shoulders and walked round to the driver's door. Before the doors were shut properly they heard Nita say sharply to him.

'And you can shut up as well!' With that they drove away.

Emma turned back into the house beginning to cry softly. Closing the door, Stephen put his arm around her shoulder drawing her into an embrace. Resting her head on his chest she let the tears flow.

'Emma love, it'll be fine, we'll sort it somehow.' he said quietly.

She looked at him, her eyes full of tears, 'Will you Dad… really?'

He heard the doubt in her voice as she broke their embrace turned and went up to her room.

For the remainder of the day and into the early evening, Stephen sat reflecting on everything that had developed over the past three days both here and in Germany, focusing on his recent secret past, in particular, not putting Nita fully in the picture regarding his covert task informing the authorities of any sightings of the fishing boat Caspian Blue. He wrestled with his guilt for the affect his actions had had on Nita, what she'd put herself through thinking that her and Emma's incident was her fault because of the murder case she was pursuing with Alan Syms. Also there was the ongoing work of the gang masters who'd tried to silence their only witness until now. In his mind he ran through different scenarios of trying to explaining his actions to her.

Emma spent her day in her room, upset and emotional, bursting into tears from time to time feeling very confused by Stephen and Nita's reactions. Still suffering the aftereffects of the drug she'd been given she catnapped from time to time. Dusk was falling when she padded downstairs to find Stephen laid out on the settee asleep. Going into the kitchen she filled the kettle to make a drink then decided she was a little peckish and put some bread in the toaster.

The combination of the sound of the kettle boiling and the aroma of toast was enough to stir him. From the lounge she heard him call.

'Yes please, two slices will do for a start.'

Minutes later she brought a tray of tea and toast into the lounge and they sat together drinking tea eating the toast and talking about all that had occurred to the two of them.

Across Portbridge, alone in the house she shared when Stephen was away, Nita made herself a drink and went through to the lounge turned on the gas fire and curled up in one of the armchairs feeling wretched. She was angry and hurt that no-one, her boss, Stephen or anyone involved in this ever-widening enquiry, had considered keeping her in the group of 'need to knows'. Was Alan Syms up to speed or was he just as much in the dark as she was. The only clear common link in all this was the Lithuanian woman Kate. It was a definite connection, because the woman who'd approached her and Emma in the café knew Nita was a detective and appeared to know quite a bit about Kate, now she was off the case, plus Stephen had been instructed not to involve himself any further either. Why had Stephen become so involved, why hadn't Nita been included in the overall planning of whatever was on-going with this boat? For some time she tried to work through all the evidence; Patrick Doyle's suspicious death, Kate's connection with him, now there was Stephen and this boat, the attempt to harm her and Emma and Stephens's assault. The bang of the front door closing brought her up with a start and she realised that she must have fallen asleep. Moira poked her head around the door to the lounge.

'Hello you, are you okay after the accident?' She looked anxiously at her. 'Alan has kept us up to speed, we were so worried. How's Emma, it must have been awful! By all accounts you were so lucky that the truck driver had his wits about him. God Nita it doesn't bear thinking about.'

She paused briefly before adding. 'Anyway what are you doing here? Alan said Stephen was coming home, I'd have thought you'd be cosy and all loved up at his place.'

Nita looked at her friend, eyes full of tears and just held her hand up.

'Oh Nita, what's wrong?'

Dropping her bags in the doorway she came and knelt by the side of the chair taking her hand repeating the question again.

'Hun, what's wrong, why the tears?'

The two girls sat together, Moira waited patiently for Nita to compose herself enough to speak, eventually she took a deep breath.

'It's all a bloody mess, I'm thinking the accident was all my fault because of what I've been working on with Alan. Now it seems it wasn't an accident but a warning because Stephens been beaten up again, this time in Germany.'

'God is he all right?' Moira asked.

'Bruised and bloodied but he's ok. It's not that so much it's the fact that there's been an operation on-going all this time that I've not known about or even been involved in.'

Her voice began to rise a little as she became annoyed and emotional again.

'Everyone and his dog knows about it except me, even Stephen was involved. I feel stupid Moira, I'm hurt, I'm so angry and I feel so guilty because this time Emma's involved and she's just a kid and I thought it was down to me and… Ohh I could spit!'

It wasn't long before Louise arrived home. Seeing Nita in the lounge she went to her give her a cuddle and so started the whole de-brief once again. In answering the questions the girls kept firing at her, she began to get a clearer picture of the past few days that helped her to see things a little more objectively. They eventually turned in for the night and whilst not wholly at peace, she did feel easier in herself. Instead of the anger she'd felt before and the feeling of being let down by Stephen, she'd actually started to feel sorry for overreacting, she fell asleep promising to make things right between them.

Stephen meanwhile, unable to sleep just kept going over and over the events of the past three days, he'd been surprised and shocked at Nita's reaction in learning about his involvement from the DI. He thought she'd understand him reporting these sightings were covert in building a case before initiating a full-on operation to bring whoever was involved to book. What troubled him more though was the affect it appeared to have had on their relationship. Half asleep he rolled onto his back and sighed, somehow he had to find a way of making it right between them and for Emma too. He'd seen his daughter change since meeting Nita, she'd suddenly grown up. He'd watched her adopt some of Nita's mannerisms, perhaps begun to see Nita as a role model. Something of herself in Nita's independent side, her rebelliousness. Finally surrendering to the fact that he couldn't sleep, he threw off the covers and padded downstairs, brewed himself a mug of tea and sat at the breakfast bar resolved to try and make things up with Nita. He sat there until the dawn came up just thinking.

~~~~~~~~~~~~~~~~~~~~~~~~~~~~~~~~

The aroma of bacon and coffee gently invaded Stephens's senses and woke him from the deep sleep he slipped into after eventually returning to bed. He made his way down to the kitchen to find Emma dressed, looking all domesticated. Hair up, apron on attending to a variety of pans on the cooker. To her right on the work surface wisps of blue smoke rose from the toaster to blend with the general blue haze enveloping the kitchen. Moments later the shrill pulses of the fire alarm made both of them jump. Stephen moved to the toaster as he heard Emma exclaim.

'SHIT…!'

'Hey… there's no need for that!' he said as he popped the release on the side of the toaster then grabbing the kitchen towel stood by the alarm wafting it back and forth until it ceased its noise.

Emma glanced at him guiltily. 'Sorry dad, I'd forgotten I'd put the toast on. Is it edible?'
~~~~~~~~~~~~~~~~~~~~~~~~~~~~~~~~

'Erm not unless you're into charcoal!' he replied, 'No!' grinning and holding up two blackened pieces of what used to be bread. 'I'll put some more on love.'

Emma took two plates from the oven and plated up bacon, eggs, baked beans and mushrooms and presented one of the plates on the breakfast bar in front of him. She put a cafetiere of coffee beside two mugs. The toaster popped once more and Stephen reached for the two slices of toast. Sitting facing each other they consumed their 'full English' without really speaking. Refilling his mug he looked at Emma.

'How are you this morning?'

She shrugged. 'Okay I suppose, still upset about yesterday. I slept really deeply but I'm sad dad. How are you?'

'Still a bit sore but a lot better, thinking about yesterday kept me awake too. I was up thinking about all sorts, I'm going to try and sort things with Nita this weekend if I can.'

'You've got to dad she's just so much part of us now! Even Nan and Granddad think of her as family.'

Stephen glanced at her.

'You know sweetheart, I've watched you change so much over the last year, it's really scary because my little girl is becoming a young lady.'

Emma smiled warmly, picked up their plates and took them to the sink.

'For age's dad I've wanted you to meet someone, I miss mum so much although I never really got to know her other than my mum; not like knowing Nita now like a grown up a friend. I sometimes wonder how it would have been with mum, how would we get on shopping and talking about grown up things? I know Nan's always there and we've talked about girl stuff, women's things.' She glanced at Stephen quickly. 'Since you've been with Nita it's all different, you're different. You've always been dad and it's really been us two for ever! But now with Nita around it feels like we're... a family. You have to go and see her dad, you said you would last night.'

He studied Emma, once again she'd surprised him with her

maturity. She turned to face him holding his stare.

'Yes, I will, she means an awful lot to me too Em. Up 'til now I've avoided any sort of friendship with anyone because it would have thrown up all sorts of problems, loads of what ifs you know.'

'Such as?' Em asked.

'Well... er... what if they didn't get on with you or tried to change me or... well lots of things, I can't think of any right now.'

'No and that's the thing dad, with Nita it was different because the circumstances were different. You didn't meet her in a pub or a club but something must have clicked at the hospital or through the summer when you two were Skyping or texting all day. Come on dad you were messaging one way or the other all through the last holiday. We all wondered who this person was 'cause nobody has ever had that effect on you since I can remember. You even had Nan and Granddad guessing.'

He smirked at Emma's logical observation.

'Okay yes guilty I have avoided getting involved, Nita's taken me to task so many times over my attitude. It was her who basically got us into this relationship, I'd have run off back to Europe in the truck and never come back given half a chance but she kept showing me that it was me in my head putting up all sorts of barriers to escape making any effort to meet someone.'

'Exactly, mum wouldn't have not wanted you not to see someone, be with someone, if they were the right person and okay, for me too.'

He nodded. 'You're right, I was my own worst enemy.'

'Yeah... and look how everything's changed. You might not see it but the rest of us can, Nita's made such a difference, so you need to do something to sort it out... now... today!'

Getting to his feet he walked round the breakfast bar and enfolded her in his arms kissing her on the top of her head.

'Emma Leigh-Grace you've no idea how much I love you lady, your mother would be so proud of the way you are growing up, I'm proud of you too.'

'I love you too dad,' she said against his chest, 'and I'm proud of you and will be even prouder when you sort this out with Nita. She needs to be part of us dad, really she does. I just love spending time with her.'

'I will, I'll call her and meet up promise, if not this weekend then next week. I am missing her too you know! Now do we need shopping for you or us before you go back to Nan and Granddads on Monday?'

Emma disengaged herself to finish the washing up.

'I got all I needed when I was with Nita last week but I want to see Grandpa Harold before I go.'

'Okay, we'll shop today and then go to the Currergate on Sunday, all right?'

On Sunday they drove the fifty minutes to Harold's home and took him out for a carvery lunch. Stephen sat quietly watching how his father came alive in Emma's company, he couldn't help smiling as he heard him laugh at the stories Emma was telling him about school and her friends and the antics they got up to. Returning to the home they had tea with the old man and Sylvie before saying goodbye.

'How do you think Grandpa looked today love?'

Stephen asked as they drove home.

'He's changed a bit since I saw him at Christmas, a bit frailer but all his slates are on. What do think, you see him more than I do!'

'He slowed down quite a bit at first but now he's been there for the last year and made some friends he seems a bit more settled.' he laughed briefly, 'A sight happier than when we moved him into the place. Remember how he thought we just wanted rid of him and were putting him in a home to get him out of our lives.'

Emma smiled at the thought from a year ago. 'Oh yes but he is in the best place. There's less chance of him having little accidents with people to watch him, plus he's got Sylvie around, it's lovely.'

Nita spent her weekend with Louise and Moira shopping and eating out in Portbridge. Moira left them to meet her fiancé while the two girls went to the cinema and then a club bar. Sunday morning was a slow painful start for both of them suffering the excesses from last night but by lunch time and the benefits of a greasy home cooked breakfast and strong coffee they'd both pretty well recovered. Nita spent the day making notes on the previous week's happenings, still trying to see if she could see some sort of pattern how things had got so out of hand. Everything always came back to how involved Stephen had been since they'd seen that boat in York at Easter. In the end she decided to go into work on Monday and speak to DI Allen or her sergeant.

Monday morning was all hustle and bustle. The girls dashing around collecting files and papers they needed for today, while Nita kept them supplied with coffee until she was finally on her own. Standing in the silence of the kitchen she couldn't help smiling, she'd forgotten just what life was like before Stephen, when all three of them would be falling over one another to get off to work on time. Making herself a drink she sat for some time thinking about Stephen and Emma. Glancing at the clock on the mantel piece she saw the time and thought of Emma getting her stuff together to travel back to Poole. Meanwhile at Stephen's house, standing at the foot of the stairs he called out.

'Emma! If you don't get a rush on we're going to miss your train! All your stuff's in the car so what do you need now?'

She replied from her room. 'I'm coming dad now.'

This was followed moments later by the thundering of Emma's footsteps on the stairs.

'Sarnies dad, where are my snacks and things?'

He held up her back bag which she grabbed then pulling her coat off the stand in the hall she stood looking at him.

Right... I'm here, ready... are we going then?'

Shaking his head he set off following her out of the house to the car.

'I don't know how you manage to do this every time Em? Yesterday you were packed and sorted, this morning it's like it's all fallen apart, what happens?'

Emma shrugged, 'Dunno, I just remember things I want.'

'Unbelievable!'

Very little was said on the drive to the station but once parked and walking to the platform Emma said.

'Dad, promise you'll take care and please don't get involved in anything again.'

'Promise sweetheart and yes before you ask, I'm going to speak to Nita sometime today and sort us out too, I'll call you and let you know how it goes. Now you've got your exams this term, I'm really proud of how hard you've worked Em, all you can do now is your best. Whatever the outcome love we all know how hard you're trying.'

Standing by the carriage door they hugged one another tightly.

'Love you Emma, soooo much!'

'You too dad, love you too.'

She boarded the train and he walked down the platform following her to her seat then standing by the window waited until the automatic doors closed. Moments later the train began to move and they waved to each other. Returning to his car he saw Nita's sergeant hovering at the station entrance.

'Mr Leigh-Grace, detective sergeant Ruth Dawson.'

Stephen nodded. 'Yes I remember, we met last week.'

The detective smiled falling into step with him as they walked across the car park.

'DI Allen just wanted to put your mind at rest and let you know there are two detectives from our regional unit on the train with Emma. They will travel with her all the way to Poole where the officer charged with keeping in contact with her will take over.'

'Thank you, that's comforting to know, I must admit I'm torn, a huge part of me wants to be down there with her. The alternative was to keep her up here with me.'

The detective smiled again.

'Understandable but for this operation to work we all have to try and live normally to avoid spooking whoever's running this gang.'

Standing beside his car Stephen turned to the detective.

'I wonder, would you do something for me?'

'If I can, yes.'

'If possible can you explain to Nita, DC Patel, what has happened and why I couldn't say anything about my part in this. She just went off on Friday and I've not been able to get hold of her all weekend. Emma's really upset and I've also realised this weekend how important she has become to me as well.'

Touching his arm briefly, she replied.

'Not sure how much influence I have, but yes I'll have a word if that'll help.'

Stephen nodded, they shook hands and the detective walked to her car. Stephen got into his car and phoned Mary and Richard to let them know Emma was on her way back to them, then made his way back home.

~~~~~~

Pressing her pass code into the door lock Nita entered her office and made her way up three flights of stairs to the detective's office. Entering the large room, one or two heads turned to glance who was coming in. Quite quickly a general silence fell across the room making her feel a little uncomfortable as a dozen pairs of eyes fixed on her. Trying to feel confident she said brightly.

'Morning all, I'm sort of back and okay.'

Linda walked over to her, 'Hey you, are you sure you should be in?'

Nita looked at her nodding. 'Yeah, I'm okay, a bit woozy about things at times but okay.'

Alan Syms had come across to them.

'Why have you come in so soon you could've stayed off another day or two the boss would understand?'

'There's so much shit going on, I need to see the boss or at least the sarge to get it all clear in my head.' Looking directly at Alan she asked him, 'Did you know anything about this other operation that the world and his dog is involved in, except us?'
~~~~~~

Alan shrugged. 'Nita, what operation, what are you talking about? All we're investigating is Patrick Doyle's death and you're looking into that assault on the Lithuanian girl… what's this other operation you're on about?'

She stared at him for a moment.

'Right! I need to see the boss, is he in yet?' then realising it was Monday morning, answered her own question. 'Cause he is, it's bloody Monday.' Glancing at Linda she asked, 'Have you had the Monday briefing?'

Linda nodded adding. 'He went straight off to a meeting at division.'

'Sarge?'

Linda shook her head. 'She wasn't here this morning.'

'Where the chuff is everyone?' Nita exclaimed angrily.

Both Alan and Linda were watching her, Alan said.

'Nita, what are you on about?'

Exhaling to release her frustration she walked to her desk followed by the other two officers. Those few moments gave her time to get her head together allowing her to remember the meeting on Friday and the emphasis for absolute secrecy. Choosing her words carefully she began to explain.

'It appears my accident…. wasn't an accident. The boss and the guys at division think it might have been a warning connected with Patrick's disappearance and death.'

Alan looked at her shocked.

'Bloody hell Nita, does that mean something similar could happen to me then?'

Nita shrugged. 'Who knows, don't forget I'm involved with both cases, the warning could be connected with Katterine's case also.'

'So what's going to happen now?' he said.

The banging of the office door distracted the three of them, turning they saw that the sergeant had just come in, as she walked to her office she pointed at Nita and Alan and gestured for them to follow. Once in her office she dragged an extra chair to her desk.

'Alan go get some drinks will you, black coffee two sugars for me, Nita?'

'Tea no sugar please.'

Alan left to get the drinks.

'Have you said anything?'

Nita shrugged, 'Just asked Alan if he knew anything.'

'And...?'

'He's as much in the dark as me sarge, how much do you know?'

'Nothing lovie, nada...zilch! Until Thursday that was and your accident, before that absolutely bloody nothing honest, then the DI and me were called up to headquarters for a briefing; by that time HQ knew of Stephens attack in Germany. This is all linked to him reporting to immigration and Special Branch on some boat's movements when he's been on his travels. Apparently there is a link to your inquiry into Katterine's assault and the Doyle murder. It seems pretty obvious that this gang have been doing their research, so we must be rattling someone's cage quite a bit.'

Alan Syms crashed through the office door carrying three mugs, placing them on the desk he sat down.

'Okay you two, this is how things are going to happen. Nita knows some of this already, Alan your enquiries into Patrick Doyle's death and the assault on Katterine have turned up an international trafficking gang that so far have been able to stay below anyone's radar. For some time Special branch and Immigration have been working with an informant working abroad.'

She didn't look at Nita but just carried on giving the facts to Alan.

'Together a case is being put together to try and net the whole lot here in the UK, Holland and Germany, it's not quite there yet so absolute secrecy is essential.'

Glancing from one detective to the other, 'Keeping up?' They both nodded, 'Good, so...'

She took a breath and a sip of her drink.

'So what happened to Nita can't be hidden and we feel we can run with the theory that the attack on her was a warning from some group, gang, whatever but a small-time lot trying to flex their muscles. Both of you are to continue your enquiries into the Doyle case, but Nita's case with Katterine is being taken over by the wooden tops. Nita you will still need to keep the contact with the woman because she relies on you... but it will be, errmm... sort of supervised, for your own safety, okay? Alan you carry on as usual, but you will have company as well. That however, will be at a discreet distance so don't get paranoid, these guys know who they are looking for trust me. Remember simple stories are believable and easy to maintain, work together on it but 'Mums the word' absolute secrecy! Okay?' They both nodded again. 'Right, Alan you carry on, Nita a word.'

Alan Syms got up to leave the office touching Nita's shoulder momentarily as he moved past her, they exchanged a look. Once he was out of the office the sergeant pushed the door slightly too.

'Right... as a friend lovie, you need to go and see Stephen and sort this out. I was at the station this morning to see that Emma got off okay with her shadows. They are both struggling, Emma hasn't the faintest idea what has occurred and why. Her world just seems to have crashed and burned around her and she's trying to understand if she's anything to do with it. Stephen has been in an intolerable place since Easter and your original, albeit innocent enquiry to division about that boat and the van. Division passed your sighting to immigration and they got the wooden tops involved who then linked in with Interpol. As I understand it, Immigration met Stephen off the ferry one trip and he agreed to feed them information each time he saw this boat or the van. Because of the nature of the enquiry he nearly had to sign the official secrets act, you understand, that's why until last week he couldn't say anything. Nita sweetie, your reaction was understandable, Stephen accepts that but cut him a bit of slack! You are very significant in that family's lives now and I think you know that plus I know what that man means to you! You show it in how you've changed over the last year, even I've noticed from this desk. Go see the man for god's sake and sort it... as your friend lovie I'm asking, as your sergeant that's an order!'

She held Nita in a firm stare for some time before adding.

'Now sod off home for the rest of the day and only come in tomorrow if you're feeling okay, right.'

Nita stood up. 'Thanks sarge, I was going to go and find him today after I'd spoken to you or the boss.' The sergeant grinned and nodded. 'Close the door on your way out.'

Stopping by the desk she shared with Alan, she perched on the edge.

'We need to talk, when's best for you?'

'Any time really but where's best?' Alan replied looking round the office, 'There are some sharp ears round here!'

'Mmm... I'll call you later.

'Okay, are you all right? You know that was something else, you must have wondered what was happening, is Emma all right?'

'Emma! ... she's fine we both recovered quickly once they'd got us to hospital. To be honest Alan I can't remember a thing, all I know is what people have told me but I gather we were both lucky.'

'Oh yes!... When you're up to it ask the traffic lads to show you the pictures... scary trust me!'

She stood up and touched his shoulder. 'I'll call you.'

~~~~~~
~~~~~~

MAKING UP THE BEST WAY

Everything Stephen did round the house through the morning was half hearted, he was distracted what was going to be the best way to sort things out with Nita. He sat at the breakfast bar staring at his mobile phone fully intending to call her, at the fourth attempt he pressed the call button. He heard the connection click, it rang for some time and his nerve started to fade, almost at the point of cancelling the call he heard Nita say.

'Hello… that's funny I was going to call you actually.'

He breathed a huge sigh of relief.

'Are you all right Ferryman?'

'Yeah… I'm all right, it's good to hear your voice.'

'You too.'

Silence for some time, neither of them spoke.

'Listen.' Nita began, at the same time as Stephen said, 'I need.'

They stopped speaking, Stephen began again.

'Nita I need to see you to planex.'

'To what?'

'To planex… I mean explain, sorry got my words mixed up.'

'Yeah just a bit! Listen what I said the other day was unfair, I'm sorry.'

He interrupted, 'No you were right, I should have trusted that if I'd said anything you'd have worked with me on the importance of secrecy.'

Silence once more.

'Did you say you wanted to meet?' Nita ventured.

'Yes, I'd like to see you.'

Another pause before Nita said.

'Okay, should we say the Duchess then, about seven, are you all right with that?'

'Yeah seven's good.'

'See you there then.'

The line went dead. He sat now contemplating what he could do, or say to show it had never been his intention to exclude her from this escalating operation. That the need for absolute secrecy had been so forcefully emphasized to him that he'd felt pressured into not saying anything. Deep down though he knew he could have trusted her to maintain the secrecy. Perhaps tonight they could try and put their relationship on an even keel again, not just for himself but for Emma too.

Nita on the other hand felt so relieved, the feelings of guilt she'd experienced following the accident; that Emma had been caught up in it all, had grown and grown into a nightmare. It had helped that she'd talked out those feelings with her housemates. Her anger had given way to a feeling of regret that she'd instantly blamed Stephen for everything without giving him chance to explain. Having spoken to the sergeant today and been given more of the details about the case she'd realised that her over-reaction had probably contributed to the situation they were in now; she'd actually begun to feel some sympathy for him. Tonight she would say sorry and try and make up for the past three days. She felt bad for Emma too, the way she'd left, the look on Emma's face haunted her, it was important that she got her message over to them but the bottom line was she wanted to stay in touch, she wanted Stephen in her life,

Driving into Portbridge he parked in the Duchess's car park just before seven. The pub was very quiet compared to the last time they were here but it was a Monday. Ordering a lager and white wine spritzer for Nita he sat in the lounge area. A few minutes later she walked through the main entrance, standing by the bar she turned glancing round the room, her eyes fell on him. He gestured that he had a drink waiting for her and stood up as she approached the table. For a few fleeting moments they stood looking at one another before he reached for her hand and drew her into an embrace. He inhaled the scent she was wearing experiencing that feeling of closeness she always seemed to give him. She allowed herself to relax in his embrace feeling warm and secure herself. Stepping apart they sat down studying one another, he picked up his drink. 'Cheers.'

Nita couldn't help grinning at the formality, picking up her glass she responded.

'Cheers to you too. That was very formal.'

He chuckled. 'I don't know what to say.'

'Hmm, neither do I... except perhaps I'm sorry.'

Over the rim of her glass she watched for his reaction, he smiled.

'Maybe it should be me saying sorry, after all in your job integrity is a watch word. By not saying anything to you I put you and Em in a position where you could have been seriously injured. If you'd have known what I'd been asked to do then perhaps what happened at the café wouldn't have happened, if you see what I mean?'

'All right apology accepted and just for the record it wasn't just what you were doing that brought this situation about. It appears to be connected with two enquiries I'm involved in as well. The 'powers at be' think that Alan and I are rattling someone's door nearer to home which is possibly connected to what you've been involved in on your travels.'

They sat in silence sipping their drinks, draining his glass Stephen looked at Nita.

'Another?'

'Why not.'

When he returned with their drinks he sat next to her they touched glasses.

'Where do we go from here Ferryman...?' she said quietly.

It took a while for him to answer.

'I'm under strict instructions to sort this out and make it right, apparently you being in my life has changed me...for the better I'm told!'

Nita rocked back a little on the settee silently giggling.

'What?' he said

Well, 'sort it out' is pretty much the same instructions I've had too.'

'Who from?'

'The girls at the house and my sergeant would you believe? It seems I'm not such a grumpy cow these days.'

He smiled, 'Okay, well I'm home now until further notice on the pretext of being a character witness for that driver last year.

They sat together quietly there was no need to speak, Nita chuckled briefly and when he looked at her, she said.

'Look at us just like a content old married couple sitting here drinking in silence.'

He shrugged, 'Listen, I've really missed you these last few days and it's made me realise that having you around does make all the difference in my life, you've given me my confidence back. Not talking to you every day makes me feel lost again, vulnerable, like I was last September.'

He glanced at her. She was watching him with a smile on her face.

'What... doesn't that make sense?'

She shook her head slightly,

'Mmm yes but maybe a bit, how should I say... obtuse. You could have been a lot more economical and just simply told me,' she shuffling closer to him she placed her hands on his thigh, 'you love me!'

Closing the gap she kissed him gently. Still only inches apart he whispered.

'I love you.

This time they hugged one another and gently kissed again.

'Phew, I need a drink!' he said.

'I need the little girl's room.'

When she returned he handed her a brandy, she noticed he had a whisky on the rocks.

'Err aren't you driving?'

He grinned. 'Not tonight, I've taken the liberty of booking us a room. Is that a problem?'

She looked steadily at him.

'You do realise I'm at work in the morning.'

'Hmm... okay, you'll have to do the walk of shame then.'

'Scuse me, aren't you rushing things here a bit. We're still sort of trying to resolve what's happened and who did what, or have I missed something?'

He gave her a wry smile...

'I thought we could arrive at a better agreement in private! However if you feel you aren't ready to reach some sort of compromise, then we...'

Reaching for the lapels of his jacket she pulled him closer looking straight into his eyes.

'Shut up! Kiss me.'

They kissed and hugged once more. Nita whispered in his ear.

'I have an ache in my tummy to have you.'

'Better finish our drinks then.'

They finished their drinks and left the bar trying to look as casual as possible and not raise any suspicion to their sudden departure. As he unlocked the bedroom door he could hear Nita behind him trying to stifle a giggle. Crashing into the room they fell onto the bed laughing like teenagers. Taking a breath to control himself he spluttered.

'We're adults, why are we behaving like guilty teenagers?'

'Do you think anyone noticed?'

'Nita! You think...! We arrive separately, we have a couple of drinks, I get a room and we sneak off! And you wonder if anyone noticed! I'll bet everyone in that bar is thinking 'we know what you're doing'!'

Calling on all her powers of self-control she calmed herself, rolled off the bed she closed the curtains.

'Better not prove them wrong then!'

Crossing back to the bed she sat astride his prone body, leaning forward she planted her lips on his. He responded, they matched each other's urges with ever increasing passion somehow managing to remove every stitch of clothing without breaking the kiss. Finally with Stephen sitting upright against the bedhead they joined together in a slow very deliberate act of making love until they orgasmed together. The intensity of their shared orgasm was so strong that Nita's body convulsed as her orgasm tore through her. Stephen clung to her holding her in a bear hug as he too reacted to such an intense orgasm. Remaining in this position, it was quite some time before they recovered enough to speak. With her head resting on his shoulder her lips by his neck, she said.

'I have missed you these last few days. I felt so wretched at the way I left, being so angry and blaming you for everything, I am so sorry.'

She lifted her head staring into his eyes, repeating softly, 'So sorry.'

Releasing his hold of her slim body he replied.

'You've nothing to be sorry for sugar, I think what has happened is mainly down to me, I was watching them and didn't realise how clever they were at adding two and two together. When I was told about you and Emma, I was so sick with worry and guilt for getting us into this mess. It hit me then, what would I do if either of you were seriously injured. I realised just how much you mean to me... just how much I've grown to love you!'

She placed her arms around his neck drawing him onto her breasts. They stayed like this for some time until Stephen said.

'I think you need to move I can't feel my legs anymore!'

Nita giggled and grabbing a few tissues from the box on the bedside cabinet and scrambled off to the bathroom. When she returned they quickly snuggled together under the duvet.

'Mmm this is nice, when I was back at the house with the girls I couldn't get settled. Funny isn't it, we haven't been sleeping together for that long but when you're not here I don't sleep as well.'

He said softly. 'For the past few years I've never had a problem sleeping in the wagon but yes, since I met you I don't seem to sleep so well on my own. These last few days have been awful.' A few moments later he asked.

'Are we okay now? You and me, are we okay?'

Lifting her head slightly she looked at him. 'Mmm, yes, very okay.'

Placing her head back under his chin she hugged him tightly repeating herself. 'Very okay.'

~~~~~~~~~~~~~~~~~~~~~~~~~~~~~~~~

The pair walked into the dining room at seven forty-five to be greeted by Jean who seemed surprised to see them.

'Hello you two to what do we owe the pleasure to have you staying over?'

They glanced at each other then back to Jean, Stephen replying.

'Should we say an excess!'

She laughed at them.

'Not the first, did you sleep well?'

They replied in unison, 'Yes we did.'

'Right well there are the juices and cereals,' she said pointing to the long table against the wall at the back of the dining room. 'Help yourselves; so tea or coffee and would you like some toast?'

Stephen replied. 'Coffee for me please,' glancing at Nita he continued 'and ... tea for Nita

and yes toast, thank you.'

'I've put you in the window, have a look at the menu and I'll be back in a minute.'

They selected fruit juices from the table, Nita picked up two yoghurts and after a quick look around popped one into her bag.

'I saw that and you a police officer to boot!'

'Shush! I can have that for my lunch.'

She'd just managed to hide it in her bag before an elderly couple walked into the dining room followed moments later by a single man. Stephen shook his head tutting as she took a banana from the selection of fruit on the table.
~~~~~~~~~~~~~~~~~~~~~~~~~~~~~~~~

The landlady returned. 'Tea, coffee and toast. What else can I get you?'

Stephen ordered a full English, Nita poached eggs. Settled at their table he said.

'Are you going to come up to the house tonight?'

'Not tonight, the girls will be wondering where I've got to, I'll get the stuff I took back and come over tomorrow night. What are you doing today?'

'As I'm in town I'll nip through to the depot and badger the boss again.'

Their breakfasts arrived and once eaten they left, going to the reception desk. Stephen rang the bell and they waited for someone to respond, he chuckled.

'What?'

'The bell reminds me of Fawlty Towers, I'm kind of waiting for Basil to appear through the door all fussy you know, 'Yes dear, don't mind me, I'll see to it...' he mimicked.

'Fool!' Nita said as Jean appeared.

'Everything all right for you two?'

'Fine thanks, what's the damage?' Stephen asked.

Smiling broadly she said. 'For cash at 'mates' rates let's say fifty, is that okay.'

They exchanged looks and Nita said, 'Are you sure?'

'Oh yes you're locals, well sort of. If Mick found out I'd charged you the going rate he'd have quite a lot to say don't you think?'

Between them they found the fifty pounds, said their goodbyes and walked to the car park. Standing close together Stephen took hold of Nita's hands.

'Do you think this how people feel when they've had an illicit night of passion?'

Nita laughed nervously, 'I feel really naughty you know, excited, sort of on a high all tingly!'

Putting her arms around his waist she drew him into a close embrace.

'You were very passionate.'

They stood in this embrace for quite some time just enjoying the closeness, until Nita said against his chest.

'If this is making up then we ought to do it more often... but without the drama hhmm? however I am sorry but duty calls and I have to go Ferryman.'

'I just hope we're all going to be safer now as it's out of our hands.' he said quietly.

'Well just tell me next time you want to be a hero then I'm prepared for whatever shit you stir up. Okay?'

'Okay.'

'Good, right I'm off I'll see you tomorrow at yours, yes?'

Nodding Stephen replied, 'Yes.'

Planting a noisy kiss on his lips she turned, opened her car door saying as she sat down.

'Love you!'

Raising his hand he replied. 'You too.'

Starting the engine and reversing into the centre of the car park she tooted her horn and drove out of the parking area. Moments later he followed going towards his depot.

Nita arrived at her office with a happy face and a smile she couldn't hide. Stephen drove to his depot with an equally broad grin on his face. Both experiencing a huge sense of relief that they'd sorted everything out.

That evening he called Emma to see how she was coping with her undercover shadow, having listened to her telling him about the detective working with her she wanted to know how he was and what he'd done with himself. Eventually the subject came around to him and Nita.

'So dad, have you seen her, have you sorted things out?'

'Yes Em we've met and I think everything is all right.'

'Way to go dad! I'm so pleased, that means I can message her again. Ohh you've just made my day, I'll sleep happy now.'

'Good, well be good work hard okay! Give my love to your Nan and Granddad. Night Em, love you loads.'

'Love you back dad, night.'

Just after six that evening Nita arrived back at her house all bubbly with a big smile much to the surprise of the girls. Moira was the first to comment.

'Oh-oh, someone's made up! We wondered where you'd got to last night, we considered reporting you as missing but thought we'd wait until tonight.'

Nita grinned broadly as Louise added.

'I take it that that huge void in your shattered heart has been mended?'

'Mmm work in process you could say, I'm here tonight then back to his tomorrow.'

The two housemates exchanged glances and raised eyebrows.

'Fickle, very fickle.' Moira said, Louise nodded in agreement. The three of them giggled as Louise gave Nita a tight hug. Periodically through the evening they both found themselves reflecting on last night. They both felt this sense of relief but more significantly the realization that in just a year they had fallen in love.

~~~~~~~~~~~~~~~~~~~~~~~~~~~~~~~~~~~~~

The first full week back at work for Stephen was quite difficult. He faced the boss questioning him about the whole incident on the German border, his mood not improved by having to explain to a customer why his delivery was delayed; added to that was the fact he had a truck stuck in Frankfurt until a driver could get there to complete the run. Stephen's other problem was running with the 'story' as to why he had to remain in the UK. He quickly realised that being an informant for 'Operation Hawkeye' was so much easier than having to watch what he said to mates and friends hoping he didn't inadvertently blurt out the real reason for staying local. When he said as much to Nita one evening she chuckled.
~~~~~~~~~~~~~~~~~~~~~~~~~~~~~~~~~~~~~

'Now you know what it's like for us. There's a definite art in dodging awkward questions and finding plausible answers that satisfy inquisitive folk.' To put him at ease she added, 'Anyway we've only got six weeks before the holidays. Tell you what I'm ready for a break, this last six months has been tough.'

He nodded.

'Certainly has, actually it's lasted over a year really.

She couldn't help a little giggle, he looked at her.

'Well if you didn't get yourself into these scrapes like some superhero life would be much simpler for all of us! I'm getting paranoid you know, every time my phone rings and I don't recognise the number I answer it with bated breath expecting someone to say they're calling from this hospital or that police station and not worry but...'

Looking directly at him, she raised an eyebrow giving him the look! He grinned.

'Yeah I know and I promise I'll try to stay out of other people's problems in future!'

He crossed his heart as he said this.

Over the next month Stephen worked UK runs, away Mondays until the Friday night or Saturday morning. Occasionally he managed to get home mid-week to spend the night with Nita. Conveniently the work gave him time to think about his request to permanently come back onto home runs allowing him to compare the difference between his earnings on the European runs against UK home jobs. With the annual five-week cruise looming, every moment he had available was spent phoning and e-mailing the family finalising what had still to be done. Who was doing what, had Emma and her friend got their things ready, were the travel arrangements sorted because this year the holiday would start from Dover not Poole. They were all going to have to travel to Dover to collect *Finbar*. He asked Mary to organise a delivery of provisions from one of the supermarkets, so for the first few days until they could shop somewhere together they'd have food on board. Listening to all the chit-chat Nita felt a little left out because she was still going to have to work for an additional three weeks before flying out to join them all.

The Friday of the holiday finally arrived, Stephen was back at the depot that afternoon and having signed off all his paperwork bade everyone in the office goodbye before travelling home. They sat and ate dinner talking through last minute plans both for his departure in the morning, and Nita's in three weeks' time. He asked her if she was sure she wanted to remain at the house on her own rather than return to the one she shared with the girls.

'Listen I'll be quite happy here, the last few weeks has been good for me, I didn't feel so lonely with you so much nearer; as in the UK and not hundreds of miles away in Sweden or Germany. I can always up sticks if I'm not happy you know!'

He smiled. 'I know, just wanted to be sure you were going to be okay.'

Packing the last bits of kit he needed, they went to bed quite early. Snuggling together they talked quietly, face to face until Nita realised he'd fallen asleep, kissing his forehead she slid away from him and was soon asleep herself.

They were both up early Saturday morning and loaded Stephen's case and two sailing bags into Nita's new car. Standing together on the platform they embraced kissed, hugged, and just held one another. Tearfully she studied his face, she wanted to say something but couldn't find the right words. Wiping her cheeks with his thumbs he kissed her softly.

'Hey, it's going to be okay, you'll be with us in three Saturdays and we'll have a great time, promise?'

She nodded holding back the tears squeezing him tightly.

'I'm being silly I know, and we've said bye so many times through the last year but this feels different. I think it's because you're going to be with the family and not trucking, I am going to miss you!' The tears came again and she finished by saying, 'I love you so much.'

A horn sounded just outside the station announcing the arrival of the train. A few minutes later with Stephen safely aboard a station guard blew his whistle and the train started to roll, they both waved, Nita blowing kisses. She watched the train disappearing into the distance before turning and walking back to her car. Pulling her mobile from her bag she called the girls number. Leaning against her car wing waiting for a reply she realised she was crying again.

'Come on stupid, get a grip.' she thought.

'Hello?' a voice said.

'Moira, hi it's Nita.'

'Hey sweetie, how's you?'

'Okay… well sort of okay, I've just seen Stephen off and…' The tears came again. 'Sorry…' Nita said through a sob.

'Nita, Nita sweetie, where are you?'

'At the station, I'll be alright, Are you both in? I need a hug and a coffee.'

'Surely, get yourself here there'll be one ready when you arrive okay? Hey, be safe don't rush!'

'Okay fifteen minutes, thank you.'

In the background she heard Louise asking what the problem was and Moira saying she was a bit upset and was coming over for a bit of TLC. She heard Louise shout, 'You take care Nita, see you soon.' The line went dead.

In twenty minutes she was being consoled by the two girls and feeling calmer. They talked about the holiday and when she was going to join them.

'In three weeks' time in Jersey.'

The girls began to tease her about life on a 'floating gin palace' and she was on a slippery slope to a very decadent life. Soon she'd disown them… shun them in the street. It was just envy really and they all ended up laughing about the whole scenario particularly when Nita said she'd arrange for them all to have a weekend away on *Finbar* at some point. Later they all went off to Leeds for some retail therapy to brighten her up, not returning until quite late in the evening. Collecting a take-away from one of the curry houses in Portbridge and three bottles of wine from the off-licence they finally landed back at the house deciding Nita would stay the night. Stephen called during the evening to say he'd arrived safely in Dover, met up with all the others and everything was aboard *Finbar*, tomorrow they'd depart for the French coast. Finishing the call Nita sent her love to everyone and wished them 'bon voyage'. With her workload reduced now she was off the Patrick Doyle case, she found time to clear some minor cases, even taking some of Alan Syms's misdemeanour case work. She made two visits to Katterine to check how she was and updated her regarding her asylum application. She visited Vivienne Doyle too, updating her on the investigation into Patrick's death. Returning to the office she told Alan that Vivienne seemed to have really turned her life around, she looked well the flat was still clean. Her daughter was at a nursery and she was taking her son to a mother and toddler group.

The Thursday before she was due to fly to Jersey she personally filed all her completed cases, closing the filing cabinet with a flourish then apologising to everyone as the draw slammed shut a little harder than she'd intended making a few people start at the bang. At five she left saying to Alan.

'You still on for tomorrow at nine?'

'Surely, I'm going to wave you off... you know tears in my eyes waving a white hanky at the prospect of two whole weeks without you bending my ear,' he smiled, 'ahh bliss!'

She scowled at him, 'Bog off sod pot!'

They both laughed and as she walked to the door Alan called after her.

'Nine then... set your alarm.' Nita waved and left.

~~~~~~~~~~~~~~~~~~~~~~~~~~~~~~
~~~~~~~~~~~~~~~~~~~~~~~~~~~~~~

SUMMER JOLLIES

Alan Syms parked his car in the drop off zone at Leeds Bradford airport, Nita and Louise piled out onto the pavement while Alan opened the tailgate pulling Nita's suitcase and holdall out.

'Thanks Alan.'

He smiled at her as she put her arms round Louise hugging her.

'Have a fabulous holiday. I'm so jealous of you, a fella, a boat, and holidays who knows

where. Look at me pale and wan after two wet weeks in the Lake District. If you come back all tanned I'll just ignore you until you're pale again.'

They giggled at each other before Louise added.

'Have fun Nita, see you in two weeks.'

Getting back into the car she added, 'Love you.'

'You too Lou.' Nita replied, 'and thanks a million for driving Alan.'

She said to him through the passenger door.

'No probs, like Lou said have a great holiday. We've worked bloody hard these past three months. See you in two weeks then.'

Standing by her luggage she waved the pair off and as the car disappeared she sighed, she could feel herself relaxing and broke out in a beaming smile. 'Wahoo... I'm on holiday.' she thought. Throwing the strap of her hold-all over her shoulder she turned and walked through to departures and after checking her bags in for the flight made her way to the departure lounge. She could feel butterflies in her stomach, it was happening whenever she was going to see Stephen. The time they spent together seemed so much more important these days since the attack eight weeks ago. She felt a tingle of excitement run down her spine anticipating holidaying on a boat, more importantly being with Stephen for longer than three or four days. She gave an involuntary shudder then caught sight of herself in a foyer mirror and realised she was smiling openly, looking around at the other passengers waiting she wondered if any of them guessed what she was thinking; she gave a little shrug and giggled quietly to herself.

'Stop it silly woman,' she said to herself, 'you're acting like a smitten schoolgirl.'

Realising suddenly that in fact she really was quite smitten and totally in love with this man.

It was mid-afternoon when she walked through the arrival doors of Jersey's airport. Even though this little island was part of the United Kingdom, it felt so continental. It was warm and sunny it could almost have been in the Mediterranean. Standing for a moment she scanned the faces of people waiting around the arrivals lounge. Someone touched her shoulder, she started, surprised turned and looked straight into Stephen's eyes, they were smiley and he was grinning broadly at her.

'Hello, welcome to Jersey.' he said simply.

Dropping her holdall next to her suitcase she threw her arms around his neck and kissed him passionately. She wasn't bothered what people might think right now she just wanted to show how happy she was to see him. Their embrace lasted for some time to the total exclusion of everyone around them; ignoring the fact people were having to manoeuvre around them. The airport PA system suddenly made an announcement asking people meeting arrivals to keep the walkway in front of the arrival doors clear. They parted smiling, embarrassed at the thought that they could have been the subject of the announcement. Taking her holdall and throwing it over his shoulder he grabbed the handle of her suitcase and guided her out of the terminal building joining the queue at the taxi rank, she put both arms around his waist and squeezed him looking into his eyes.

'You've had your hair cut!' he commented.

'Hmm, just shortened a little. I get hot and sweaty in my neck if it's too long and the weather's hot. Anyway, look at you T-shirt, shorts looking all tanned, I've missed you so much Ferryman. The thought of you all here together and wherever else you've been over the past three weeks has been total garbage.'

'Mmmm,' Stephen answered kissing the top of her head. 'I've missed you too sugar. You know you really have messed my head since we took *Finbar* up to the Grahams yard.'

'Messed your head up…' she cuffed his arm playfully, 'do you realise you turned my normally organised life and my career, into mush! I can't focus when you're away, I can't sleep in my own bed anymore because I miss you next to me, I ache to love you, here.' she said holding her hands against her stomach.

They shuffled forward in the line as another taxi took some people away. Stephen didn't answer immediately but studied her face. Reaching out he stroked her cheek tenderly, gently pushing some strands of her long jet-black hair away from her face, catching it behind an ear. He looked deeply into her beautiful bright brown eyes.

'I know,' he said, 'since that weekend in York at Easter I've found the job so difficult particularly since I got us accidently involved yet again in someone else's problems.'

He paused as they moved forward again to stand at the front of the queue now.

'I've been doing the sums since we've been away and coming back onto UK runs, I can manage everything.'

A Yellow cab pulled up beside them, the driver got out opened the boot and put her bags into it as they climbed into the back seats. Settled back in the front again he turned to look at Stephen.

'Where too?'

'Gorey Castle, the slipway please.'

The driver nodded, turned back, set the meter and drove off away from the airport.

Nita was watching Stephen.

'Are you serious?'

He nodded, 'Absolutely! I'm making too many mistakes these

days. My mind's not on the job, and that can be dangerous in the long run, so yes I'm serious.'

The taxi driver interrupted trying to start up a conversation.

'Sailing then are you?' he inquired.

Stephen and Nita looked at him in his rear-view mirror.

'Erm, yes.' Stephen replied.

'Going far or just cruising around the Channel Islands?' he asked.

'Just cruising for now.' Stephen answered.

'Where's your home then?'

'Poole.'

'Right, been here before?'

Stephen nodded, 'A couple of times, I dodge between Northern France and here during the summer with my family.'

'Right.' The taxi driver replied, adding. 'Not been a bad year this year has it.'

Nita heard Stephen sigh quietly.

'No, we've had some great weather over the past three weeks, just hope it holds for the next two until we get back to Poole.'

'Aye,' the driver agreed, 'the last thing you want is bad weather.'

Stephen feigned a false, interested smile back to the mirror image of the driver. Turning his attention back to Nita, he picked up the thread of their conversation.

'Like I've said, it will mean I'm still away but only for the week you know goodbye Monday hello Friday or Saturday. That's got to be better than the weeks on the long runs, yes?'

She didn't reply but nodded thoughtfully, beginning to run various scenarios through in her mind. After a while she said.

'Are you sure you can afford to come back and still support Em and the boat?'

'Just, I'm working on that.'

The journey to Gorey took a little over an hour ending with the taxi was wending its way through the streets of Gorey towards the harbour slipway. Shuffling closer to him she slipped her arm through his.

'Where is everyone then? I was expecting a grand welcome, you know a banner and flowers.'

He smirked.

'We considered that actually, but then Mary thought it might be good if I came on my own so we could have a little us time.'

She gave a little laugh.

'Bless, always thinking of others and practical things.'

He gazed at her for a moment.

'You've known her less than a year and you've got the measure of her so soon.' He laughed, then at an afterthought saying, 'She'll love you for that, she always claims men are about as sensitive as a goat.'

'A goat?' Nita looked at him, 'where does that come from?'

He smiled at her and winked.

'Eat anything they can, always take a chance at the other... you know?' winking again he nudged her with his elbow... 'you know?'

'Right...!' Nita suddenly twigged, 'well she's not too wrong there,' and giggled.

'Just a minute,' he began to say but she closed the gap and kissed him quickly before saying.

'We however, are the exception to the rule for the next two weeks.'

Glancing at her quizzically, he wondered what she was on about. She grinned and this time she nudged him with her elbow.

'Well we're still in first flush of this relationship... and,' she hesitated for a moment lowering her voice, 'we've been celibate for the past four weeks.'

Looking at her wide eyed, 'Well Nita Patel!' he exclaimed, 'who would have thought you'd think such things, I'm shocked!'

She giggled as he added.

'Mary and Richard have gone shopping and will cook for us tonight.'

'And the girls, where are they?' she asked.

'Right now, probably with a gang of others from a couple of boats in the harbour. They'll be wandering around the town eyeing up the local lads, they'll come back when they're hungry, a bit like homing pigeons. Tonight I think the parents of a girl we've met from another boat are taking them up into town to see the night life. Em's been nattering to go 'clubbing' since we dropped the hook here on Thursday. Be aware sugar she'll be on to you like a rash.'

Resting her head on his shoulder she sighed.

'I've been so looking forward to this holiday, I'm going to have such fun just being with you all.' She looked into his eyes, 'Thank you.'

'For what?'

'Oh just being this wonderful man who hid himself away until the right person came along.'

Sitting up suddenly she chuckled.

'It's like a fairy tale in reverse. The princess comes along and saves the knight.' She laughed again and ended saying, 'a knight in tarnished armour but he's shining and very brave again.'

The taxi driver interrupted their conversation. 'Anywhere in particular boss?'

Stephen peered between the front seats and once he'd got his bearings pointed to a big fishing boat moored alongside the quay. 'Just by that boat there please.'

Two minutes later they were standing on the harbour side with Nita's bags looking across the bay at the array of yachts, cruisers and working boats. Stephen paid off the taxi and as it turned behind them to drive back towards the town put his arm around her shoulder.

'I'm glad you're here sugar. If someone had told me a year ago that I'd find someone who'd bowl me over, change my life back to how it was before Suzanne died, I'd have said they were talking rubbish.' Giving her a little squeeze, he continued, 'but here I am, a new man thanks to you. Even Emma says it's been different this year, in the past we've had a great time wherever we've been but she can see now that I was always closed to other people.'

Reaching and putting her hands on his face she turned his head to face her and gently, but with tender passion kissed him. The moment was broken suddenly by someone shouting further along the harbour.

'Dad, Nita, Wahoo you're here!'

Thirty seconds later Emma and Rachel were standing by their side. Emma threw her arms around Nita in a bear hug, then Rachel embraced her too.

'Have you called Granddad yet?' Emma said.

'No, why are they back already, we've just got here.'

Emma looked at him rolling her eyes.

'Durrr… Where's the tender…!'

As she said this she swept her arm along the harbour side and tutted. Turning to Nita again she added excitedly.

'We are going to have an absolute ball now you're here, there's this club we can go to later. The music's mind blowing, you'll love it.'

'Whoa missey.' Stephen interjected. 'Just how old are you?'

'You know how old I am dad, but I don't look it when I'm dressed up neither does Rach and we'll be okay with Nita won't we?'

'No!' Stephen said.

Emma looked at him hard, her eyes fixed on his, angry. To make his point he repeated himself.

'No Em, you're underage, you know the rules.'

'Dad!' she shouted.

'Enough Emma, talk to me normally or be quiet.' he said firmly.

'Nita,'

Emma appealed to her now.

'It's not fair, if you come with us we're not going to drink, not with you there. We just want to go to a real club, a disco.' To both of them she pleaded now, 'Oh please!'

'No Emma.'

Stephen repeated himself. Before she could say anything else Nita took a firm hold of her arm to get her attention and looking directly at her said.

'Emma, I don't appreciate you trying to use me as a pawn against your dad and drawing me into this. Just leave it for now, I've just got here let me get sorted first, okay!'

Emma went to say something but Nita tightened her hand on Emma's arm slightly. Emma looked at her quickly and saw a look in her eyes, she nodded. Nita released her hold and the two girls walked away to stand looking out over the harbour.

'Sorry,' Stephen began to say, 'She was totally out...'

Nita held her hand up.

'That's okay, don't worry, she's growing up and wanting to run wild before she can walk properly, its fine.'

He reached out and caressed her shoulder. She smiled at him adding quietly.

'Take me, my family still see me as a rebel, remember what I told you at dinner last year and you saw my mothers' reaction at Christmas, it's fine honestly.'

Reaching round the belt on his shorts he unclipped a small walkie-talkie radio.

'*Finbar*, you there Richard? Can you bring the tender to the quay by the French trawler please?'

Moments later the radio crackled.

'*Hi Stephen, five minutes. Just siding the stuff we've brought back.*'

Richard had to make two trips to *Finbar* but within fifteen minutes everyone was on-board all talking at once as Mary made drinks. As things settled down Stephen took Nita's bags to the cabin. The girls disappeared up to the flying bridge and Mary sat round the galley table talking to Nita. Returning to the galley table Stephen asked.

'Right, does anyone want to do anything special just now?' looking from one to another; faced by shaking heads, he grinned.

'Ok, here's what I think, I'd like to get up to St Catharine's tomorrow. I'm going to move *Finbar* now to the harbour side for the night, if not we're stuck here as the harbour dries out at low tide and there's just enough draft to move her now. We can eat then the girls are going into Gorey for the evening with that family we've met. We can go to the pub if you're up to it sugar,' he glanced at Nita, 'or stay here for a quiet night if you're knackered after the flight.'

Nita shrugged her shoulders. 'No, I'm ok if we want a drink.'

Richard interrupted. 'Actually, Mary and I had a mind to walk up to the castle and watch the sunset. I might get some good shots on the camera.'

Mary was nodding, 'It gives you two some 'you' time too…' she said.

They exchanged quick glances before he replied. 'Ok, sounds like a plan. That's settled then.'

Pushing himself upright he moved to the saloon. 'Let's get this boat shifted.'

As he started the engines he called to Emma.

'Em, will you and Rachel put the fenders out starboard side please.'

From up on the flying bridge the girls replied, turning to Richard he added, 'Can you and Nita get the hook up?'

Richard nodded saying to Nita.

'Come on crew, time to get your hands dirty!'

As they made their way through the saloon Richard winked at Stephen, Nita following, glanced at him quizzically. He watched the pair on the fore deck as Richard explained how they pulled the anchor up.

'*Finbar* has an electric winch' he said, 'but it takes so long that the quickest way is to do by hand, at least until the chain and cable are straight up and down.'

From the saloon Stephen continued watching until Richard raised an arm showing Nita the different signals they used. He saw Richard nod his head and Nita raised her arm. Waiting a few moments longer so that the anchor plough would be clear of the seabed, he sounded *Finbar's* horn and put the throttle controls astern at the same time turning the wheel to bring the boat around to face the harbour wall. Slowly they moved between other boats until they came alongside the wall. Richard clambered up a ladder to the quayside taking the stern line Emma threw up to him and securing it to a bollard. He moved to the bow and took that line from Nita. She missed with her first throw but quickly gathered the first few feet into a coil and tried again, successfully this time. Richard caught it and secured it to another bollard. Safely tethered Stephen shut the engines down. As everyone came back into the saloon, Emma asked.

'Can we go onto the harbour dad, the girl from the yacht is up there?'

He nodded then said, 'Hang on a minute.' turning, he called down to the galley.

'Mary, how long to dinner?'

'Oh a while yet,' came the reply.

Looking at Emma he said, 'Half an hour love, are you going to sort this evening out with her?'

Emma nodded and the two girls left.

'Drink?' Stephen asked.

'Please.' Nita answered.

He glanced at Richard who shook his head. 'Not for me, I'm going to read the paper and sit with my other half thanks.'

'Go and sit up on the bridge love, I'll bring the tea up.'

'Ok'

Alone for a few minutes she looked around the harbour and the town taking in the view. Sighing she sank down on one of the settees that ran around the edge of the bridge.

'I'm on holiday for two whole weeks' she thought and exhaling felt her body release a whole lot of tension. Stephens head appeared at the top of the saloon staircase as he brought their tea up. Placing the tray on the table he smiled at her.

'You're spoiled you know, no-one else gets cream cakes.'

Nita saw two delicious cakes on the tray with the mugs of tea. 'Why me?' she asked.

'Because Mary likes you, thinks you're good for me.'

She chuckled, 'Doesn't she know I'm only after your body.'

'Oh I think she's got a rough idea what your motives are!'

She chuckled again using a finger to clean some wayward cream from her lips. Stephen slid across the seat until his face was in hers and kissed her sticky lips. 'Yum,' he said, and they both chuckled as their lips stuck together momentarily. Sitting back they studied the view of the castle out on the point of the harbour.

'It's just so beautiful here.' Nita said quietly.

After a few moments he replied, 'Yeah, I've always loved coming across to any of the Channel Islands. It's sort of French but in an English way, do you know what I mean?'

She shrugged, 'Can't answer that really, this being my first visit.'

'Yeah,' Stephen said. 'Suzanne would have loved it here,' he hesitated, '… but that wasn't to be was it.'

Nita reached out taking his hand, he glanced down at their hands clasped together then into her eyes.

'I'm glad you're here. This year's trip wouldn't have been complete without you sharing part of it.'

Leaning across to him she kissed his cheek affectionately. They sat in silence for some time before she said.

'Why did we move to the harbour wall?'

'The harbour dries out at low tide so *Finbar* would have rolled slightly onto one side and that would've made the next 12 hours uncomfortable. We managed last night but this way we'll lean against the wall until the tide floods again. Tomorrow we'll move round to St Catharine's which doesn't dry out and spend a couple of days there. We can explore Jersey from there, come on I'll show you on the chart.'

Taking her hand he led the way down the stairs through the saloon to where the chart table was in the corner of the galley. Nita inhaled the aromas coming from the pans, peering over her shoulder she said into Mary's ear.

'That smells gorgeous, I've just realised how famished I am, mmmm…' she inhaled again, Mary glanced at her and smiled. Turning back to Stephen she squeezed into the narrow navigation area and looked at the chart he'd just unrolled.

'This is Gorey,' he said pointing to the chart, 'and here's St

Catharine's.'

Tracing his finger over the chart he circumnavigate all the way round to the north of the island.

'I'd like to get all the way round here to Grozney point this week if we can, but that'll depend on the weather and how keen we are to push on.'

Nita studied the chart for a while.

'What are all these numbers dotted around and these lines here?'

'They're depth soundings, they will, should correspond with our echo sounder as we enter a harbour or a bay. And these are compass bearings that we will follow as leading marks into a harbour. If you look closely, somewhere on shore will be some marks or posts that we line up on and then just run into the mooring.'

She studied all the different information on the chart closely then pointing at a sign and some sort of code on one headland said. 'And this?'

'That's a light house, flashing every 35 seconds, green to this bearing, then white to this bearing and then red to there. We would stay in the white area to avoid rocks either side in the coloured zones, and that's the frequency that the foghorn sounds.'

Looking at the chart again she said.

'Are all charts like this, everywhere?'

'Yeah at least around our coast line. Trinity House ships and the navy continue to check the figures.'

'Wow!' she repeated herself.

'Way back, I mean over three hundred years or more ago the Navy and explorers sailed all over the world making charts. Ships today can mostly navigate any waters anywhere in relative safety putting their trust in charts like this. Some mistakes still happen and then you end up with a big problem, remember reading about the Torrey Canyon off Cornwall, or the Exon Valdez in Canada. Serious human errors caused those catastrophes because they didn't follow their charts. Trinity House keeps all charts up to date around the

UK and most of the seas around our coasts these days. They also maintain all the different buoys you see and the lighthouses around our coast and Ireland.'

Nita studied the chart for a while.

'So you understand all this and how to get from home say to France or Ireland?'

'Enough to set a course and work out tides and times, yes.'

'Ohh you are clever.' she said putting an arm round his waist.

From the galley Mary interrupted them.

'If you two have finished canoodling in there, we need to set for dinner and call the girls back'

Richard slid out from the oval table and began setting the table. Stephen disappeared up to the saloon and Nita went to stand by Mary's side.

'Anything I can do?'

'No my dear, just sit I think.' She replied.

Stephen returned to the galley carrying a bottle of red wine. Shortly after the four of them had settled around the table Emma and Rachel clambered down the harbour wall ladder into the sun deck and appeared in the galley all of a rush.

'What we having Nan?' Emma asked.

Mary replied instantly.

'Bread and a pennyworth of dripping miss!'

Emma glanced at her quickly realising she'd just had a warning.

'Sorry... wait and see.'

She said apologetically, Mary answered quietly.

'Yes, now just settle down.'

This simple rebuke was accompanied by a look that Emma knew only too well. Shuffling to the back of the oval table with Rachel she sat quietly. Richard brought a folding chair from the saloon and set it down by the table for Mary. Stephen gently caressed Nita's thigh under the table as they watched Mary put a large casserole in the middle of the table accompanied by a bowl of rice and another with salad.

Looking briefly at Emma she said.

'Now help yourselves everyone and enjoy.'

Emma smiled warmly at Mary who returned a soft affectionate smile. Nita looked at the dishes and bowls on the table as a plate of chicken in a white sauce on rice appeared in front of her.

'How do you do all this on that cooker Mary? I'd need a full kitchen before I'd even try!'

Mary chuckled. 'Practice my dear, I've had nearly seven years of this so I've become quite proficient.'

There was a muffled choke from the back of the table, and wiping her mouth Emma said, laughing.

'Sorry Nan, do you remember when you tried that fish dish those guys told you about in Scotland when we first went off on *Finbar*?'

Richard chuckled immediately receiving a gentle slap on his arm from Mary.

'Did you have to bring that up?'

Stephen laughed. 'Did you mean that literally?'

Everyone was laughing now as he added.

'I think the gulls in Ullapool probably never recovered from the experience.'

'You know what,' Mary said firmly, 'if any of you can do better, I'm happy to sit up on the bridge and get a tan.'

Nita spoke now, 'I'm sure it wasn't that bad.'

Mary, laughing now, replied.

'Oh it was Nita, trust me, it was pretty bad but in my defence, Emma was too young to cook and these two louts would have had us drinking cup-a-soups, eating crisps and biscuits if they'd had their way... am I right boys?'

Richard shrugged as Stephen said. 'Yeah, but we'd have eaten out when we hit a port.'

Richard was nodding in agreement.

'To be fair that was a while ago, now she can cook up a Sunday roast with all the trimmings... and a crumble that Keith Floyd would be proud of.'

Mary bowed her head slightly acknowledging the compliment, the remainder of their meal passed quickly with light-hearted conversation. Dinner finished the two girls went to the saloon to get ready for their evening out whilst the others cleared away. Richard in the meantime had dropped the table to make up the double berth where he and Mary were to sleep.

Nita followed Stephen out to the sun deck and they settled themselves on one of the settees.

'It's just so peaceful, it's only seven and still warm, Mmmm perfect. Has it been like this for the last three weeks?'

'Pretty well, we've had wet mornings or half days but never washed out'

'Did you get across to France?'

'That first week we made the west side of the Cherbourg peninsular, remember that's where I Skyped you from.'

'Oh yes, that's where it was wet.'

He'd started to say something when they were distracted by someone calling from the harbour wall.

'Hello there, are the girls ready.'

Quickly scanning the harbour side they saw a lady looking down at them, her daughter standing by her side. Stephen stood up and waved then called into the saloon.

'Emma, Rach, come on time to go.'

The girls rushed from the saloon and went to climb the ladder to the harbour side.

'Hang on.' Stephen stopped them. 'Have you got money?'

Taking his wallet from his pocket he took out a note giving It to Emma.

'Thanks Dad, but I've got my spends.'

'I know but this is a treat ok. I'll have the change though... if there is any.'

Emma kissed him on the cheek and ascended the ladder followed by Rachel.

'Back in a minute.'

Stephen said to Nita and followed them up to the top. She

watched as he spoke to the woman and her daughter. Richard and Mary joined Nita now following her gaze to the harbour side.

'We're off too.' Richard said. 'Want to catch the sunset by the castle if we can. Watch for the flood lights at the castle Nita, they're pretty good I'm told.'

She smiled and watched them climb the ladder. All alone now she wandered into the saloon and through to the master cabin. Picking up her case she opened it on the bed and began taking things out. Checking through some of the drawers in the fitted dressing table she found one empty and pushed her 'smalls' into it. Opening the wardrobe she found some hangers and put some of her clothes on those. Taking her PJs and dressing gown she laid them across the bed. Finally she put her vanity bag in the en-suite shower room. Turning back into the cabin, she started, surprised to see Stephen standing there watching her.

'Shit... don't do that, you scared me.' she exclaimed.

Opening his arms, inviting her to come to him, he smiled at her.

'We've got *Finbar* to ourselves for, oh, two hours at least. Sooo...I thought...'

Nita shuddered, Stephen pushed her away to look at her.

'You ok Sugar, you shook just then.'

'Mmm, I know. It was at the thought of making love to you. Are we going to be ok, I mean I've never been so close to people with you before, it's kind of confining. Do you know what I mean?'

'Neither have I, we'll just have to pick our moments and you'll have to be quiet.'

'How the hell am I going to be quiet, I can't help it it's what you do to me.'

Grinning he said, 'Well I'll have to use a pillow... Anyway we've got two hours on our own so, want a practice?'

As he was saying this his fingers had begun to open her shirt. She watched his fingers deliberately move down her shirt opening it down to her waist.

Looking directly at him she said softly.

'You're awful, and yes, of course I want a practice.'

Pulling open her shirt he saw her breasts captive in a pretty lace bra. Slipping his hands inside her shirt he encircled her and in a moment she felt her bra released. He began to caress her naked breasts inside the loosened bra, she sighed and shuddered at his touch. Yielding completely she leaned against him.

'Ohh god I've missed you so much.'

Nuzzling her neck he responded. 'I want to love you so much.'

Still in the embrace she pulled her shirt from the waist band of her trousers, undid the remaining buttons and wriggled her arms out of it. She released her hair before returning to the embrace moving her head slightly to alter the angle where Stephen's head was buried in the nape of her neck. They remained like this for some time before he said.

'I miss your smell when I'm away. I'd like to bottle it and release it in my cab at night.'

He gave her neck a very gentle bite, she squirmed and giggled. As the space between them opened up he reached out and cupped her face in his hands. They kissed deeply, their tongues searching each other's mouth. Their passion rose quickly and in no time they were sprawled, naked across the bed caressing one another wantonly. Unable to restrain himself any longer, he pushed Nita onto her back, from deep in her throat she emitted a low growl.

'Oh god, yes! don't stop, I want you so much…Oh you're going to make me cum!'

Moved by her sudden orgasm he felt her body stiffen. She arched her back lifting them both up from the bed, her face contorted as though she was in pain, she moaned from the back of her throat again, shuddered violently then collapsed back onto the bed. He quickened his movements rushing towards his own inevitable climax. Nita began to sigh once more in time to his thrusts reaching a second orgasm of her own. As he orgasmed he felt her body go ridged once more as she emitted a high-pitched squeal.

Later, lying together in the after-glow lovers share, arms and legs all entwined.

'You surprise me sometimes,' he said wistfully, 'to look at you or talk to you, you give the impression that butter wouldn't melt... but'

He paused, she watched him wondering what was coming next.

'But?' she said.

'When you're aroused you're quite vocal and very demanding in what you want!'

Pushing herself up onto an elbow she stroked his chest.

'Problem...?'

He shook his head, 'No, far from it, you get me more aroused!'

She grinned cheekily. 'I've learned that if you want something you need to ask for it.'

Flopping back beside him she added giggling. 'Sometimes... you need to demand it!'

A little while later she moved her hand and began to caress him. Turning over he looked into her eyes but before he could say anything she increased the pressure of her hand saying.

'I'm not sure that we got that quite right, I think we need another practice. After all you've had a holiday and may have forgotten a few of the finer points of making love to me!'

'See what I mean...' he said, 'you're being demanding again! I'm only a mere mortal man, whereas you Nita Patel are a siren, I have no willpower to resist you!'

Still caressing him she lifted herself from the bed, straddling his thighs. Leaning forward she butterfly kissed his eyes, mouth and then moved to his chest butterfly kissing all the way down his body. He groaned at the warmth and moistness of her mouth. Releasing him she slid back up his body to sit astride him again. He moaned as he felt her muscles contract around him. Leaning forward until they were face to face she said.

'Do you want me, hmmm?'

'Stupid question woman, of course I want you!'

She felt his hands on her hips, she put hers over his and felt him lift her slightly then release her to sink down on him again, repeating this movement a number of times she began to move on her own. For a few minutes they moved in unison, her breathing short, hot on his face.

He saw the look in her eyes, she kissed his lips quickly.

'Take me from behind… please.' She purred the words. 'I love it when you have me that way.'

Pushing himself up from the bed until he was sitting, Nita still astride him, he held her close pressing her smooth form against his.

'I love you!'

She returned this embrace, 'I want you now.'

Pushing herself away from him in one flowing movement she turned. He knelt behind her. Neither of them could hold back any longer finally collapsing onto the bed moulded together.

'I am so into you Ferryman,' she said softly, 'you make me feel so naughty when we make love. I just want you in so many ways.'

He replied against her back, between her shoulder blades his free hand gently caressing her breasts.

'Maybe we should get a copy of the Karma Sutra then.'

'Oh I think we can make up our own positions, don't you?'

'Hmmm…' he responded, 'We ought to make a move you know or we're going to be caught out like naughty teenagers.'

He moved to sit up, affectionately smacking her bottom.

'You have a peach of a bum you know, when you wear a skirt I just want to walk behind you and watch you move. Even in jeans you look so sexy! Right quick shower I think.'

'Hang on I need the loo and a shower, you've made me all sticky.'

'Sorry me first, but if you need the loo go now sexy lady.'

Nita climbed off the bed and into the en-suite room closing the door. Moments later Stephen heard the toilet flush followed straight away by the sound of *Finbar's* pump working.

'Hey monkey!' Stephen protested, knocking on the door. 'I was going to have a shower first!'

He heard her giggle.

'Sorry, I won't be long, but I thought as I was here I'd…'

'Yeah yeah, yeah!'

Resigned to the fact that she was showering he knew to protest would be useless. Selecting some clothes he grabbed a towel and padded through the galley to the other heads to shower.

He'd been sitting on the flying bridge with a beer for a good fifteen minutes watching the sun sink to sea level creating a strengthening aurora of colours in a clear sky. He heard Nita climb the stairs from the saloon, turning he saw her appear through the deck hatch and watched as she seemed to unfurl like a beautiful butterfly emerging from its pupae. Sitting together they looked to the western horizon where the sun had almost disappeared now leaving vivid orange and red colours that lit the whole sky, he heard her sigh and smiled.

'I brought you up a spritzer, are you okay with that or do you want a beer?'

Reaching out to the small table she picked up the long glass taking a sip.

'Mmm perfect thank you.'

Together they watched nature's 'Son et Lumière' until the colours changed leaving softer pinks and yellows that gradually softened to leave pale soft purple tones like a colour wash on a canvas.

'I can't believe that its way past nine thirty and we're sitting here with drinks and it's still so warm.' she said.

'This is what grabs you when you start cruising, it's totally relaxing, in two or three days you'll feel completely different.' Rotating slightly he turned to her. 'If I didn't have *Finbar* then Emma and I and the rest of us, even you would have gone abroad, or gambled that the weather was going to be good at home and found somewhere to stay. Think of how stressful that could... might be! Noisy hotels, noisy fractious kids and families, set mealtimes and then having to find things to do all the time.' Sweeping his arm in an arc across *Finbar* with the harbour and the surrounding houses, he said. 'Whereas here we choose what to do, when.'

She watched him smiling, he'd become quite animated using his hands to emphasize the points he wanted to make.

'Look, you and I both have jobs that are hard and stressful. After two or three weeks of this we go back to work completely relaxed, batteries re-charged, ready to face whatever gets thrown at us. If we were in a hotel or self-catering even and the place wasn't as we'd thought it was going to be, or the weather turned, what would we do?'

He looked at her for a moment waiting for an answer, she shrugged lost for an idea. Answering his own question he said.

'We'd run out of things to do or just do the same, day after day, hmmm...?'

She nodded agreeing then said.

'Surely the weather's bad sometimes, then you're slightly confined here on top of each other, aren't you?'

'True but that's the beauty of having *Finbar*, it allows us to slip off and find somewhere else to stay. Okay you could do the same with a caravan or if you camped but there's still all the hassle of traffic jams and noisy sites. I owe nothing on the boat, I pay insurance and mooring fees that's all. For what we'd pay to stay somewhere as a family here or abroad costs about the same as I spend on running *Finbar*, It's a no brainer for me!'

Sliding across the settee cushion she snuggled up under his arm and rested her head on his chest.

'Right now I'm just looking forward to the next two weeks with you and the family doing absolutely nada... zilch.'

He kissed the crown of her head.

'Ah well, whilst I said you become totally relaxed cruising around, there are one or two duties, chores, house keeping things which have to be done regularly. So while you do zilch you'll have to turn to and do your share too.'

Raising her head from his chest she looked closely at him.

'Would these chores include deck washing for example?'

'Yes and other necessary tasks towards the efficiency and smooth running of the boat.'

'Hmmm.' she dropped her head back onto his chest. They sat like this for some time watching the sky darken. At some point Stephen became aware her breathing had changed.

From the harbour side he heard Mary and Richard talking as they approached.

'Awe look they're asleep.'

'No we're awake just sitting and watching the sunset. Did you get the picture at the castle then?'

Stephen asked, Nita sighed nestling herself into Stephens chest a little more.

'Correction… I'm awake, this one's asleep.'

The three of them laughed quietly. There was a flash and Richard said.

'Couldn't miss that one, got to be one for the album I think.'

Climbing down the wall ladder, Richards head popped up through the saloon hatch a minute later. 'Beer, tea, coffee, anything?' he asked.

'Beer please, cheers.'

'Coming up.'

They joined Stephen and the slumbering Nita on the bridge and sat chatting about the evening; making plans for the next few days to entertain Nita and the girls. They'd been sitting quietly for some time when a car engine travelling along the harbour distracted them. They watched above their heads as the vehicle obviously turned round, its headlight beams sweeping in an arc above them. They heard doors open and close followed by animated chatter as the car drove away. Two silhouettes appeared at the steps at the top of the harbour wall calling to an unseen person.

'Thank you so much, it's been really cool, see you before you leave.'

The person responded and the silhouette at the top of the ladder replied.

'Yes, thanks, we've had an absolute blast, your dad's off the wall Heather.'

With that they descended the ladder onto *Finbar's* deck. Stephen and the others listened to the clumping footsteps on the bridge stairway as Emma and Rachel clattered up to them. Before either could launch into telling them of the evenings events, Stephen held his hand up saying quietly.

'This one's asleep,' pointing to the top of Nita's head nestled into his chest, 'will you turn the gantry lights on please Em.'

She skirted round the group and switched on the lights. Richard disappeared below returning with more refreshment. All settled again Stephen, Richard and Mary listened under the glow of the overhead lights as the girls relate their evenings exploits, both trying to speak at the same time. Mary raised her hand after a few minutes.

'Girls… one at a time please, you're both gabbling so fast I can't understand either of you. Now I got to the part about the street café and something about Heathers father, go on from there.'

The girls began again, explaining where they'd been and what had happened, occasionally breaking into peals of laughter. After an hour listening to them, Stephen decided now would be a good time to call an end to the day and evenings events.

'Right, I'm calling lights out. Let's turn in and see what tomorrow brings.'

Gently lifting Nita's slumbering form slightly upright he said quietly.

'Hey sleeping beauty,' she moaned trying to snuggle into him again. 'Hey… It's time to turn in my lovely, you can't really sleep up here.'

'Mmmm, what?' came the response.

'Bed… now!'

'OK, will you carry me?'

Stephen chuckled, replying. 'NO, you're on your own lady.'

'You're mean…!'

'You'd have a hell of a headache in the morning if I were to carry you trust me. I'd be bouncing your head off every doorframe.'

Reaching to the control panel he turned the deck lights off, then helped Nita to her feet and to the top of the stairway. Once down in the saloon he secured the hatch then guiding Nita through to the master cabin said goodnight to the girls as they got their duvets and pillows out of the settee lockers, repeating himself as they passed through the galley to Mary and Richard making up their berth. Once in their cabin Nita flopped down on the bed and slipped sideways onto her pillow. He stood for a while waiting for her to stir but it soon became clear that unless he undressed her that's where she was going to remain until morning. Sighing, he reached over her slumbering form and gently began the task of removing her clothes leaving her in just her bra and pants. Heaving the duvet from under her, he covered her up, a soft moan came from her as she shuffled a little and settled. Minutes later he lay beside her listening to the stillness that had descended on the boat. From her occasional movement, gently bumping against the wall, he realised the tide was flooding again and she was beginning to float off the sandy harbour bed. Turning onto his side he breathed deeply closed his eyes and in minutes was asleep along with everyone else on board.

There was a knock on the cabin door that suddenly brought Stephen wide awake.

'Yes?'

He heard Mary say through the door. 'Tea and toast, are you decent?'

'Thank you Mary, yes I am Nita's still buried under the duvet.'

The door opened and she came in with two mugs and a plate piled high with toast. Placing them on the dressing table she said as she left.

'We're all up and cleared away looks like it could be another good day.'

Throwing back the covers he collected the tray from the dresser returning to sit in bed.

'Come on sugar we've got to get on or we'll miss the best of the day.'

The duvet on the other side of the bed moved and an arm appeared followed by a head peering at him. She scanned the cabin.

'How did I get here?' she asked sleepily.

'You staggered.'

Quickly looking back under the quilt and then tightening it round her neck a little surprised, she looked at Stephen. 'Who undressed me?'

'I did… problem?'

Shuffling herself upright with the quilt still pulled tightly around her neck, she stared at him.

'How long have I been asleep?'

Passing her a mug of tea, he said, 'You've almost slept the clock round.'

'I was so tired.' she said taking a slice of toast from the plate he'd offered her.

Beyond the cabin door there were occasional sounds from other parts of the boat, the odd bump or thud from above their heads as the others moved about the deck.

'Come on madam we need to get sorted, we've got a boat to attend to and some sightseeing to do. You don't want to waste your day lazing about do you?'

Throwing on some clothes he disappeared into the bathroom, the heads. Minutes later he emerged, bent to kiss her and turned to leave the cabin, collecting the mugs and plate as he went. He got as far as the door and turned.

'I have this really odd feeling in my belly,' he said softly.

His voice quivered very slightly. She watched him wondering what was coming next.

'You being here is a first for me. I know we've done the run from Portbridge and back twice, but this is the first time I've had anyone to stay on board for me… ever. It feels strange, nice- strange but strange, I feel good inside, complete… do you know what I mean? Thank you!'

Nita felt tears welling up in her eyes she didn't trust herself to say anything just now. She just smiled at him, he smiled back and left closing the door. Alone Nita slid out of the bed and dressed. Once she'd put everything away she brushed her hair and made herself presentable she went to find where everyone else was.

Arriving through the patio doors onto the sundeck she was surprised to find that she could see the top of the harbour wall not just the sides. Stepping onto *Finbar's* gunnel she stepped across the gap between the boat and the harbour and walked over to where Stephen and the others were gathered talking to some other people. Stephen introduced her to the group and told her this was the family the girls had gone into town with. Up to speed now she listened to the general conversation and gathered this family were leaving Gorey to sail back to the South Coast. Final farewells were said, Emma and Rachel exchanged numbers with the daughter before the family returned to their yacht.

Stephen and Nita stood together after the others went back on board *Finbar*. Looking around Gorey harbour bathed in bright sunshine, Nita took a firm hold of his arm.

'It looks so different from yesterday evening, it's beautiful with the castle standing over the harbour and all these lovely boats moored around.'

'Hmm,' Stephen began, 'this is the difference between driving to a place or coming at it from the sea. A place can look so different from this perspective.'

'Ferryman,' she began to say squeezing his arm gently, 'What you said this morning.'

He watched her.

'Yes I do know how you feel… I think. I'm sorry Suzanne never got to see *Finbar*, I'm sure she'd have loved all the exploring you've done over the years.'

He put his arm around her shoulder.

'You know as well as I do if it wasn't for you I'd have done this summer trip on my own just for the family's sake. You've made the difference, this feeling in here is lovely,' he said rubbing his tummy, 'it's warm, I've not felt this since Suzanne until now with you, it makes me feel complete again, I love you for that.'

They kissed quickly; wrinkling her nose she smiled finally finishing off what she'd started to say.

'It's not one way this you know. You've made me very happy too and I love you for that.'

A horn sounded out in the harbour attracting their attention, they looked to see the family from the girls' friends' yacht waving as they passed *Finbar* heading seaward. They watched from the harbour side with the rest of their family waving too from *Finbar's* flying bridge.

'Right lady, let's go and decide what we're all going to do for the rest of the day.'

Taking her hand they walked across to the boats side.

'Listen folks, I know I said we'd move today but as the weather's so nice I think we could explore a bit more round here, show Nita some of the sights, you know St Helier and maybe move tomorrow. We're against the wall so we won't keel over at low tide, how do you feel about it?' They all looked at each other nodding.

'Okay,' Richard said, 'I think we can all work with that, let's get stuff together.'

Twenty minutes later the entire family piled into a taxi bus with swimming stuff and picnic bags and headed off for the day. Having discussed the various options open to them, it was decided to 'do the tourist bit' around St Helier, visit some of the WWII relics that covered the island from the German occupation then go to a beach and crash for the rest of the day.

Had Stephen happened to have been near Corbiere light house on the South-West corner of Jersey around this time, he might well have observed the familiar outline of a fishing boat passing the point through the haze of the day. It was a vessel he was beginning to be more aware of lately on his trips across to Euro port and Scandinavia one he'd now been warned off having anything to do with. It was standing some six miles off the point quietly heading towards the French coastline. Apart from two crewmen working on the fore deck and the silhouettes of people in the wheelhouse, she appeared to any observer as a boat just going about its business, just like on all the other occasions he'd seen her.

It was falling dusk when a taxi brought them back to the harbour. As the minibus drove away back towards the town they stood looking around their surroundings. The castle was floodlit again highlighting some of its features.

'I'm shattered!' Mary said breaking the silence.

'Me too Nan.' Emma added quietly.

'Right then,' Stephen said, 'night cap and bed I think.'

Everyone nodded as he added.

'I think we'll move to St Catherine's tomorrow, we'll be sheltered there if the weather turns.'

Making their way down the ladder to *Finbar*'s deck Richard gathered a rope and threw the coil up to Stephen. He tied some of the bags to the end and lowered it to the boats deck in a continuous loop. Having lowered the last bag he climbed down the steps to the boats deck, closing and securing the patio doors for the night. Looking around the room he smiled, Emma and Rachel were legged out on the long settee, Richard was sitting on the helms seat, Mary and Nita must have gone down to the galley. They'd definitely had a good day around St Helier and spent the afternoon on the beach enjoying the sun and sea. He rubbed his arms feeling the heat of the day's sun on them. 'There'll be some sore bits and strap lines in the morning he thought.' Mary appeared through the galley door with a tray of drinks, Nita followed with two plates of cakes and biscuits. There was little conversation as they sipped their drinks, it was obvious everyone was worn out. Eventually Richard stirred from the helms seat.

'Right I'm going to make our bed up, I don't know about you lot but I'm wiped out.'

Placing his mug on the tray as he passed it he disappeared down the galley steps and they heard the bumps and bangs as he turned the galley table into their berth. The girls started to set their berths up on the long settee. Mary gathered the remaining mugs and saying night night to everyone took them down to the galley.

'Night girls.' Stephen said as he moved to follow Nita and Mary to the galley then into the master cabin. In just a few minutes everyone was in bed and a sense of stillness fell over *Finbar*. Snuggling up to Stephen, resting her head on his chest.

'What a great day,' she said quietly, 'I feel I've been away for ages and it's only the first day.'

Squeezing her he replied. 'That's the thing about a sailing holiday, if the weathers good then you feel great at the end of the day. Once you're back on the boat it's all quiet and peaceful unlike a hotel, you're not disturbed by folk coming in at all hours pissed and noisy.'

She giggled, 'I can imagine coming back to the boat totally smashed and ending up in the sea or worse the mud, having mis-judged where the boat is!'

'It happens!' Stephen said, 'It happens, I've seen people go out for the night and come back expecting the boat to be where they'd left it but the tides gone out and the gormless pillocks just step into thin air and end up in a moaning heap on the deck six or eight feet lower down than they expected.'

He felt Nita shaking beside him in silent laughter, she looked up at him, her eyes bright.

'Seriously!'

Nodding he replied, 'Yep, seriously.... Wheee, thud!'

She laughed again. They shuffled about getting comfortable before drifting off into a deep sleep.

Day two began with breakfast on the sun deck with Mary, Emma and Rachel were still tucked up in their duvets, awake but reluctant to get up. Looking around the harbour Nita felt she could be in the Mediterranean it was so warm and bright sitting in the sun. As yesterday morning the tide had come in and *Finbar* was again level with the harbour side. Richard and Stephen came through the patio doors.

'Okay, the plan today,' Stephen started to explain, 'we need fuel, we need to water up and empty the foul tank then sail round to St Catherine's, how does that sound?'

The three of them nodded.

'Right we need to get the crew up and get tidied away.'

Turning to the girls he called out. 'You've got fifteen minutes to sort yourselves out girls, we're sailing and I'm sure you don't want to let the local lads on the fuel pier see you in bed!'

True enough fifteen minutes later Stephen and Richard slipped the moorings and motored *Finbar* across the harbour to the pier where they could replenish fuel and drinking water and empty the foul tank. The girls were still rushing around the saloon tidying up and trying to look presentable for the local lads who worked on the pier. Just as Stephen brought *Finbar* alongside the pier they appeared up the steps to the flying bridge in shorts and bikini tops draping themselves on the seats on the bridge. Stephen glanced across to where Nita was sitting, smiled and winked.

'Works a treat, every time.'

It took the best part of an hour to complete the jobs and pay for the fuel they'd taken on. It was obvious that the girls had attracted the boy's attention because quite a group had gathered on the pier busying themselves about the various tasks, plus another yacht had come alongside to take on fuel and water as well. When *Finbar* was ready to leave it was the girls who took the bow line, standing together on the foredeck exchanging cheeky banter with two or three of the local lads. Nita, sitting beside the helms position watched their antics. She looked at Stephen and chuckled quietly.

'You know you're going to have your hands full in the next few years? She's going to be gorgeous do you realise that!'

Stephen looked towards Emma and smiled.

'I'd like to think you'd be around to give her some clues... hmm?'

Nita laughed.

'Yeah right! Remember that 'chat' you had with my Dad?' She used her fingers to create the comprehension marks for the word 'chat'. 'Remember the bit about...' she hesitated for a moment, before adding, 'she never listened to me and she was such a rebel!'

Stephen shrugged. 'Okay... Forgot that bit, we'll cross that bridge when we come to it.'

Nita laughed out loud this time, her arms describing an ark to emphasise her point.

'Ohh... we is it now! You're jumping to some huge conclusions here Stephen Leigh-Grace, what makes you think she'll take any notice of what I have to say... hmmm?'

From the foredeck Emma shouted, 'Are we clear to let go?'

He quickly looked around to see all was clear before replying. 'Let go...' he called, then to Richard holding the stern rope gave the same command. Running astern until the boat was clear of the dock and the other yacht, he turned the wheel hard left, to port and changed the engines to slow ahead. Slowly they navigated their way through some moored boats and out to the open sea. Richard came up to the bridge.

'I called our departure and destination into the harbour masters office, I take it you'd have remembered at some point!'

Stephen grinned at him and nodded, 'Thanks, slipped my mind!'

Out in the open sea he increased the engines to cruising speed. For Nita this was the first time she'd experienced the feeling of speed. Until now she'd been used to hearing the engines running on the canal or river at four knots, five miles an hour. Now with both engines running she felt a surge of excitement sending a shiver through her as *Finbar* picked up speed. It felt exhilarating, the wind blowing in her face as they seemed to skim across the sea rising and falling ever so slightly following the contours of the waves. The sea surface was flat calm, like a mirror. Sliding onto the seat nearest to Stephen she said.

'How fast are we going now?'

'About twelve knots say sixteen miles an hour.'

'How fast will she go?'

Stephen looked at her for a moment then called to Richard and the girls.

'Nita wants to know how fast *Finbar* will go.'

The girls giggled, Richard sucked in air through his teeth.

'Ohh that's going to be very expensive!'

Looking at Nita he nodded. 'Very expensive!' he said, adding, 'On a good day twenty knots that's around twenty six miles an hour. Not a lot on land but on water that's pretty fast. Now at thirty mph a car will do about forty, forty-five miles to the gallon. *Finbar* on the other hand uses about a gallon of fuel in around three hours at cruising speed, but on full throttle she gets through a gallon an hour.'

Nita held his gaze and nodded accepting his explanation. 'Expensive then.' she said.

'Yep!'

A silence fell on the bridge a strange sense of tension, anticipation almost. Richard suddenly got up and moved to the stairs to the saloon.

'I'll tell Mary to batten down then.'

Stephen glanced over his shoulder nodding, Nita looked a little confused.

'What are we going to do?'

'Erm, well I thought we'd blow the cob-webs out of the engines. They run more smoothly if I give them a good blast after a winter chugging up and down the canal, blow all the sh..1..t out of them.' He mouthed the last words to her before calling.

'Hold tight everyone!' then pushed both throttle levers to 'Full'. There was a moment's hesitation then Nita felt *Finbar* shudder slightly. At the same time she clearly heard the pitch of the engines change. The stern sank slightly raising the bow up so sight of the horizon was lost. The shuddering lasted for some seconds then ceased, *Finbar* seemed to level out again and Nita could see the horizon once more. The engine note had changed, it was less noisy. The breeze she'd felt on her face earlier had become much stronger if anything it was increasing more. There was a shriek from her side that made her start with surprise, she glanced to see Emma grinning like a demented witch, her hair blowing wildly in the wind. Nita grinned, her hair would be the same had she not tied it back in the morning. Both girls were laughing but the sound was lost, all Nita could see was their open mouths, all she could hear was the wind roaring past her ears and *Finbars* engines, they were humming in perfect harmony. Her gaze fell on Stephen although he was concentrating on their course he was grinning too. Sliding up close to him gave his arm a squeeze exclaiming.

'Oh my god this is so much fun!'

'Look behind us.'

Turning to look back she was amazed to see a white furrow on the surface. It was arrow straight disappearing into the distance behind them. She noticed a slight haze too which she deduced was the result of the muck being blown out of the engines. Looking forward again, she saw the gently rolling waves being flattened by the boats speed and her hull throwing flat sheets of spray out to the sides as they powered on. Kissing Stephens cheek she said quietly in his ear.

'It's like the thrill you give me when we make love, it sends shivers through me, I'm tingling all over. I want you right now, I want to feel you in me, possessing me, making me tingle... oh god Stephen I want sooo much!' She kissed him again.

For the next ten minutes he kept the boat at full speed by which time Nita was beginning to feel uncomfortable with the noise from the pitch of the engines and the continuous buffeting of the wind at this speed. Reaching for the throttle levers he slowly pulled them back to 'half'.

Finbar quickly slowed, her stern sinking down into the water as her speed reduced then levelling off again as she settled down to her cruising speed

'How was it for you?' Stephen said looking into her eyes raising an eyebrow. She pushed his shoulder playfully grinning at him.

'You're so cheeky sometimes Ferryman, but yes that was fun.'

From the saloon they heard Mary shout.

'Well... now you've got that out of your system, can I get on?'

Collectively they all answered in unison, 'Yes!'

'Good!'

The remainder of the passage to St Catherine's was uneventful and by mid-afternoon they were anchored in the shelter of the breakwater and small harbour. The tender was inflated and alongside ready for a run ashore. Later over dinner in a pub close to the harbour they chatted about the day. Nita shared her feelings of her first experience travelling at full speed.

'And?' Richard enquired.

'Amazing... really! it kind of took over my senses, I can see why people get this thing about speed, going fast. On a boat though that's special it's a totally different feeling. I said to Stephen that I was tingling all over, it sent a shivers through me.'

Stephen reached and held her hand as she explained how she'd felt. Richard added.

'Can you imagine what a thrill it must be on one of those racing power boats with the big engines?'

Stephen nodded. 'Really fancy that one day,' he said looking around the table saying, 'You can all club together for my fortieth as a gift experience day power boat driving.'

That brought a peel of laughter from all of them.

As the evening sun settled on the western horizon sinking into the still calm sea the six of them made their way back to the harbour slipway and launched the tender. Stephen took Mary and the girls first then returned for Richard and Nita the dinghy's little outboard puttering over to where *Finbar* swung gently on her mooring. All safely back on-board with the tender secured alongside they closed everything up for the night.

'Been a good day, yeah.' Richard said.

'Yeah,' Stephen replied, 'it felt good opening her up.'

'Too right, you haven't done that for... ohh two years or more, such a great feeling when you let her run.'

Richard rested his arm about his son-in-law's shoulder momentarily.

'Night cap?' Stephen said.

'Yeah.'

Opening the wall cabinet he took two bottles out putting them on the low table in the saloon, reaching back for some glasses he called through the boat.

'Splicing the main brace, nightcap anyone?'

Emma and Rachel were first to appear enthusiastically from the galley closely followed by Mary.

'I was just making a drink for us all but this tops tea or coffee.' she said.

'If the weather holds I think we'll stay here until the weekend,' Stephen said, 'then how do you feel about sailing to Alderney?'

A general murmur of approval ran around the room everyone nodding in agreement.

'It's been a while since we've been up there, it's on our way home and there's a lot to explore.'

'Didn't we put in there once just after you got Finbar?' Mary said.

'Yeah, that was the first year we ventured further away than the south coast, remember I'd underestimated how much water and fuel we'd use, well remembered Mary.' Stephen replied. 'Right, that's the plan then.'

Rising from the settee Mary asked,

'Anyone want that drink I was making?'

'Please Nan.' The girls replied, she glanced at Stephen, 'Coffee?'

'Please.'

Nita followed her down to the galley, said goodnight and went forward to the master suite. The girls began pulling their bedding out from the settee lockers, Richard disappeared down to galley. Mary came up from the galley with two coffees for the girls.

'Yours is on the side.' She said to Stephen.

'Night you two sleep tight.' He said and kissed Emma on the forehead as he walked past her.

'Night dad.'

Sitting on the edge of the bed he began to undress as Nita came out of the bathroom. He didn't turn around but felt the bed depress slightly as she climbed onto it. Bare to the waist he was about to stand up when he felt her arms encircle his shoulders. He became aware that he could feel her naked breasts gently pressing into his back.

Glancing over his shoulder he saw that she was naked. He caught his breath as she tightened her embrace saying softly into his ear.

'You made me shiver all over this morning, I had a mini orgasm as we sped over the water, I was all tingly inside just like I am when we've made love. I want to feel that again now, with you!'

Turning, he slid his arms around her smooth brown body excited and aroused by her nakedness. Struggling to control his breathing he whispered.

'We're going to have to be so quiet or everyone will guess what's going on.'

Putting a finger to her lips she replied.

'Shhh.... Like a church mouse... promise.'

He pushed her away a little and while she lay on the bed squirming with anticipation he finished undressing. Lying beside now her she reached out and grasped him, they kissed while he caressed her breasts. Whispering he said softly.

'Which way's the quietest do you think?'

'You sitting against the headboard and me on top.' she whispered back.

He looked at her a little surprised, she added.

'It won't rock the boat too much and give us away!'

Unable to stop herself, she giggled, instantly clamping a hand over her mouth to stifle it but even so spluttered through her fingers. That set Stephen off and he silently laughed gasping for breath before putting a finger to his lips and puffing like a steam train as he tried to say.

'Shh... shhhh... shh.'

Their need to make love helped them regain some composure and focus on what they both wanted. Changing positions as gently as possible they resumed their kissing and caressing. With her head on his shoulder her voice husky with desire she pleaded.

'Now...! Take me now, I'm aching I want you so much.'

She allowed herself to sink slowly down until she was resting on his thighs letting out a soft low moan against his neck feeling him deep inside her. Clinging tightly to one another to reduce any chance of rocking the boat with their movements they moved together until, unable to restrain themselves surged to a shared climax. Fortunately the wake of a passing tender puttering by *Finbar* returning to a yacht moored a little way off caused her to rock gently masking the final moments of their uncontrollable passion, that otherwise may well have given them away to the others on-board. Oblivious to this fortunate intervention they clung to one another breathing heavily from their combined efforts to cause as little movement as possible.

It took a little time for them to recover before they could speak.

'Bloody hell that was something else!' he whispered.

Sweeping her hair back from her face with one hand she looked deeply into his eyes.

'That was so good!' she replied, 'do you think we were quiet enough at the end? I tell you I really struggled to keep from squealing!'

'Tell me about it,' Stephen said, 'I thought you were going to take a chunk out of my neck!'

He felt round his neck where Nita's head had rested rubbing the spot, she grinned kissing his neck.

'There, all better now.' she whispered.

Still sitting astride him she reached across to the bedside cabinet pulling a handful of tissues from the box, slipped off him and made a dash for the bathroom.

Snuggling together on her return they listened to the sounds around the boat, the water rippling along the hull the distant sounds coming from the direction of the town until they both drifted off to sleep.

~~~~~~~~~~~~~~~~~~~~~~~~~~~~~~~~~~

A bright sunny morning greeted them all as they sat round the table
~~~~~~~~~~~~~~~~~~~~~~~~~~~~~~~~~~

at breakfast time.

'Reckon there was a wind shift last night, brought a bit of a swell on I think.'

Richard said in conversation. Nita felt sure she'd suddenly flushed and nervously cleared her throat taking a mouthful of tea to hide her embarrassment. Stephen quickly glanced across the table at her, replying.

'Yeah, could have been.'

Later with chores done around the boat, Stephen, Nita, Mary and Richard clambered aboard the tender and motored across the harbour to the slipway and wandered into St Catherine's leaving the girls on *Finbar* to entertain themselves. Later as lunch time loomed Richard went back and brought them ashore to join them at a street café. They had lunch sitting until late in the afternoon soaking up the warm sunshine and watching the world go by just talking and snacking before finally deciding to have their evening meal at the café as well.

'Little point in going back to the boat really is there if we're quite happy here?'

Stephen said, Mary gave a little chuckle replying. '

Let's me off the hook making dinner.'

A little later Nita casually commented.

'You know I don't think I've ever spent the best part of a day sitting in one place watching people. I'm usually chasing my tail trying to nail the bad guys, it's really fascinating trying to guess what they're about.'

'Can you tell if someone's up to no good?' Rachel asked.

'When I'm working and my heads in the right place yes, I can spot them sometimes. You get a feeling about someone, their behaviour, their body language, it kind of shouts at you.'

Richard nudged Emma. 'Are you listening to this miss?' she glanced at her Granddad putting her hand across her mouth and feigned a look of innocent surprise.

'Me!' she exclaimed, 'I'm a good girl!'

'Have you ever had to solve a murder or anything like that?'

Nita hesitated for a moment.

'Over the years I've investigated all sorts from missing persons to drugs and yes suspicious deaths. You can't say that something's a murder until all the facts have been put together. Something might appear as an assault that leads to a person dying but it may well be an accidental death when it all comes out in the wash. Then another case might seem like an accident but on deeper investigation you find someone's gone to a lot of trouble to make it appear like one. You start every case with a blank piece of paper and build a timeline, a sort of story that if it goes to court hopefully gets the bad guy off the street.'

'Have you ever been attacked or in danger, like you know your life's been threatened?'

Nita glanced quickly at Emma then Stephen but before she could decide how to answer this question, Mary interrupted saying to Richard.

'Darling, go get us some more drinks will you, oh and the menus please.'

That interruption gave Nita enough time to formulate a suitable reply.

'No, not really, I've always had someone who'd have my back. If there is ever a risk of violence then we deal with it mob handed! You know we make sure we're going to come out on top.'

Richard came back to the table with menus for everyone handing them out he said.

'The waiters bringing the drinks out in a minute and he'll take our order then.'

While they waited for the drinks to arrive they poured over the menus deciding what to have.

It seemed ages before their food arrived but when it did they were all delighted with their choices. As two waiters cleared their dishes away later, Mary commented.

'My goodness that was filling.'

'Certainly was.' Nita added.

Remaining at the restaurant for the rest of the evening, Richard and Mary went for a wander through town, Stephen and Nita walked along the seafront and breakwater while Emma and Rachel went to listen to some street musicians playing a little way off from the café. As the church clock struck ten they were all back together again around the table.

Stephen said. 'Well I guess it's time to make tracks folks.'

He and Richard went into the café and settled the bill returning to the table with a bottle of wine.

'What's with the wine?' Nita enquired.

'Err it appears the waiter who took our order also took a shine to the girls, he thought our children were gorgeous!' Stephen said, 'and gave us this bottle...'

Nita laughed, 'The tall Mediterranean looking guy?'

He nodded, she continued.

'Thought he was very attentive to them when we ordered, did you notice he just served them and the young girl served the rest of us!'

The girls suddenly went all coy starting to giggle. Turning, Stephen nudged Nita who followed his gaze to see the waiter in question standing in the doorway of the café. Realising he'd been spotted he casually threw a cloth over his shoulder and with a simple bow turned back inside.

'Told you...' Nita said quietly, 'a pair of bum magnets these two, you'll have to watch them in a couple of years!'

Mary interrupted. 'What do you mean 'he'll have to watch them in a couple of years' it's happening right now!' she said nodding in Stephens's direction, 'we're getting all this now whilst he's driving round who knows where!'

Nita gave him a sideways glance.

'Told you.' she repeated.

They left the café making their way back to the break water. Stephen and Nita strolled along the break water while Richard ferried the others back to the boat. They watched the sun setting on the horizon over a flat calm sea mirroring perfectly the oranges and purples of the suns reflection. Back on the boat they sat until it was dark and a blanket of bright stars shone all around then.

'You having a good time sugar?'

'Mmm, it's not a week yet and all the stress of work and the assault has gone, I feel just so relaxed; mind you some sunshine helps,' she paused looking around to see they weren't being overheard, adding in a whisper.

'Oh and screwing the arse off you! I just can't get enough, it's an insatiable need.'

She giggled knowing it would get a reaction from him. He slapped her bottom quite hard with the arm that was around her shoulders. She went to pinch his ribs with her free arm in retaliation but it was half hearted, they laughed and hugged each other tightly. Some time passed until he inhaled deeply and said quietly.

'I never got to spend time like this with Suz and that hurts, it was our dream really to do something like this, that's when I miss her. I didn't want to carry on you know, but Emma was only a tot and needed love... so much love and that kind of gave me a purpose. Mary and Richard helped, after all they'd lost their only daughter and helping bring up Emma gave them a focus. For them and me and dad even, he loved Suzanne so much, having Emma got us all through the grief of her passing.

Nita squeezed his waist. 'I'm sorry.'

'No, it's fine, honestly, then I go and get involved in all that who-ha in Portbridge and you appeared! Right from day one, well what I can remember of day one, you've been on my case.

The rest of the family think you've worked a miracle you know, they feel you've got the old Stephen back for them, Mary said as much when we were all in York. Once I'd got used to letting myself relax around you then the barricades fell apart, now I find you're in my thoughts all the time.'

Kissing the top of her head he spoke into her hair. 'I love you

Nita Patel.'

'Hmm, love you too Ferryman.' she responded.

'Come on our watch has ended bed.'

They went through the saloon saying goodnight to the girls then tip-toed past the sleeping forms of Richard and Mary, a soft purring snore was coming from one of them. Nita put her hand to her mouth to stifle a giggle but once in their cabin she giggled uncontrollably. Stephen looked at her shaking his head.

'Don't make the mistake of thinking that was Richard, its Mary and some nights she can wake the dead, trust me...'

Sliding under the duvet they kissed one another and drifted off into a restful sleep.

~~~~~~

They stayed at St Catherine's for the rest of the week touring around the East and Northern parts of Jersey. Saturday Morning literally began with a bang as they were all woken by a shattering thunderstorm that shook *Finbar* to her very keel. It was accompanied by torrential rain which lasted for a couple of hours. Confined to the 'lower deck' they sat around after breakfast and talked. Stephen summarised the past week.

'To be honest I half expected the weather to break sooner, we've had some pretty hot days recently. Hopefully, this will clear the air for the rest of the week. Alderneys somewhere I've wanted to stop at and explore, the island is beautiful and unspoilt I've been told. It's going to take a couple of days, we'll lay-over in a bay up north and then see what the weathers like. We've got options to stay if it brightens up or carry on up. If the weathers broken then it's only six hours maybe a bit more to Poole. We can decide there whether to stay or head back to the south coast and just bay hop for the rest of the holiday, are we all, all right with that?'

They all agreed, so when the storm had passed Stephen and
~~~~~~

Nita took the tender ashore to settle the mooring fees and advise the harbour office of their intended plans. Finally back on *Finbar* with the tender and its little outboard engine stowed, all was ready to set off north.

Raising the anchor they motored slowly to the end of the breakwater and out into the open sea. Having plotted their course up the north east coast Stephen gave Richard the bearing then sat by him. A sense of peace washed over him, not something he'd felt since Suzannes' death. He thought about all the years the family had cruised whilst he and *Finbar* provided them with the 'wear-with-all' to have a good time. He smiled briefly, 'Stupid sod!' he thought and caught sight of Richard looking at him out the corner of his eye.

'You okay?'

Thoughtfully he replied. 'Yeah, just having a moment a bit of reflection I guess.'

Richard nodded and a few moments later added.

'You know we've said already that me and Mary are okay you being with Nita. It's nearly eight years since Suzanne passed, we've said for some time you should meet someone. You've been there for all of us all this time, either tramping round Europe or taking every opportunity to use *Finbar* for our breaks. Emma's well made up for you plus she's got someone she can get close to and do girly things with. Okay Mary's always there to go shopping with,' Richard chuckled, 'she keeps telling me she sees so much of Suzanne in her it's frightening at times. Nita's modern, fashionable, okay Mary and Em are fine together… Nita and Emma together are an eruption at times and that's just since Easter.'

Stephen laughed, 'Yeah Nita's already warning me to be ready. You're right though I see Suzanne in Em too. It feels odd really, this is the first time we've had our summer cruise and I'm not on my own, I don't know if it's a feeling of guilt or pleasure but I feel so relaxed sharing it with Nita.'

'Don't analyse it Stephen just enjoy it, we're fine with it. I'm sure Suzanne would be if you could ask her.' The two men grinned at each other.

'Thanks Richard, that means a lot.'

Richard simply nodded and concentrated on their course. They sat in silence listening to the steady thrum of the boats engines driving them northwards. Stephen woke with a start.

'What... problem?'

Nita was sitting beside him gently stroking the side of his head smiling at him, she kissed his cheek.

'No, you were hard on and Richard was worried you'd get burnt so he called me, anyway it's... err, what do you call it... mess time.'

Sitting upright he stretched feeling the heat from the sun on the parts of his body that it had touched while he was asleep. Looking at Richard he saw him nod.

'You eat first then send Emma up, I'm okay just now.'

He touched Richards shoulder as he made his way down the stairs to the saloon and the galley where a spread of cold meats and salad met his gaze.

'My you're doing us proud today Mary, this looks gorgeous.'

He shuffled round the table to sit beside Emma as Mary placed a glass of white wine by his plate, the glass misting up with the cool liquid. As he picked from the selection of meat and salad, he said to Emma.

'When you're finished will you go and relieve Granddad love?'

'Sure.'

By mid-afternoon they were off the north-east corner of Jersey with Nita helming now. Stephen had disappeared down to the saloon some time ago, confident enough to leave her helming *Finbar* on her course. He re-appeared on the bridge holding one of the charts and two glasses of lager placing them in the holders by her side.

'I've decided to put in at Boulay bay for tonight and if it's nice tomorrow we can stay over for a day and mess around. From there to Braye bay on Alderney will take the day, we could carry on now but I don't fancy a night passage then having to seek an anchorage in the dark.'

Throwing him a half salute she replied. 'Aye aye cappen!' and grinned at him.

'Come on out! I'll take over.'

They shuffled around swapping seats; she kissed him as he adjusted the seat and settled at the wheel.

'What was that for?'

'Just 'cause I love you and I'm having a wonderful time. You know this is the first proper holiday I've had for ten years or more, I mean where I've done nothing but enjoyed the sun and scenery, and the company… especially the company. Thank you.'

Reaching across he stroked her thigh.

'You know I was just thinking the same this morning, I talked to Richard about it, he told me to just enjoy it and not analyse it too much. I'm having the best time ever sugar so thank you.'

He reached into his pocket and pulled out a notebook setting it down beside the wheel.

'Where are we going then?'

Studying his notes for a minute he replied.

'Boulay bay it's just on the northern shoreline. Never been to it before but it looks nice so we'll see.'

Opening a locker by his side he took out a gadget with earphones attached.

'Interesting, what does that do?' she asked.

'Ahh, I can take bearings with this and fix my position so we can get into the bay without hitting anything.'

Putting the earphones on, he plugged the small jack plug into a socket on *Finbars* control panel. Holding the device up he rotated it too and fro a few times explaining what he was listening for.

'Lighthouses and radio beacons transmit a signal this bit of kit picks up. I need two signals, three ideally, to fix our position then I can plot our run safely into the bay.'

He stopped moving for a moment and wrote down a bearing the device was showing on the compass before aiming it forward of them and repeating the exercise. Reaching for the chart he marked off the two bearings he'd taken then drew two lines until they crossed one another. 'We're here, six miles off the coast and eight miles away from the bay.'

Checking the radar repeater he compared the coastal scan with the chart, made some notes and happy with the results set *Finbar* on the course to Boulay bay.

Half an hour later he stood up and looking ahead called to Emma and Rachel sunbathing on the roof of the forward cabin.

'Changing course to run into this bay for the night so you might want to clear away, we'll drop the hook I think.'

The girls waved and began to tidy things up. Richard appeared on the bridge.

'What's happening?'

'Going into Boulay bay for tonight I didn't fancy the night passage to Alderney.'

'Okay.' Richard said looking at the chart. 'Bit different from the south coast.'

'Yeah,' Stephen replied, 'looks like mixed bed I think, mainly rock at least that's what the companion says. We'll drop the hook and see what's what then.'

Looking at the radar for a while then the coastal layout from the chart and turned the wheel to port. *Finbar* responded straight away swinging in towards the coast.

Richard touched Nita's shoulder, 'You coming with me to get the anchor ready then?'

Approaching the bay Stephen reduced their speed and studied the entrance, it was an open bay affording little shelter from strong winds and seas. Close inshore was a Jetty that had clearly seen better days, and one he would be reluctant to moor against. There was an assortment of small fishing boats all on long lines that ran ashore. More into the centre of the bay were three cruisers and a couple of yachts at anchor. He stopped engines allowing *Finbar* to drift, checking the depth on the chart.

'Now?' came a shout from the bow.

'NO,' he replied, 'just checking.'

Pushing one engine throttle forward he set the speed used on the canals taking them into the bay until they were in two fathoms of water, he stopped the engine calling.

'Okay let go!'

He saw Richard launch the anchor forwards as Nita released the ratchet lock on the winch a moment later. He waited until the rattle of the chain slowed then went slow astern drawing her back from where the anchor was on the sea bed laying firstly chain then strong warp until there was as much cable and chain out as he thought would be needed to hold *Finbar* steady but allow her to swing with the tide without colliding with the other boats then shut the engines down. A few minutes passed before everyone was up on the bridge.

'Well this place looks alive dad...' Emma said sarcastically.

'It's just for tonight... that is unless you want to do a night passage to Alderney. Personally love I don't, okay.' Stephen said.

Emma shrugged, 'Yeah okay.'

Looking over the side of the bridge Nita commented.

'The waters really clear look you can see the seabed and the rocks.'

Stephen said straight away.

'So we'll get the tender out if anyone wants to go ashore for a look around or we can swim off the stern.'

Richard added, 'Get the rods out, I've spotted some good-sized fish, we could have fresh fish for dinner.

They heard Mary say under her breath, 'You can top and tail them and gut them then, that's not my department!'

Emma giggled saying, 'Ohh Nan we had to dissect a rat's eye when I started biology, gutting a fish can't be that bad.'

Mary fixed Emma with 'the look' over the rim of her reading glasses. Putting a hand over her mouth Emma stifled a chuckle. Mary inhaled loudly.

'I dissected a rat when I was at school young lady... and I have gutted fish in the past but Granddad can deal with anything he catches now.'

Nita chuckled, turning to Stephen.

'I'm going to change I want to dive off the side and see if I can get to the bottom it looks so clear.'

'We're in twelve feet of water, it'll be twenty odd feet at full tide so now's the best time.'

In a flash everyone cleared the bridge. Stephen followed Mary down the stairs to the saloon.

'Are you going to take the plunge then?'

She turned and looked at him cynically then grinned.

'Stephen, if I swim you need to get your camera because it'll be the closest you'll ever get to a Moby Dick look-a-like!'

'Go on, I bet you swim well.'

'Oh Stephen Grace you're a terrible liar.'

They laughed together as they made their way through to the galley. Stephen went through to the fore cabin, knocking on the door he said, 'Can I come in?'

The door opened and he saw Nita in a canary yellow bikini adjusting the bra to cover her breasts.

'Wow, stunning!' he said.

She grinned at him, 'I'd never be brave enough to wear this if any of my family were likely to see me, they'd have an absolute fit me revealing so much flesh.'

Standing behind her he circled his arms around her and looked at their reflection in the long mirror.

'You are stunningly beautiful do you know that?'

She snuggled her body back into his.

'I like what I wear for you because you say how nice I look and it makes me feel good.'

As he kissed her long neck she spun in his embrace and they kissed tenderly.

'Are you coming for a swim too?'

'I'll get changed and then see.'

'Okay, I'm off.'

Disengaging herself, she slipped out of the cabin. Stephen got changed and made his way to the sun deck. Richard had pulled the tender out of its locker and was putting the formers into the hull that strengthen it. Stephen took the small outboard from its locker resting it on one of the seats. Rummaging in the locker he pulled out two oars and the small electric pump plugging the nozzle into the dinghy and switched it on. In ten minutes the boat was fully inflated the engine attached and alongside in the water. Richard appeared from the saloon with a fishing rod, a reel of line, some pretty vicious looking hooks and a large plastic tub. Stephen looked at everything saying quietly.

'Got the foot pump with you... just in case? Don't put any holes in it will you!'

Richard studied him for a moment. 'Really, Stephen...'

Shuffling through the narrow door onto the swim deck he loaded everything into the tender and clambered in. Priming the engine he gave it two, three, pulls before it fired into life. Stephen slipped the painter and watched as Richard puttered away further out of the bay.

A sudden shriek from the bow attracted his attention, he turned to see two splashes alongside *Finbars* hull followed a moment later by a third splash. Mary came out of the saloon wearing a swimming costume and sporting a wide brimmed hat.

'Not a word you! I'm changed but I'm going to sit in the sun and read, all right.'

Stephen held his hands up in surrender.

'Dad can you rig the ladder please?'

Turning he saw three heads bobbing by the swim deck like inquisitive seals. Opening a locker he took out a steel ladder and after a bit of fiddling got it into its fixings so the girls could climb back on board. Nita stalked her way towards him, mischief in her eye. He backed away into the sun deck to give himself space, saying. 'Cold?'

Nita stopped, 'Actually no very refreshing and so clear. Are you coming in?'

'Of course, it's not often we get to anchor where we can swim.'

Two more shrieks came from the bow again as the girls repeated their first leap, they both laughed at the joy in the girls shrieks.

'Listen I've got some goggles and snorkels somewhere and I think flippers if you want to dive.' He began rummaging through one of the lockers finally hauling out two sets of kit. The girls had reappeared through the swim deck door now and pounced on the stuff lying around.

'Hey,' Stephen spoke firmly, 'That's for all to share, okay!'

The girls nodded as they clambered back to the swim deck pulling the goggles over their heads and stuffing the breathing tubes into their mouths. Nita and Stephen followed them and holding hands launched themselves off the deck into the clear blue water. Moments later the girls slid off the deck all fitted out and began flapping about half submerged as they looked at the seabed.

The afternoon passed off with everyone swimming, diving and snorkelling. By the time the sun began to settled low over the headland and it began to cool down they'd all had their fill of 'water sports'. Stephen turned looking across the bay as he heard the tenders little outboard approaching and watched until Richard brought it alongside the swim platform. Taking the painter he secured the dingy and reached to take some of the fishing gear from Richard.

'Bloody hell Richard, have you been trawling?'

In the bucket and on the bottom of the tender was an assortment of fish plus a lobster.

Richard grinned. 'Never had a day like this... ever, they were jumping in.'

Picking up the lobster he added. 'This greedy bugger was fighting for a prawn, I got all three of them!'

'So what have we got then?'

'Mackerel, I think this is a turbort, there's this lobster and some others I'm not sure what, Pollock maybe and rock fish. Do you think we could cook up a barbie on the beach tonight just for a change?'

Stephen nodded, 'Why not we've got all the gear.'

Throwing a sheet over his catch Richard climbed onto the swim deck and patted Stephen on his shoulder.

'Let's get sorted then.'

With a bit of organising and switching around they managed to get everything for the bar-b-que ashore. Stephen got the charcoal fired up whilst Richard ferried everyone and the food from boat to the beach. Having cleaned his catch he gave the fish to Mary and Stephen to cook. They had the best evening of the holiday so far, the fish were cooked perfectly, tasty and succulent with hot potato wedges and salad followed by cheese, biscuits, fruit and wine. As darkness fell everyone was ferried back to the boat. The afternoons sport had worn them all out and by ten they'd all turned in.

Not only had yesterday ended early after a really restful day, but everyone overslept. It was nine before the first sounds of life began to rattle through *Finbar,* starting with the clatter of the kettle being filled and the clink of mugs being set up to make drinks, soon followed with the smell of bacon cooking wafting through the boat. Always a sure magnet to get people up and paying attention and by ten everyone was in the galley eating bacon sandwiches with toast on the side. Glancing at everyone around the table Stephen said.

'Looks like another good day, is everyone happy to carry onto Alderney? We had a fun yesterday but there's nothing here and like I said it's going to take most of the day to get up there.'

Nods and murmurs of agreement round the table carried the vote.

'Right, Richard you and Nita see to the anchor, there's about five fathoms of cable out,' he smiled adding, 'that's your morning workout. Emma helm please, a back bearing of our course yesterday until I've re-plotted. Steady out of the bay love, watch the echo sounder. Mary, you okay doing your thing?'

She nodded, 'Any requests for lunch?'

No-one replied straight away so she said.

'Okay think about it and let me know, it'll have to be light mind, I'm not spending all day down here.'

They all moved to get underway as Stephen said to Richard.

'I'll stow the engine and bits but we'll tow the tender just in case we need it tonight.'

Nita followed him slipping an arm around his waist and kissed him, saying quietly.

'I do fancy you when you're being assertive!'

He gave her a playful smack on her bottom as she passed him. Hearing the engines fire up he went out to the swim platform and began sorting the tender out. With the outboard and oars stowed back in their locker and the tender tethered on two tow lines astern. He returned to the chart table in the galley and plotted their course to Blaye Bay on Alderney. It wasn't long before he heard Emma shout to Richard and Nita then heard the windlass start up to pull the anchor free of the seabed. Moments later *Finbar* gave a little shudder as they went slowly astern and then ahead. Going back through the galley he said to Mary.

'You all right?'

'Fine, I've decided I'm doing sandwiches, I want to see what's what today.'

'Why not, it looks like another nice day so you should be upstairs enjoying it.'

Continuing on through the saloon he met Nita in the saloon doorway.

'Phew, that's pretty physical work pulling up all that rope and chain, my arms are killing me.'

'Its good exercise and it's quicker to pull it in by hand until the chain is up and down rather than use the windlass.'

'Why do you put so much rope out, doesn't the anchor hold you?

Turning her round he gently propelled her back out into the sun deck and sat her down. He turned and called up to Emma on the bridge. 'Em, once you're clear of the headland say a mile out steer 090 degrees, I'll change course in an hour or so.'

'Okay, 090.' She acknowledged.

Sitting with Nita he started to explain.

'It's not the anchor that holds a boat, it's the amount of cable you lay out, it should be roughly three times the depth, plus you have to bear in mind too how you will swing when the tide changes if other boats are anchored by you.'

'Right.' Nita replied.

They felt *Finbar* accelerate and realised they were clear of the bay. An hour out of Boulay bay Stephen climbed up to the bridge and took over from Emma and changed course north heading for Alderney in a gentle rolling sea. Everyone lounged around until lunchtime. The girls stayed below in the shade of the sun deck. Stephen and Richard donned sun hats and continued to helm from the bridge.

Quite some time later Richard reached for the binoculars on the console and scanned the horizon to starboard. Fixing on something he called to everyone.

'I can see land, look over there!' They all looked in the direction he was pointing, as he added, 'and there's more, further over.'

'That'll be Sark and the other one in the distance is Herm.' Stephen said, 'We're about halfway then.'

Through the afternoon they motored steadily towards Alderney. Apart from the two men on the bridge everyone slept for part of the passage. Just after four they both saw the outline of Alderney on the horizon. Switching places Stephen went below to check their approach to the anchorage and the state of the tide. It took another two hours for them to navigate into the harbour at Braye bay. As at Boulay bay they dropped anchor as there was no room at the sea wall. Pulling the tender alongside they put the engine back on and everyone was ferried ashore going in search of somewhere to eat as it was late.

~~~~~~~~~~~~~~~~~~~~~~~~~~~~~~~~~~~~~
~~~~~~~~~~~~~~~~~~~~~~~~~~~~~~~~~~~~~

They woke in the morning to a sea fret so thick they could just make out the shoreline and jetty, also the temperature had dropped noticeably from the pleasant low to mid-twenties they'd experienced all the time they'd been around Jersey. Sitting around the galley after breakfast they talked about what to do for the day in the hope the sun would burn off the mist. Stephen said.

'Look, we do need to do some housekeeping stuff, with the weather being so good recently we've neglected the jobs and the old girls looking a bit dishevelled. If we concentrate on the chores this morning, I reckon that when the tide turns it'll brighten up and we can go and explore the island, what do you think?'

Everyone agreed, so they all turned too and spent the morning washing down the decks and superstructure, cleaning through *Finbars* interior, galley and cabins until she looked bright and clean throughout. By the time all the housekeeping tasks were completed the fret had gone, burned off by the sun, and the bay was shimmering in bright sunshine just as Stephen had predicted. Reporting to the harbour office once they'd got everyone ashore the two men were told that they could moor up by the harbour wall now if they chose and could replenish the fuel and water immediately. They made their way back to *Finbar* then slowly motored to the inner harbour and the utility pier. Over the next hour they emptied the foul tank, replenished fuel and fresh water then moved into the bay again to the long breakwater and moored alongside another cruiser, having asked permission from the owner to cross his boat and secure their lines. With *Finbar* safely moored they wandered back into the village eventually finding Mary, Nita and later the girls. They found a small restaurant down a side street that appeared to serve a great selection of French dishes so decided rather than return to the boat and cook they'd eat at the restaurant. Replete from the meal and rehydrated having sampled some very pleasant French wine the little group wandered back to the harbour. Later, with all their shopping stowed away they settled down for a quiet evening. Mary produced a snacky supper that they ate sitting on the sun deck later getting into conversation with the family on the neighbouring boat.

The Sun was up and hot to greet them in the morning when.

'Looks like a cracking day folks, what do we want to do?' Stephen said.

'What's on the island dad, are there any good beaches to go to if it's going to be hot?'

Emma asked.

He chuckled a little under his breath.

'Humm, St Anne's is the only town, don't know much about it except it's in the middle of the island and is supposed to be very quaint. Yes there is a beach about a ten-minute walk from here to a place called... Crabbys would you believe!'

This brought a smile from everyone as Mary interrupted.

'I've read a bit about Alderney, St Anne's has got little squares that are all cobbled, I think I'd like to see the town.'

'How long are we staying?' Richard asked.

'I was thinking leave Thursday get onto our coast in daylight anchor for the night and finish off and home Friday. So town today or beach... It's going to be hot for the next few days.'

In the end the beach came out favourite for the day and they began gathering their stuff together. Passing a small general store en-route to the beach they bought fruit and snacks and a guidebook about the island before arriving at a beautiful white sandy beach that seemed to stretch miles. In no time towels were laid out, sun cream liberally applied before the girls ran off into the sea with lilos. Richard and Mary settled themselves to sunbathe, while Stephen and Nita wandered off along the beach hand in hand to explore where it went. So the day passed until by mid-afternoon when they'd all had their fill of the sun and sea. Gathering their bits and pieces they wandered back to *Finbar*.

'That was a good day don't you think.' Stephen said to Nita as they got ready for bed.

Smiling she said quietly, 'It's like a wonderful dream and I don't want to wake up yet.'

He nodded, 'I always feel rested by the time this holiday is over; this year though is so so different 'cause you're here, I feel complete for once.'

They hugged one another tightly, kissed and fell asleep, limbs entwined.

Thursday began in a rush as the family on the cruiser moored in-between them and the wall were ready to leave. It took twenty minutes of manoeuvring to extricate their boat then moor themselves against the wall. Piling into a taxi they travelled into St Anne's spending the rest of the day wandering around the streets of the town taking in its quaint architecture. After lunch Stephen and Richard took off to investigate the old fort on the coast arranging to meet everyone back at the restaurant. In the evening they were drawn towards a bar by the sounds of singing and folk music. Richard bought a round of drinks and they settled themselves at a street side table joining in the songs they knew. The evening drifted on everyone enjoying the warmth radiating from the brightly decorated cottages surrounding the square. Emma and Rachel fell into conversation with two young couples sitting at a nearby table. At times, their conversation dissolved into periods of near hysteria.

As the four of them walked back to the harbour when the bar closed, Nita asked Emma

'So what was so funny then you two?'

The girls giggled each contributing to part of their conversation.

'One of the girls lives here, all of them have just finished Uni and are spending some time here before looking for jobs. They were telling us about life at Uni.'

Emma added, 'Honestly dad it sounds mental at times can't wait until next year if my grades are good and I get into my choice Uni, wow!'

Rachel laughed agreeing with Em.

'Okay you two, by all means have fun the first year, but you're there to work not waste your time and our money.' Stephen said.

Next morning Stephen was up with the lark plotting their passage back to Poole then checking everything was all right with the boat, engines, filters, fuel and so on. So far in seven years of cruising they'd never suffered a breakdown. He knew that the time he thought everything was okay and didn't do these checks would be the time something would fail. It was the same when he was away in the truck, always checking his unit and paperwork, there had been times when he'd been delayed because of faulty documents.

As with the past few days it was already very warm and it wasn't yet eight-o-clock. Another hot one he thought to himself. Over breakfast Stephen was lobbied to delay their departure so they could enjoy this last day of their holiday in the sun. Despite expressing his concerns about delaying their departure, such as the risk of the weather breaking or that to stay was going to necessitate a night passage leaving them with no margin for the unexpected, he eventually gave in.

'Alright,' he said. 'alright, we'll stay and cope with a night passage provided you all take turns 'on watch'.

Everyone agreed they'd do a watch during the night so by mid-morning they were all laid out on the beach they'd first gone to when they'd arrived on Alderney.

Just after mid-day Stephen went back to the boat to catch the noon shipping forecast. Tuning the radio to radio four he listened for the sea areas they were in and surrounding areas.

"The Met office issued the following gale warning to shipping at 1145 BST today Friday, August 26th. Sole, Plymouth, Portland, south-westerly gale force eight imminent. That is the end of the gale warning, we now return you to the programme.'

Sitting back in his chair he swore under his breath, they could have been four hours nearer home if he'd been firmer at breakfast, now they were likely to get a battering in the next few hours. Shaking his head he made his way back to the beach. Approaching the group he announced.

'Grab the gear folks, we need to get off now, there's a gale brewing and we're too far from home for my liking. I want to see how far we can get before it hits.'

Within the hour everyone was back on board, Stephen had been to the Harbour office to log their passage to Poole. The Harbour Master advised him of the gale warning which he acknowledged. By the time he got back to the boat all was ready to leave, the engines were running. Slipping the lines they made way to the end of the long breakwater and turned to skirt round the island then headed north. Once they had some sea room Stephen opened the engines to make fifteen knots while the sea was still calm. Richard climbed up to the flying bridge bringing a mug of tea for him.

'Bet you're spitting fur and feathers?'

Stephen looked at him. 'I wish I'd stuck to my guns this morning, we'd be nearly on the coast by now, but hey-hoe everyone wanted the last of the sun so we'll do the best we can. Has Mary hit the Stematil then? I think it would be a good idea to make some sarnies and boil up some flasks.'

Richard nodded, 'She's given Nita and Rachel some too.'

He got up and left him alone at the helm.

~~~~~~~~~~~~~~~~~~~~~~~~~~~~~~~~~~~~
~~~~~~~~~~~~~~~~~~~~~~~~~~~~~~~~~~~~

THROUGH THE STORM

'Dad... Dad, wake up.'

Instantly he was awake, his eyes focusing on his surroundings lit by the glow of the red night light above the chart table. Lying on the bed in the galley he felt the boats motion listening for any tell-tale sounds that would suggest she'd developed a problem. Everything sounded okay, even though she was pitching and rolling quite a bit. There was an occasional thud or judder as she ploughed through a big wave.

Focusing his eyes on Emma, 'What's up love?'

'Can you come Granddads just picked up a mayday.'

Sitting up he slipped his feet into his shoes picked up his sweater and sailing smock and followed Emma up to the saloon bracing himself against the door jamb as *Finbar* pitched on a big wave. Pulling his sweater over his head he looked at Richard.

'What is it?'

'Just heard a mayday on channel 16 from a yacht. Partial dismasting one of the crew has been injured. Sounds like they're just three up one of them is a child. The skipper's asking for immediate assistance.'

'Did you get his position?' Richard nodded, 'Em got it.'

'What's his position love?' Emma handed over a piece paper. Glancing at it he turned going back to the chart table in corner of the galley. Before he returned to the saloon the radio came live once more.

'Mayday relay, mayday relay, mayday relay. All stations, all stations, all stations, this is Falmouth Coastguard, Falmouth Coastguard, Falmouth Coastguard. Yacht Spring Dawn, information number one. Following received from Yacht Spring Dawn on VHF

channel 16. Yacht Spring Dawn requests immediate assistance. They have been partially dismasted. There are three persons on board one a minor, the other crew member has sustained a crush injury and requires immediate medical assistance.'

The message continued with the Coastguard giving the yachts position, Stephen reached for a pencil and scribbled the yachts position down. The Coastguard ended the transmission giving the time at 0115 hours. Sorting through the charts he found one and went back up to the saloon with the relevant chart in hand. Laying it on the coffee table he studied it and plotted the yachts position. Sure now of where everyone was, he came and stood by Richard's shoulder.

'He's about 20 miles west of us, if we change course towards him and he steers towards us we could be there in...' Stephen did a quick calculation, '... in three hours, four maybe give or take.' Glancing at Richard he said. 'How's she handling?'

'The seas calmer but there are still the occasional big ones running.'

Glancing at the control panel he added.

'We're doing 6 knots, and she's taking that alright.'

Stephen stood sensing the boats motion for a while. He knew if possible they were required to give all possible assistance to any vessel in distress, he also knew that if they were in trouble in the middle of a storm driven sea, it could be an extremely lonely and frightening place to be especially if someone with you was injured. So to know that help was on the way would be so reassuring.

'Okay,' he said over Richards shoulder, 'steer 250 degrees, and see if you can make eight knots.' Looking at Emma he said. 'How's everyone else coping?'

She grinned, as Richard turned the wheel bringing them onto the new course.

'Nan's in your cabin dying as usual Rachel is in with her. Nita's crashed out on the settee,' she said pointing at the slumbering hump under a quilt. 'She's coping considering this is her first experience of a rough sea. I'm okay now, I did feel rough earlier but I've slept for three hours until Granddad called me to get you.'

Stephen glanced at Richard.

'Hey, I'm okay.'

Turning back to Emma he said. 'Do you want to make some tea love?'

'Okay.'

As she disappeared down to the galley, he called after her. 'If it's not too rough try and fill some flasks. We may well need them later.'

'No probs.' she replied.

Looking at Richard he said quietly. 'Are we going to be okay do you think? Are we going to be able to do anything when we get there?'

Richard shrugged his shoulders, 'Who knows, but they'll know we're there and won't feel so alone. We've got the fuel to reach them and at least we can stand by until the cavalry arrive, whoever that's going to be.'

He fell silent for a moment, Stephen could see he was thinking. 'What?'

Richard looked at him steadily. 'I was thinking, 'There but for Grace' as the saying goes, it might as well be us, we're the nearest!'

Stephen nodded.

'Just what I thought earlier, I wouldn't fancy being out here alone, not in this! No matter how much I trusted my boat.' he said patting the coving above *Finbar's* control panel affectionately. 'Have you had some rest?'

He nodded as he turned the wheel slightly to keep them on the right heading and meet a large wave which threw them slightly off course.

'Nita did almost two hours after you'd turned in I dozed in case she had a problem. She did okay though I was impressed.'

Emma lurched through the door from the galley as another wave broke alongside *Finbar* throwing her into a roll and showering the saloon windows in spray and spume. Bracing herself against the galley door expertly she waited until the boat settled again before handing out three insulated mugs. Another wave crest broke alongside the spray splattering on the cabin windows. Stephen said to Richard.

'Right, I'll take the helm. You go and crash on the galley berth. Are you okay Em, do you want try and get some rest?'

Thinking for a moment she replied.

'Yeah, I'll leg out for a while dad, but listen call If you need me, yeah.'

Putting her mug into a recessed holder in the arm of the settee she lay down on the other long settee, pulled up the board from underneath and dragged a spare quilt up over her head. Richard and Stephen changed places. He patted Stephen's shoulder and taking his mug wobbled through the door to the galley trying to keep his balance as *Finbar* dropped into a trough, shuddering as she hit the back of the next wave. Stephen watched the eerie green light of the compass as it spun and gyrated frantically until the boat settled back on her course again before rising to the top of the next wave. He adjusted their course to compensate for the pitch and slight roll and picked up the radio handset.

'Mayday, Falmouth Coastguard, Falmouth Coastguard, Falmouth Coastguard. This is the motor cruiser Finbar Two, Finbar Two Finbar Two on passage to Poole from Alderney. We are some 20 miles south east of yacht Spring Dawn. We have changed course to assist her. Our ETA is about three hours, over.'

Replacing the handset he peered into the night watching the sea rise and fall. Occasionally a wave broke etched with white as its crest, illuminated by the gantry lights on the bridge, was driven away in the wind. Eventually Falmouth acknowledged Stephen's message. Glancing around their position he could just make out to the east the horizon and the brightening edge of dawn. Almost an hour passed as Stephen kept *Finbar* on course between six and eight knots towards *Spring Dawn*. Dawn had chased along behind them and now it was properly light. He couldn't help a little smile thinking this morning was anything but a spring Dawn. From the radio messages it was obvious that the yacht could only manage enough way to provide steerage so they were going to have to go all the way to assist her. Everyone slept despite *Finbars* occasional lunge or shudder as she ploughed into a trough or big wave. He listened to the latest shipping forecast issued by Falmouth Coastguard, taking note of the conditions for the sea areas round them, Wight, Portland, Plymouth and Sole. It was obvious that the storm had just blown up out of nowhere as many sailors have previously found to their cost at this end of the English Channel. The weather was set to improve over the next twelve hours and that would make a rescue much easier. Focusing on keeping *Finba*r on course and listening to the radio traffic, he started a little when something touched his shoulder. It was Nita resting her hand there.

'Bloody hell woman, you gave me a start!'

'Sorry.' she said kissing his cheek.

'How are we doing? Has the storm passed yet?'

She grabbed the back of his seat and reached for the small grab handle by the side of the control panel as *Finbar* dropped into a trough with a thud that echoed and shuddered through the hull then ploughed into the back of the following wave which lifted them on the body of water to rise to the waves summit and burst through it in a wall of spray that splattered back driven by the wind onto the cabin windows; The wiper blades on the windows, moving incessantly side to side quickly clearing the screen.

'We changed course two hours ago to help a yacht in distress.'

Nita looked at him aghast. 'What's happened?'

'A family have got caught in this storm, they've broken their mast and one of the crew has a crush injury. There are only three of them on board, one is a child and the skipper can't handle her on his own.'

As he filled Nita in with the details he continued to fight *Finbar* through what was now quite a turbulent sea. Checking the depth sounder he saw that they were running through quite a shallow area which was causing the sea to break up more easily.

'Why us, what can we do?' Nita asked.

'It's maritime law my love, any vessel in the vicinity of a vessel in distress has to render assistance if at all possible. Take a look at the radar.'

She turned and studied the VDU screen as he continued explaining.

'See that big echo and the tiny one near it.'

Nita pointed at the screen, he nodded, 'Yeah, those two blips.'

'Well the big one is a thirty-thousand-ton container ship, and the little one is the yacht, *Spring Dawn*, who we're going to help.'

'Why can't the big ship get them?'

'Just look at the size of her she's far too big love. If they tried to get alongside in this sea they could roll onto them and crush them. However, they'll stay there to shield them until someone else can get there to help.'

The radio suddenly broke into their conversation.

'Mayday relay, mayday relay, mayday relay. All stations, all stations, all stations. This is Falmouth Coastguard, Falmouth Coastguard, Falmouth Coastguard. Yacht Spring Dawn, information number five. Container ship 'Mauri Carrier' is standing 500 metres to windward of yacht Spring Dawn. Motor cruiser Finbar Two is enroute to assist, Alderney and Salcombe Lifeboats have launched, ETA expected in next three hours. French patrol boat Cormoran has diverted to the area, ETA two hours.'

The Coastguard ended the message giving the time of the transmission. Reaching for the mic intending to respond to the message, a large rogue wave came in from *Finbars* port quarter lifting her up and almost throwing her over sideways into the back of another wave. A dark grey green mass of water engulfed them from the port side, Nita shrieked out aloud.

'HOLD ON!' Stephen shouted.

Instinctively he braced himself against his side of the cabin as he shouted the warning. Nita made a grab for the helm seat and grab rail but the size and force of the wave simply lifted *Finbar* throwing her onto Stephen. Her whole-body weight landed on him hitting him hard in the chest.

'Aagghh...!'

Stephen let go of the wheel, which, once released, spun one way and then back the other way. Out of control, *Finbar* gyrated furiously. Stephen grasped his chest at the same time gasping breathlessly to her.

'The wheel... Get the wheel!'

She made a grab for the spinning wheel it slipped through her hands a couple of times as she fought to bring *Finbar* back under control. Stephen slowly sank down the side of the cabin wall, by the seat and slumped on the floor moaning. Panicking Nita looked over her shoulder towards where Emma lay. Seeing she'd been disturbed from her sleep, she shuffled then settled again.

'Emma,' Nita called, 'EMMA...' she shouted this time.

Emma surfaced from under the quilt looking towards Nita, blurry eyed. Seeing her dad heaped in the corner she sat up fully alert. Clambering of the settee bed she lurched across the saloon, grabbing the seat for support she made a grab for Stephen.

'No... NO leave me, leave me, let me get my breath back.'

Having regained control of *Finbar*, Nita said quietly but firmly to her.

'Leave him, go and get Richard.'

Emma just stood looking at her dad, then at Nita vacantly. Nita repeated herself.

'Emma go and get Granddad.'

She nodded and handing herself round Nita got to the doorway to the galley just as Richard appeared up the steps.

'Gramps... dad's hurt, we need you to help us move him!'

Richard nodded, 'Heard the thud, rogue one was it? It nearly had me out of the bed.'

Seeing Stephen still in a heap behind the helm seat pillar, he quickly moved to help him. Stephen shook his head vigorously.

'No... Leave me...! Please, just leave me. I'll get myself out.'

Seated on the helms seat, Nita glanced down at him by her feet saying, her voice full of concern.

'Are you alright? Have you damaged your ribs again?'

'Don't think so, just badly winded.'

Carefully he turned onto his side and began to edge himself out from under her feet then around the large stainless-steel shaft that supported the seat. Once his shoulders were clear Richard and Emma helped him to his feet. He stretched and arched his back and did some gentle rotations whilst trying to retain his balance as *Finbar* did her utmost to knock him off his feet again.

'Okay,' he said, 'I haven't broken anything but I'm going to have a massive bruise on my back.'

Reaching for Nita, he rested his hands on her shoulders.

'Are you okay sweetness? You took a big hit as well.'

'No, I'm okay. You make a nice cushion to land on.'

She said glancing at him briefly smiling.

Relieved that he seemed okay, Richard turned to Emma.

'Go and see if Nan and Rachel are okay will you love.'

She disappeared down to the galley and forward to the main cabin. Opening the door to peek in she saw that things were in a bit of a state due to the rogue wave.

'Rach,' Emma called quietly. 'Rachel, are you alright?'

Her friend lifted her head from the pillow and looked towards the door and Emma.

'Oh god Em, I'm dying. What the chuff just happened?'

'Rogue wave threw us about a bit.'

'Bloody hell Em, is it always this bad?'

'No, this is a nasty storm and we're trying to get to a boat that's in trouble so it feels worse.'

'Ohh.' Rachel answered, burying her head in her pillow again groaning as *Finbar* dropped into yet another trough.

'How are you Nan?' Emma asked.

Without moving off the bed she replied.

'Oh you know me sweetheart, anything more than a duck's wake and I'm ill.'

Emma smiled, 'Sorry Nan.'

Mary lifted her arm and waved. As she left shutting the door *Finbar* lifted on a wave and she heard both the women moan in unison.

'Well?' Stephen said as she appeared through the galley door, he was sitting on the settee gently massaging his side.

'Dying according to Rachel.'

The radio came alive. *'Mayday, Finbar Two, Finbar Two, Finbar Two This is Falmouth Coastguard, Falmouth Coastguard, Falmouth Coastguard, over.'*

Richard, being nearest to the radio set picked up the mic. 'Mayday, Falmouth Coastguard, this is *Finbar Two*, go ahead, over.'

'Mayday, Finbar Two, Falmouth Coastguard. You should be able to talk directly with Spring Dawn on channel 16, over'

Stephen nodded to Richard then gingerly stood up and moved across the cabin. Taking the mic from him he took a quick look at the radar to confirm where they were in relation to *Spring Dawn*. Glancing at Nita who had remained at the wheel he said, 'Steer 225° love. Keep an eye on your heading, just make a bee-line for the two blips, okay.'

'Yep, okay.' She replied making a small adjustment with the wheel.

Keying the mic he responded.

'Mayday Falmouth Coastguard this is *Finbar Two* Message received thank you, out.'

He waited for a minute before keying the mic again.

'Yacht *Spring Dawn, Spring Dawn, Spring Dawn*, this is Motor cruiser *Finbar Two Finbar Two, Finbar Two*. Are you receiving, over?'

He rested his chin on his hand on the top of the galley bulkhead waiting for a reply gently massaging his side where he'd hit the cabin wall. Looking at the state of the sea again he felt it was calmer. The wave height seemed lower and *Finbar* wasn't pitching quite as much. He jumped when a little voice came through on the radio.

'Finbar Two, Finbar Two,' it said. In the background he could

hear someone else's voice coaxing him, telling him what to say next.

'A third time,' they said.

The small voice spoke again. '*Finbar Two.*' There was a moment of hesitation. '*This is yacht Spring Dawn, Spring Dawn, Spring Dawn, over.*'

Stephen assessed that the young person on the other end of the radio was probably terrified and all they wanted was someone there to help. He could probably see the big container ship standing off from them, but a smaller boat a lot nearer, even alongside would be so very reassuring.

'Spring Dawn, this is *Finbar Two*. My name's Stephen, what's yours, over?'

'*I'm Charley.*' The reply came.

'Well Charley, we think we'll be with you in very soon. Can you hang on that long for us? Over.'

After a brief pause Charley called back.

'*Dad says okay, we're looking forward to seeing you.*' There was a pause and then Charley said. '*Sorry, I forgot… over.*'

'Good Charley, can you tell me firstly who is hurt and then ask your dad what state your boat is in okay, over.'

There was another pause before Charley answered.

'*Mummy's hand got trapped in one of the winches last night and some of her fingers have been crushed. She can't move them and they're bleeding quite a lot. I feel very sick the sea is very rough. Dad says to tell you, we've rigged a storm jib and we're just keeping steerage way. He says the top of the mast is bent above the crosstrees.*' another pause then '*Over.*'

Stephen replied. 'Thank you Charley. Now can you tell me what you've done about wrapping your mum's hand up? Over'

'*I got a tea towel and put that round it, and she has put a sling on… over.*'

'Good one Charley. We'll be there before you know it, okay. Over.'

'*Okay. Bye, I mean out.*'

Putting the mic down by the radio, Stephen said eventually.

'Right Richard call Falmouth and see if they copied all that, are you okay on the wheel for the moment sugar?'

Nita nodded. 'The sea seems a lot calmer than an hour ago.'

Stephen had to agree the waves weren't as big or as steep as they had been around dawn. Turning to Emma.

'Em, get the proper First Aid kit from the locker under the chart table, then break out the waterproofs, don't forget the life vests and harnesses love. No-one goes outside without a suit, a vest and a harness on understand? Richard, Nita?'

'Okay' they both replied.

'How many flasks did you manage to fill Em?'

Emma was headfirst in one of the base lockers under the settee, pulling out bright yellow suits. Lifting her head up and blowing upwards through her lips she blew a straggling hair from over her face.

'Erm, two of the big ones.'

'Okay, when you've finished there see if you can make up two more will you?' she nodded.

Richard returning to the saloon said.

'Falmouth Coastguard copied that transmission and has said that because Charley is only quite young and obviously a bit distressed, we can contact *Spring Dawn* directly anytime. They're keeping a listening watch on 16.'

'Okay good.' Stephen said. 'I think when we get alongside, Richard you need to go across with Nita.' He turned to look at her. 'You'll be more use there initially sugar until we know how bad the mum's hand is. Once we know that I think her and Charley need to be here on *Finbar*. They'll be warmer and we'll be able to treat them better. Em, you helm until the cavalry arrive, I'll be on deck to help with the transfers.'

Richard added the comment. 'I guess the owner could do with being relieved for a while.'

'You're probably right.'

Stephen continued out-lining his plan.

'Take two of the flasks with you, I reckon he'll appreciate a hot drink.

Turning to Nita once more he asked.

'Are you still okay on the wheel sugar?'

Oblivious to Stephens's question, she ignored him. She was concentrating on the radar screen, he asked the question again.

'Nita, are you okay for the moment? ... Nita!'

He raised his voice this time to get her attention. She looked at him surprised.

'What... yes, I'm okay.'

Whilst she'd answered his question, he sensed that she was a little distracted. Moving over by her side he scanned the VDU screen. 'What's up love?' He said watching the screen with her. Pointing at the screen, she said.

'Look, there's *Spring Dawn* and the container ship, right. That must be the French patrol boat which has only just come up on the screen, and we're here in the middle. Yes?'

She looked at Stephen for confirmation that she'd got everybody correctly placed,

'That's right.' He answered.

'So, who or what is that blip?' she asked pointing at the screen and looking at Stephen, 'because it's not coming this way, so it's not going to offer assistance. Isn't that wrong?'

He watched the VDU as the green arm swept round in its arc three or four times. It appeared that the boat Nita had pointed out was going to pass the other side of the container ship by some distance, ignoring *Spring Dawn's* emergency. Richard had just come back into the saloon and moved so he could see the screen.

'You know,' he said, 'I was watching that echo earlier. Its maybe ten miles or so further North West of us on just about the same course as we are. Interestingly the French patrol boat was maybe fifteen miles or so behind but on the same course as the boat until the Mayday call.'

They all watched the VDU for a few moments as the scanner

rotated again refreshing all the images in the area with every sweep. A message on the radio broke their concentration.

'Finbar Two Finbar two, Finbar two, Zis is the French patrol boat Cormoran, Cormoran, Cormoran calling on channel 16, receiving, over.'

The patrol boat's radio operator spoke with a heavy French accent. Stephen picked up the mic to respond.

'*Cormoran, Cormoran, Cormoran*. This is *Finbar Two, Finbar Two, Finbar Two*. Go ahead, over.'

The operator began to update Stephen on how long it would be before they too would be alongside *Spring Dawn*. He told him that they had a qualified sick berth attendant on board and depending how bad the injury was to the lady's hand could take her on board their boat for treatment if a transfer was possible. Stephen acknowledged Cormoran's message.

Nita touched his arm. 'Look, there!' she said quietly.

He glanced quickly at Nita, and then to where she was looking. 'What? Where?'

'Wait until the next wave lifts us.' she said.

As *Finbar* rose and crested the oncoming wave in a plume of spray the four of them, Stephen, Nita, Richard and Emma saw on the horizon the black bulk of a large merchant ship and nestled beneath it the tiny white silhouette of a yacht, its mast bent over halfway down to ninety degrees.

'Bingo!' Richard said, 'That's them, right on the button. Well done Stephen, well done.'

'Hey, I didn't do anything. We've just followed a heading and the radar.'

'Well I think you're wonderful.' Nita said planting a noisy kiss on his lips.

Emma went. 'Oh gross... but you are dead cool dad.' and she kissed him as well.

'Alright, alright, we've still a lot to do.' he said.

Looking at Richard he asked, 'What about Mary and Rachel. Are they going to be able to help us?'

'Not sure, Mary will be the quickest to recover because she's always like this when it's bad, you know?' Stephen nodded. 'Rachel's still ill, but as you say, by the time we are up to Spring Dawn, she might be on the mend.'

Stephen thought for a moment, forming the next part of the plan.

'Right, Emma finish the flasks. Richard waterproofs, and don't forget the harness. Sugar pie,' he said, 'I'll take the wheel you get into your waterproofs, let Richard put your harness on.'

As they swapped places she kissed Stephen again.

'My real-life hero.' she said quietly scrunching her nose up as she said it. 'I do love you.'

Sitting on the helm's seat he took the mic from the clip on the bulkhead.

'*Spring Dawn, Spring Dawn, Spring Dawn.* This is *Finbar Two*, you receiving Charley? It's Stephen, over.'

There was silence for a few moments just a faint crackling sound of the open radio wavelength.

'*Finbar Two, this is Spring Dawn.*'

He heard Charley's father's voice in the background.

'Pass your message, over.' and then Charley repeat, '*Pass your message over.*'

'*Spring Dawn, Finbar Two*, we can see you Charley. We'll be with you in half an hour son okay, Over.'

There was the sound of Charley keying the mic to reply, at the same time he heard him shouting to his father. He could hear the excitement and relief in the boy's voice.

'They're nearly here dad. Did you hear?'

Stephen called Charley again. '*Spring Dawn, Finbar two*, listen Charley. How is your mum? Over.'

The young lad replied instantly. '*She's still bleeding a lot, and says it really hurts... Over.*'

'Okay Charley. Ask your dad if there is any gear in the water around you? Over'

Stephen heard him talk to his dad again.

'Finbar Two, dad says you'd be best on our starboard side because of the mast and rigging, over'

'Alright Charley. When we can get alongside, Richard and Nita are going to come across to help. Now I've got a job for you to do, can you see that your mum has a sea jacket or something warm on and you'll need to wrap up too. Got that, over?'

Charley answered, *'Yes.'*

Stephen continued with his instructions, making them as simple as possible.

'I want you and your mum to come onto my boat because it'll be warmer and we can care for your mum here. It will help your seasickness too understand? Over'

'Yes.' The answer came back.

'Good, Richard is going to stay with your dad to help him and give him a rest until the French Navy get here or one of the lifeboats. Do you understand, over?'

'Okay, I'll go and help mummy get ready.'

'Good lad, you get yourself and your mum ready, and call me when you've done that. *Finbar Two*, listening out.'

Stephen called the Coastguard and he updated them with the latest information, including his plan to treat the injured lady. The Coastguard repeated that they were keeping a listening watch and plotting all the vessels involved in the rescue. They informed him that the first lifeboat would be on the scene in about an hour, as the sea state was improving. They also said that after re-fuelling the helicopter from the Naval station at Culdrose would fly out to them and airlift anyone needing hospitalising. Whilst he was listening to the update he heard a rustling by his side. Turning slightly to see what it was he did a double take. Standing next to him was a yellow teddy bear at least that's what he thought. He couldn't help a chuckle as he looked at her, she smiled back at him, and reading his thoughts playfully punched his arm.

'Do I look fat in this?' she said quietly.

'Mmm... not fat, cuddlier I'd say...'

Emma came up from the galley carrying a small a cool box in one hand and four insulated mugs in the other hand. Taking one look at Nita she let out a little shriek of laughter. Nita threw her a deep frown.

'Not a word or I'll turn you into a mermaid... Okay!'

Still smirking Emma replied, putting the cool box down by the coffee table and handing out the mugs.

'Me... I'm not saying a word.'

They hugged one another as Emma gave her her drink. Nearer now, they could clearly see *Spring Dawn* dwarfed against the dark background of the container ship *Mauri Carrier*. She was bobbing about like a toy boat in an enormous bath, while the container ship appeared just to be rolling slightly. Through his binoculars Stephen could see the bent upper mast which explained why the main sail was only partially lowered, the remainder was trailing over the port side in the sea. He deduced that when the mast snapped it must have trapped the thick binding on the edge of the main sail trapping it in the channel which ran up the mast track. From the bow of *Spring Dawn* to the top of what was left of the mast a small triangular sail, a storm jib was set providing some steerage way to allow the skipper a little bit of manoeuvrability otherwise they would have just drifted at the mercy of the storm. He turned to Emma.

'Take the wheel love I'm going to get into my suit.'

He struggled to get himself into the awkwardly fitting waterproof suit, wincing from time to time as his side and ribs reminded him of his earlier fall, finally he fastened his life vest and harness on. The radio crackled into life once more and someone with an Asian or Oriental accent called them.

'Finbar Two Finbar Two Finbar Two, this is CS Mauri Carrier, Mauri Carrier, Mauri Carrier, Good day. We have open view of you coming. We will stand here until you are alongside Spring Dawn and other boat helps arrive. Is there any things more we can help you do, over?'

Richard being nearest, picked up the mic.

'*Mauri Carrier* this is *Finbar Two,* Good morning, we should be up to *Spring Dawn* very soon. We have all the equipment we need for the moment to get alongside and give first aid to the injured woman and the sick son. Thank you, over.'

The container ship replied straight away. '*Finbar Two*, all received listening out.'

Glancing at Stephen he said tentatively.

'I hope to god we can cope with this woman's hand. It sounds pretty smashed up you know.'

'I know, but at least we'll be doing something pro-active and that must be reassuring for them all. If it is as bad as that, then the French Navy guys will have to take over.'

'*Finbar Two Finbar Two Finbar Two, its Charley. I've got mum into her jacket and I'm ready as well. Dad says he's seen you coming, over*'

Richard, still with the mic in his hand, grinned and replied.

'Hello Charley, I'm Richard. Thanks for the update, we'll be there very soon to look after you and your mum. Well done young man. Over.'

Stephen took a deep breath, exhaled before saying.

'They need our help guys all we can do is our best. Just listen to the lad's voice he's full of confidence in us. Right, I'm going on deck to put the fenders out. Nita get a couple of clean tea towels just in case mums' hand is worse than we've been told.'

Opening one of the patio doors he stepped out onto the sun deck taking two of the sausage fenders with him. Instantly he smelt the salt on the wind and tasted it on his lips. Securing the short rope on one of the fenders to a cleat on *Finbars* port side, he tossed it over the side. Taking the other one, he stepped up onto the narrow decking that ran down the sides of the superstructure pausing for a moment he clipped his lifeline onto the grab rail that ran the whole length of the cabin sides. Holding onto the rail with one hand he moved forward to where he wanted the other fender secured. He felt that although *Finbar* was still pitching and rolling showering him in sheets of spray as she burst through a wave, or dropped into a trough, the sea was definitely calmer. He could feel the benefit of being in the lee of the container ship that had sheltered *Spring Dawn* from the worst of the storm. Twice he was caught off-balance once his foot slipped off the side causing him to wince. Getting to where he wanted the other fender placed he had to let go of the grab rail and crouching fastened the rope to a cleat before dropping that fender over the side. For this brief time his lifeline was the only thing fastening him safely to the boat preventing him being washed, or worse, fall overboard. He retraced his way back to the sun deck and the safety of the saloon. By now they were a matter of a few hundred yards from *Spring Dawn*, Charley and his dad were visible now sitting in the yacht's cockpit. She looked about the same length as *Finbar* around 30 feet, under normal circumstances she would have made a pretty picture with her sails set, now she looked as though she'd just come through the battle of Trafalgar. A broken mast the main sail trapped in the mast channel, wire rigging, ropes and sheets, as they are known in sailing terms all trailing in the sea.

A head appeared through the galley door as Mary unexpectedly came into the saloon. She looked dreadful, her pallor was a pale green hue as she very gingerly came up the three steps. She looked around at everyone a little surprised at their various states of dress and smiled.

'Am I imagining it or has it suddenly got calmer?'

Richard winked at Stephen. 'Reinforcements...' he said smiling.

Stephen quickly explained the events of the last four hours ending by saying.

'It would be a huge bonus if you would oversee refreshments once we get the woman and the lad across here, can you cope with that?'

Peering through the salt coated saloon windows towards *Spring Dawn* and the huge container ship nearby, she replied firmly.

'No problem you know me, if I've got something to keep me busy then I can manage the sea-sickness.'

Looking at Richard she smiled and quite deliberately took the insulated mug out of his hand and took a drink replacing it back in his hand.

'Oh... I think I need one of my own.'

Emma gently pushed past her down into the galley.

'I'll make you one Nan. Do you want a tablet?'

'Yes love, that's probably a good idea, better make it two.'

They were now only yards from *Spring Dawn's* starboard side and because of the shield the container vessel was providing the sea was considerably calmer. Richard reduced their speed to allow for a slow approach to the yachts side. Emma came back from the galley handing her Nan a mug and tablets.

'Right, Emma you're on the wheel,' Stephen said, 'you two get the box of flasks and we'll get on deck.'

Gathering the cool box up Nita moved out onto the sun deck. From the patio doors he turned back to Emma.

'Slow and steady Em watch for my signals.' She nodded.

Stephen and Nita stood together in the shelter of the sun deck as Emma brought them alongside the yacht, Richard emerged couple of minutes later.

'Thought I'd take a walkie-talkie with me, we can talk without going through channels, plus if there is anything unpleasant to do the world needn't know about it just yet.'

Stephen nodded taking the second radio, 'Good idea.'

They could make out Charley sitting by his father wrapped in yellow waterproofs. Stephen looked closely at Charley's dad, he could see the strain on his face from the last seven hours or so. He looked totally worn out after fighting to keep his boat in one piece and his family safe. Richard must have had the same thoughts.

'My God, he's absolutely done in, poor sod.'

Stephen glanced at him then called to Emma.

'Slow ahead Em, bring her up onto the same course and then just let her drift alongside. Watch the sea love.'

'Okay.' She replied.

'You two ready then? I'll go first and get the boat hook. Once we're alongside you get across from here.' He said pointing to the side of the gunnel that would be the nearest point to *Spring Dawn.*

'Nita you first then Richard, get Charley over here soon as and then see to his mother. That's going to be up to you sugar okay?'

They answered together. 'Okay' and 'All right.'

Finbar gave a sudden lurch and they all heard the sausage fenders screech in protest as the two boats suddenly came together. A flume of water and spray erupted between them like a siphon, forcing the water upwards. Stephen climbed up from the sun deck, clipped his lifeline onto the grab rail then moved forward until he could un-clip the boathook from its spring cleats on the cabin roof. Returning to the sun deck he reached across the constantly varying gap and hooked onto the base of one of the yachts deck stanchions, pulled hard to close the gap between them just long enough for Nita to scramble across down into the cockpit of the yacht. Richard passed the chill box over then he stepped across onto *Spring Dawn.* Stephen saw him shake hands with Charley's dad and Nita ruffle Charley's hair, she said something to him and he pointed to the cabin. She looked through the hatch then disappeared into the cabin. Charley's father leant towards to his son saying something to him. Charley got to his feet and with Richard steadying him climbed out of the cockpit and waited for the two boats to come close together again. When the next wave brought them up on the crest side by side, Richard helped the lad over the wires. Stephen held out one hand to steady him and he stepped across the gap and down into *Finbars* sun deck. Giving the lad a big smile he said.

'Hello Charley, I'm Stephen, are you alright son?' The youth nodded, Stephen continued, 'Well welcome aboard *Finbar* you get yourself inside the saloon where it's warm, my daughter's there she's called Emma and her Nan too, she's Mary okay?'

'Thank you.' Charley said disappearing through the door.

Looking back to *Spring Dawn* he saw that Richard had taken the helm from Charley's father who had moved to this side of the cockpit closest to *Finbar.* Again the boats were forced against each other by the seas motion and another flume of water and spray erupted dowsing them both. Despite all the waterproof gear he was wearing Stephen could see how wet and tired he looked after the last seven hours. He guessed he must be absolutely perished from the continual dowsing from the sea and spray he'd endured while waiting for help to arrive.

'Bloody hell am I glad to see you.' He called across the gap. 'I'm Edwin Gates, I can't thank you enough for coming.'

Stephen called back. 'Stephen Leigh-Grace and it's not a problem, pleased we were near enough to help. How's your wife, do you know?'

'No, your friend went below to help her.'

Nita's head popped up out of the hatch and she called Edwin. He turned, listened to what she had to say then moved to the hatch. Moments later his wife appeared wearing a green and grey anorak and around her neck a sling to support her right arm. Taking a firm grip of the boat hook he pulled hard to bring the two boats as close together as possible. Edwin supported his wife until Nita had climbed out of the hatch then together they helped her to the side of the yacht. Nita climbed back onto *Finbar* then Edwin, giving his wife a kiss, carefully assisted her over the gap. Once across the gap and safely on the sun deck, Nita put her arm round the woman's waist and led her into the saloon giving Stephen a glance and a quick shake of the head as she passed him. Releasing the boat hook from the stanchion he called across to *Spring Dawn*.

'Edwin, I'm going to give us some sea room, Richard will stay with you until the French Navy arrives or one of the lifeboats, okay?'

Edwin waved, 'Okay, keep in touch and let me know how Susan is will you.'

Instantly an ice-cold chill ran down Stephen's spine, just hearing the name Susan. Quickly recovering his composure he replied.

'Richard has a walkie talkie and some flasks with him, I suggest you get a hot drink and try and get a little rest, you must be absolutely knackered.'

'I am but so relieved you're here. I know the container ship has been here most of the night but she was far too big to be able to do anything really.'

Stephen nodded as Edwin finished off saying.

'Still they've been able to give us so much shelter from the worst of the gale.'

Stephen waved, 'Get a hot drink and some rest okay!'

Emma steered away when she'd felt him release them from the yachts side, Stephen moved back into the warmth of the saloon closing the patio doors.

'Keep us twenty-five yards off Em, I don't want to risk damaging either boat. If it gets choppy, go another twenty-five but keep them in sight, where are Nita and your nan?'

'Galley.'

'Charley.'

Emma smiled and nodded towards the heap of quilts lying on the long settee.

'The warmth got him in five minutes, Nan covered him up poor kid. What an experience dad, he must've been shit scared.'

Stephen just looked at her.

'Sorry...' she mumbled.

'Mmm... but you're right love. You okay there for the moment I want to see how her hand is.' Emma nodded.

Stephen went to go through to the galley but stopped at the door and glanced across to his daughter.

'She's called Susan by the way!' he said quietly, the look from Emma said it all.

In the galley the dining area the table had reappeared and Nita and Mary had begun to gently remove the outer layers of tea towels that had been the dressings for Susan's hand. As each layer was taken off so the next one was bloodier and as each layer was removed so the pain from the crushed hand and fingers grew more intense. Stephen watched Susan's face as the next towel was taken off. This was the third one and he saw the pain etched on her face.

'Stop,' he said. 'Leave it. This is beyond our limited first aid skills. Susan needs a hospital pronto.'

Both Nita and Mary looked at him agreeing, he came and sat on the edge of the semi-circle of seats surrounding the table.

'Susan, all we can do really is make you as comfortable as possible until we can get you off *Finbar* and away to hospital.'

She was watching him, concentrating on what he was saying. He could see in her eyes she was as exhausted as Edwin. She appeared to be on the edge of collapse both from her injury and sheer exhaustion after seven hours of being thrown around by the storm.

'We have a number of options to work with. One, there is a French Navy vessel coming, it should be here in the next half hour and they have a medic on board. Two, there are two lifeboats coming their ETA is within the hour. The third option and for me, given how serious this looks to be honest, there is a helicopter coming. I suggest we get you and Charley airlifted to hospital as soon as.'

At the suggestion of the helicopter both Nita and Mary nodded. Struggling against the exhaustion and her general weakened state, she said quietly.

'I just feel so tired and weary, I can't think clearly and the pain is awful it feels like my hand is going to burst open. Whatever you think is best and Charley has been so ill, I think he needs to be off the sea too. Is he alright where is he?'

'Charley's okay,' he said, 'he fell asleep almost as soon as he got into the warmth of the saloon. Mary covered him up on the settee.'

Susan looked at the three of them sitting around her.

'Thank you so much for coming I was so frightened. We've never been in a storm like this before. It just came out of nowhere.'

Stephen said, 'Like I said to your husband I'm glad we were near enough to be able to help. Now, I need to set things in motion to get you and Charley away to hospital, you rest okay?'

As he got up to leave he touched Nita on the shoulder. 'Got a minute love?' she shuffled out from her seat and followed him up into the saloon.

'It's serious yes,' he said unzipping his sea suit and wriggled his shoulders out of the top part, tying the sleeves around his waist.

'Yes, I think it is.'

Stephen added. 'She needs fluids now and I know it's a bit of a cliché but go with hot sweet tea for the moment and give her some pain killers. I'm going to ask for advice and see if the Coastguard can whistle up the helicopter ASAP.'

'Okay.' she squeezed his arm affectionately, turned and went back to the galley.

'Is it bad then dad?' Emma asked.

'Think so love... seriously bad.'

Picking up the mic from the side of the radio, he turned the channel selector to 16.

'Mayday, Falmouth Coastguard, Falmouth Coastguard, Falmouth Coastguard, *Finbar Two, Finbar Two, Finbar Two*, over.'

The Coastguard replied instantly.

'Mayday, Finbar Two this is Falmouth Coastguard, go ahead, over.'

'Falmouth Coastguard, *Finbar Two*. We have taken the injured woman and her son off *Spring Dawn*. One of my crew has gone on board to assist the owner until more help arrives. We have assessed the crush injury sustained by the woman and consider that she requires immediate, repeat immediate evacuation to hospital. She has crushed three fingers there is considerable swelling around the injury causing acute pain. She has suffered some blood loss. We have given her warm sweet tea to drink as she is dehydrated. We have also given her some basic pain killers. Can you give me an ETA for the helicopter? Over.'

'Finbar Two, Falmouth Coastguard wait one.'

The walkie talkie on Stephen's belt crackled.

'Stephen, Richard, Edwin would like an up-date, any news? Over'

Unclipping his handset from his belt he replied.

'Richard, I've asked the Coastguard if they can arrange for immediate casevac. Susan's crush injury is outside our limited first aid skills, her hand is badly swollen and she's in acute pain. I'm going ask if I can send Charley as well, he's asleep just now but I think they both need rehydrating. How's Edwin? How's the boat? Over.'

'He's okay,' Richard answered, 'He's had two mugs of tea with sugar and they've perked him up. He's heard what you've suggested. The boats is in a bit of a state and handling like a bathtub, but we've got some steerage way with the storm jib he set, so we'll manage until the cavalry arrive. Over.'

A few minutes elapsed before Falmouth Coastguard came back to him with the information he'd asked for. Nita had come up into the saloon to stand with him and Emma. Going over to the long settees, she peeked at Charley under the quilt, nodding as she came back saying.

'Out for the count and mums gone to sleep as well. We've made her as comfortable as we can, she's had some pain killers and a mug of sweet tea. Mary's staying with her to see she's all right. How long do you think before help gets here?'

Stephen glanced at the clock the middle of the roof coving then at the radar screen. He waited for the green line to sweep round again and pointed to one of the green blips.

'That's the French patrol boat, five miles or so away say fifteen to twenty minutes.'

On the next sweep of the radar he added.

'Those two blips are the two lifeboats, and they're twelve miles or so off. I reckon three quarters of an hour. Falmouth say that the chopper should be over us in about twenty-five minutes.'

The radio broke into their conversation.

'*Finbar Two, Finbar Two, Finbar Two, zis is French Naval patrol boat Cormoran, over.*'

Stephen reached up to the radio and keying the mic replied.

'*Cormoran, Cormoran, Cormoran. Finbar Two, Finbar Two, Finbar Two,* go ahead, over.'

'*Finbar Two* we `ave you on radar and our lookouts 'ave seen you and the yacht *Spring Dawn*. Can you give us any information on your status and if you require any assistance over.'

Stephen thought about their options for a moment, and then said to Nita and Emma.

'Okay, I think we need medical help now, certainly until the RNLI or chopper arrive. These guys have a medic and I'm inclined to get them here soon as. Yes?'

Nita replied nodding. 'For sure yes. My guess is they'll be able to give Susan something stronger than Paracetamol.'

Emma simply nodded. Keying the mic he called the French patrol boat, giving them all the up-to-date information regarding Susan's injuries and what they had done to do to make her comfortable. Nearly ten minutes elapsed before the French boat called again. By now they could see the boat quite clearly only a matter of a mile away.

'*Finbar Two, Finbar Two, Finbar Two. Comoran. Falmouth Coastguard `ave asked if we could provide medical `elp. We will be wiz you in a few minutes and will send away our Zodiac wiz our medic and some ratings to `elp, over.*'

Relieved Stephen sighed replying. '*Comoran, Finbar Two*. I'm most obliged to you, we will be waiting.'

Picking up a pair of binoculars from the shelf that ran along the front of the cabin windows, he scanned the sea surface in the direction of the French boat, and in a moment saw the dark shape of a Zodiac rigid hulled boat about twenty feet long, similar to the type the marines use, wave hopping towards them. Making his way onto the sun deck he watched its approach. In minutes it was alongside and two of the crew quickly transferred onto *Finbars* sun deck in a very practised boarding manoeuvre. As soon as they were on the deck a third crew member passed over two bags. The rib sheared off taking station some yards away on *Finbars* starboard side and just astern of them. Stephen held his hand out to the first French crewman.

'Stephen Leigh-Grace.' he said.

Taking his hand briefly the sailor shook it at the same time throwing off the hood of their sea-suit. The sailor was quite petite and very pretty, her dark hair pulled back into a perfect bun. For a moment Stephen was caught off guard, a woman was not who he'd expected to be greeting just now.

'Officier Marinier Yvonne Merrs.' she said and then turned to the second sailor. 'Zis is our sick bay orderly. Matelot Bernard Rochere.'

Looking straight back at Stephen she continued, 'Where is ze injured lady and ze boy please?'

Opening the patio doors, Stephen ushered them into the saloon. 'This way,' he said, explaining to the officer as they moved into the saloon.

'The boy, Charley, is asleep under there.' he said pointing to the heaped duvet cover on the long settee. 'As soon as we got him on board he relaxed and the warmth just put him to sleep.'

The French officer smiled lifting the edge of the duvet to look at Charley.

'Benir.' she said quietly, replacing the cover over the young lad again. Turning to Stephen she added, 'So sweet.'

The two sailors followed him through the saloon to the galley doorway. 'This is my daughter, Emma.' Stephen introduced her.

'Mademoiselle.' The officer replied courteously, the seaman, Bernard, nodded and smiled at her. Emma felt herself colour up and smiled back at him saying coyly, 'Hello.'

They went down into the galley where Stephen introduced everyone to Yvonne and Bernard. Nita and Mary moved out of the way to allow the two sailors to get closer to Susan and begin to assess her injury. Mary asked them if they would like a drink. Yvonne spoke to her colleague he nodded to her, she turned back to Mary answering.

'Oui, madam, yes please two coffees black, sugar in one of them merci, thank you.'

A few minutes passed as they assessed the injury to Susan's hand. Following a brief conversation, Yvonne stood up and moved to stand beside Stephen, Nita and Mary. Quietly she began to say.

'Bernard thinks zat we leave zis dressing as it is. To disturb it now could, erm,' she thought for a moment of the English word that she wanted, 'bad things, no, make things more badly, we understand zat the Navy or RAF are flying a `elecopter to you, yes?'

Stephen nodded, the officer continued.

'Bon, good, then we need to improve zis lady's fluids, he is going to put a drip up.'

She turned to speak to the medic again and listened as he explained further she acknowledged him.

'Oui, oui...bon.' Turning to Stephen she said. 'Can you explain to Susan zat he is going to give `er some fluids and a little morphine to `elp ze pain, please.' She smiled adding. 'My English is not so good I think.'

Stephen chuckled replying. 'Huh... It's better than my French any day, much better.'

Moving to sit opposite Susan Stephen explained they were going to help ease her pain. She just nodded and watched as the orderly drew up a small amount of morphine into a syringe. He rummaged in one of the bags they'd brought taking out a pouch of saline and a sealed bag with a cannula in. When he was ready he turned to Yvonne and said something to her. She pushed up Susan's sweater sleeve on her un-injured arm. Bernard wiped the back of her hand with a swab and having found a vein slid the needle of the cannula into it. Taping it in place he connected the tube to the saline pouch. Holding the pouch out to Nita he gestured for her to hold it up above Susan. Next he injected the morphine into her through the small shunt valve that branched out of the side of the cannula. The effect was almost instant, in less than a minute she had visibly relaxed, released from the acute pain the injury was causing her. Holding her wrist for a few moments checked her pulse then looked at the Officer, 'Bon.'

From the saloon Emma called. 'Dad, Granddads on the walkie-talkie.'

'Right love, coming.'

Stephen slipped out of the seat and went up to the saloon. Taking the walkie talkie he pressed the send key.

'Richard, okay or problem?'

As he spoke he looked across to the yacht as she wallowed in the troughs. To be fair the sea was generally calmer in spite of the shelter the huge container ship was still providing for them.

'No,' Richard replied, 'no problem, apart from the fact I'd sooner be helming a bathtub right now. The jury rig's just giving her enough way to keep her on this tack but she's handling like our old Enterprise did after a capsize remember?'

Stephen chuckled remembering when he'd first met Suzanne, Richard had taken him sailing in an Enterprise dinghy and because of his total inexperience at the time they often capsized. An Enterprise full of water always seemed to just wallow no matter how much water you bailed out. Memories he thought and smiled, Richard continued.

'No, Edwin would like to know what the French medics have said about Susan.'

Stephen saw Edwin's head at the hatch entrance to the yachts cabin as he updated them. He was just finishing his message off when *Finbars* radio came alive.

'Mayday Finbar Two this is Falmouth Coastguard over.'

Quickly Stephen explained to Richard that Falmouth were calling then reaching for the mic responded to the call.

'Falmouth Coastguard this is *Finbar Two*. Go ahead, over.'

The Coastguard came back. *'Finbar Two, Falmouth Coastguard. Expect Rescue 251 with you in approximately fifteen minutes, repeat, one five minutes. Over.'*

'Falmouth Coastguard, *Finbar Two* all received, out.'

'I'll take the wheel love, will you go and fill the others in, I'll tell Granddad and I suppose we ought to wake Charley and get him and Susan ready to move.'

Emma looked at the heaped duvet on the settee and smiled prodding Stephen nodding for him to look at the long settee. Beneath one edge of the quilt a pair of small feet protruded, and an arm hung down at the side, he grinned back at Emma.

'Seems a shame to disturb him, but I think he'd be better off on dry land. I reckon he'll not forget this holiday in a rush, do you?'

Emma glanced back at her dad then to the settee again as she went through the doorway to the galley.

'He can write about it when he goes back to school,' she said drawing her hand across her front as though she was reading a headline. 'What I did on my holidays..!'

They both laughed briefly. Stephen called Richard and updated him. As he finished his conversation the French officer came up into the saloon.

'Can I be permitted to use your radio please, I need to speak wis my ship.'

Stephen gestured to her the direction of the radio. She switched the channel selector to a new one, picked up the mic and called *Cormoran*. He listened as he assumed she was making a brief report. Conversation over, she replaced the mic and reselected channel 16.

'Merci.' She said then using her own handheld radio called their rib that was still just off *Finbars* starboard side. Turning to look at the rib as she spoke to the crew she watched the helmsman on the boat wave to acknowledge her message. Immediately the rib sheared off heading back towards the patrol boat.

'A lot calmer now... the sea.' Stephen said.

The officer studied him quizzically for a moment trying to translate what he'd just said into French. He used his hand, waving it up and down to simulate a rough sea then describing a smooth arc. 'Calmer.' he said.

'Ah... oui.' she said, 'apaiser oui.'

Emma and Nita came up into the saloon, Emma went over to the long settee and lifting the duvet edge revealing the sleeping Charley they heard her say softly.

'Charley... Charley, wake up.'

The young lad sat bolt up-right peering around, he looked

startled for a moment as he scanned his unfamiliar surroundings. Emma touched his shoulder gently.

'Remember I'm Emma, you and your mum came onto *Finbar*. Look over there, there's *Spring Dawn*. My Granddad's gone to help you dad until the lifeboats arrive, okay.'

The lad nodded still a little bewildered, Emma continued.

'We've got to get you ready to go with your mum to hospital so she can have her hand seen to properly.'

'Where's mummy now?' he asked watching Emma.

She took his hand and steadied him as he stood up then led him towards the door to the galley.

'These French sailors have come to help your mum,' she said, 'they've given her something to help the pain so she's a bit sleepy right now.'

Charley looked at Yvonne and the others as they went down the steps to the galley. They heard Emma say to Charlie.

'There's a helicopter coming to take you both to hospital, have you ever been in one?'

They saw him shake his head.

'*Finbar Two,*' the radio broke into the chat as Emma and Charlie disappeared through the doorway. '*Finbar Two, Finbar Two. Rescue two five one, two five one, two five one on channel 16. Over.*'

Stephen took the mic. 'Rescue two five one, *Finbar Two*. Go ahead. Over'

'*Finbar Two, rescue two five one. We have you on radar, our eta is six minutes. Have you any aerials or upper structure that could cause a problem for our winchman? Over*'

'Rescue two five one, Negative,' Stephen replied, 'We have a flying bridge with a radar cone mounted. The aft sun deck is open. Over.'

'*Roger that.*' The operator responded. '*Can you change course to head bow into the sea and maintain eight knots if possible. Over.*'

Acknowledging the helicopter, Stephen looked at the Petty Officer.

'Can you get everyone up here and tell them to hang on it's going to get a bit choppy.' Then to Nita said, 'Better get yourself back into that sea-suit sugar and get ready to welcome our guest.'

Nita giggled at the thought of someone just dropping out of the sky as she struggled to get herself back into the top half of her suit once again.

Off to the starboard Stephen suddenly picked out the pinprick of light high in the sky approaching them quickly. Within seconds he was able to make out the shape and colour of a Sea King search and rescue helicopter. Everyone was up in the saloon now, either seated or hanging onto something. Even Rachel had managed to crawl out of the forward cabin.

'Hang on!' Stephen said, 'I'm changing course.'

To warn *Spring Dawn,* he gave two long blasts on *Finbars* horn and turning the wheel brought the boat up into the sea. He pushed the throttles forward to increase their speed to eight knots however it was evident they weren't going to be able to maintain that speed as they just plunged into every wave, the boat burying her bow into each one and throwing up sheets of spray that were whisked away in the wind. He throttled the back to six knots, which he felt was comfortable for the boat and everyone on board. Plunging into one deep trough he heard Mary moan a little, Rachel echoed it as it knocked her off balance into the cabinet by the galley door.

'Here we go again...' Mary said, 'but at least it's only for a little while.'

The medical orderly reached to help Rachel to her feet, she looked at him for a moment and just like Emma earlier, blushed and said coyly. 'Thank you.'

The seaman grinned at her. 'Mademoiselle.' he replied politely.

'Finbar Two, rescue two five one.' The radio broke into life again. *'Are you able to maintain that heading and speed? Over.'*

Stephen responded. 'That's affirmative, yes, over.'

'Finbar Two, recue two five one, our winchman is lowering to you now.'

Turning to Nita, Stephen said, 'Go on, go and welcome our guest.'

As she got to the patio door he called, 'Use your harness!' then turning to Emma said.

'Take the walkie talkie and call granddad, see if Charlie wants to speak to his dad before they leave.'

Holding *Finbar* on this new heading they began to pitch and dive into the sea more heavily. Overhead now the noise of the approaching Sea King was becoming deafening so much so that it was impossible to hear anyone without shouting. Like some conjuring trick an orange suit suddenly appeared on the sun deck. Having landed the crewman the helicopter pulled away and the noise of the rotors faded. Nita ushered the person into the saloon, closing the patio door behind them. Their new visitor removed their helmet and introduced himself.

'Morning all, I'm flight sergeant Ray Hughes.'

Standing to attention for a moment, he nodded to the French officer, 'Ma'am,'

'Sergeant.' She responded.

Ray looked towards the French medic and they acknowledged each other with a nod.

Stephen went around the room introducing everyone else.

'Right, let's see what we can do about you.'

Ray said moving to crouch by Susan. Through Yvonne the orderly explained the treatment she'd had so far to stabilize her while Ray made brief notes on the thigh pad of his flying suit. Emma led Charley to the back of the saloon and called her Granddad on the walkie talkie. Explaining what was happening now she said that Charley wanted to speak to his dad before being airlifted to the hospital. Giving the lad the radio she showed him which buttons to press then left him to talk to his father.

'Take the wheel love,' Stephen said, 'I'm going to help on the sun deck. Keep her on this heading at six knots, all right?'

Slipping onto the helms seat she nodded. 'Okay.'

The flight sergeant stood up, 'Right I'll call the chopper back, I'll take Susan first and then come back for the son, Charley did you say?' He glanced round the saloon for the young lad.

Emma called to him, 'Charley come and meet Ray.'

He came back through the group of people holding the radio out to her.

'Daddy wants to speak to mummy.'

Nita took the radio and went to sit by Susan whilst, Ray explained to Charley what was going to happen over the next few minutes. The young lad listened nodding as he went through each phase of the lift. Replacing his helmet he called the helicopter.

'Okay, all sorted,' he said, 'let's get Susan out onto the sun deck.'

Nita and the French Officer helped her to stand and supported her as she walked towards the patio doors onto the sun deck. Stopping for a moment she looked back at Charley, he came towards her and hugged her round the waist, she kissed his head and briefly stroked his shoulders. Emerging onto the open deck Stephen looked up at the sky and smiled, how perverse he thought. For the past seven hours they'd battled through one of the worst storms he'd ever had to sail in and now, as he stood with Ray, Nita and the others the grey skies had begun to break and shafts of weak sun light had begun to illuminate patches of the sea around them. Even *Spring Dawn,* some distance away was in the centre of a sun ray.

Nita stood supporting Susan at the patio doors with Charley by them.

'Thank you...' she said, 'all of you so much, thank you for being here and helping; we'll never forget this.' To the two French sailors she said. 'Merci.'

They nodded to her as Stephen said.

'Glad we were able to get to you, listen take care of that hand, okay.'

Nita added, 'Yes look after yourself, I think it will take some time.'

Stephen said, 'You should be very proud of young Charley here, he was the hero in all this.'

Susan smiled weakly glancing at her son, 'He was wasn't he?'

With *Finbar* still heading up into the running sea throwing up the occasional shower of spray the noise of the approaching Sea King grew to an ear-splitting crescendo stopping any further conversation. They were all being buffeted by the rotor wash as it hovered above them. A rope fell onto the sun deck, Ray grabbed it and guided a harness down onto the deck. He waved to Stephen to come to him and shouted above the noise of the rotor.

'Keep hold of this and feed it out as they lift us. Okay?'

Stephen gave a thumb's up as Ray gestured to Nita to bring Susan to him. Helped by the French orderly they supported her as Ray slipped the halter around her. Satisfied she was comfortable and ready for the lift without causing too much discomfort to her injured hand he waved his arm in a circular motion. Instantly they were lifted from the deck at the same time travelling backwards. Ray had his legs straddled around Susan and protected her head with his arms while Stephen fed out the line until it slipped from his fingers. At the door of the Sea King they watched as Ray rotated slightly as they were both pulled inside. The Sea King turned and flew round in a wide arc and began its second run into *Finbar*. Moments later Ray was approaching the boats stern about ten feet above the waves gesturing with his arm again until finally landing plumb in the centre of the sun deck. Releasing the harness he went to the door to the saloon.

'Right young'un,' he shouted above the noise of the rotors, 'ready for the fastest lift you're ever likely to go in?'

Charley looked at him for a moment then turned and dashed back into the saloon to Emma.

Throwing his arms around her and the seat he said.

'Thank you, goodbye.'

Taken aback by his show of affection she put her arm round him and squeezed him.

'That's alright,' she said, 'take care Charley look after your Mum, go on, go for your ride, Bye.'

From the other end of the saloon Ray called out gently but firmly.

'Put her down son you don't know where she's been! Come on

we've got to get your Mum to hospital sharpish.'

'Bye Charley.' Emma called as he got to the door, as he passed Nita he gave her a hug too.

'Bye Charley.' she said.

Ray guided him to the centre of the sun deck and taking the harness from Stephen slipped it over Charley fitting it snugly round his body before clipping his own harness onto it. Saluting the deck briefly, he waved his arm, and the pair were whisked upwards and backwards as before. Everyone craned their necks to watch the lift completed. Moments later the big side door slid shut and the helicopter banked round heading back to the English coast. They watched for a while until it became a speck in the sky before returning to the saloon. Emma called to them.

'The helicopter has just called Falmouth Coastguard to say the rescue has been completed. They're taking them to Truro.'

The French Officer pulled her personal radio from her jacket calling her patrol boat. Meanwhile the medical orderly gathered all his equipment together sealing it into the waterproof bags. Fastening their sea suits they went around shaking hands with everyone. Stephen and Nita went out onto the sun deck again, the sun was even stronger than before. Yvonne waved her arm to the rib as it appeared wave hopping again back to *Finbar*. The helmsman brought the craft expertly alongside adjusting his speed to match Finbars.

Yvonne turned to the two of them. 'Au`voir Missuer Stephen, Mademoiselle Nita, safe passage back `ome to Angletere.'

Thank you, glad you were here.' Stephen said, 'Au`voir, goodbye.'

With the rib alongside the two sailors stepped up to the gunnel as the next wave brought the two boats level then stepped across onto the rib helped by one of their crew mates. When the next wave brought them close again, Stephen and Nita passed the medical bags to them. The rib sheared away and with a final wave from the two sailors sped back towards the *Cormoran*.

Returning to the warmth of the saloon Stephen and Nita helped each other out of their sea suits as Mary appeared from the galley with five mugs of hot tea. 'Reckon we've earned this.' she said handing them round.

'Bring us about sweetheart, take us back to *Spring Dawn*.' Stephen said.

Although the sea state had settled to just a big swell, it still took almost twenty minutes for them to come up alongside yacht again. In that time Stephen called Falmouth Coastguard reporting that everything had gone well with the rescue. Falmouth up dated him that the first lifeboat to arrive on scene was likely to be the Alderney boat, and that would be in the next fifteen minutes. Glancing at the radar screen, he saw the two green blips of the boats coming from two directions. They heard Falmouth calling the container ship releasing her to continue her voyage thanking them for their assistance. As the big ship began to increase speed and draw away from the two tiny boats that it had sheltered like a mother duck sheltering her ducklings, she gave three long blasts on her siren. Even at the couple of hundred metres it was deafening making some of the fittings vibrate quite violently. Emma responded on *Finbars* horn. She couldn't help giggling as she pressed the button three times.

Stephen laughed at her. 'You enjoyed that, didn't you?'

'Yeah,' she replied, 'I always thought ours was quite loud, until now!'

That brief moment seemed to shake everyone out of a mood of melancholy that had overtaken them since rescue two five one and the French crew had left. Stephen turned to Emma.

'Take us alongside Granddad Em, I want to see how they're doing.'

Turning the wheel slightly she manoeuvred them in close to the yacht's side adjusting their speed allowing them to stay alongside the yacht. Taking his anorak from the set of hooks beneath the staircase to the flying bridge he went out to the sun deck. Mary pushed herself up from the long settee and began to straighten the duvets. Nita helped lifting the seats and pushing the quilts into the lockers beneath, occasionally grabbing onto something to steady herself as *Finbar* pitched or rolled on the odd wave. She went to the coat hooks and hung up the waterproofs to dry off properly. In a matter of minutes the saloon looked neat once more.

'Right,' Mary said, 'I'm going to make another brew and Rachel love,' she said looking at the girl, 'now that everything has calmed down, do you feel you could eat something?'

Rachel was huddled in the corner of the settee, arms folded around herself hugging her sides. She looked so pale which spoiled her tan from the five weeks she'd been with them. She replied softly.

'I don't know I don't want to be sick again. It's such an awful feeling. What do you think?'

Mary smiled sympathetically at her. 'I know just how you feel darling,' she said, 'trust me you need something inside you now. I'll make you some toast and maybe a little later some soup. That will help.'

Emma nodded vigorously. 'Nan's right Rach, she's the voice of experience when it comes to suffering mal-de-mare,' then glancing at Mary added, pleadingly. 'If you're doing toast Nan can I have some too... please?'

'I suppose...' Mary replied with a long-suffering sigh and glancing at Nita said, 'What about you, do you want some too?'

She smirked and shrugged. 'Well if it's not too much trouble, yes please. A couple of slices would be very nice. Thank you.' Rubbing her tummy she added as innocently as she could. 'After the past few hours it should help settle my tummy too. I mean you said so yourself just now.'

She stood gazing at Mary with the most pleading of looks, trying hard not to smile. Turning to go into the galley they all heard her say in a stage whisper.

'I don't know, what is the world coming to you try your best and see what happens they just take advantage, a galley slave that's all I am... huh!'

Giggling softly Emma shouted to her.

'We all love you, you know that, you're the best Nan ever.'

From the galley came the reply.

'Emma Leigh-Grace... that's just cupboard love, nothing more and well you know it!'

The three girls exchanged glances with each other and laughed. Nita went to the end of the saloon and opened the door. Standing in the shelter of the superstructure she saw Stephen braced against the side of the bridge swaying with the boats motion. She heard him calling across to Richard.

'How are you doing, how's she handling?'

'Manageable, just,' he replied, 'just enough way on so she responds to the helm.'

'Good, did you hear the message from Falmouth, the Alderney boat should be with us pretty soon.'

'Yes, but I think they're going to have to tow us. There's too much damage to the mast, the jury rig is only just giving us steerage. Edwin's worked bloody miracles just to rig the jib.'

'How is he?' Stephen asked.

'Better now, relieved that Susan and Charley are safe and out of it. He's had a couple of hot drinks with a nip. He's got a really good malt on board...' Richard grinned adding 'So I've joined him... yum yum. He's had a bit of a kip too and feels better now.'

Stephen waved, 'Right, good, I'm going for a brew. Do you want some food sending across?'

Richard nodded, 'Could be a plan... yeah, now you mention, that would be good.'

Stephen waved and turned to come back to the warmth of *Finbars* saloon. Nita stood in the doorway unmoved, he looked at her.

'Sugar,' he said resting his hands on her hips and kissing her nose. 'You're keeping a man from his pot of tea, that isn't always a sensible thing to do you know.'

She nodded, her eyes fixed on his. 'I know' she said linking her arms around his waist, still looking deeply into his eyes she added. 'I am so proud of you. You really are a living action man, an absolute hero and I love you.'

She offered up her face to him for a kiss.

'Thank you.' He said against her lips and kissed her.

With their lips still together in the kiss he gently lifted her off her feet. She sighed against his lips but was a little surprised when he rotated her through 180 degrees before setting her back on her feet again. Breaking the kiss he stepped back into the saloon, closed the doors and said through the glass, 'I love you too.'

She now found herself on the outside with the door closed and Stephen inside. Through the glass he grinned and waved his fingers at her. Pulling the door open sharply she pursued him into the saloon. 'You bugger!' she called after him and slapped his backside as she caught up with him. Quickly he enveloped her in his arms to prevent her slapping him again and resumed the kiss.

'My hero.' she said.

Still holding her in his arms he looked at everyone in the saloon.

'You were all heroes today, that's the first and I hope the only rescue we come across ever again. Well done all of you.'

Standing by the galley door with a plate stacked with buttered toast Mary beamed at Nita, Emma reached across from the helm's seat and took his hand.

'You were brilliant dad, you deserve one of those medals they give out on TV for bravery.'

He squeezed Emma's hand and was about to reply when something attracted his attention off the port side of *Finbars* stern. Disengaging himself from Nita he picked up the binoculars focusing them on the area where he thought he'd just seen something. He waited watching, then with the magnified view through the lenses saw a huge wall of spray erupt and a dark blue hull topped by orange superstructure burst through the spray before plunging into the back of the next wave throwing up more spray that blew away in the remnants of the gale.

'Yes!' he exclaimed, 'What a beautiful sight. Nita love go tell Richard and Edwin the cavalry have arrived, it's the RNLI.'

She went to the saloon doors and moments later he heard

Richard give a whoop as she gave him the news.

Finbars radio burst into life. '*Finbar Two, Finbar Two, Finbar Two, this is the Alderney lifeboat, Alderney lifeboat, Alderney lifeboat. We have visual sight of you and will be there in a few minutes, over.*'

Stephen felt elated, sighing deeply. He replied to the message and like felt a huge weight had suddenly been lifted off his shoulders. He hadn't realised until now the huge commitment, and responsibility he'd taken on when he'd answered *Spring Dawn's* mayday. Only now was he truly aware of the risks he'd put Nita, Richard, Mary, Emma and Rachel through. As it turned out everyone was okay and to all intents and purposes he and *Finbar* and everyone else were the heroes of the moment. Now he could relax, the professional rescuers were here in the shape of six men and a boat from Alderney, and somewhere pretty near the same number of people on another boat from Salcombe. Emma was aware that, just for a moment, he was pre-occupied somewhere else in his head. Reaching out she said quietly.

'Dad you okay?'

He looked at her and smiled.

'Yeah... I'm alright love, just thinking,' adding, 'well done Em, well done love.'

For a brief moment this was a 'them' moment, reserved for the bond between parent and child excluding everyone else, Emma squeezed his hand once more

'What's up you two?' Nita asked.

'Nothing sugar, we just had a moment.'

She didn't need to know anything else, she nodded stroking his cheek affectionately.

Within an hour of receiving that first call from the Alderney lifeboat everything seemed to happen so quickly. Stephen felt swept along by the pace of change and just watched with respect at the professionalism firstly from the crew of the Alderney boat and twenty minutes later the Salcombe boat when it arrived. Richard had re-joined them as two crew members from the Alderney boat went onto

Spring Dawn. Edwin called across to them to thank them just before they changed places with the lifeboat.

Stephen stood *Finbar* off for another half an hour and watched as the two crews combined to sort out the broken mast, sails and rigging and listened to the radio as the two coxswains came to the decision to take the stricken yacht in tow to Salcombe. Having informed the Coastguard of their plan, he waited for a break in their transmissions before calling Falmouth himself.

'Falmouth coastguard, Falmouth coastguard, Falmouth coast guard. *Finbar Two, Finbar Two, Finbar Two*. As the RNLI have taken over here, are we clear to continue our passage to Poole. Over.'

'*Finbar Two, Falmouth Coastguard. Yes you are clear to continue your passage to Poole. Thank you for your assistance throughout this incident. Safe passage, Falmouth Coastguard listening, out.*'

Replacing the mic on its rest he looked around the saloon.

'Well I suppose we should be on our way then. Take the wheel will you sugar, head in that direction,' he said pointing where he wanted her to go, adding, 'I'll go and work out a course.'

Nita swapped places with Emma sliding onto the helm seat as Stephen moved to go down to the chart table. Everybody else just sat or stood where they were for quite some time. It was Mary who eventually broke the silence.

'Do you know I feel absolutely drained after all this, I'm going to make something proper for us all to eat?'

Richard grinned. 'That's my Mary, a full stomach helps get everything in proportion and the brain functioning better, plus it's very comforting, never fails.'

Mary looked at him briefly in a particular way, words weren't necessary the look said it all. They smiled affectionately at each other. From the chart table in the galley Stephen called.

'Nita bring her round to a heading of 080 will you, try eight knots for the moment.'

'Ok 080.' she replied.

Richard moved over beside Nita and sounded their horn three

times as they turned away from *Spring Dawn* and the lifeboats onto their new heading. Moments later the boat's radio crackled.

'Finbar Two, Finbar Two, Finbar Two, Spring Dawn. Richard give everyone my heartfelt thanks for today. I can't think of anything else to say really except just how much it has meant having you stand by and help. Safe journey, Spring Dawn out.

Stephen emerged from the galley as Edwin finished his message going straight out to the sun deck.

'Nita sound the horn again love.' He said as he passed her.

Richard went and joined him on the sun deck, as she sounded the horn again. The two men waved to the yacht and saw Edwin wave back. For a while they watched the three boats gradually becoming smaller as they pulled away. Returning to the saloon they stood beside Nita.

'She's good you know.' Stephen said quietly to Richard, they both watched her.

Richard nodded. 'You're not thinking of offering her a permanent berth are you?'

'Mmm thinking...'

'Hhmm... trust me, you can't afford me!'

Nita interrupted without taking her eyes off the compass.

'Bit of an anti-climax now isn't it?' Richard said.

Stephen huffed down his nose in agreement.

'I'm absolutely knackered, that's an experience I'd not wish to repeat ever again whichever way you look at it.'

Richard nodded, 'Mmmm.'

Turning, Stephen reached across to the drinks cabinet opening the glass door, he said.

'Did you say Edwin had a good malt with him?'

'I did, yes.'

'Can't manage a malt but I've got that Cognac we bought in Honfluer, fancy a drop?'

'Definitely, help settle the stomach don't you think?'

The two men grinned at one another. From behind them Nita

said.

'You men, what are you like, any excuse and out comes the booze...'

Stephen looked at her feigning a surprised expression. Taking a deep breath he set about defending his logic.

'Excuse me lady, this is purely for medicinal reasons, Richard is cold suffering from mild hypothermia after the events of the past few hours and me, well I'm exhausted from all the pressure of managing the rescue. Rachel is so ill this will perk her up and help settle her stomach!'

Realising that his reasoning wasn't working he stopped talking and simply gave Nita a long, hung-dog stare. She looked at his poor man's look then shook her head and tutting.

'Right well if that's the case then,' she began, 'Mary and I need a tot each because we're both traumatised from treating Susan's injured hand. You've no idea how distressing it was coping with such a shocking injury...!'

Trying to maintain a serious expression, she talked up her reasoning why she thought Mary and she deserved a 'medicinal tot. It didn't last long though, the forlorn look on his face won it for the men in the end. The sight of him standing there with a bottle of Cognac in one hand and an empty glass in the other hand was just too much, glancing at Richard briefly she saw a huge grin on his face. He'd listened to the two of them, fascinated by the rapport between them, it reminded him of some American TV soap the title of which escaped him for the moment. That was it though her attempt to remain serious crumbled and she gave in to a giggle. The two men looked at each other breaking into a laugh as well. It was like a release valve for them all and they laughed out loud.

Mary and Emma came up from the galley to see what all the laughter was about. They realised they weren't going to get any sensible explanation from any of them so looking across at Rachel sitting in the corner of the long settee sought the answer. She couldn't help but smile at the three of them and their silliness and shrugging said to Mary and Emma as Stephen filled the two glasses.

'It's medicinal apparently,' trying to sound convincing, 'they say they're suffering from trauma and hypothermia! Personally, I think it's some sort of age thing or a break down.' then added, 'Emma I think you'd best take the wheel, it'd be safer.'

Immediately, Mary turned to Stephen and took hold of the bottle of cognac wrestling it from his grasp and taking two more glasses from the cabinet proceeded to fill them with a measure of the cognac passing one to Nita.

Rachel continued. 'I think we should lock them in forward cabin and call the coastguard to have them removed for their own protection.'

Nita protested, 'Just a minute, don't include me with them just look at the evidence they're the ones with the bottle and glasses, I'm the innocent party here...!'

Mary tutted at the two men then taking two more glasses from the cabinet poured two smaller measures of the tan liquor before passing them to the girls. She glanced quickly at Stephen and saw the slightest of nods

'This is definitely medicinal where Rachel's concerned,' she said, 'just sip it, it will definitely settle your tummy.'

They drank the spirit in silence feeling the warmth from the liquid travel down their throats and spread in their stomachs.

'Mmm,' Mary said, 'that was lovely, very settling.'

Glancing at Emma for a moment she added. '

Come on you, lunch won't prepare itself.'

She turned to go back to the galley, still holding the bottle.

'Err...excuse me, where are you off to with that?' Stephen said.

Looking at him, then at the bottle in her hand and back at Stephen she replied.

'We need it for cooking... as an additive to one of my dishes.'

As she said this she gave him a look of shocked surprise.

'Stephen Leigh-Grace you didn't think I was going to have another drink?'

Eyes wide accusingly, she added.

'You did! Well I'm shocked... really!'

He reached out to take the bottle from her but she turned away from him wrapping her arms around it defensively. He got hold of the bottle neck pulling it out of her grip.

'You are not using my best cognac for cooking!' he said. 'You can have another tot and use some of that if you need to!'

She held out her glass and he topped it up. 'Huh.' She said going down the steps to the galley. Rachel got up from the settee and followed them into the galley. After this light hearted interlude, the atmosphere throughout the boat, that feeling of weariness that had hung over them was all but gone now.

The afternoon passed quietly, the sea becoming increasingly calmer the further east they progressed then north to finally run into Poole. After a tasty lunch Mary and Emma cooked for them everyone managed to grab some rest, taking turns to steer them home such a contrast to last night's passage and the morning's difficulties getting to *Spring Dawn*. There were moments when they all found themselves talking about some of the morning's events. Stephen listened and more than once reflected on his decision to help, he had a lot of 'what ifs' churning through his mind and felt very guilty that without consulting the others he'd been the one who'd ultimately made the decision to go to the yacht's aid.

Nita knew by his manner he was troubled, he was withdrawn lost in thought, periodically she gave him a hug or a kiss to reassure him. At one point with Richard helming, Mary was by his side, Emma and Rachel dozing in the easy chairs, he took his anorak and climbed up to the flying bridge. She let him go but later went and joined him, he was sitting on the helms seat; snuggling up to him she said softly.

'What's the matter Ferryman you're not all here?'

Putting his arm round her shoulder he squeezed her gently kissing her forehead. He was watching their approach and the navigation channel emerging from the land mass in front of them.

'I'm okay sugar lots of what ifs milling around in my head.'

'What more could you have done? You got us there you did an amazing job of helping, I'm so proud of my action man.'

She squeezed his arm and kissed his cheek, he glanced at her.

'Not me sugar, you and the others we all helped.'

'I know but you made the decision to change course to go and help.'

'That's what I mean, I made the decision,' he said quietly. 'I made the decision Nita, I never even thought of the consequences for you or the others, or *Finbar*.'

'Stephen it was okay we all survived, *Finbar* survived. You've said it yourself often she's a strong boat.'

He just nodded. They sat quietly for a while.

'If it helps, write it all down like a report, write it down it might help. We have to write up reports and sometimes it helps to ease your mind thinking about what action you took, what decisions you made, particularly if it's an awkward or nasty case. Do that, it might help you put things into perspective you know.'

He looked at her smiled then hugged her. 'Yeah... I'll do that, you are clever.'

They kissed then sat snuggled together watching the land enlarging before their eyes, they could smell it on the wind, something Nita felt was odd, that you could smell the land as you approached it.

~~~~~~~~~~~~~~~~~~~~~~~~~~~~~~~~~~~~~
~~~~~~~~~~~~~~~~~~~~~~~~~~~~~~~~~~~~~

A FINAL RESOLUTION

It was quite dark when two taxis pulled into Mary and Richard's driveway some seven miles outside Poole. It took quite some time to unload all their bags and cases but finally they watched the two cars drive away leaving them standing beside quite a collection of kit as Richard unlocked the front door. They'd cleaned *Finbar* down and she was moored up at her berth in the marina and all sheeted up. All the perishable food they'd brought home with them or thrown away.

Stephen and Nita would catch the train back to Portbridge tomorrow, Rachel was staying tonight her parents would pick her up tomorrow and she and Emma would return to school mid-week for their final year to study and to sit their 'A' level exams. Richard and Mary would once again take on the role of caring for Emma for this last year before she hopefully went to university. As was the tradition established over the years the first meal on returning home from the long summer cruise was a takeaway. There was the discussion whether it was to be Indian, Chinese or fish and chips, it invariably ended with the latter winning out. Mary always found this northern trait for fish and chips with bread and butter plus tea quite strange. Even Suzanne, when she was alive relished any opportunity to consume this delicacy joining the debate as to where the best ones came from.

Supper completed and the house feeling warm after its five week closure everyone lounged about. Richard started to work through the mountain of post that had arrived in their absence, the girls had retreated to Emma's room, Stephen, Nita and Mary sat together watching television for the first time in almost ten days. The news had just begun and the presenter reading the headlines was saying.

'*Following last night's sudden storm in the South West a number of properties were damaged and flash floods disrupted road and rail travel. There was a dramatic rescue in the Western approaches in the early hours involving two lifeboats, a helicopter from RAF Culdrose and other boats in the area, including a French navy vessel that culminated in two crew members from a yacht being airlifted to Truro hospital for emergency treatment. The yacht was eventually towed into Salcombe in an operation lasting some fifteen hours. We go live now to Truro hospital for an update on the two crew members.*'

Mary rushed into the hall calling Richard and the girls to come and watch. By the time they'd all congregated in the living room the news channel had gone live to a reporter outside the hospital. She was giving an update on the condition of an injured woman and her son airlifted from the scene by the helicopter, she continued with a brief outline of the rescue, how the joint operation was controlled by Falmouth Coastguard. Her report ended she handed back to the studio where the news presenter went on to say.

'*In a separate incident off the North Cornwall coast a fisheries protection vessel and a lifeboat went to the aid of a converted fishing boat also reported to be in difficulties. The vessel, Caspian Blue, had lost all power at the height of the storm and was drifting. A number of people were taken off the boat for safety and it was eventually towed into Padstow.*

The bulletin then went on to report about other damage around the coast caused by this freak storm. Stephen and Nita looked at each other.

'Bloody hell,' Stephen exclaimed, 'What happens now?'

Nita picked up her handbag and rummaged through it for her mobile.

'Don't know, but I'll find out.'

She left the room and went through to the kitchen. Pulling his phone from his pocket he scrolled through the numbers found one and pressed call. Waiting for some time for an answer, he eventually spoke.

'My name is Stephen Leigh-Grace can you put me through to the extension for Hawkeye.'

The operator asked him a question, he replied, 'Valarie Jane.' He waited then said, 'Thank you.'

A minute later someone spoke to him and at the end of a very one-way conversation Stephen said.

'No, thank you, it appears all bases have been covered and you're sure there will be no further threat?'

Having got the reassurance he wanted he ended the call. Emma was watching him for any reaction.

'What about school dad, will Heather be my contact again do you think?'

She was breathing heavily and sounded anxious. Rachel listened to what was unfolding around her, wondering what all the panic was about.

'Em, what's going on, why are you all panicking like this?'

'Nita's calling someone now let's wait and see.'

Emma quickly glanced at him waiting for an answer but Mary reached out taking Rachel by the arm and gently led her out of the room saying to her and Emma.

'Come on you two, let's go up to your room... Em come on.'

The three of them made their way upstairs passing Nita as she came back to the living room from the kitchen, she closed the door.

'Right, this is what's happened, for once the boat had a genuine breakdown. It turns out that the French patrol boat was actually shadowing *Caspian Blue* but left to assist us with *Spring Dawn*. The original plan was that HMC and E and fisheries protection were waiting to intercept them as they came into territorial waters, the French were to shut the back door. Immigration believes they have enough evidence now to grab most of the operation here in the UK and in France and Holland. As we speak arrests are being made across these countries. It seems that last night's storm kind of put a spanner in the operation to start with but ended up doing everyone a favour, albeit a little prematurely.'

Richard had followed Nita into the room, he exchanged a glance with Stephen saying.

'There but for grace again… aye!'

Raising an eyebrow Stephen asked.

'Who was on the boat sugar?'

'They arrested three crewmen and another man and found four girls in one of the cabins. Caught bang to rights you could say.'

Richard asked, 'Are the girls all right?'

'Apparently,' Nita replied, 'traumatised I imagine but at least they're safe. The operation commander is going to brief the boss tomorrow and he'll tell me what's likely to happen next.'

'Good, got the bastards!' Richard said harshly.

Mary had come downstairs and stood in the living room doorway.

'Are they alright?' Stephen asked.

She nodded. 'Emma's a bit anxious, Rachel's stunned but I've sworn her to secrecy. Not even her parents to know.'

'Will she keep quiet do you think?' he asked.

Mary shrugged, 'Who knows, we're just going to have to hope she can.'

Richard went to the sideboard opened it to reveal a collection of bottles of spirits.

'Drink anyone?'

'Brandy please.' Stephen said, 'I'm just going to see Emma for a minute.'

'Same.' Nita said, Mary asked for a sherry, stopping at the door he turned.

'Was anything said about keeping an eye on Emma?'

'Yes, don't worry, the DC assigned to her before is going to be in touch when she goes back this week. To all intents and purposes they are just going to catch up on her summer adventures. She'll be watched for the next week then depending how the case develops, it will be reviewed after that.'

'Thanks, that's a relief.'

Upstairs he knocked on Emma's bedroom door, 'Yes.' came her

reply

'It's dad love.'

'Come in.'

Opening the door he saw Emma getting up from her bed dabbing her eyes. She went to him and he took her in his arms.

'Listen sweetie, it's going to be okay. From what Nita has just said this could be an end to the whole thing, they've arrested a lot of people all over the place.'

'Am I going to be all right back at school?'

'Yes love Heather is going to get in touch again and she'll be around until all the dust has settled okay!'

'Do you mean you've got a bodyguard Em?' Rachel asked. 'That's really cool.'

Stephen walked into the bedroom, Emma dropped back onto the bed while he sat on the chair by the dressing table.

'Rachel, this is really important,' he said focusing on her to hold her attention. 'Last year something happened that brought me and Nita together in the first instance, okay.' she nodded. 'You know Nita is a detective?' another nod, 'Long story short, I ended up in hospital after helping some people, Nita was one of the detectives involved in the case and we kind of clicked and here we are today, okay!' She nodded again. 'Nita has been working on a case and quite separately, I've seen some things on my travels in Europe that have sort of involved me quite by accident yet again. Unknowingly this is all related to the same case. The result is that Emma and Nita have been at risk since our Easter break.'

'And you too dad, you were attacked in Germany.'

'Yes Em but that's not what this is about here and now, okay.'

He focused on Rachel again.

'Rachel, seriously! You cannot speak to anyone for the moment, not even your mum or dad, do you understand!'

Rachel was just staring at him.

'Rachel do you understand!' he said forcefully, 'To say anything could put Emma at risk again, I'm sure you wouldn't want that.'

She simply nodded while Stephen continued to drive the point home.

'Promise me you won't say anything! You girls can keep secrets when you want, I know you can'

'Yes,' she said glancing quickly at Emma, 'I promise, not a word, honest.'

'Thank you.'

'It'll be all right dad.' Emma said. 'It will!'

Stephen smiled at her and as he left the room heard Rachel say.

'So that friend of yours you met up with last term is a detective?'

The door clicked shut and he went downstairs to join the others. Although they couldn't help the conversation re-visiting tonight's news from time to time, they spent the rest of the evening talking about the rescue. When the girls came down the conversation centred on the three weeks before Nita had joined them as they'd cruised around the harbours and bays of Northern France. Eventually the chat got to focusing on the work the girls were facing in this last year in the upper sixth. Both Emma and Rachel were undecided at the moment what they wanted to do career wise. It was quite late when conversation ebbed into long moments of silence and Richard and Mary declared that they were absolutely 'whacked' after the rough passage from Alderney and tonight's developments and they were going to bed. That seemed to be the signal for everyone to turn in.

~~~~~~

In the morning everyone seemed to appear downstairs about the same time, Stephen and Nita put all the baggage from the holiday into Richards's car ready to get away. Finally gathered in the kitchen they said their goodbyes, Stephen addressed the group.

'Well here we are again, the end of another years cruising, I know we're all feeling a bit low at the thought of getting back to work and
~~~~~~

studying. For me this year has been a bit special because of this lady,' he reached out drawing Nita to his side, 'If anyone had said this time last year that I'd be standing here with someone in my life, I'd have laughed and replied, 'yeah right' and the channel might freeze over this Christmas! Well here I am and here she is!'

'You took your time though.' Mary interrupted, they all chuckled.

'Okay,' Stephen held a hand up, 'I did yes and the circumstances were very strange too.'

'Too right, but that's not unusual for you!' Richard interjected.

Stephen grinned, 'But everything worked out in the end and I've had a great time this year, I hope you have as well.'

'This one has been a one off I hope,' Richard said, 'With the security operation hanging over our heads for the past three months or more, I hope next year's cruise is back to restful... boring even.'

'Yeah, but it was fun, well sort of.' Stephen added.

Nita stepped away from Stephen saying.

'I want to say thank you too. Since Easter in York you've drawn me into your family and it's just so lovely to share everything with you all, so thank you.'

Turning to look at the girls, she said quietly to them.

'Right listen to me, I've got my working head on now. Emma knows only too well what the last three months has been like.' She rested her arm on her shoulder. 'I'm very proud of you, I think you've coped with it so well Em. Now regrettably Rachel has become involved, I can't stress this enough girls, you cannot say anything to anyone at all for the moment, got it, not a word! Rachel if you find you're struggling then please speak to the DC who's with Emma or phone me or Stephen okay, we will help you. Hopefully, it should be all over within the next month.'

Standing at the front door Mary and the girls watched as Richard drove Stephen and Nita to the station. They shook hands and embraced one another then went and found their seats on the train. Both sat in silence for some time as the train pulled away from Poole. Neither could think of anything to say to lighten their mood after leaving the family. They both managed to sleep a little during the six-hour journey arriving back in Portbridge in the early evening where they got a taxi home. Once inside Nita made a snack and a drink for them while Stephen set the heating and began the task of sorting the washing so they had the necessary clothes to wear next week. The remainder of the evening was spent listening to the score of answer-phone messages and sorting through the mountain of post.

Nita, resting her head on his chest when they'd turned in for the night said.

'Is it me or is this bed rocking ever so gently? The bed at Richard and Mary's did it too.'

He gently squeezed her.

'No your head thinks you're still on the boat. Can you hear the water lapping along the hull as well?'

She listened for a moment before answering, giggling.

'Oh yes, that's really weird. How long does it last?'

'The balance thing will go in a day or so but the water thing, who knows. Every now and again you'll be sure you can hear the water.'

Lying there she found herself listening for the different creaks around the house compared to those of the boat. Sub-consciously Stephen had begun stroking lower back and bottom, she responded stroking his side and thigh. Parting slightly they looked at one another, kissed and began caressing one another passionately their kisses deep and searching their caresses wanton, urgent!

'Ohh that's so good, I've missed you...Ohh!'

She shuddered as a mini orgasm shook her whole body, throwing her arms around him tightly they lay locked together hardly moving but revelling in the thrilling sensations they were generating for each other, he whispered close to her ear.

'Your muscles are squeezing me and I'm sorry but I can't help it... I'm going to cum... ohh god!'

Nita clamped a hand over her mouth responding with a stifled shriek. Later she soothed him gently until they were both calm again.

'Where did that come from Ferryman that was amazing, I just can't get enough of you?'

He laughed quietly. 'Two weeks of being quiet and trying not to rock the boat!'

She spluttered dissolving into an uncontrollable giggles.

'Was that an intended pun?'

He realised what he'd just said and laughed with her.

'NO... I meant we needn't be quiet no no-one is going to hear us!'

~~~~~~
~~~~~~

BACK TO WORK

Up early in the morning, refreshed and ready for the challenges of the first day back at the coal face! Leaving the house together he waited to see if Nita's car would start after the break, it struggled initially but finally fired up. Hugging each other he watched her drive down the street before getting into his car and driving to the depot.

'Morning all.' he said as he walked into the transport office. 'How are we all, any disasters while I've been away?'

A chuckle ran around the room as Chris answered him from her desk.

'Did you know there's less drama when you're away the job runs like a well-oiled machine, I actually sleep better because you're not out there somewhere pretending to be a hero! Any way how the was your holiday?'

He spent a little time telling them about the family's holiday exploits and the storm as they sailed home. Taking a sheaf of papers from under the front desk she handed them to him saying.

'The boss wants to see you when he comes in, so make yourself useful and do us all a brew... please.'

Sometime later the man walked into the general office and through to his own office gesturing to Stephen. Following him they sat and talked about his holiday, where he'd got to and how everyone had got on in such a confined space.

'I just don't know how you do it,' he said, 'I've got more than enough trouble coping with our lass and mi' daughter in a hotel! At least I can escape to't bar if I need space.'

Sorting through some papers on his desk, he eventually found his diary.

'Right, your move is on, maybe in a month okay? I am trying to get you back on UK runs. We've set a new driver on who's happy to take on the Scan-Euro run. You'll need to do a trip out twinned up so the new guy can get some idea of the routes etc. Now, the next question is what're we going to do with you? Will you find out if the police will release you to do more UK stuff.'

Stephen nodded, 'I'll speak to Nita now and find out okay.'

'Go on then get that sorted and let me know, now bugger off then I can get something done.'

Stephen left the office beaming and walked through the outer to office. Chris looked at him and grinned.

'And just when I thought things were settling down... let me guess, UK only?'

Glancing at her he replied, 'Oh yes... r e s u l t!' he said punching the air and continued out of the office saying, 'Get in!'

The phone rang a few times before it was answered.

'Hello Portbridge police, DCs Syms and Patel's phone, they are away from their desks at the moment, can I help?'

'Oh hi, yes possibly. My names Stephen Leigh-Grace I need to speak with DC Patel or DI Allen if possible.'

'Okay I'm sorry but the three of them are out of the office at the moment, they should be back this afternoon do you want to leave a message?'

'Could you ask DC Patel to call me when she can.?'

'Your number is?'

'She has my number, thank you.'

'All right, I'll see she gets the message.'

'Thanks, bye.'

'Bye.'

Stephen returned to the office and sat with the route planner to discuss his options at home or away for the rest of the week before leaving the office and returning home.

Mid-afternoon his phone buzzed in his pocket, the screen said Nita when he looked at it.

'Hello sugar, I guess you're off chasing felons already, I've got some news for you job wise.'

'Hello, Alan and me and the DI were up at a meeting at division. Is it good news then?'

'Yes, sort of, they've got someone to do the Scan-Euro run starting next month so I'll be on UK stuff pretty soon. I need to know if I can resume working the run now or am I still stuck here.'

'I was going to tell you all about it tonight but I'll see the boss now and just confirm we can all get back to normal.'

'Okay, that sounds promising, I'll see you tonight, Take care.'

'Love you Ferryman, bye.'

A short time later his mobile buzzed again. 'Hello?' he said.

'Hey, it's me can you come to the office for five tonight. The boss is going to brief us both on what's happening now.'

'Okay yes but I thought you were at the same meeting so why can't you tell me?

'After the general stuff and updates on mine and Alan's cases, he went off for a word with the top brass.'

'Oh okay, five then?'

'Yep.'

'Okay, bye.'

Five pm and Stephen climbed the two flights of stairs to the detective's office in the centre of Portbridge. On his way up he exchanged nods and brief 'hellos' as he passed one or two people descending obviously going home at the end of their day. Arriving at the office door he knocked, a few moments passed before a woman opened the door on her way out.

'Hello, can I help you?'

'I've come to see DC Patel and DI Allen.'

'Are you Stephen?'

'Yes'

Offering her hand he shock it, a bit surprised,.

'I'm Linda, I've heard a so much about you it seems you're a bit of an all-round hero. Do you often rescue damsels in distress?'

Unsure just who this lady was, he shrugged and smiled at her, he was going to say something when Nita appeared behind Linda. Quietly she said.

'Leave him alone you, he's my hero go and find your own action man.'

The two women laughed, Stephen smiled a little awkwardly as Linda moved to slide past him, she glanced at Nita then Stephen smiling.

'I'll go home to my singles flat and my cat and my ready meal for one and think about the one that got away,' she sighed loudly, flashed Nita a glance saying, 'I'll call you sweetie if I need rescuing!'

Nita gave her a gentle shove.

'Get away, you've got your Barry at home cooking for you!'

Looking at Stephen she nodded towards Linda.

'Married to a rugby league forward, three kids and crazy…! Goodnight Linda.'

'Night sweetie.'

She replied giving Stephen a glance and a wink and continued down the stairs.

Stephen followed Nita into the general office and through to DI Allen's office, she knocked on the door. Looking up from his desk he motioned them to come in saying to Nita.

'Go and get the sergeant will you.'

She turned and disappeared briefly returning with Ruth the DS, they all settled down around DI Allen's desk. Pulling a piece of paper from under the heap of work on his desk, he said.

'Okay, listen carefully, I'm only going to say this once, to coin a phrase.'

He searched now for another piece of paper adding that to the one he'd just found.

'Having pulled you off anything to do with this case since your attack, the agencies involved from our teams here, to those across Europe have been beavering away to search out as much info as possible on this organisation.'

Shaking his head briefly he said thoughtfully.

'It really beggars' belief given all the techy stuff we have available today, that they were able to stay below all the alerts, given what they've been involved in. Someone has been very clever working out ways of firstly trafficking the girls and then all the other contraband. The interesting thing is they don't appear to have been selling the stuff on the open market otherwise someone somewhere would have flagged it up. No, everything was moved on in house so it never affected any street sales anywhere. He looked at Nita and then Stephen briefly. Had our Mr Doyle not turned up dead, then the young lady in hospital followed by your inquisitiveness Mr Leigh-Grace regarding the number times you spotted that boat in so many places and DC Patel asking the Special Branch boys one question, then they would quite likely still be operating.'

He sighed and took a deep breath.

'The operation to net this lot began the day you were returning to Poole. The Dutch police were controlling the whole thing co-ordinating customs and immigration departments in Germany, Belgium, France, and here in the UK plus a special task force in Georgia. The French coastal patrol was working with one of our fisheries protection boats heading up the marine contingent. 'Once the boat,' he glanced at one of his notes, 'the *Caspian Blue* made port here and met with whoever, that would be the signal for all the teams in each country to begin their raids on the known clubs and places where either the girls were being kept, or the stores of drugs and everything else were. Immigration, medical and care teams were to look after the girls and get them any treatment or help needed. Everything else would be taken care of by the various law enforcement agencies. I don't think any of us wanted any loopholes left open for them to wriggle out of, not this lot! Finally the task force in Georgia would move on the root of the operation. It seems the Georgian authorities knew of this family and that they were into something big but had been unable to discover just what until we began to unravel it from this end. Like I said, someone has been very clever planning and running this in such a way it stayed very low key. Using small coastal harbours with satellite custom offices, using engine breakdowns as the way of having transport available supposedly bringing spare parts to the boat meant they were able to move the girls around and all the other stuff. You know they sedated them packing them in ridged boxes. That's just bloody cruel, bloody cruel.'

In a brief moment of silence, Stephen said.

'So, where does this leave Nita, me and Emma, are we still confined?'

'Yes, well I've been told that as the whole operation in the UK has been closed down you can resume life as before. I'm going to get the DC in Poole to meet with Emma and give her the same briefing I've just given you so she'll understand where we are. There'll be no further need for the detective to be there then.'

'You're sure any threat is done with?' Stephen asked seeking reassurance.

DI Allen nodded. 'I'm assured that there should be no further trouble.'

Stephen nodded, 'Okay, as long as Emma is going to be safe, I can go back on the road again.'

The DI smiled adding, 'You certainly can.'

Sighing he said to them.

'Right home time for everyone, thank you for your time.'

They filed out of the DI's office, the sergeant said good night to Nita and Stephen and returned to her office. Nita collected her bag and things from her desk and led the way out of the office and down to the street.

'So home or eat out, any thoughts?'

Stephen said. Nita studied him for a while thinking.

'Do you know I really fancy a curry, what about you?'

'Mmm yeah, I can go with that.'

'Good, Mahmoud's Balti then?'

'Okay, see you there.'

They kissed briefly, Nita turned setting off to the car park at the rear of the building just as DI Allen came out of the building. He nodded to Stephen then fell into step with Nita disappearing around the corner of the office block. Twenty minutes later the two of them were seated at a table in the curry house with a beer each sharing a pickle tray with poppadums' waiting for their food to come. Bill paid and standing on the street again they embraced and walked to their respective vehicles.

See you at home sugar.'

She smiled and waved as she climbed into her car, he quickly caught her up and followed her back to his house. They parked as near as they could to the house, once inside with the gas fire on low lights and a bottle of wine they relaxed watching the television. Sometime later Nita shuffled round to look at Stephen.

'Do you feel relieved, happier after the boss spoke to us tonight?'

'Yeah I suppose I do when I think about it, relieved. Relieved that Emma isn't at risk anymore, and you too. I know it comes with the territory for you but this was too close to home, I felt physically sick when I heard that you and Em had been hurt, I just felt so useless and I was angry as well.'

Nita nodded and shuffled closer taking his arm and draping it around her shoulder. Quietly she said.

'Please, don't go being the hero again, just walk away and call someone okay? In the two years I've known you I've started to go grey with you getting into all these scrapes. I dread the call that comes up *'unknown'* on my phone when you're away so no more please!'

She heard him chuckle softly and gently prodded him in the ribs. When the television drama finished and the evening news began they shut everything down and went to bed.

~~~~~~
~~~~~~

Sitting opposite each other at the breakfast bar in the morning, Nita asked.

'So what now that you're free to work again?'

'Well you know I'm coming back to UK runs in a month or so. The boss wants me to run one, maybe two trips with the new guy just to help if he has any problems. So I'll tell him to set a run up soon as pos.'

She shrugged and pouted.

'Shame… I've got used to you being around over these past weeks it's going to be hard going back to the old routine.'

'Yeah but it's only for the next couple of months and then I'll be running UK stuff.'

She nodded and pushed out her bottom lip again feigning a sulk. Getting off his stool he went around the bar and cuddled her resting his head on her shoulder and kissing the nape of her neck.

'I didn't know you could sulk.'

She stroked his head as he nuzzled her neck before exclaiming.

'I know… Oh shoot! look at the time I'm going to be late!'

The next few minutes were manic as she rushed around gathering her bits and pieces together and making her way to the door, she turned to Stephen.

'Call me, I'll try and get out for lunch if you want?'

He followed her to the door to kiss her goodbye.

'Okay, I'll let you know.'

Having tidied around he drove to the depot where he spent time arranging some sort of a timetable for his return to work. The possible lunch date was cancelled because she was being de-briefed on her case relating to Patrick Doyle's death and her involvement with Katterine. She also told him that she would be going back to the house she shared with her two friends for a girly night and to tell them all about her holiday and it's dramatic end.

Facing an evening on his own he called Emma's school arranging through her year tutor to speak with her in their office rather than in one of the corridors where friends might overhear their conversation.

Later Emma called him back, she told him she'd seen Heather, the detective and she had given her the same information he and Nita had heard from DI Allen the previous evening. She sounded relieved everything could return to normal once more. She sounded very happy too when he confirmed that he would be working back in the UK very soon. Giggling, she told him how Rachel had found all the protection stuff exciting and how on more than one occasion had nearly told friends about it, something she would be able to do now. Emma added she reckoned Rachel's popularity at school would go sky high when she told everyone and knowing her so well the drama would be elaborated some! He asked about the work she was facing for this year as she worked up to her 'A' level exams. Their call finished with Stephen saying goodbye adding finally 'Love you Em'.

After speaking to Emma he called Richard and Mary bringing them up to speed too and telling them that he would be working back in the UK soon. Like Emma, they said how relieved they both were that the risk of further attacks was over for all of them. The conversation ended with Stephen saying he would speak to them as usual when he was back from this last trip.

Sitting quietly now in the cosy living room he began reflecting on the changes that had happened in his life in the last twelve months, thinking about the past year and recalling some of its high points; there was his relationship with Nita, he smiled: the passion, the friendship and subtle support that was there whenever he thought he was floundering. There was the family, Emma, Mary and Richard, and Harold; it felt complete once again now Nita had been accepted and welcomed by them all. He hadn't had this sense of wholeness since Suzanne had died over eight years ago. It was a long time to be alone he thought, but there again that was his own doing, it had been Nita who'd quietly changed all that and through their relationship bringing them all so close again. They'd had some fun together, lots of laughs some great moments cruising on *Finbar,* some dramatic ones too that would stay with him for years to come. There'd been some low points through the year, painful ones that he'd sooner forget.

From now on he'd do his utmost to avoid getting into such situations, he'd promised Nita that he'd turn the other way, better still walk or drive away! He smiled thinking what she'd said to him.

'Just drive into the sunset, let someone else be the hero from now on... okay, got it!'

Going into the kitchen he picked up the bottle of malt whiskey on the side, a glass and some ice out of the fridge returning to the lounge. Settling on the settee he put some of his favourite music on the hi-fi, poured a measure of whiskey onto ice and sat back, relaxed. He truly felt life was good just now.

~~~~~~
~~~~~~

FOOTNOTE

For Stephen, Nita, Emma and the rest of the family's as their lives began to return to normality, the net that was operation 'Hawkeye' continued to close on the clubs and warehouses in the UK, Holland, France and Germany. By the time the operation was concluded authorities in these countries had arrested almost one hundred people, released some thirty-eight young women from lives as sex slaves who'd been enticed to travel to new countries by promises of well-paid work. Alcohol, cigarettes and tobacco plus quantities of banned substances were also seized: in total the value of all this contraband was estimated at more than seven hundred thousand euros. Once all the clubs were closed down, the Georgian police and security forces moved on the core of the operation sealing off a heavily forested area in the west of the country and surrounding a large residential property. A stand-off ensued which continued for four days before the occupants eventually surrendered thus avoiding any direct action by the security authorities and any bloodshed; nine people were taken into custody. At this present time, they are being detained by the Georgian justice system while extradition notices are being presented to have them brought to the UK or other European countries to face trial.

Closer to home the team of detectives in Portbridge were able to close their investigations into the death of Patrick Doyle, as during the raid on the club in Hull, evidence and DNA was collected both from the club but more importantly the van that directly incriminated the manager and his staff in Patricks' death; four men arrested, they are awaiting trial for conspiracy to murder. Katterine and two other women rescued from there have been granted temporary work permits and are waiting to see if they can acquire more permanent residency here. Life in Portbridge seemed slow after all the statements and case history gathered was sent forward to the CPC to be reviewed.

For Stephen there have been times he has occasionally missed the open roads of Northern Europe and Scandinavia, of travelling for days through amazing scenery; but being 'local' as he calls it, on UK runs, has had the added bonus that he gets to spend more time with Nita. This year for the first time in six years Stephen, Nita and the whole family including Harold and Sylvia were able to get together for the entire Christmas holiday.

As has happened every autumn, Finbar was brought back up the river to winter at the Grahams yard where necessary maintenance could be carried out on her, unfortunately this year Stephen was unable to moor up at the NCB wharf as the site had been closed and the area sold to a developer with plans passed to turn it into offices shops and apartments. However, both Stephen and Nita got to meet Mick Holmes at the Duchess and discovered he'd been given a very favorable redundancy package. He is planning to do a bit of travelling and visit his brother and other friends.

When in spring the time came to move the boat again it felt very strange to sail past the old site and see the new buildings taking shape. Easter this year was a low-key affair as Emma was to begin her 'A' levels exams and was totally focused on revising and completing two study papers. Stephen and Nita travelled down to Poole and spent the four days they had off with Mary and Richard. Having kept *Finbar* at the estuary marina, the summer cruise this year headed north for the first time, visiting many of the bays and harbours along the Yorkshire coast up as far as Holy Island in Northumberland. The cruise ended on a high as they celebrated Emma passing her 'A' levels and being accepted for Manchester Uni to study Engineering Science.

~~~~~~~~~~~~~~~~~~~~~~~~~~~~~~~~~~~~~~~
~~~~~~~~~~~~~~~~~~~~~~~~~~~~~~~~~~~~~~~